Series

Paranormal

Moons of Mystery
Sara's Moon (MF)
Charline's Solstice (MF)
Diana's Eclipse (MF)

War on Darkness
Darkness Defined (MM)
Order of Light (MM)
Knights of Nyx (MM)

Kisin Novels
Courting Death (MM)
Death, Love, & Tacos (MM)

True Mates
Truth in Exile (MM)
The Inescapable Truth (MM)
Truth in Lies (MM)

Lycan Detective Duet
Hart's Betrayal (MM)
Hart's Redemption (MM)

Contemporary

Ulwich Preparatory Academy
Our Last Fall (MM)
Our Secret Winter (MM)
Our Epic Spring (MM)

Oak Haven Romance
One Brave Thing (Enby/M)
All the Hype (MM)
The Bright Side (MM)

Copyright © 2024 by Chaotic Neutral Press LLC

All rights reserved.

No part of this publication may be reproduced, distributed, or transmitted in any form or by any means, including photocopying, recording, or other electronic or mechanical methods, without the prior written permission of the publisher, except as permitted by U.S. copyright law. For permission requests, contact info@booksb ysbolanos.com.

NO AI TRAINING: Without in any way limiting the author's [and publisher's] exclusive rights under copyright, any use of this publication to "train" generative artificial intelligence (AI) technologies to generate text is expressly prohibited.

The story, all names, characters, and incidents portrayed in this production are fictitious. No identification with actual persons (living or deceased), places, buildings, and products is intended or should be inferred.

Cover Design by Yellow Butterfly Editing & Design Services

Version 2

Courting Death

A KISIN NOVEL

S BOLANOS

Contents

Chapter 1 — 1

Chapter 2 — 11

Chapter 3 — 18

Chapter 4 — 29

Chapter 5 — 36

Chapter 6 — 46

Chapter 7 — 56

Chapter 8 — 70

Chapter 9 — 81

Chapter 10 — 96

Chapter 11 — 107

Chapter 12   114

Chapter 13   125

Chapter 14   138

Chapter 15   149

Chapter 16   157

Chapter 17   170

Chapter 18   180

Chapter 19   195

Chapter 20   206

Chapter 21   216

Chapter 22   229

Chapter 23   241

Chapter 24   254

Chapter 25   266

Chapter 26   274

Chapter 27   289

Chapter 28   299

Chapter 29   309

Chapter 30   322

Chapter 31   331

Chapter 32   338

Chapter 1

Theo

Why the fuck did I agree to seduce a demon?

The question resonated in my mind as I slipped into the classroom... late. Not that I cared, it wasn't like I needed a Demonic History credit for my major. I located an empty seat in the auditorium-style classroom and made a beeline for it. My bag slumped to the ground loudly enough to earn reproachful glares from around the nearly packed room.

I held up my hands in silent apology while I searched for the sole reason I'd transferred from my very prestigious private college. Arminius University may only be four hundred kilometers west of Vienna and an acclaimed place of higher learning in its own right, but the curriculum couldn't hold a candle to the oldest institute of arcana in the world.

When my gaze finally landed on the wiry guy with dark hair and glasses, he was also glaring at me. He scowled a moment longer, making his dark, golden skin seem darker, then adjusted his focus back to the board at the front of the room. I let out an involuntary groan.

This is going to be harder than I thought.

"Hey," the girl next to me hissed. Her aqua eyes spoke of storms, while her chestnut hair streamed over her shoulder, obscuring dark skin the color of driftwood, light gray with soft undertones of the same brown that defined her hair. "Some of us are actually here to learn."

I bit back the knee-jerk response to tell her to go drown herself. Selkies might not be as human as I was, but they weren't any more demonic either. "Sorry, I'll be quieter."

She sniffed disapprovingly and returned to her less than subtle drooling over the professor.

I rolled my eyes and slumped deeper into my seat, even as my gaze once more sought my target. On the upside, at least Carlos Barrera was sort of cute in that I've-been-a-geek-my-whole-life way. I wondered again if it was worth tempting fate and getting tangled up with a demon who literally had the power to separate my soul from my body.

The classroom slowly faded out and a feeling of being wrapped in warm blankets surrounded me. The hand cupping my face was almost as soft as the plush lips pressing into mine. Contentment and love pulsed in my chest, radiating to every particle of my being. Our breaths mingled as the gentle kiss lingered.

"Theo, I..."

The promise in those whispered words set my pulse racing. I needed to hear the rest of that sentence, needed to know who this was that called to my heart so completely. I pulled away, eager to get a look at this mystery man.

Lips still tingling, I willed my eyes to open.
I had to know.

I blinked, and the classroom came back into focus. My heart sank at the realization that I would get no answer. Foresight was super helpful that way. As visions went, it was a mild one, but that it had happened *here* was a problem. I absently ran a hand through my hair, not caring what color it was supposed to be today, while my gaze yet again slid over to the object of my quest.

The memory of absolute love from the vision came back to me, the warmth and total peace I'd felt in the caress of some unknown lover, and my resolve solidified. It would absolutely be worth *anything* to get to that feeling. I was tired of living a half-life, avoiding some indeterminate future. It was past time I took my fate into my own hands. But before I could even think about finding true happiness, I had to subvert a prophecy of certain death—and Carlos Barrera was going to help me, whether he knew it or not.

Carlos

The loud crash of books hitting the floor echoed around the room, stealing everyone's focus. I turned to see the source of the disruption and was unsurprised to find a blond guy waving at the class in apology with a decidedly unapologetic expression on his face. His gaze slipped in my direction. I turned away and back to the lesson Professor Roman was attempting to teach.

Two weeks was all it had taken to fall madly in love with my Advanced Demonic History professor. He was tall, confident, sexy as sin, and unquestionably not interested in a lowly fourth-year taking his course.

He turned to address the class once he finished writing on the board, his startlingly green eyes flashing brightly in the early morning light from the windows. "Who can tell me what really happened at the Battle of Gaugamela?"

I let out a wistful sigh at the sultry sound of his voice carrying across the large room. The hand holding my face slipped enough to push my glasses up. I adjusted them and continued my blatant mooning. Like the good little overachiever I was, I'd already read the material and could have easily passed a pop quiz, but I wasn't dumb enough to open my mouth while I was also busy fantasizing about the professor naked. Somewhere in the room, a student paying more attention to the actual lesson than the man teaching it supplied the answer. I sighed again as the professor smiled in response to what I assumed was the correct answer.

A guy sitting near me offered a derisive snort. I glanced over at him to find him doodling away on a page and paying no more attention than I was. Everything from his messy brown hair and wide shoulders to the casual way he'd his feet propped on the desk screamed troublemaker. I dismissed his unwelcome intrusion and returned to my mental fantasy of Professor Roman doing something decidedly more engaging with those fingers than scribbling dates.

"Interesting class," the guy beside me said.

I glanced over at my unwelcome companion. "Yes."

He flipped to a fresh page and resumed sketching as if he hadn't spoken at all. Irritation slithered through my gut. I shifted in my chair, determined to ignore him. After only a few minutes, he turned loudly to yet another page, and my annoyance won out. I twisted to face him once more.

"Are you new? I don't think I've seen you here before. Did you register late?" Though how he could have managed that in a class that filled up weeks in advance was beyond me.

His pen continued to scratch along the page. "I'm just here for him." He gestured subtly at the professor, who was now talking animatedly about some battle involving Alexander the Great using the same hands I'd been admiring moments before.

Is he not even a student?

"He is kind of worth the insane amount of homework," I ventured tentatively.

A smile twitched at the corner of the guy's mouth. "Shame he's married."

The word was like a dagger straight to my heart. I looked back at the professor. The morning light fractured around him in a multitude of rainbows, much like my dreams, shattering into a thousand tiny pieces. My wistful sigh was decidedly more disheartened as my gaze latched onto the band encircling his right ring finger.

Of course. He's European and doesn't wear it on his left. Unattainable and unavailable. I'm such an idiot.

"His wife is a lucky woman." I couldn't even imagine how amazing it would be to come home to a man like that every day.

"Husband."

My gaze flicked sharply to my unlikely classmate. "What did you say?"

"He has a husband, not a wife," he supplied in greater detail, still not looking up from his latest drawing. From what I could tell, this one was a rather impressive sketch of the class.

I huffed. "And how would you know that? I've never seen him with anyone—man, woman, or anything else."

The guy finally glanced up from his drawing. His dark hair fanned across his forehead, and alarmingly blue eyes peered back at me. "Because I'm his husband."

My tongue stuck to the roof of my mouth, then promptly lodged itself in my throat. I choked and spluttered as the reality of who I'd been talking to and about whom burned itself across my face and down my neck.

"Matthew."

The guy next to me and I both swiveled forward at the commanding tone. Professor Roman stared back with such intensity it was like someone peeling my skin back to reveal the bones beneath. I attempted to swallow my embarrassment, which only prompted another series of painful coughs. The guy next to me—Matthew—slapped my back hard enough to knock my glasses askew.

"How many times have I told you not to harass my students?"

Matthew's lips quirked in a crooked smile. "I was merely clarifying something for him."

Professor Roman's eyes narrowed, but he didn't dispute the obvious subversion. Instead, his gaze shifted to me. "Are you alright, Barrera?"

I waved away his concern with one hand and pushed my glasses back up with the other, all while silently praying to spontaneously combust so this mortifying moment in my life would finally end. Matthew—Professor Roman's husband—passed me a water. I graciously accepted it, twisted the sealed cap until it popped free, then downed the cool contents.

Why? Why do I bother to talk to anyone at all?

With half the bottle of water now sitting in my churning stomach, I made to pass it back.

"Keep it," Matthew said, once again completely absorbed in his art.

I refrained from smacking myself in the head. "Claro que sí. Sorry, thank you."

Ay Dios mío. Please just let me die.

"You know, perhaps if you weren't so focused on the instructor, you'd see other people noticing you." He nodded his head almost imperceptibly at another corner of the room.

There sat a guy about my age with platinum hair and the fairest skin I'd ever seen staring at me. It also happened to be the same pendejo that had shown up late and disrupted the class. When he realized I was looking back, he blinked what I suspected were blue eyes and quickly averted his gaze to the open textbook before him.

Uncertain about what exactly I'd just witnessed, I turned to address Matthew once more. "What makes you think..." My words trailed off when my gaze landed on an empty seat. I startled, knocking my pen to clatter loudly on the floor. I raced to retrieve the offending stationery before I could attract any more attention than I already had.

By the time class let out, my embarrassment finally seemed to be under control. It had been an unfortunate moment for sure, but that's all it was, a moment. I stood by the exit and waited to catch up with my study group to determine what time we'd be meeting at the library for the assignment. Advanced Demon History was a popular class and, unsurprisingly, full, though I suspected it had nothing to do with Professor Roman's passion for the subject and everything to do with the fact that he was hands-down the hottest professor in the department.

I shook my head to fend off the wayward thought. It was decidedly more disturbing to think about the man like that after getting caught drooling by his husband. That Professor Roman had a husband at all was like a gut punch.

I might have actually stood a chance... if he weren't already taken.

Who am I kidding? Why would anyone who looks like that be interested in my bony self?

Right in time with my miserable thought, Matthew sauntered through the throng, Professor Roman hot on his heels. I quickly spun away and pretended with all my might that I was one with the wooden walls.

"Give me a minute?" Matthew's voice pierced through my cocoon of self-imposed oblivion, as did the professor's sweet response that he would wait outside and the intimate sound of a shared kiss. At this rate, if I tried any harder to be invisible, I'd become part of the paneling.

I jumped straight up with a yelp at a light touch on my shoulder. When I spun around, it was to find Matthew staring at me with his head cocked to the side. I nudged my glasses further up my nose, even though they hadn't slipped. "H-hi," I stammered, my voice tipping high and cracking. The heat already dominating my face intensified. I cleared my throat and tried to get a grip. "Thanks again for the water."

"No problem." He stared at me for a long moment, those icy eyes seeming to see all the way to my soul. "I wanted to apologize for earlier. I shouldn't have baited you like that."

"What? No. Oh God, no. I'm the one who should apologize. I never should have—"

His sudden burst of laughter cut me off. "It's not your fault my husband is attractive. I meant what I said before, though. Perhaps a look around would enlighten you to other opportunities." He passed me a folded piece of paper and winked.

"What's this?" I asked, but he'd already moved down the hall, presumably to join said husband.

My heart rate shamefully picked up at the thought that it might be the image I'd seen him sketching of the professor. Only when I opened it, the image was of the student I'd caught staring at me.

"Hey."

I glanced up from the picture at the unfamiliar voice. To my horror, it was the same guy in the picture. I quickly folded up the incriminating page and shoved it in a pocket. The guy's eyebrows rose in delicate arches, only a shade or two darker than his hair. "Um, hi. ¿Qué quieres?"

He blinked sky-blue eyes. "I'm sorry, I don't speak Spanish. I'm Theo, by the way. Theo Kendal."

Santa Muerte, I'm such a dolt. At least he doesn't know how rude I was.

"Right, yeah, of course. I'm—"

"Carlos!" The shout from my friend Patty sliced through the roaring in my ears.

My head snapped from the guy standing before me to focus on her frizzy curls bobbing towards us.

"We all still on for the study group?" she asked excitedly.

"Claro."

"Perfect. Be there at six, the usual table. I've already checked with the others." Message delivered, she made to flow out the door with the rest of the class. I desperately wanted to cling to her warm sepia arm and beg her not to leave me alone with this guy, but she was gone before I had a chance to so much as twitch.

I turned a wary gaze back to the blond cutie who, by some stroke of insanity, was still standing there.

"Study group?" he asked, turning those baby blues on me once more.

"Uh, yeah." I took off my glasses and cleaned the lenses on my shirt to avoid his intense gaze. "We meet up every Tuesday and Thursday in the library. Our table is over by the astronomy stacks," I babbled, unable to stop myself.

"Six o'clock. Every time?"

"Ye-ah." My voice cracked for the second time that day, and I squeezed my eyes shut at the sheer humiliation of it.

I'm not thirteen anymore. What the hell is wrong with me? I can't possibly be that hard up for attractive people to talk to me. Can I?

"Sounds great. I'll see you there."

My head shot up. "What?" My luck fared no better this time than it had the rest of the day. *Theo* was already gone and somehow had gotten the impression I'd invited him to join my study group.

   Mierda.

Chapter 2

Theo

Standing in the hall talking to Carlos, I was reminded of the terrified field mouse my feline familiar had once brought me. He even squeaked. Not at all what I would have expected from a fear-inspiring Kisin Demon. Carlos Barrera looked more likely to faint at the sight of a dead body than ferry their soul beyond the veil.

I combed fingers through my hair and let out a heavy breath before swinging into the Witch's College. Whether Carlos was in any way dangerous was irrelevant. He was a soul-stealer, and that was exactly the type of demon we'd been searching for. Kisin tended to be a close-knit group that traditionally didn't venture beyond their cultural borders. That I'd stumbled across one at Uni over ten thousand kilometers away from his traditional territory was nothing short of a miracle.

Between one step and the next, the hallway vanished.

I sat at a round table with four other people. Books lay strewn about the table in various states of open, their pages highlighted in bright neon yellow. Only two of the surrounding faces looked familiar. One belonged to the girl that had shouted at Carlos earlier; the other, of course, was Carlos.
I met his gaze, and he quickly looked elsewhere, choosing instead to hyper-focus on his notes. He was cute in an odd, self-conscious way, with his deeply tanned skin and long lashes fanning darkly over his cheeks behind those round frames. I couldn't help but wonder if his baby face was as soft as it looked.

"You growing roots or something?"

The vision dissolved as abruptly as it had taken hold. I sneaked a quick glance at my reflection in the reflective glass of a nearby portrait to make sure my hair and eyes were still the desired color. Satisfied that the magic still held, I turned my attention to the source of the voice.

"What's the matter, Walter? Jealous I know better spells than you?" I offered a smug grin to hide my unease at having a vision forced upon me in such a public place for the second time. In class was bad enough, but now walking?

Walter Pielton rolled his eyes. As a member of one of the older covens that had survived both the Regency and the Shadow Wars, he had as much access to magic as he could stand. Of course, he didn't know that I also belonged to one of the oldest and most distinguished families of witches.

The Wisterias had long since learned that our rare gift of foresight, while highly sought after, also made us targets. Fortunately, we had more than enough ancient magic to protect ourselves. Unfortunately, those with the gift were identifiable on sight, hence my own manufactured appearance and false last name. Purple hair might not be all that remarkable these days, but purple eyes were.

"Are you coming or not? Albright won't be pleased if we're late," Walter grumbled, ignoring my dig.

Now it was my turn to roll my eyes. "Albright won't know if we're late if she's already asleep."

"You say that now, but I swear she cheats and uses magic to keep attendance."

"Is that cheating, though?" I asked as we fell in step and made our way to our alchemy class.

We continued to debate the topic even after we picked up several more classmates and walked into the laboratory where Professor Albright was, in fact, already asleep. Not even the collective snickers could prod the old crone out of her deep slumber. I shook my head and set up my things at my assigned station. Albright may be asleep now, but she'd eventually wake up and start circling the room to inspect our progress.

The class took on a peaceful calm interspersed with soft whispers as we independently tackled the assignment on the board. My attention was focused solely on measuring out the ingredients needed to create a scrying crystal when a less savory classmate sidled up next to me.

"You seem to be going a little heavy on the winter wisps."

"Probably because I'm a Winter Witch and my magic is stronger in that area. There's more than one way to bless a crystal, Kavren." The lie was easy enough. Given how strong my latent magic was anyway, I could pass for virtually any kind of witch I needed to. However, maintaining that cover was tricky. I'd always favored magic that flourished in the cold, thus the assumed identity of a Winter Witch, but it still wasn't my specialty and I had to be careful to avoid common missteps that could betray that.

Kavren snorted and made himself comfortable on the stool beside me, even though I hadn't invited any such companionship. "Whatever. Did you find him?"

My gaze darted around the room in search of any prying ears. I mumbled a silencing spell beneath my breath that was virtually undetectable and leagues ahead of what anyone in this room was capable of, the ancient Professor Albright notwithstanding.

"I found him." The crystallized particles of moonlight settled into my beaker, mixing with the bluish liquid of winter wisps like glitter. The unstable components started to glow and pulse in their fragile container.

"And?"

I added a teaspoon of powdered bat's wing, and the solution faded to a modest glow of nearly transparent blue. "And what? He was in the class, just like I told you. I also don't see why I'm the one who had to sign up for the damn thing. I don't need any more history credits."

Kavren leaned forward, resting one arm on the metal table as he took a glass stirrer and swirled the contents of my potion. I bit my tongue to prevent myself from tearing into him and attracting unwanted attention. You did *not* touch another witch's magic.

"My dear Theo, you're the one who wanted in on this little venture. Besides, you catch more flies with honey, wouldn't you say?" He tapped the stirrer on the glass, and the contents flared.

I quickly secured the beaker before he could ruin the solution. "And what exactly is that supposed to mean?"

"Let's just say some of us are aware of your reputation as a charmer." His gaze slid less than subtly over to where Maverick was openly staring at the two of us.

I checked my reflexive sigh. Sleeping with Maverick on summer break had been a mistake. How was I to know that he'd end up being a stage-five clinger? Only after weeks of dodging him and then telling him to his face that I wasn't interested in pursuing anything more than the casual fling had gotten him to back off. Though judging by the hurt look in his eyes as he took in the sight of Kavren and me standing a little too close, it would seem that more drastic measures would need to be taken.

I carefully stirred in a reduction of seawater and sealed the container to set overnight. The cork popped into place with a squeak that reminded me of Carlos' own peculiar sound at finding me unexpectedly behind him. "Are you suggesting I seduce him in order to get what we need?"

"I'm just saying you seem to have a vested interest in this project succeeding. I'd think you'd want to do whatever it took."

I barely didn't outwardly grimace at the astute assessment of my situation. If we could pull this off and really harness dominion over death, then I might actually subvert my grandmother's prophecy before it was too late. While those with foresight typically couldn't see their own deaths, it didn't stop them from seeing other people's. She'd informed me at the tender age of six that I'd be courted by death and life as I knew it would end.

A shiver ran through me, as it did every time I thought of Grandmother Wisteria's ominous foretelling. She hadn't told me when this prophecy would come to pass, but I saw the truth of it in her eyes with each year that passed and my time was running out. Twenty-three was simply too young to leave this mortal coil. There was still so much I wanted to do, including things I'd put off in my desperate quest to prevent the prophecy from ever coming to pass.

Kavren reached out to clap me on the shoulder, and I dropped the silence spell just in time not to draw attention to our eerie lack of sound. The clap rang sharply through the room, and Professor Albright startled awake. She gazed blearily out at the room, then shuffled to her feet to start the rounds.

Kavren leaned in close and whispered, "We're going to be gods." Then he slipped away to deal with his own assignment and left me to my musings.

I stared intently at the solution spinning in the beaker like a miniature bottled galaxy. I didn't want to be a god; I just wanted to not be dead. Using a demon's true name to control them was a fable as old as magic. But if Kavren and his consortium of delusional sycophants had actually struck upon the origin of the mythos, then I could look forward to a long, bright future, one where I could finally enjoy all the pleasures I'd put off. In the meantime, there was a demon to seduce.

The vision hit hard and without warning.

Once again, I was back at the round table. This time, there was no one sitting between Carlos and me. He was leaning towards me with an array of untouched books before him. Tears sat heavy on his lashes while his hand cupped the side of my face.

I had no idea why he was so sad, but I knew it tore at my heart. I'd do anything to see him smile. The vision didn't show me what had happened to get to this moment, but I felt a sparkle of something in my chest that reminded me of flying.

I licked my lips, tasting the bittersweetness of a kiss on them, and smiled. The fluttery feeling in my chest intensified. Then I heard myself say, "I knew I could get you to say I love you first."

Air tore through my lungs in a painful gasp, and I collapsed forward, barely catching myself in time to prevent the scrying potion from crashing to the ground and shattering into explosive motes of magic. I braced myself on unsteady arms as my body shook with the force of receding emotion. I hated when the visions tapped into all the senses and even more when they included feelings.

I raked both hands through my hair, assuming that the powerful vision had destroyed the previous platinum and returned my hair to its natural lavender shade. Magic trailed through the tresses, reasserting the desired color in one sweep. With shaking hands, I slipped on a pair of dark sunglasses in case my eyes had shifted as well. That would take substantially more than a passive magic charm. The solution that would restore them to blue sat prepped and ready on my dresser back at the apartment.

Albright didn't even notice when I put the day's potion on the shelf and slipped out of the room. I officially had four and a half hours to make sure I'd gotten the eye solution right for quick doses, shake loose the disturbing vision, and figure out how the hell I was going to pull this off, preferably *without* Carlos Barrera falling in love with me.

Chapter 3

Carlos

I glared across the table with something akin to resentment. Patty had secured the intimate, round table in the library two years previously and we'd been meeting at it ever since. Only now, our core four had grown to encompass an interloper.

After inviting himself to the semester's first study group, Theo had continued to show up like a bad penny. He leaned into a laugh at some joke Lena, our resident dryad, had told. Grisham joined in on the hilarity, his deep voice rumbling like the earth from which he'd sprung. My glare morphed into a glower.

Bunch of traitors is what they were. Patty, Grisham, and Lena had all thrown veritable hissy fits when I'd broken the news of our party crasher moments before he'd arrived. Not even a week later, they hung on his every word, apparently having forgotten he was the enemy.

Every higher magical being in creation knew not to trust a witch. Granted, that distrust went deeper with demons. Our combined history was long and sordid, namely with witches exploiting any demon they could get their hands on for power.

I shoved my glasses forcibly up my nose and ignored the tick starting in my eyebrow. The fact that *my* friends had taken to the charismatic witch with hardly any protest added insult to injury. Theo caught my eye as he brushed back straight locks of bright blue from his forehead. While the abrasive color made his eyes pop, it looked terrible against his fair skin. Quite frankly, he looked a bit like death warmed over and I would know, death was kind of my thing.

"What's the matter, Barrera? Don't like the joke?" Theo asked playfully.

I averted my gaze from his penetrating look. As the only demon at the table, his attention made me more than a little anxious. "I was under the impression we were here to study, not mess around."

"Don't be like that," Patty said at the same time Theo countered with, "What's wrong with messing around?"

The suggestive undercurrent of his question instantly shed new light on his persistent presence. I debated telling him that both Lena and Patty were in relationships and Grisham was currently trying to win back his ex, just to knock him down a few pegs. It would have been awesome to see the look on his face when he realized all of this effort was for naught, but confrontation wasn't really something I handled well. Instead, I stacked my books and notes and avoided his searching gaze.

"If it's all right with guys, I'm going to duck out," I said to the table at large.

Lena pouted and gave a huff. "Aw, Carlos, don't say we've scared you away."

"Nunca," I responded with a reassuring smile. "I promised mi primo that I'd help him with his math homework. Es un idiota and still thinks he can be an architect without a basic understanding of engineering."

Lena's pout shifted to a roguish grin. "You tell that Latin hottie I said hi."

Patty snickered. "And how would your beau feel about that?"

Lena shrugged delicate shoulders. "He might be up for it... if I pitch it right." She winked and Grisham barked out a gravelly laugh.

"And with that, I'm out of here." I shouldered my bag and turned to leave. With each step, I had to resist the urge to turn and see if Theo was staring at me. The hair raised on the back of my neck would have to be confirmation enough. I wouldn't give him the satisfaction of seeing how he unnerved me.

The escape wasn't a total fabrication. I really was meeting my cousin Miguel to help with his math homework... in half an hour. I settled down at a discreet table outside the commissary and prepared to wait. The day's weather was expectedly warm for an August afternoon, but cooling down significantly with the approach of evening. Though the Austrian summer had boasted record highs, the heat didn't hold a candle to summers in my hometown in Mexico. No matter the temperature, my brothers and I could be found running around and playing in the stream near our house.

I smiled to myself, as I did anytime I thought of my family. Sure, having four older brothers had put a major crimp in my love life—if they weren't grilling potential boyfriends, then said potentials were lusting after one of them—but I wouldn't trade them for anything. Even Julissa, my baby sister, could be sweet when she wasn't being an absolute, spoiled terror.

"Oye, primo. ¿Qué paso?"

I looked up and smiled at the guy several inches shorter than me, with substantially curlier hair and a grin that split his dark face in two. "Hey, Miguel. You're early."

"So are you," he countered as he took a seat. "Also, you didn't answer the question."

I rolled my eyes. Miguel may have been a year behind me in school, but it was only because he'd chosen to have an off year before transferring to Arminius. Although he could be pushy, we'd always been close. "What makes you think something's up?"

"Now we're answering questions with questions?" He laughed and nudged me in the ribs. "Pregunto porque, you never leave that precious study group of yours early."

At the reminder of my infiltrated oasis, my face fell.

"Ah-ha!" Miguel loudly proclaimed.

"Shut up. No pasó nada."

"Mentiroso."

I threw my hands up, nearly dislodging my glasses and successfully toppling my backpack so its contents could scatter over the ground. But he wasn't wrong. I was a liar. The nose pads of my glasses dug painfully into the bridge of my nose as I forced the lenses back in place and bent to retrieve the spilled notes. "Ugh, fine. Tú ganas. There's a new guy. Un intruso."

"Intruder? That seems a bit harsh. I've met tus amigos. They wouldn't put up with some jerk."

"Yeah, well, those friends are traitors. They've all been suckered by his good looks and charisma."

Miguel snickered. "Good looks, ¿eh primo?"

My head snapped up from where I was shoving papers unceremoniously back in my bag. "What? No, that's not... Eres un idiota."

He ignored the insult and leaned on the concrete table. "Tell me more about these good looks."

"It doesn't matter how cute he is, he's a nuisance."

"Oh, now he's cute?"

"Dios mío, Miguel. Fine, yes, he's stupid cute and yeah, okay, he's a little funny, but he's a witch."

My cousin blinked back at me in silent judgment.

"What?" I finally snapped.

"You need to get laid, primo."

"Seriously? That's what you got out of all of this? I thought we were working on your abysmal math skills." I let out a huff and slammed the calculus book on the table with a loud thud.

Miguel followed suit, taking out his notes, but sadly did not let it drop. "Si, you absolutely need to get laid. Are you sure you're not interested in me setting you up? I know a lot of people..."

"The last thing I want is mi familia getting me dates. Could you just imagine how much heckling I would get if mis hermanos found out? José would never let me live it down and don't even get me started with Javier."

"Pft. Tus hermanos aren't so bad. They just want you to be happy."

"Como infierno que hacen," I scoffed. "No way, no blind dates."

"Okay, then. What about this witch of yours?"

"Theo is not *my* witch, and I'm not sleeping with him."

"Why not? You already admitted you think he's attractive."

I threw my hands up again, this time more mindful of my open bag. "Because he's a witch, Miguel."

"So what? No one said you had to take him home to meet Tía Lina o Abuela."

The blood drained from my face at the thought of what my mother, or even worse, my *grandmother*, would say if they found out I'd been cavorting with a witch. "No. ¡Absolutamente no!"

Miguel shifted beside me and grumbled beneath his breath, "Couldn't hurt."

I refrained from pointing out the obvious, that it absolutely could hurt. "Can we just do your math homework already?"

He rolled his eyes and opened his book. "Si, primo. But you could at least tell me more about this cuteness. Like, how stupid cute?" he teased.

"Voy a asesinarte. Murder, you hear me? I will unalive your ass."

His crooked grin brought out his dimple. "You're the one who called him cute, not me," he pressed relentlessly. And that's how we spent the next two hours—bickering on and off between formulas. It was almost like being home again.

Theo

It is incredibly difficult to seduce someone who doesn't like you. I was beginning to wonder if Carlos was even gay. He certainly had seemed so when he'd been openly ogling our history professor and when he'd stumbled over his words when I first introduced myself. Now, I wasn't so sure. I wasn't vain enough to believe I was some Adonis, but the fact that he barely spared me a look was downright insulting. Three weeks of inviting myself to his little study group and I'd managed to win over everyone... everyone but him.

Maybe I wasn't his type. It was possible. Unlikely, but possible. Either way, I was running out of hair colors, and even more concerning, options. My clock was ticking down, which meant drastic measures would have to be taken. I briefly considered whipping up a love spell just to hurry things along, but promptly dismissed it. Love spells were dangerous, unpredictable, and inevitably bit you in the ass. Not to mention the added bonus that if I got caught with one, I'd be expelled and possibly imprisoned.

I'm not that desperate. Not yet.

If I could just catch him alone again.

On cue, Patty heaved an over-the-top sigh. "That's it for me. I can't take another second of staring at dates. I'm going cross-eyed. I could use a real date if you catch my drift."

Carlos' gaze flicked up at her statement, and did I detect a glint of envy? Was our quiet Carlos lonely?

Lena pushed back from the table, her long, dark brown hair falling over fawn-colored skin. "Thank goodness. I thought I was going to have to message Derek that I'd be late."

Grisham glanced between the ladies vacating their seats, and Carlos stubbornly fixated on his notes. "You know I'd stay if..."

"No es problema. You all can go. I... I'm going to stay a bit longer."

I smothered a cheer of victory while the concerned trio shared knowing looks.

"You sure, chipmunk?" Lena asked.

Carlos sank deeper into his chair and pushed his glasses further up his nose. "You all go have fun."

Patty spared her friend a worried glance before caving. "Okay, sweetie. I'll catch up with you later."

Carlos raised a hand in farewell without looking up or even cracking so much as a fake smile. Meanwhile, I remained perfectly still as the others grabbed their respective books and notes, then ventured off. Lena flashed me a wink before dancing out of sight.

At least someone knows what's up.

Once it was clear everyone was gone, Carlos let out a heavy sigh and shoved his round frames up his face in order to massage the bridge of his nose. He let out a groan of relief that slipped right past all of my defenses and went right to my dick. Devoting so much time to chasing Carlos meant I hadn't had much time to chase anyone else.

I shifted to the seat closest to him. When he didn't open his eyes to investigate, I steeled my resolve.

It's now or never.

"I thought they'd never leave."

Carlos

My eyes flew open, and I dropped my hand at the unexpected sound of a voice right beside me. But not just any voice, Theo's voice.

"You squeak a lot," he commented, his blue eyes sparkling with mischief.

"What, what are you still doing here?" To my chagrin, my voice pitched high and cracked.

Hijo de puta. What is my problem?

I cleared my throat and tried again. "Don't you have somewhere else you need to be? Plans or something?"

The corner of his mouth twitched with a hint of a smile. "These *are* my plans."

I barely didn't roll my eyes. "I doubt you need the extra study time and, in case you missed it, the rest of the group already left."

"Oh, I definitely noticed." There was a hint of something else in that, but I shied away from delving deeper.

I shifted to put away my things since any chance of quiet study was a pipe dream while Theo was still there with his pretty blond hair, pretty pink lips, and stupid, pretty blue eyes. Unfortunately, I didn't consider the fact that leaning down to grab my bag would put me at eye level with Theo's crotch.

I squeezed my eyes shut, but it was too late. The damage was done, and I could feel the telltale burn creeping past my collar. It took every ounce of calm I could scrounge up to pretend I hadn't just eyed his junk and continue about my business.

"Why are you still here?" I repeated, determined to put the focus anywhere but on my ridiculous blush.

"You're fucking adorable, you know that?"

My ears burned even hotter while my rebellious gaze sought his face to determine the depth of the insult. "You still haven't answered the question," I countered.

He leaned forward, and I stubbornly held my ground, unwilling to betray how much his presence was getting to me. Without my buffer of friends, there was no ignoring the desperate want crawling its way up my spine. Maybe Miguel was right. I definitely needed to get laid if I was acting like this over innocent banter. How long had it been? That no answer immediately sprang to mind was telling.

Theo's baby blues searched mine, and his tongue darted out to wet his lips. There was no way to hide the fact that my gaze tracked the path it took before returning to his eyes. "I'm still here because I want to be. Also, I don't think your friends would particularly appreciate seeing this."

I frowned in confusion. "See what?"

He placed a finger beneath my chin and tipped my face up. I had just enough time to register how close he'd gotten when his lips pressed against mine. Awareness of the library fell away. Every particle of focus zeroed in on Theo's soft lips against mine. It didn't matter that I was on the verge of falling out of my chair or that the kiss was on full display for everyone on campus. A part of me was sending up a solid chant of *Yes, yes, yes*, while another part fought to remind me of where we were, *who* we were. The tip of Theo's tongue teased my top lip, and the yes-part won.

My lips parted with a soft sigh and a silent cry of *More, please.*

Someone loudly clearing their throat finally brought me back to my senses, but Theo was still holding my face hostage with that solitary finger. He unhurriedly pulled away, leaving me hanging in the air. I quickly sat back in my seat and swallowed several times, not a hundred percent sure I wasn't actually asleep.

Theo shifted in his chair to glance back towards whoever had interrupted us before returning his focus to me. "Like I was saying... *studying* is what I had planned for tonight."

The sound of my heart hammering away made thinking difficult, which is probably how my mouth managed to open and start spouting words it wouldn't normally. "We could study at my place. My roommate is out for the night. Dorm isn't far from here. We could walk there and hang out or study or whatever."

I did not just ask him back to my place like some bumbling fool. There's a better chance of a chupacabra popping out of an aisle and swallowing me whole than a guy like Theo Kendal actually agreeing to that insanity.

Theo's lips tipped into a half smile. He reached out a hand, and I went stiller than a statue as he pushed my glasses up my nose with the same finger that had held me captive earlier. "Sure." By the time I remembered how to breathe, Theo was already standing with his backpack hanging off one shoulder. "Lead the way, Carlos." The way his tongue caressed my name sent dizzying thoughts of what else it could caress tumbling through my mind and on a straight track south.

I surged to my feet, zipping my bag as I made my way out of the library, Theo following quietly in my wake. He didn't speak as we ventured across the campus towards Starling Hall, which was unfortunate, as it gave me far too much time to doubt what I was doing. Had I really just invited Theo back to my dorm to "study"? What was with the kiss? Just how desperate was I?

Theo was a witch. I knew better. This couldn't possibly end well.

Chapter 4

Carlos

All too soon, the faded wood of my dorm room door loomed before us. I swallowed and took out the antique key, grateful that my roommate would already be gone for the evening and wouldn't be able to see the epic fool I was making of myself. I turned the key in the lock and pushed my glasses up, still waffling between telling Theo to go and begging him not to change his mind.

"You said your roommate is out?" Theo asked.

The sudden question after so much silence startled me right out of my circuitous thoughts, and I virtually fell into the room. "Y-yeah."

Theo nodded as he stepped inside, far more put together than I was currently managing. He glanced around the shared living area, taking in the simple couch and kitchenette, as well as the two opposing doors that led to the bedrooms.

"I'm on this side." I pointed unnecessarily to the door closest to us.

"And he'll be gone all night?" Theo asked in continuation of his previous question.

"He has a club he goes to on Tuesdays and Thursdays. It's doubtful I'll see him at all before tomorrow afternoon."

"Good." Theo nudged the door closed with his foot and dropped his bag. That was all the warning I had before he pressed me against the wall and conquered my mouth with a vengeance. I gasped into him, but with both of his hands holding my face, I wasn't going anywhere. Not that I wanted to.

My bag slid to the ground from numb fingers that I promptly used to grab Theo's waist and pull him closer. A hungry groan tore free at the feel of his erection grinding into my hip. The obnoxious *Yes* chant started up again, desperate and needy.

He abandoned my mouth to lay a trail of hot kisses down my neck. I swallowed hard as he tasted the sensitive flesh and arched into him, my fingers hooking into his belt loops and pulling him tighter against me. A moan vibrated against my throat.

Suddenly, our hands traded places. I clutched Theo's face as I brought that succulent mouth back to mine, while his hands snaked between us to work at the buttons of our pants. My fingers slipped through his silken hair, and I canted my hips forward to aid in his endeavor to see us both liberated.

No sooner did it look like he would succeed than he shifted his efforts to removing my shirt. I released his head in order to lose my polo. His hands returned to my face, a finger tugging at my already swollen bottom lip.

"Fuck, Carlos, I've been dying to get my lips on these." He mashed his mouth back onto mine in a quick, punishing kiss. "I'm generally a top. That okay?"

I nodded dumbly, and he jerked my hips away from the wall to start steering me back towards my room. My undone khakis slipped down my hips. That, combined with shuffling backwards, instantly became a recipe for disaster. I tripped and went down with a squeak in a tangle of limbs.

Despite my instant mortification, Theo remained unperturbed. He followed after me, his mouth still plastered on mine. The intense kiss deepened, and I forgot all about my embarrassment as he owned me with a confidence that far surpassed my own. One thing quickly became apparent: Theo definitely had more experience than me.

No sooner did the niggling doubt about my performance surface than Theo pulled back. His fingers delicately hooked on my wire frames. "May I?"

I nodded, unable to formulate words.

Without another word, he carefully removed my glasses, folded them, and set them safely on the side table. My chest rose and fell in heavy pants as I fought both my insecurity and the urge to blow from the single hottest sexual encounter I'd ever had, and all we'd done was kiss.

He leaned forward to taste my lips again, and his fingers curled around the waist of my briefs and failing khakis. He jerked them down in one decisive move, and I fell back onto the floor. A low groan drifted above me. "I misspoke earlier."

"What?"

"You're not adorable. You're fucking hot, Carlos. Hecate save me." I was still trying to process the statement when his hand wrapped around my length. All thoughts fled at the sensation of someone else's touch. "Hands and knees, hot stuff."

I was so far gone that by the time I registered the bossy command, I'd already complied.

What the hell am I doing? Theo is a witch. I don't care how horny I am. This is a mistake.

"I swear to all the ancestors, this ass." He dug his fingers into the round globes and kneaded like a cat. "I've been dying to get my hands on it."

I angled my head to see him. "Which is it, Theo? My mouth or my ass?"

His eyes were dark pools of lust when he looked at me. "Why can't it be both?"

I rolled my eyes and gave up trying to look back at him. Doubt pulled at me like the tide going out. I yelped in surprise at a sudden tingling sensation that spread everywhere his hands roved. "What the hell is that?"

"Magic," he quipped.

"For what?" My head fell between my shoulders as the feeling of sparklers playing along my skin continued. Once the initial shock wore off, the tingle felt incredible, subtle electricity dancing over every nerve, increasing sensation.

He trailed a finger down my crevice, and the sparklers followed in its wake. I nearly bit off my tongue with a strangled moan. "Seemed safe to assume you didn't expect to get lucky tonight."

There's fucking magic for that? Mierda. Am I really doing this?

The flat of Theo's tongue traced the same path as his finger. My arms gave out, and I collapsed to the floor.

Yes. I'm totally doing this.

"Still with me, sexy?"

"Sí. Santa mierda que se siente tan bien. No pares." Seriously, *holy shit,* he had a gifted tongue.

"Mmm," Theo hummed from where his face nestled between my cheeks, "still don't speak Spanish."

"Don't... don't stop," I panted. His teeth sank into a light nip, and I sucked in a breath. My entire body shook with the force of staving off my orgasm. "Dios mío, Theo. Fuck. Shit. Condom. We need a condom."

In a heartbeat, Theo's tongue was gone. I let out a pathetic whine that nearly eclipsed the sound of first one zipper and then another. I was already tilting my head to figure out what had happened to all the delicious sensation when a slick finger slipped inside.

"¡Santa mierda!"

Theo's lips brushed along my spine in light kisses as his fingers established a mind-blowing rhythm. "I've got you, baby. Just relax."

Easier said than done when every nerve in my body was screaming for release. When his finger curled against my prostate, I was positive that was it.

Theo

"Wait, wait, wait. Por favor, espera." I stalled at Carlos' sudden brake-check. If he wasn't into this, I was going to feel like a real ass. Maybe I'd misunderstood his response to my check-in. Which would really fucking suck, because now that I'd finally gotten a taste of the quiet nerd, I wanted to taste the rest of him.

I pushed down my trepidation. "You okay?"

"Yeah," he gasped. "I just... need a minute."

I was kind of glad that Carlos couldn't see what was likely a feral smile spread across my face. My hands caressed and kneaded the spectacular globes of his ass while he fought to bring himself under control. Finally, the shaking subsided.

"O-okay."

I placed a kiss on one cheek, fully prepared to pick up where I'd left off.

"But not here. Nessa will fucking kill me if I get cum on the carpet."

His roommate sounded like a Class A douche to me, but I didn't have to live with the guy. "Bedroom?"

Carlos' head nodded between his shoulders. "Bedroom."

I sneaked another ass grab before rocking back on my heels and standing up. Then, I reached down to help Carlos up. He accepted the extended hand, and I hauled him to his feet. It wasn't until he was fully upright that he seemed to realize I was naked now. His gaze traveled down my near ghost-white torso down to my jutting cock. Unable to control the impulse, I took hold of myself and gave a lazy stroke. Another one of those insanely adorable squeaks slipped out of him.

He seemed to realize that he was openly staring and brought his gaze back to mine. "Bedroom. Now."

I snagged the supplies I'd fished out of my backpack. "Don't have to tell me twice."

"Pretty sure I just did," he countered as he ushered us into his room.

I laughed, both because he was right and because I kind of loved that he was a little all over the place. The door clicked closed, and I turned in time to see Carlos sink to his knees. My eyes rolled back as he put those full lips to work in the best way possible. My suspicion that Carlos might not be all that experienced went up in smoke with each expert swirl of his tongue around my dick. It was a solid toss-up whether it had really been that long for me or if Carlos was just that good.

A deep groan pushed its way out of my chest, and I forced myself to look down at the beautiful man before me. The sight of his deep brown eyes framed with dark lashes and that lush mouth wrapped around me stole my breath away. I reached out and brushed the wavy locks from his forehead with a tenderness that surprised me. The moment was so intense I feared the onset of a vision. At last, Carlos blinked, breaking the spell that had ensnared me.

"On the bed," I croaked. With a self-satisfied smirk, he moved. Panic shot through my chest when it became apparent he was going to lie on his back. "Knees," I managed without any of my usual suave. Ancestors help me if I had to look into those rich eyes while I sank into him. I wouldn't survive it. Already, this entire encounter had flown past all of my careful plans and expectations.

I waited for Carlos to get settled. My heart thundered in anticipation as I took in the stunning sight of his gloriously tanned skin and lean body waiting for me. I'd been wrong to think he was too skinny. He was perfect. The slight hint of his hipbones only accentuated the stunning curve of his ass. His smooth back held the barest hint of definition, and the subtle dip of his spine invited hours of kissing.

He gave me an impatient look over his shoulder, and I flashed him my best Cheshire grin. Before he could decide I was absolutely not worth this interlude, I suited up and joined him on the bed. "Last chance. Still on board? Because once I start, I'm going to plow you into the fucking mattress, Carlos Barrera." His resulting groan at the threat went straight to my already aching balls.

"Deja de hablar y hazlo ya," he fired off.

"I'll take that as a yes." I pressed the blunt head of my cock against his slick rim and got the confirmation I'd been seeking.

"Ay, sí, yes. Mierda. Oh fuck! Yes, yes, yes."

His intense heat sucked me deeper until I was mentally chanting complex spell components to bring myself down. Then my gaze fixed on the contrast of my pale hand against his darker back, and all bets were off.

Chapter 5

Theo

There was a very good chance I'd slept through my first class by the time I finally stirred the next morning, but fuck if it wasn't worth it. I sent up a silent thanks that Carlos' brand of demon was decidedly more human than elemental. As it was, we'd worn each other out until we'd collapsed with barely enough strength to clean up.

I smiled to myself, recalling his totally blissed-out face falling gracelessly into the pillow. To be fair, he wasn't the only one who'd ended up a boneless pool of satiated jelly. My toes curled into the rumpled sheets, and my fingers did the same, drawing my attention to the fact that my arm was draped across Carlos' back. It had taken all of point-five seconds for me to become completely obsessed with the way our skin looked against each other.

My gaze traveled over Carlos' still passed out form. He lay on his stomach in a near-perfect mirror of myself with his head pillowed on his arms, allowing his dark hair to stick up in a gloriously mussed mess. Insanely long lashes fanned in dark feathers against his cheek, and those full lips that had tortured me for weeks parted slightly in deep sleep. I couldn't help but wonder if he'd missed classes as well and if he would be upset.

Carlos shifted in his sleep and took a deep inhale that drew my gaze once again to where my hand rested on his lower back. I debated removing it and getting dressed, but a morbid curiosity about what his reaction would be stayed my hand.

His lashes fluttered in conjunction with a sigh, and I quickly shut my eyes. I forced my breathing to become shallow in replication of the deep slumber he was coming out of and relaxed into the bed. He jerked beneath my touch, and I held my breath, fighting the smile that wanted to emerge.

"You're still here."

I feigned being startled awake and blinked open my eyes to find him staring at me in open disbelief. Rather than respond right away, I sat up and stretched my arms towards the ceiling. His gaze on my body was like a physical touch. After a few seconds more, I dropped my arms into my lap and looked over at him. "Why wouldn't I be?"

His mouth opened and closed a couple of times in an effort to get words out. While he struggled, I slipped free of the sheets and reached for the clothes I'd acquired from the living room in the wee hours of the morning before slipping back into bed. "You just strike me as the kind of guy who'd slip out after... after..." He trailed off and his cheeks darkened to a dusky rose.

I bit my cheek to keep from laughing. Carlos Barrera was one of the most adorable creatures I'd ever had the pleasure of encountering. A nervous field mouse staring down a barnyard tabby. "After killer sex?" I finished for him. His blush deepened, and I leaned over to steal a kiss.

Carlos squeaked in response to the unanticipated intimacy and scrambled out of the bed. I didn't bother to keep my eyes to myself as he scurried to pull on light sweats and a t-shirt with a skull and crossbones on it.

My laugh slipped free before I could stop it. "That's cute."

Carlos pulled out the shirt to get a better look at it. "Ugh. Maldita ridícula. My brother got it for me." He promptly ripped off the shirt to no complaints from yours truly and dug out a plain green one.

I leaned down to grab my shirt. "And in answer to your assumption, I've never understood why I should have to sneak out in the dead of night just because it's not my bed. Pretty sure I earned the right to clock out just as much as you did."

He ducked his head, no doubt, to hide a fresh blush, and I used the opportunity to slip into the bathroom. A quick hunt revealed that Carlos was absolutely the kind of guy who kept spare toothbrushes. I finished brushing and stepped back into the bedroom, where Carlos was pointedly avoiding my reappearance.

We can't have that.

Before he could try to make a break for it, like the terrified little mouse he appeared, I walked up and planted one on him. He blinked in confusion and glanced behind me towards the bathroom and back again. I watched him connect the dots as to why my breath was suddenly minty fresh, then stole a deeper kiss. He staggered back when I released him, wearing the best stupefied expression I'd ever seen.

"Also, I'm not an asshole," I added cheekily.

His tongue darted out to taste his lips. "Oh." My eyebrows rose at the surprised response. He cleared his throat. "I mean... uh... of course not. I didn't mean to imply..." He reached out to grab his glasses from the dresser where I'd moved them. He slipped them on and unnecessarily pushed them up. "Would you like some breakfast?"

I smiled and stepped back to give him room to breathe. He took the opening and made a beeline for the door. "I don't really do breakfast," I said as he opened the door to the living room and a supremely angry voice.

"What the fuck is this shit?" an unfamiliar gruff voice demanded.

Carlos

Horror replaced my confusion about Theo's answer. My head snapped up to meet the angry glare of my one-hundred percent pissed roommate.

"Nessa." His name came out more of a squeak, and I didn't even have the wherewithal to be embarrassed about it. Nessa was an undeniably terrifying figure of a wyvern with red scales that glistened like wet blood and bulging muscles that could absolutely break my scrawny ass in two.

His glare transferred to Theo right behind me. "You're bringing guys back to the dorm now? Isn't putting up with your queer ass enough?" The biting comment had the desired effect, and I shrunk in on myself, heedless of Theo bearing witness to this humiliating scene. Nessa was one of the few people I'd met outside of my family who knew what type of demon I was and wasn't the least bit intimidated. Even if he had been, Kisin weren't exactly known for their prowess in combat, and I abhorred confrontation.

"Who the fuck are you calling a queer ass?" Theo said from behind me, his voice bristling with indignation.

I spun to quiet him before he could get us both killed. My hand closed around his arm, and Nessa's gaze zeroed in on the contact like a laser.

"You better not have had sex in here. I swear to the sky, you little shitstain, if I catch so much as a whiff, I'll peel your skin back and we can all see what you really look like."

I snatched my hand from Theo like I'd been burned. "Th-that w-won't be n-n-necessary," I stammered. My hand shook as I tried to push my glasses back up.

Nessa snorted through his nose, and while it was probably a product of a terrified mind, I could've sworn smoke curled out of his flared nostrils. All I could think was that my brothers would never have put up with this shit. That if I told them what a monster my roommate was, they'd pool money for a pop-up portal and take care of everything. But that humiliation would be even worse than what I endured daily with Nessa and his strict demands. Poor Carlos can't stick up for himself. Poor Carlos needed his hermanos to fight his battles for him. Poor Carlos, still the baby.

I'd die before I admitted to my family that I couldn't hack it on my own. Which is exactly why I stood there like a statue as Nessa crossed the room and fisted a hand in my shirt. He jerked me up closer to his wide face. "I'm heading out. When I get back, this place better be fucking spotless. Not a trace of your extracurriculars," he snarled. "Got it?"

"Sí. Entiendo," I mumbled.

"English, you freak," he demanded, shaking me forcefully.

"Y-yes. Yes, I understand."

He released his hold on my shirt, and I barely didn't crumple to the ground. I was shaking so badly I couldn't even see straight. The world was just one loud roar punctuated by muffled voices and a slammed door. I stumbled into the kitchenette and braced myself on the peninsula, where I devoted all of my energy to dragging in more than a scant breath of air.

Theo

Carlos didn't even try to fight back as the blatantly homophobic brute lifted him to his toes and continued to berate him for fucking existing.

"What the fuck is your problem?" I snapped when it was apparent Carlos had no intention of sticking up for either of us. Nessa may have had a hundred kilos on me, but he didn't know what I was capable of. Hell, most of the school didn't know.

"You got something to say, pipsqueak?"

I stepped around a shaking Carlos, who seemed to have forgotten I was there altogether, in order to stand toe to toe with this asshole. "Yeah, I do. This room is fucking spotless. I would know. I cleaned it. And what we do behind closed doors is none of your goddamn business." I was sorely tempted to mention what we *had* done in the living room, but didn't want to risk putting Carlos in any more danger than he clearly already was.

"You think you can take me? I'm a damn wyvern, asshat. What are you?"

"The last thing you'll ever see if you don't back the fuck off."

He barked a laugh that sounded like water hitting hot coals. "I'd like to see you try."

In hindsight, I probably should have thought through the consequences before losing my temper. The lightning that had been low-key playing along my skin as the confrontation escalated skittered down my arm to form a living ball of electricity in my hand. A ball I promptly lobbed at Nessa's chest. He let out a pained grunt as the sphere hit him full force.

"What... the fuck?" he wheezed.

"Get out. And leave Carlos alone. Or next time, I won't check the voltage."

It took a moment for the implications of the threat to sink in, then he hobbled out the door, tail tucked between his legs.

"Son of a bitch." I shook my head and released the rest of the latent energy into a colorful explosion of sparks.

Suddenly, I realized Carlos wasn't standing beside me anymore. I frantically swept the small space until I found him shaking like the last leaf of autumn during a winter gale and gasping for air. I'd seen enough of the symptoms from my aunt to recognize that I had no desire to find out what happened when a Kisin Demon had a panic attack.

I raced into the kitchen just as Carlos removed his glasses with violently shaking hands. They clattered onto the counter while his fingers tugged at his collar as if it were somehow restricting his ability to breathe properly.

"Hey, hey, he's gone now," I tried. When that didn't work, I stepped up behind him and carefully placed my hands on his arms. The last thing I wanted to do was startle him into a power surge, especially since I had no idea what such a surge might entail. I'd never actually seen a Kisin in action, only knew the stories.

"Hey, shhhh, it's okay. You're alright. Breathe for me, baby." I rubbed my hands along his arms, and just like the night before, excess magic poured out of me to swirl in glittering motes of purple on his tanned skin.

He shuddered at the touch, but didn't freak. I kept up the steady motion, letting the magic cover every inch of exposed skin. At last, he let out a deep breath and relaxed against me.

"There you go," I crooned into his ear and followed it up with a kiss behind the shell. His shaking stopped altogether, and he rested more of his weight on me. I nuzzled the back of his neck, inhaling the musky scent of spices I'd picked up on the night before. "I've got you," I whispered and placed a lingering kiss on his neck while my hands ventured from his arms to his torso. I rucked up his shirt so my fingers could lay the magic directly on his skin and continued to whisper reassurances in his ear as I lay more kisses along the back of his shoulders.

He let out a light moan, and my fingers reflexively raked along his abdomen. Suddenly, the full weight of what I'd done crashed over me. I never should have used such volatile magic in close quarters, and I definitely shouldn't have planted myself behind the man currently wreaking havoc on my already over-keyed senses.

This isn't right. I'm taking advantage of him. I need to stop.

Logical judgment went right out the window when Carlos reached back to angle me in for a kiss. I devoured his mouth, pressing him firmly against my already straining pants with one hand and questing into his sweats with the other. His breath caught when my fingers tipped his erection.

I brought my hand back up and offered it to him. He sucked my fingers like it was his damn job, and I groaned into his collarbone. At this rate, I was going to have to borrow pants for my walk of shame. When he finally relented, he stared at me with dark pools of incoherent lust. I snatched at his lips again and shoved my hand back into his pants.

He keened into my mouth as my now slick fingers wrapped around his length. I pressed my forehead into his, eager for more kisses, but also desperate for breath as I worked him over.

"Theo," he panted.

Suddenly, the dorm was gone.

We stood face to face in a confined space, surrounded by darkness. The only source of light was the magic sparkling along Carlos' arm as my other hand continued to slide up and down his shaft.

Adrenaline and joy wove together in a tangled knot while Carlos kissed the hell out of me. I moaned into him and wanted more than anything for this feeling to last forever. To be his rock and safe harbor. To be the reason he was brave. To be—

Carlos' cry ripped me out of the vision. His fingers clenched tightly around my hand not currently wrapped around his dick, which had somehow found its way over his heart. The last of his release left him, and he sagged in my embrace.

"Santa mierda, Theo."

I wanted to purr at the way he said my name, but opted for a kiss on his neck. "How about that breakfast?"

Carlos blinked uncertainly, still somewhat in a daze. "I thought you said..."

"I know, but now I'm hungry. What are you feeling?"

He shook his head as if he were shaking off a fog. "You're going to laugh."

"No, I won't. What?"

He gave me a crooked smile that made me want to kiss the damn thing right off his face. "Seriously, you're gonna laugh. It's so stereotypical."

I turned to wash my hands. "Well, now you have to tell me. Promise, I won't laugh."

"I could really go for a taco."

I didn't laugh, but I did grin. "That actually sounds pretty good. Shame there's nowhere around here to get one."

"Don't be so sure. I know a place. Real, authentic stuff. It's even edible." His eyes sparkled with merriment. Playful Carlos was definitely something I could get used to.

I leaned forward to cage him against the counter. "Then what are you waiting for?"

The joy left his eyes, and his gaze darted to the ribbon of white decorating the counter. "I—"

Before he could fall too far down the rabbit hole, I interrupted. "Wanna see a magic trick?"

With an absent wave and a mumbled spell, I restored the counter and floor to their previously pristine condition. It wouldn't do a damn thing about the smell of sex lingering in the air that the sensitive nose of a steroid-riddled wyvern would easily pick up, but after my earlier display, I didn't foresee Nessa being much of a problem for Carlos. At least, not as long as I was around.

Chapter 6

Carlos

I couldn't believe this was actually happening. I'd had mind-blowing sex with Theo Kendal—a witch—and now we were going to get breakfast, which he didn't do. I glanced at him out of the corner of my eye as we made our way into town and ground to a halt.

"Wasn't your hair blond before?"

Theo gave a chuckle and dragged his fingers through his hair. As they passed through, the light lavender turned into a dark auburn. Staring at the darker tresses, I wondered if it was his natural color, if I'd ever even seen his natural color. At the same time, my fingers itched to slide through the silken strands and pull him close for a taste of those sweet lips.

I shook off the renegade impulse and resumed walking. It was one night. One really incredible standard-setting night. Even if

Theo didn't "do breakfast". I cleared my throat and kept my gaze straight ahead. "That's neat."

"Keeps things interesting. So where are you taking me?" he asked as we turned down a side street off the main road. Aged brick rose up on either side of us, crowding our steps as we made our way down the narrow alley. So what if I'd chosen this one out of five others simply because it would force Theo to be closer to me?

"A hole in the wall and an absolute treasure."

We walked a few more paces in easy silence when Theo spoke again. "Question for you."

I glanced over my shoulder and smiled. "No, I'm not sneaking you off to a secluded place to sacrifice you."

He paused for a moment to absorb the unanticipated response, then laughed. "Get that one a lot, do you?"

I rolled my eyes and faced forward again. "You'd be surprised." It was the truth. Far too many people still believed the Kisin sacrificed wayward souls to appease the Mayan gods. If that had ever been true, those gods hadn't bothered to chat me up once, not so much as a text.

"No offense, but I'm not really worried you'll decide to off me in full daylight, even if we are in the smallest alley I've ever seen." The playful banter brought a smile to my lips that faded just as quickly when he got to his point. "I was actually wondering why you haven't reported your roommate."

My steps stalled out for the second time that morning. I swallowed thickly past all the embarrassment that decided now was an excellent time to show up. "He hasn't... he hasn't actually hurt me." I cast a wary glance back at Theo and was met with a dubious expression. "Seriously. What he did earlier... that's really the most he's ever done."

"But he's done it before."

I fixed my gaze on the concrete at my feet, my mind awash with what Theo must think of me.

I'm such a fucking coward. Jodido cobarde.

Theo slid a hand along my arm, and I jumped, doubly ashamed of my reaction and utter lack of one earlier. "You shouldn't have to put up with abuse like that. Request a different assignment. Demand one if you have to. Why aren't you rooming with another demon, anyway?"

I shook my head. "I don't know how it is in the Witch's College, but the room assignment was random. Besides, it's not worth the trouble. Like I said, he doesn't really do anything to me." I left out the part that I wasn't Nessa's first roommate and that he basically treated me like the help. The silence hung heavy around us, and I dragged my gaze up to the end of the alley only a few yards away. "The stand is just down here."

Theo's hand slipped off my arm. "Good, I'm starving." He brushed past me, and a sudden spike of panic lanced through my chest, prompting me to reach out and pull him up short.

"Please don't say anything."

He cocked his head to the side, causing the auburn strands to glint in the dappled light. "To who?"

I glanced at the opening and debated the wisdom of my confession. "My cousin kind of works at this place. I'm not sure if he'll be there today, but I really don't want him to know about the situation with Nessa."

Theo stared at me for a long minute, his face betraying absolutely nothing about his thoughts. At last, he gave a shallow nod. "Okay, Carlos."

I let out a breath I hadn't realized I was holding and released him to take the last few steps. The alley opened up to an intimate square with a smattering of tiny iron tables and matching chairs as well as the food stand we'd come for. Sure enough, Miguel was behind the counter.

"Primo!"

I rolled my eyes at his enthusiastic greeting. "Buenos días, primo. ¿Cuáles son los especiales hoy?"

"Sabes cuáles son los especiales. Son los mismos todos los días." That was fair. The specials never changed here, which he hated. Miguel tilted his chin toward Theo, who was eyeing the place behind me. "Quién es?"

Like hell was I going to voluntarily tell him who my companion was. It was none of his damn business. "No es asunto tuyo."

He laughed loudly, scaring a flock of mourning doves. "¿Es este el brujo?" Of course, he fucking guessed this was the witch I'd told him about. "Es muy guapo. Subestimaste su buena apariencia."

I cut my cousin a nasty look and ignored the implication that Theo was substantially cuter than I'd led him to believe. Instead, I turned to Theo. "What'll it be? Miguel's treat. Bacon, eggs, potato…"

Theo's smile sparkled in his eyes. "Should have thought it'd be pretty obvious I have a penchant for sausage."

I was so enraptured with the wicked glint in Theo's eyes, I barely even heard Miguel choke on his laugh.

"Closest I've got is chorizo," Miguel supplied behind me.

Theo ignored him and addressed his question to me. "And what's chorizo?"

"It's a kind of spicy sausage. But I admit, I've never really been a fan of all that much spice."

"Broken Mexican," Miguel fake-coughed. I made a mental note to kill him later.

"And what will *you* be having?" Theo asked, totally disregarding my cousin's snide comment.

My grin widened so much I was positive I looked half-manic. "The barbacoa definitely. Tons of savory flavor, not a lot of spice."

Theo's gaze swept unabashedly over me from head to toe and back again. "Sounds perfect. I'll have that. I'll go grab a table." He turned to claim one of the five sets, all currently sitting unoccupied.

I swiveled around to hide my hard-on and had to fight the need to palm my cock. Theo's gaze might as well have stripped me bare and bent me over to fuck me right here.

"Mierda primo. You blush any harder. People are gonna start thinking *you're* chorizo."

"Callate la boca. Just hand over the food, you meddling busy-body."

"Oy, what about payment?" he asked as I took the two hefty, foil-wrapped tacos.

"You're buying."

He snorted. "Fine, but I want details, primo. Like all of them."

"Estàs loco. Not happening." I ignored Miguel's wounded look and walked over to where Theo was already sitting. I passed him a taco and settled down. He spared me a wink before peeling back the foil and sinking his teeth into it. The second his tongue touched the food, he let out a deep groan that simultaneously made me want to grin like a fool and drag him back to the bedroom.

"Fuck, Carlos, this is amazing," he said around a mouthful.

I hid my idiotic grin behind a bite. "Glad you like it."

He mumbled something that might have been about finding heaven and took another bite. "And your *cousin* made this?"

"Yep. I keep telling him he should switch from architectural engineering to culinary arts, but he won't hear it. He's determined to build a skyscraper one day."

"Lofty goal," Theo deadpanned.

Half a beat went by, then I dissolved into laughter. I balled up the foil as I sobered up. "Thanks for this morning, by the way."

"Which part?"

I bit my bottom lip and pretended the heat suffusing my neck was from the sun overhead. "Why can't it be both?"

Theo ducked his head as he chuckled, and his hair shone copper in the early morning light. "Well played, Barrera, well played." He pushed his chair back and stood. "I should be getting back to campus and to my next class."

"Yeah, of course." I slid my chair back so I could stand. Before I got the chance, though, Theo leaned down and stole a kiss that certainly didn't feel like we were out in broad daylight.

"Thanks for breakfast."

"Uh-huh."

He smirked and pushed my sliding frames back up my nose. Then he turned and wandered back down the alley we'd used to get here. I was still watching the last place I'd seen him before he disappeared when my cousin let out a vulgar whistle.

"Madre de Díos. Do you want the whole village to hear you?" I snapped as I vacated my chair and stomped up to my pain in the ass cousin.

He walked out from behind the shop window and wrapped me in a big hug. "Aw primo, I'm so proud of you."

I tried unsuccessfully to shove him off. "Eres un asno."

At last, he relented and pushed me back to arm's length. "Tu madre te va a matar."

My eyes widened. I hadn't even thought about what my mother would do if she found out I'd slept with a witch. Death would be a mercy. "Díselo y te mataré."

He ignored my threat to kill him if he told her and feigned sorrow as he combed fingers through my hair like my mother did. "Ay mi'jo, you used to be such a good boy."

"Cut it out, asshole." I swatted his hand away. "It was your idea."

"Exactly. Now how about those details?"

Theo

I dropped my overloaded pack on the floor and slumped into the armchair. Exhaustion weighed heavy on my bones right next to a heavy dose of guilt. In classic Theo-style, I'd taken what I wanted and then acted like nothing had happened, like my entire world hadn't been turned on its axis. I pinched the bridge of my nose as the image of Carlos's confused expression swam in my mind.

I'm such a fucking dick.

Forget the fact that I needed to stay close in order to win his trust and eventually his true name, or that the sex really had been killer. The visions were freaking me out. Never had I ever had so many in such a short amount of time and never all around the same person. Add to that how many of them seemed to be hints of a near future, and my mind was shot.

I cast a wary glance at the calendar hanging on the wall. Tiny colored stars decorated the otherwise blank canvas, each one denoting a vision and its subject matter. Green for something school related, gray for strangers, purple for anything directly involving me, red for death... and black for Carlos.

I stared at the current week. It was only Wednesday, and already there were more stars than there'd ever been before. I could add up every single star of any color for the entire year and the last two weeks would take the pot. Ever since I'd slept with Carlos, there'd been at least a vision a day, four of which had two. Each occurrence stood out with a star of black... and purple, always together.

I let out a groan and scrubbed at my face. "Ugh, what does any of it mean?"

An enormous gray cat with long hair and a bushy tail landed gracefully, if heavily, in my lap. My hand automatically came up to smooth the silken fur.

"Do you know, Sigurd?" I scratched behind his ears and was rewarded with a purr that rumbled like thunder. "You like that, don't you?" The purring increased, and Sigurd aggressively bumped my hand to keep the pets going. "Tell me, is he the one that's going to kill me?"

My familiar turned luminescent green eyes on me that shone even in the half-gloom.

"I don't know why I'm asking you. You probably wouldn't tell me even if you did know."

He let out a low growl of disapproval.

"You disagree?"

His tail switched in response.

"That thing is a menace."

I lurched forward at the unexpected voice, effectively tossing Sigurd to land on the ground with an indignant yowl. My gaze landed on Kavren leaning against the wall and watching me.

"What the fuck?" I asked while I mentally went through all the wards on my apartment. None of them seemed to be broken. But if that was true, then how had the witch gotten inside? I watched Sigurd approach the intruder as he levered off the wall. When Sigurd walked through what appeared to be solid legs, I let out a breath.

Astral projection. Of course. Always forget about that one.

Kavren sneered at the cat, who glared defiantly back. "I still don't understand why you insist on having such a beast as a familiar. Why not a normal cat, or a raven, or fuck, a lizard?"

"What do you want? There is such a thing as a phone. You could have called or at least texted." I settled back into the chair and diligently didn't glance toward the calendar.

"You've been avoiding me," he said as he picked his way around the room, no doubt searching for any hint as to my coven.

"No, I haven't."

He ceased snooping and walked over to stand in front of my chair. He crossed his arms over his chest and scowled down at me. "Yes, you have. I want a status update. How are things going with our project?"

I winced at his choice of words and the rude reminder of why I'd sought out Carlos in the first place.

"What's the matter? Sex with a Kisin not quite what you expected?" he prodded. As if *he'd* ever have sex with a demon, let alone a Kisin.

That's one way to put it.

"Not exactly," I responded when it was clear Kavren was waiting for an answer.

"Well, suck it up, buttercup. You're taking one for the team."

"You're revolting."

He shrugged, not disputing it. "Look, it's either you or someone else. What'll it be? Do I need to find a different partner in this?"

Two months ago, my answer would have been fueled by my need to be in on this endeavor, but now my motivations seemed more muddled. The thought of someone else touching Carlos made my skin crawl.

"No."

Kavren leaned forward and cupped his ear. "Sorry, I didn't catch that."

"No," I repeated louder. "I've got this."

"Good. Don't fuck it up. I mean, you can fuck it if you think it will help. You can deal with a little bad sex for the greater purpose."

His assumption that the sex had been anything short of stellar got my ire up. I blamed a fragile ego. I pushed myself up out of the chair. "I can take care of my own business, thank you. Now get out before I have 'the beast' expel you."

Kavren's lip curled at Sigurd, who was already advancing in anticipation of sending our guest packing. In a blink, Kavren was gone. I stared a moment longer at the now blank space and let the sense of inevitability settle over me.

"Guess I'm asking him out," I told Sigurd as I raked my fingers through my hair. Just as Kavren had vanished, so too did the apartment, to be replaced by a familiar hallway.

I glanced around to get my bearings and recognized the antique wallpaper of Starling Hall. Suddenly, I turned and sprinted down the corridor until I skidded to a stop in front of a large wooden door. My fist pounded on it with hollow thuds a few times before I braced myself on the frame, still panting from my inexplicable run.

The door swung inward in a matter of moments. My gaze fixed on Carlos' bright smile and shining brown eyes. That same sense of inevitability wrapped around my chest.

"Hello again." His voice was playful, and the humor of it danced in his eyes.

"I don't know what I was thinking," I panted.

I stepped forward to meet him and out of the vision. My deep groan irritated Sigurd as I walked over to the calendar and added the third set of stars for the day.

Chapter 7

Carlos

I stole a glance at Theo chatting with Patty about her latest riddle quest. While I was by no means an expert at one-night stands, I thought I was handling Theo's peculiar attitude about the whole thing quite well.

Who am I kidding? I suck at one-night stands.

The bottom line was that I simply didn't get it. I thought the sex had been great, so why pretend it hadn't happened? Maybe I was deluding myself, and I really was that hard up for a good time. Maybe it was me. Maybe I hadn't lived up to his expectations. Or maybe I was just another one of his conquests. It didn't take a genius to put together that someone as charming as Theo didn't have problems getting laid regularly, which led me back to my original doubt.

Was it something I did?

I pulled my glasses off and cleaned them on the hem of my shirt. Out of the corner of my eye, I noticed Theo's gaze flick over to me. On a whim, I quirked a small smile that no one else could see. The corners of his eyes crinkled in a responding smile that didn't quite touch his lips before he turned back to Patty's rant about how Sphinxes were capable of more than riddles despite the fact that she'd just told one.

Mierda. It is me. It's not like I gave him any indication that I'd be interested in continuing this. Whatever this is.

Frankly, even if the proverbial "this" started and stopped with sex, I was still on board. All that was left to do was figure out how to start, or restart, as it were. And that was exactly where I stalled out. I wasn't outgoing like mis hermanos o mis primos. Hell, the first date I ever went on, I didn't even realize what was happening until Paolo Rivera had kissed me.

I slid my glasses back on and let out an unintentional sigh. There was only one word for guys like me—hopeless.

"Hey, chipmunk, are you all right over there? I can tell Miss Smarty Pants here to lay off the riddles and get back to studying." Theo covered his mouth to hide a chuckle at Lena's blatant suggestion about what the root of the problem was. Meanwhile, Patty gawped like a fish out of water and Grisham suddenly became very absorbed in his notes.

"Lo siento," I apologized. "I didn't mean to detract from the story. Guess I'm just bummed that I'm gonna have the dorm all to myself this weekend and all you perdedores are gonna be busy elsewhere."

Lena pouted, and Patty finally found some words. "You could always come to Cairo with me."

"And have to deal with sand up my ass?" I shook my head and pushed out a laugh. "No me interesa. Hard pass."

Lena's eyes lit up the way only a Dryad's could. "I know! Why don't you and Theo hang out?"

I looked over at Theo, expecting to see a rejection of the idea stamped plain as day across his face. To my surprise, he shrugged.

"I'm not doing anything. What do you say, Barrera? We could always work on the term paper."

Grisham's hand came down hard enough on the table that we all jumped. "No studying. You two can hang out like normal blokes, or I'm dragging both your over-achieving necks down to the mines." As a dwarf, the mines were Grisham's favorite threat, and one I'd learned the hard way wasn't empty.

"Calmate, take it easy. Fine, no studying. Won't even take the books out of my bag, Saturday," I said, holding my hands up defensively.

Grisham narrowed beady eyes at me, then swiveled his penetrating gaze to Theo, who promptly drew an "X" over his heart and held up his hands in equal surrender. My grumpy friend nodded once and resumed his perusal of his notes. The rest of us shared curious looks as to his outburst until Lena mouthed something about things not going well with his ex.

The brief outburst done, we resumed our dissemination of that week's lesson. Truthfully, I probably could have stood a cramming session before the exam on Tuesday, but I now apparently had other plans... with Theo. My gaze slid over to where today's impressive shade of magenta was falling into Theo's eyes. While it obscured his baby blues, it did nothing to hide the smirk playing at the edges of mouth.

Well, that was easier than expected.

Theo

I will not use Carlos for sex. I will not use Carlos for sex...
Even though I really want to.

My sigh of defeat bounced back at me from the vacant hall, an appropriate rebuff to the incongruous thought. After having actually slept with Carlos, the plan to seduce him into giving me his true name felt skeezy and wrong. I'd have to get my kicks elsewhere and not give in to the temptation to jump his bones.

I'll earn his trust as a friend instead of a lover. Maybe then I won't feel so much like the amoral douche I really am.

I knocked on the ancient wooden door and flinched at the physical reminder of the vision from a few days ago. My deep breath was shakier than I would have liked, but helped steady my nerves.

This isn't the vision. And I'm not here to have sex with him. We're hanging out as friends. That's all. I can do this.

The pep talk might have been more believable if I hadn't whimpered when the door finally opened. The object of my inner turmoil stood there in a red shirt plastered to his body with sweat. He pushed his glasses up, which had slid down his nose, bringing my attention to the smear of dusty white on his cheek. Carlos Barrera really was the cutest fucking thing, and he didn't even know it.

"You have flour on your face," I said, my hand already reaching out of its own accord to brush it clear. He beat me to it, and I quickly snatched down the rogue appendage before he could take notice.

"Mierda. I was helping Miguel earlier." He rubbed the fine powder between his fingers and laughed. "That sounds like I was a willing volunteer. More like volun-told. Come on in." He stepped aside so I could enter. "What have you got there?"

I held up the two movies I'd scared up. "I noticed you had a player the last time I was here." The moment the words left my mouth, I regretted them. Now all I could think about was miles of dark, tanned skin warm beneath my hands.

Fuck me, I didn't even make it three seconds before thinking about sex with Carlos.

"So, not going out then."

I was hard-pressed to figure out if it was a question or a statement. Truthfully, I had considered going to the local club, but I'd just as quickly dismissed the idea. I'd likely end up dry humping him on the dance floor for half a song before dragging that sumptuous ass somewhere more private.

Damn it. Stop thinking about sex.

I forced all thoughts of humping Carlos from my mind, dry or otherwise. "I'm not really up for going out. That okay?" I asked, and it was the truth. After spending most of the day working on potions and research, I didn't really have the energy for crowds of people.

His smile made his whole face light up. "Está bien. But, hey, do you mind if I finish cleaning up real quick? You're earlier than I expected."

I blinked, momentarily distracted by thoughts of helping Carlos out of his sweaty clothes, before finally nodding.

Am I early? I pulled out my phone to check the time as he vanished into his room. *Fuck, I'm early.*

I popped in one of the movies at random and dropped onto the couch. The cushions sank invitingly beneath me, leaving my mind to ruminate on things it shouldn't. Namely, if sleeping with Carlos again was worth the price of the increased visions, which in turn led me to memories of what we'd already done.

I diligently kept my gaze focused on the wall that held the TV and door lest it venture to more interesting places. Like the wall I'd pressed him up against as I got my first real taste of him. Or the floor behind the couch where I'd rimmed him until his words had turned to babble. Or the door that he was currently undressing behind.

I squeezed my eyes tightly shut, but the effort did nothing for the lust-fueled memories. Thankfully, I didn't have too long to think about how Carlos was likely naked, not twenty feet away, and how I could be naked with him.

"Since we're doing movies, how about some popcorn?" Carlos asked, announcing his return.

I hadn't even heard the door open. Agreement was already on my lips when I turned and nearly swallowed my tongue. Carlos stood in the open doorway to his bedroom wearing some kind of slinky lounge pants and a tight shirt that left nothing to the imagination. The teal tee suited his darker skin and was graced with an elaborate sugar skull with flowers for eyes and every color in the rainbow. It looked fucking great, and I wanted to peel it off of him with my teeth.

"I can't tell if that shirt is realistic or ironic," I said without thinking, my gaze riveted on his chest.

Carlos let out a rich laugh and ran a hand down his front that seemed to drag all the blood from my head straight to my dick. "A little of both, I suppose. So...popcorn?"

I tried to swallow past the zero moisture in my mouth. At last, I managed a husky, "Yeah," that only just didn't crack.

He spared me a crooked grin and turned to go into the kitchen. My stupid eyes stayed glued to his body and practically bugged out of my head at the rearview. Whatever those ridiculous pants were made of, they simultaneously clung to every minute contour of his magnificent ass and hung loosely to flow down his legs.

I swiveled forward so fast I almost pitched off the couch. I mashed my hand down on my pulsing dick, straining painfully against my zipper in search of a modicum of relief.

"What are we watching?" Carlos called out as the microwave beeped on and the unmistakable sound of kernels popping filled the room.

I scrambled to remember what I'd put in, but forming a coherent thought was exceedingly difficult with all of my blood currently occupying a different organ.

"As long as it's not a tragic love story, I'm good. My cousin tricked me into watching a movie about Tristan and Iseult, and I still haven't forgiven her," he continued to chat amicably.

"Would this be the same cousin that got you the shirt?" I asked, proud of myself for at least sounding like I wasn't fighting a raging hard-on.

Carlos emerged on the other side of the couch holding an oversized bowl, full to the brim with buttered popcorn, his head cocked to the side in obvious confusion. He absently pushed his glasses up. "How did you know my cousin got me this shirt?" Suddenly, his face lit with understanding. "Oh! No. My brother Jorge got me that one. My cousin Gabriella is the one who made me watch the movie and also got me this shirt. Though I have shirts that other well-meaning cousins got me."

"How many cousins do you have?" I asked as he passed me the bowl, mercifully too distracted in acquiring the remote to notice I didn't put it directly on my lap. He leaned forward with a low chuckle, revealing a strip of smooth skin beneath that painted-on shirt, and I nearly dropped the bowl altogether.

"Too many. But considering I have ten aunts and uncles, it comes with the territory. Thank goodness only one of my five siblings is a practicing Catholic. I don't think I could handle being an uncle to thirty people."

I almost choked. "*Five* siblings?" *Thirty* cousins?

"Yeah," he responded as he settled back. "They can be a real pain, but they're also kind of awesome. As if that makes any sense." He rolled his eyes. "What about you? Any siblings?" He snagged a handful of popcorn from the bowl perched above my lap, and it took me a second to process the question.

"Huh? No, it's just me. I have a smattering of cousins, but we're not all that close. Actually, I don't see my family very often. Hence why I'm chilling at uni with you."

"That sucks, but I'm not complaining." He pressed a button on the remote as if all of this was perfectly natural. Which it might have been given different circumstances. I set the bowl between us before I did something dumb like magic a hole in the bottom. He eyed me, but didn't comment.

I cleared my throat. "Right, so, the movie. It has a bit of everything, including romance, though not on the tragic side."

Carlos curled his legs into a pretzel and burrowed deeper into the couch. "Sounds promising. Magic or human?"

"Both actually. The main character crosses a barrier from the mundane world into a magical one in search of an item to win the affections of a woman."

"Ooh, I love magical realism."

"Not quite. It's a little older of a setting than that, more straight fantasy, but I admit, it's one of my favorites, even if the witches are seriously outdated. You see, his quest ultimately reveals that he's fighting for the wrong thing."

"Stop telling me the plot. You'll ruin the whole thing," Carlos admonished, then hit play.

Carlos

Theo had made an excellent choice with the first movie, and it would definitely be going on my list of favorites as well. Even the second one was pretty decent. We chatted throughout, adding our own commentary to the events unfolding on screen until the last credit had long since disappeared. The whole evening had gone spectacularly well if you didn't take into account that both of us were still dressed and that Theo was leaving.

So much for Gabbi's "spank pants". I never should have let her talk me into buying these things.

"Guess I'll see you next week. Let me know if you want to get together and study before the exam," Theo said as he stepped through the door.

I opened my mouth and realized he'd stolen my line. "Sure thing. See you around."

"Yeah, see you." He seemed to be stalling, then abruptly gave a weird salute and sped down the hall like he couldn't get away fast enough.

I closed the door so I wouldn't do anything as embarrassing as watch him race down the hallway in the hope he'd change his mind.

Well, fuck.

Knowing you weren't smooth was one thing. Having your best-laid seduction attempt blow up in your face was downright disheartening. I was halfway to my room, determined not to have the entire night be a total loss, when a loud banging sounded on the door. I frowned in confusion about who on Earth it could be and had to push my glasses back into place. I opened the door, and to my surprise, found Theo braced against the frame and panting.

"Hello again," I teased, one hundred percent positive I'd lit up like a damn fiesta at the sight of him.

"I don't know what I was thinking." He stepped forward, closing the door behind him. Between one blink and the next, his mouth mashed down on mine. My hands went to his face as I urged the kiss deeper, while his hands slipped around to cup my ass. He moaned into my mouth as he squeezed the globes through the flimsy material. "What the fuck are these things made of?" he groaned as he started walking us back towards my open room.

"No idea," I managed between kisses. At last we were in my room. Theo reached back, scarcely letting go of me long enough to close the door, then his hands were back on my flushed skin.

His fingers slipped beneath the waistband to grope my bare ass, and our joint moans echoed off the walls. The sound was still bouncing when he relinquished his hold in order to drag my shirt over my head. As soon as it was gone, his mouth returned to mine while his fingers dug into my sides.

"Fuck, Theo," I hissed.

He mumbled something against my neck that sounded suspiciously like loving it when I said his name.

"Quiero que me hagas perder el control." As if he had any clue that I'd just begged him to make me lose control, he yanked the flimsy lounge pants down to puddle on the floor. His resulting groan had me harder than it seemed possible.

"On the bed. I want to taste the rest of you."

The huskiness in his voice had me tripping over myself with my urgency to do as he asked. By the time my glasses were safely on the nightstand, Theo was as naked as I was and staring at me with a hunger that had goosebumps erupting on my arms. He crawled onto the bed between my legs, taking his time running light brushes of his lips along my legs.

"You're so fucking beautiful," he mumbled as his hand stroked my calf.

I had no idea what to say to that. People had said I was handsome before, but never with the level of reverence Theo did. My mind scrambled with some way to return the compliment, then his mouth wrapped around my erection and all thought fled. "Santa mierda." I reached down to slide my fingers through his silken hair while he devoured me. "Tómlo más," I moaned.

He gave a decisive swirl of his tongue and pulled up with a pop. "Come again." My abdomen quivered in anticipation as he placed an open-mouthed kiss on the muscles and coasted his soft hands along my thighs.

"Magia. Magic. Do the magic hands," I gasped out.

He flashed me a wicked smile. "Do we need it?"

I snorted. "No."

"Someone was optimistic."

"Hopeful." Sadly, the witty retort came out strangled as he teased the tip of my cock with his tongue. "I just like the way it feels." Theo froze long enough that I propped myself up on my elbows to investigate. "I'm sor—"

He surged up the rest of my body to tackle me with a dominating kiss. At the same time, his hands caressed my sides, and sparklers came alive on my skin. I gasped with the intensity of it, my body bowing off the bed into him, craving more of the electric touch.

"Please tell me you have a condom," he said as his kisses ventured to the sensitive area between my neck and shoulder. I wanted to ask why he didn't, since he had last time, but instead, I flailed blindly around for the supplies in the nightstand. My fingers closed around what we needed right as a finger buzzing with electricity brushed my entrance.

"Mierda. Voy a explotar. Sí. No pares. No pares." Sensation overwhelmed me from head to toe, and I *was* a little afraid I'd explode, but not enough to want him to stop. I didn't even notice when Theo took the bottle of lube and foil square from me.

Theo

My smile refused to be quelled as I watched Carlos collapse back onto the mattress after cleaning up. I finished my own efforts and landed beside him with a bounce. His shit-eating grin shone back at me as I settled on my side, facing him. I couldn't remember the last time I'd been so into a sexual liaison. Even exhausted, a lightness filled my chest, and I wanted to continue being around him.

"Can I stay?"

His eyes crinkled with laughter. "Oh, *now* you're asking?"

I took the humor as a good sign. "Last time you were passed out."

He rolled his eyes. "Kind of surprised I'm not now. My body feels like over-cooked fideos—pasta," he clarified. "But I don't think I could sleep even if I wanted to."

"I know what you mean. My mind is completely wired. So... was that a yes?" I prompted.

"That's a yes. Of course you can stay, Theo. After all, you earned it." He winked, and a fresh wave of giddy laughter bubbled out of me.

"Well played." As I sobered up, I couldn't help but reach out to tuck a curl of wild hair behind his ear. "Can I ask you something potentially really personal?"

His eyes danced as my fingers lingered to trace around his eye. "Guess it depends on what it is. If you're going to ask me how hopeful I was that this is where this night would lead, I'm not telling you that."

I laughed as my finger dipped down to trace his smirk. "No, that's not what I was going to ask." Though now I really wanted to know. "I was just curious why you wear glasses. Is it a personal choice, or do you actually need them?"

His smirk softened into a smile. "I actually need them."

I pulled my hand back and tucked it beneath my chest. "But why? I thought demons healed quickly. Shouldn't your vision be perfect or something?"

Carlos gave me a long, considering look. "You know what I am."

"I mean, yeah, I know you're a demon, obviously," I quipped.

"No. You know what kind. Took me a while to put it together. First it was the teasing comment about the skull and crossbones, then the quip about the sugar skull tee. You know I'm a Kisin. What I can't figure out is how you figured it out."

I swallowed thickly and tried not to let my anxiety show. "I, uh, overheard a few things and sort of put two and two together." His unblinking gaze threatened to obliterate whatever was left of the euphoria swimming through me. When he finally broke the silence, I was on the verge of excusing myself rather than continue lying to him.

"You knew what I was and slept with me, anyway?"

I blinked, taken completely aback by the question. In a heartbeat, I'd pushed him onto his back and straddled him. "There are people who won't sleep with you because of what kind of demon you are?" The dark rose that stained his cheeks as he averted his gaze from mine was all the answer I needed. "Seriously? You're fucking hot, Carlos. Fuck those guys. Or better yet, don't. They don't deserve you."

His hands came automatically to my sides but stayed still, and he refused to meet my gaze.

"Hey, look at me." At last he turned his head enough to meet my questing look with hooded eyes. "You are incredible. I've had such an amazing time tonight, and we're definitely getting tacos again in the morning." His cheeks darkened, and his gaze flicked up. "Now, explain this glasses business to me."

A smile curled his full mouth. "Kisin Demons cross the veil to the realm of the dead."

"Know that," I teased. "Keep going."

The smile widened as he relaxed beneath me. "Like I was saying, Kisin cross the veil. When we walk back into the mortal realm from our first journey across the Marigold Bridge, some part of our physical body stays behind."

I frowned in confusion.

"I'm not explaining this right," he huffed. "Every Kisin Demon sacrifices some part of their mortal form in order to return from the realm of the dead. No one knows what their sacrifice will be until they make their first walk. For my brother Jose, it was his knees. For Javier, it was his ankles. For me, it was my vision. Honestly, the fact that I'm a demon is the only reason I'm not blind."

"All magic has a price." It was a lesson as old as time, and I wondered why I'd never thought to apply it to demons. They were, after all, magical beings.

He nodded, and his hands finally started to coast enticingly up and down my sides. I pushed back thoughts of increasing want. "Then why make the journey at all if you know there's such a steep price?"

He chuckled beneath me, which sent delicious zings of pleasure radiating through my body. "Porque es nuestro proposito, our purpose, and we want to. Reuniting loved ones separated by the veil is the most rewarding thing I've ever done in my life." He carded fingers through my hair, and I momentarily got lost in the exquisite sensation.

"How old were you when you took your first journey?"

"Thirteen."

I hummed appreciatively as his fingers massaged my scalp. "Has anyone ever refused to follow the path?"

"A couple that I know of, but it's a part of us. They all come back eventually. It's simply one of those things you have to experience to truly get."

The logical part of my mind longed to delve deeper into this layer of understanding that I'd never thought to consider. But the rest of me was far more interested in the way Carlos' full mouth shaped words. Unsurprisingly, the latter won out. I leaned down to taste his lips and didn't come back up for air until late Sunday evening.

Chapter 8

Theo

I glanced up at the unassuming facade of the building where I was meeting the group. As far as I could tell, it looked nothing like the warehouse Kavren said he'd secured for the ritual. The door opened without opposition, which didn't bode well for the activities we had planned.

Summoning demons had become substantially more taboo over the last decade, and holding one against their will ranked high on the list of illegal shit that would not only get someone expelled, but bound and thrown into prison, most likely the kind without windows or visitors. My family had enough pull in the magical community that I wasn't all that worried about never seeing the light of day again if this all went horribly south, but I doubted the others had that kind of security.

Inside, I discovered my initial assessment to be correct—this was not a warehouse. My gaze wandered around the gutted apartment, which appeared to be in the midst of a renovation. The odd pieces of furniture still occupying the space sat clustered against the walls, draped with white sheets and a fine layer of dust. Light filtered in from half-closed windows, lending the room an ominous feel. I shifted the heavy bag slung over my shoulder and stepped deeper inside in search of my accomplices.

My sneaker bumped a rogue piece of drywall, and it clattered loudly across the floor. At the sound, a guy who could have passed for one of the remodelers stepped out. I, however, knew better. Warren may wear paint-splattered cargo pants and a shirt that had seen better days, but I'd yet to meet anyone with his knack for linguistics. Of course, he was also a self-righteous prat.

For a second, I debated asking if he had a good spell for translations, maybe something portable. I quickly dismissed the notion. The last thing I needed was any of this trio suspecting I might be going soft on the plan.

Warren stepped forward, dusting his hands even though they were clean. "Good, you found the place."

"Was a little worried I hadn't when the door was unlocked." My fingers tightened on the strap of my bag. I shouldn't have to point out how dangerous what we were doing was or how much trouble we could land in, even without a demon. The components in my bag alone would be condemning enough.

"Is that Theo?" A shorter witch, wearing a modest floral print dress that flowed over her curvy frame, emerged from behind Warren.

"Hey, Essen." I offered a small wave, and she took the gesture as an invitation to scurry across the room and wrap me in an exuberant embrace. Laughter bubbled out of me as if summoned.

Of everyone, I liked Essen best. She was lively, genuine, and could fly better than my grandmother. She was also the least likely person I'd have ever guessed would be interested in having dominion over death. Like all of us, though, I assumed she had her reasons, not that we'd shared those. No one asked me, and I didn't ask anyone else. Having a common goal didn't mean we had common motives.

Essen released me and floated back a few paces, unintentionally using flight magic in her excitement. I wistfully imagined what it would be like to bleed magic that didn't run the risk of electrocuting people.

Carlos likes your magic. The thought sent a giddy rush through me that didn't stand a chance of being checked. No one had ever *asked* me to use my magic on them before, and my mind still reeled that he had.

"Kavren is in the back," she said, drawing my attention to why I was here. "We just finished clearing the space to practice creating the circle."

"Did you bring the components?" Warren asked as we made our way to the back of the house.

"Nope, got bored with potions and decided to take up art. This is full of sketchbooks," I responded without missing a beat, patting the bag for good measure. The unmistakable sound of glass jars bumping into each other emanated from the sack, and Essen giggled. I gave her a wink while Warren rolled his eyes and surged ahead of us.

A few seconds later, Essen and I joined him and Kavren in a large den-like room that had been cleared. "The prodigal jokester has returned." Warren gestured dismissively toward me.

"Perfect. Now we can really get started. I have a couple of mock ups for the summoning circle to try today. The goal is to get the right pattern with the right paint and vocalization."

"Way ahead of you." I let the bag slump carefully to the ground. "I've got everything from toadstool and powdered bat wings to liquid moonlight and essence of spirit."

Warren's eyebrows raised in equal parts surprise and what I hoped was respect. Out of everyone, he'd been the most dubious about my coming on and had only become more so when it seemed my only role was to keep tabs on the Kisin demon we'd unearthed.

Essen clapped her hands together, her vibrancy suddenly all business. "Right, I'll set up the wards and aversion spells now that everyone is here. Just in case, I'll add a silencer and a latent suppression spell in case the experiments get out of hand."

I smiled, endlessly impressed with her ingenuity and professionalism, though a spell to put out fires seemed a little over the top. While she laid the spells in question, the rest of us set to work mixing and matching designs, verbal iterations, and ingredients.

By the third combusted circle, I could have kissed Essen for her foresight. Mine certainly hadn't bothered to warn me I'd catch fire not once, but twice. I grumbled as I brushed ash off my shirt and leaned down to scrape off the latest attempt at a binding circle from the floor, the paste that had started pliable, now burned into charred defiance. The only mercy was that the new flooring hadn't been installed yet and no one would ever see the remnants of magic. Just in case, I made a mental note to return with some sage. Bad circles had a nasty way of causing trouble years after the fact.

"I don't see why you included moth wings." Warren's demeanor had gone from unfriendly to downright tart with each failure.

"Do you want to be the one to do this?" I fired back, tossing a glass jar of the item in question in the bag less than delicately.

"Because I'd happily string together a bunch of bullshit lines that wouldn't bend a kitten's will, let alone a Kisin's."

"Hey, no fighting," Kavren said, smooth as silk, interjecting himself between us. "Today was about trial and error. I didn't expect everything to come out topside on the first go. We'll all hit the books and try again next week. I'll look into more creative circle structures. Warren, you can see if there are other languages or maybe dialects that have more rumored success. And Theo, think about what would be relevant to the demon we plan to hold. Essen, my sweet, you were perfect as always."

Essen effortlessly sidestepped the oily platitude and unwelcome advance. "I'll brush up on more spells to keep our efforts unnoticed. Maybe a misdirection spell," she mused aloud as she tapped a finger against her bottom lip.

"Then it's settled. We all have our homework. We'll meet back here same time every week unless otherwise conveyed. In the meantime, remember, we're doing something that's never been done before." Kavren's eyes shone with a luminescent lust for power. I may not know the others' motivations for being here, but Kavren's was plain as day.

"Cool." I shrugged on my pack, doing a quick double-check to ensure everything was in order and that both the protection spell and the illusion were solidly in place before stepping outside. Essen's silence spell must have still been in effect, because between one step and the next, the ambient sounds of a thriving town engulfed the muffled quiet I'd become accustomed to the last three hours. It was also undoubtedly how I missed someone calling my name.

"Theo." I spun around at the more demanding tone. When my gaze landed on the source, my eyes widened and my heart thumped a little harder in my chest.

"Carlos?"

Carlos

Theo appeared beyond surprised to see me, a belief reinforced by the shock plastered across his face. I still wasn't sure how he hadn't heard me calling his name or why he was standing as if struck dumb. Rather than think the worst, that he'd just come from seeing someone else—okay, that was definitely there souring my pleasure at running into him—I fell back on humor.

"Are you stalking me?" I asked in as mock-serious a tone as I could manage.

His lips turned up in a sly smile, and mischief sparkled in his eyes. "What if I am?"

I shrugged as if the concept was perfectly inconsequential. "Then, you're buying lunch."

The last of his odd air of reservation seemed to evaporate. His shoulders relaxed, and his smile broadened. "Where are we going?"

I studiously refused to let my elation at this fortuitous, albeit unlikely, chance show on my face. "Was actually going to hit up the cafe on Main."

"No tacos today?" he teased, and damn if "tacos" didn't sound like a euphemism. I ordered my libido to stand down and continued my charade of nonchalance.

"Just finished visiting with Miguel. Figured I could use a change of pace."

Theo's blue eyes darkened from sky to storm as if I'd just given him some secret code. Mierda, maybe I had. I waited for him to respond with another innuendo to our sexual exploits or maybe tease me about spending too much time with my cousin, but nothing came. In fact, his eyes seemed to have gone totally vacant, like he couldn't see me at all.

"Theo." He shuddered, but didn't so much as blink. "Theo," I tried again, more forcefully. At last, his lids closed and reopened.

"Sorry, you were saying something?" He ran an absent hand through his hair, the shade changing as his fingers slipped through the silken strands.

"It's really cool how you can do that."

"Do what?" he asked, dropping his hand.

"Change your hair. No dye or anything. One second it's a brownish sort of color, now it's platinum."

"I hadn't realized I'd changed it." His eyes darted to the side in what might have been a surprising show of self-consciousness.

"That reflexive?" I prodded in the hopes it would put him at ease.

"You could say that. Now, about this lunch, I'm starved."

I shook my head and laughed. "Then come on already. You're the holdup, not me."

Five minutes later, we were sitting at an intimate table in the popular local cafe. Thankfully, the lunch rush had already dissipated, and the place was relatively quiet. Theo took care to tuck his bag securely out of the way, and I caught the unmistakable sound of glass hitting glass.

"Were you studying for one of your witch courses?" I asked, unable to hold my curiosity at bay any longer.

"What?" he asked, and I pointed toward the sack nestled under the table. "Oh right. Yeah. Though it's more of an extracurricular project than something academic."

Before I could delve deeper, the food arrived. The next few minutes were devoted to taking the edge off of our hunger. I'd just crunched my way through half my chips when I realized Theo was staring at me, his plate forgotten. "What? Do I have something on my face?" That would be just my luck to make such an ass of myself in front of literally the only guy I had any interest in impressing.

"No. It just occurred to me we spend a lot of time together, and I have no idea what your major is."

"What makes you think it's not Demonic History?"

He scoffed and waved a chip at me. "We both know most of the people in that class are there for one reason and one reason only, and it isn't the lesson plan."

"I don't know what you're talking about. I find the subject muy interesante."

He rolled his eyes dramatically. "Please. Don't even pretend you don't think Professor Roman is hot. I've seen how you ogle him."

"How could you possibly know that?" I asked, trying not to choke on my latest bite. Theo's smile turned lascivious as he leaned across the table.

"Because *I* was ogling *you*."

Hijo de cabra. Busted.

I swallowed, my face burning with embarrassment. "About that..." Theo lightly grabbed my chin, and my gaze flicked up from the table to meet his baby blues.

"You have nothing to feel weird about. He *is* hot." He released my face and settled back to resume eating. "Now that we've cleared up that Demonic History is *not* your major, what is? What are you passionate about?"

You, my unhelpful mind supplied faster than lightning. And it was true. I'd never been more turned on than when I was with Theo. I swallowed past the impulse to say exactly that and prayed that mind-reading wasn't one of Theo's many skills. "Literature."

"Oh?" His eyebrows raised in curiosity. "Any time period or style in particular?"

I wiped my hands and put the crumpled napkin on my empty plate. "Ancient."

"Like Shakespeare?"

"Older. Think Beowulf. I'm interested in how supernatural history shaped human myths. Thus our shared class."

"That's pretty cool. Kind of like how your own culture was likely inspired by Kisin Demons way back when."

"Exactly! I can't believe you got that right away. I usually have to explain it to people, and often as not, they're still confused."

Theo shrugged as if the observation was nothing, but it wasn't. It was everything. I wanted to yank him across the table and kiss the living daylights out of him for easily grasping what not even my family really understood.

I did what I could to rein in my excitement. "Sorry, I could go on for hours about all the connections. I won't bore you."

"I don't think it's boring at all. In fact, I might even have some insights from my culture."

I blinked back at him in amazement. The late afternoon sun shone on the platinum hair he seemed to wear the most when he was with me. His eyes sparkled with sincerity, the edge of his mouth quirked in a half-smile, and a part of me fell a little in love with Theo Kendal. "What about you? What do witches specialize in?"

He threw his head back in a hearty laugh that warmed my chest. "All sorts of things, but me in particular, atmospheric science."

"Like, the weather? Is that what you're passionate about?"

"Not really, but it's good work for a witch."

I leaned forward, resting my weight on one elbow as I waved a hand. "Forget logical careers. If you could do anything, what would it be?"

"Besides you?" he quipped, immediately setting my face aflame. He ignored my very physical reaction to the taunt and carried on. "My real passion is astronomy. But that market is both cliche, and over-saturated."

"So what?" I countered, more than intrigued by this admission. "Tell me what you love about it."

His eyes got a faraway look, not like in the alley, but like he was focusing on something pleasant and treasured. "The stars hold so much power. Not just in the magical sense, but over all of our everyday lives, our pasts, our futures. I can name every single constellation and all of its historic and cultural iterations." His gaze refocused on me with a glint of shyness. "Dorky, I know."

My heart thudded stupidly in my chest. "I think it's amazing." We held each other's gaze for a long moment.

Now's as good a time as any.

"What do you say our next meal is a little more... planned? Say dinner?"

"Like a date?" The innocuous question set every nerve I had on edge. I pushed past the pervasive insecurity, determined for once to pursue what I wanted. And I definitely wanted more with Theo.

"Yeah."

Theo's smile was as warm as it had been any time I'd seen it as he gathered his things. "While I enjoy spending time with you, Carlos, I don't really date." He slung the bag over his shoulder with a subtle clatter of glass and leaned down so he was eye level again. "I'm better at casual." Without warning, he snared me in a firm yet soft kiss that edged on being inappropriate, his tongue gliding with confidence along my top lip. By the time he pulled away, I could have given the melted ice in my glass a run for its money. "Stalk you later?" The statement had just enough inflection to make it a question.

"Yeah." I sighed, silently wishing he'd invite me back to his place or at least suggest mine.

He winked and released my chin, then promptly made his way to wherever he had to go. As I sat there completely flabbergasted by the impromptu kiss, I couldn't help but wonder, if Theo didn't really date, then why had this impromptu lunch felt so much like one?

Chapter 9

Theo

Never in my entire life had I wanted to say yes so much and not done it. Rainbows had practically sprouted around Carlos when he'd nervously asked me out. I liked him far more than I should, and the thought of dating him had agreement on my lips almost too fast to stop. But I didn't date—ever. It wasn't safe. What if I had a vision so strong it ruined my disguise while we were together? What if someone tried to use him against me? What if *he* wanted to use me once he inevitably learned the truth about my family and what we could do?

I stubbornly ignored my truth—that *I* was using Carlos and that I'd eventually hurt *him*. I squeezed my eyes shut as I rested my head against the wall. All the forced darkness did was bring back to mind the vision I'd had in the alley—the one right in front of Carlos.

He'd been standing in my apartment holding Sigurd. He smiled as he pet the monstrous cat as casually as if he did it all the time. Except Sigurd hated most people. He barely even tolerated me. So why was he allowing a stranger to pet him? I could still feel my shock from inside of the vision at seeing Carlos there, surprise mixed with a heady dose of delirious joy, like he was where he belonged and I'd missed him.

I scrubbed at my eyes, willing the image to undo itself, but it remained solid and unchanged. Many of my visions had a sense of possibility about them. A future that *might* be. But most of the ones that starred Carlos held more of a sense of certainty—and that terrified me. Somehow, a simple con had turned into Carlos being entrenched in my life. More than that, I wanted him there, and I wanted to know why my prickly familiar had accepted him.

I pushed myself off the wall, only just remembering the fragile contents of my bag, and raced to my apartment. Unsurprisingly, Sigurd was stretched out in a warm swath of sunlight, his enormous body taking up nearly two feet of the floor, not counting his lengthy tail. Even for his breed, he was larger than most, the magic that had paired him as my familiar having given him both extended life and the ability to keep growing. He rolled his head to eye me with a green orb and his tail flopped a noncommittal greeting on the floor.

"We need to have a chat," I said before carefully setting the bag on the counter and adding yet another set of stars to the calendar. I paused and stared at the organization of days, days dominated by purple and black stars.

Clearly, dating Carlos was not a prerequisite for seeing him every day. I let out a groan of frustration and braced myself to more forcefully prod Sigurd into compliance. To my surprise, he was already perched expectantly on the side table beside my chair. A sudden rash of nerves hit me as I slowly sank into the seat. I met his unblinking emerald eyes and took a deep breath.

"What do you know about Carlos Barrera?"

Sigurd cocked his head to the side and twitched his ear.

I gave an exasperated sigh, more frustrated with myself for not giving him more to work with. The vision from earlier of a smiling Carlos holding and petting Sigurd filled my mind. Once it was clear, I projected it to my familiar.

I knew the moment he received the image, because his tail twitched in open agitation. He replaced the image with one of an empty room. Nothing. Sigurd knew nothing about Carlos, had never seen him before. Suddenly, the image was replaced with a memory of Sigurd rubbing against my legs and stirring loose tendrils of orange, yellow, and red. I frowned in confusion, since neither of our magic was those colors.

Sigurd reached out and bopped my nose with a soft paw.

"You're asking if that's who you've been smelling?"

Rather than respond with another image, he crossed the divide between the table and my chair, then resettled in my lap. I brushed a shaking hand over his head as he stared back at me.

"I don't know what to do." My throat felt suddenly thick at voicing the admission aloud, even if it was to my familiar. "I like him, Sigurd."

My mind filled with a picture of Sigurd batting a terrified mouse between his paws.

"Not like that."

The image dissolved into one of Sigurd sitting on a windowsill and watching a sleek Persian feline stretch gracefully on another sill across the way.

"You didn't tell me you had a lady-friend."

His eyes narrowed, and the soft purr he'd been emitting dropped to a low growl.

"You're right. I have no room to judge. Yes, I like him like that."

Like.

I blinked and smiled at him. It was rare for Sigurd to use words. They were difficult for him. My happiness at the effort, though, was diminished by the harsh reality of my situation. "You know why I can't."

He projected an image of how I looked now, with platinum hair and blue eyes beside my real self, complete with lavender hair and amethyst eyes.

"Yes, and..." I altered the image to be a dead me and added the fog that helped him to understand it was a foresight vision.

His tail swung lazily from side to side as he stared off into the distance. At last he leaned forward to brush my face with his, the light tingle of magic on my cheek likely meant to be a reassurance. He hopped down and walked over to sit before the calendar, as if considering the plethora of colored stars.

When no more images or words came from him, I took it to mean he'd consider the predicament. Sigurd was no stranger to the prophecy about my imminent demise. It was one of the first things I'd shared with him when he'd come into my life ten years ago. Even as a kitten, he'd been determined to help, vowing in his own way that we'd conquer this together.

Carlos

For someone who didn't date, Theo was really good at it. Over the next several weeks, we continued to spend more and more time together. He'd even abandoned pretense to claim the seat closest to me both in class and at the study group. Afterward, we'd either wander around campus, go to a cafe, or head back to my dorm. The name of the game was definitely confusion on my part, and I wasn't sure what to make of the situation or

Theo's behavior. I just kept thinking back to what one of my cousins had once told me: if it walks like a duck and talks like a duck, then guess what, primo. It's a fucking duck.

I glanced at Theo out of the corner of my eye as we exited the theater. The matinee had been his idea, as had the movie. A rom-com that screamed "perfect date" if ever there was one.

Maybe I should just ask.

It seemed a simple enough thing to do, except I had this deep-seated fear that so much as hinting at the word "boyfriend" would send Theo bolting to the far reaches of the planet.

But I can't not say anything. Can I?

Still unsure exactly how to broach the subject, I opened my mouth. "Theo, I—"

He turned sparkling baby blues on me. "What do you say we head back to my place?"

I swallowed whatever inane thing I was going to say and blinked back at him. Then gently pushed my frames up as I stalled for time. "Your place?" We'd never gone to his place. I didn't even know where *his* place was. I fought the urge to see this as yet another sign that we were more than casual friends who hooked up.

"Yeah. It's nearby. Figured we could relax, maybe watch another movie, if you're up for it." The hint of mischief glinting in his eyes said he had absolutely zero interest in watching another movie.

I forced myself to relax and nodded. "That sounds good. I didn't realize there were any dorms this close to town."

"I don't live in a dorm," he said over his shoulder as he led the way down a side street. I scrambled to catch up before I could lose him or, worse, he could change his mind. At last, we stopped at a modest apartment complex.

The red door was in good repair, if in need of a fresh coat of paint, and the rest of the building looked well cared for. Not as old as some parts of the town, but not new either. Theo slid his key into the lock, and suddenly I wanted more than anything to see where he lived. Was he messy? Did he have roommates? What about decor? We'd talked about all manner of likes and dislikes over the last month, but no words would ever be as revealing as seeing his personal space.

"You're not allergic to anything, are you?" he asked, turning to me before opening the door. The hint of anxiety that he'd forgotten to ask such an important question until now made all sorts of things flutter freely in my chest.

I did what I could to rein in an idiotic grin. "No, ¿por qué preguntas?"

His Adam's apple bobbed sharply. "Because I have a cat."

The stupid grin slipped free, and I stepped closer to him until we were practically plastered together. "Even if I was, I think we'd have figured it out by now. Don't you?" As I slid my hands onto his sides, I brought our lips together. Mild as the kiss was, initiating it outside of the apartment wasn't like me at all. It was bold and brazen and entirely out of character.

Theo does this to me, I thought as I teased his mouth open, only to withdraw the second his lips parted in invitation. I pulled away and removed my hands, which already ached to touch the warm skin hiding beneath his shirt. "You were going to introduce me to your familiar?"

His eyes searched mine, and I longed to ask him what he saw. A nerd who had never outgrown their awkward teenage years? Someone desperate for his attention? A guy already so enamored he hadn't so much as considered seeing anyone else? Suddenly, I knew exactly how to make my case without going anywhere near the dreaded labels. Before I got the chance, though, he spun back around and opened the door.

We stepped inside, and my gaze traveled around the room. It was airier than I would have expected, though the sparse furniture seemed on the heavier side. Small charms hung by the windows, and bright abstract paintings decorated the walls. The afternoon sun shone through lightly drawn curtains and lent the room a kind of dreamlike quality.

The door shut behind me as I continued to venture into Theo's private sanctum. I walked past a kitchen that might have actually been smaller than mine, but was similarly separated from the rest of the living space by a peninsula. The living room opened up, but instead of a couch, there were upholstered chairs, including one pushed against the wall on our left, far away from the social set-up. That chair, with its plush velvet cushion, elaborate scalloped back and side table with lamp, was clearly the place of prominence.

A ball of dark gray that I'd mistakenly taken as the bottom cushion unfurled itself, and I had a better idea of why Theo had been anxious at the door. His familiar was *huge*. It thumped onto the ground after a luxurious stretch and padded over to me. Theo made to intervene, looking for all the world like a bundle of nerves, but stopped when the feline turned emerald orbs on him.

"This is Sigurd. He, uh... isn't really fond of people."

I knelt down and extended a hand, then waited patiently. With dogs back home, I would have offered my hand palm down. With Sigurd, I held it palm up in invitation. I suspected he'd appreciate the distinction. He stopped shy of touching me, his long whiskers tickling the tips of my fingers. Then, in a move that clearly shocked Theo, pressed his head into my palm. I smiled and indulgently stroked his ears.

"How did you...? Sigurd doesn't like anyone." The flutters turned into dancing lights as I clearly passed some unspoken test.

"Skogkatt, right?"

Theo tore his gaze away from where his supposedly finicky familiar was now shamelessly rubbing himself on any part of me he could reach. "How did you know that?"

I straightened up, and Sigurd switched to doing figure eights between my legs. "I've done research on various breeds that show up in myths. Actually have a Xolo back home. Plus, it makes sense you would have the kind of cat said to pull Freyja's chariot considering your Viking heritage."

Theo didn't really seem to know what to do with all of that information. His gaze flicked between his obviously affectionate familiar and me. Finally, he swallowed and asked, "Is it true Xolos are spirit guides on the other side?"

My smile brightened. "Yes. Mine actually travels with me."

A small burst of laughter erupted out of Theo, and Sigurd stopped his dance to give him a reproachful glare. "They sacrificed hair."

I absolutely loved that he'd already put it together. "Perdóneme, Sigurd." Despite the fact that I seriously doubted the familiar was fluent in Spanish, he seemed to get the gist of my request and haughtily sauntered off to make himself comfortable on another chair clear across the room. At liberty to move freely once more, I stepped toward Theo. He was still staring off in perplexity after his cat when I snared his mouth with a kiss.

"Mmpf," he mumbled. I released him to drag my shirt over my head. His gaze followed the motion, then latched onto my exposed chest. "Carlos."

"Shirt off, Theo." He groaned and immediately moved to comply. "Pants too," I said as I dropped mine to the ground. His movements became more frantic and stalled out, his pants only half undone, when I pulled him in for another kiss. This time when I teased his lips open, I dove deep to taste the resulting moan.

I pushed him back, and he fell into the wingback chair hard enough to make it rock. His gaze remained riveted on me as I moved to straddle him. Sparklers of delicious electricity played across my skin the moment his hands caressed my back. I groaned and ground into him, promptly recapturing his mouth. I slipped my hand around his backside and snuck into his sagging back pocket to liberate the supplies we needed.

Theo arched his hips up, and I gave him enough room to finish shimmying down his pants before resettling. While I reached around to get myself ready, Theo wrapped a hand around our cocks, using the beaded liquid already there to make the tight slide smooth. I panted into his hungry mouth, desperate for more, but unwilling to give up kissing him. He took the dilemma out of my hands when he stopped jacking us and rolled the condom on.

He stole another toe-curling kiss before batting my hand away. "C'mere." The command was scarcely more than a string of consonants, but I got the message. I levered myself up, then slowly sank down onto him. "That's it, baby," he encouraged, his fingers tightening on my hips to help keep me steady on our precarious perch. "You're so hot, Carlos, so fucking hot," he whispered, edging on a moan.

My own moan got caught in my chest as one of his hands relinquished my hip to glide sparklers up my torso. "Theo." His hips canted up once more, and the sensory overload about undid me. I sank completely onto him without a second thought for whether the chair could hold us or that I was still wearing my glasses. There was just Theo and me and this unbelievable connection we had when we came together.

He continued to coast his hand up, pausing to thumb my kiss-swollen lips, before moving on to my forgotten glasses. He arched a brow in silent question, and I gave the smallest of nods. Permission granted, he carefully removed them and set them safely on the side table before returning to pull me in for another deep kiss. Our tongues tangled while I dug my fingers into his shoulders and found my rhythm.

Way down deep in a part of me I was too afraid to admit existed, I knew I would always want more from Theo Kendal, that I'd be willing to give him anything he asked, and that I'd gladly take whatever he was willing to give.

Theo

The russet orange of sunset painted the ceiling of my bedroom when I blinked open my eyes from the impromptu catnap. I turned my head to the side to find Carlos still sound asleep in his trademark position—both arms pillowed beneath his head, the sheet barely covering his round ass, his breathing deep and even. All was as it should be with one disturbing exception—a large ball of gray fluff sat curled upon his back. I still couldn't believe how Sigurd had taken to Carlos so quickly. While I'd been surprised though, it hadn't come close to what I'd experienced in the vision, nor had Carlos ever picked up Sigurd.

So much for my attempt at understanding the future. Maybe next time.

The fact that I'd risked bringing Carlos here at all made no sense. Contemplating doing it again was unfathomable. If he even guessed at a third of the things here... Ancestors help me if he asked about the calendar mottled with black and purple.

Should probably take that down. Can't even see the dates anymore.

I rolled to my side and momentarily forgot what I was doing as Carlos's long lashes fluttered in his sleep. My hand reached out with a mind of its own to tease the dark curl of hair spilled over his forehead. I lightly traced the outline of his cheek, then moved down to his shoulder and onto his back, where I was reminded that we had an uninvited guest. Rather than risk waking up Carlos, I opted for the silent, albeit somewhat unreliable, method of communicating with my familiar.

What do you think you're doing? Since when do you sleep on people?

Sigurd cracked open a green eye, but didn't deign to respond.

I fought back my impatience with his stubborn attitude. The image of him acting like a total slut upon meeting Carlos formed in my mind, and I projected it to him.

His outrageous response was to purr loud enough to wake the dead. My gaze darted from my devil cat to a miraculously still sleeping Carlos and back again.

Do you know something I don't?

He started kneading Carlos' back as if that somehow answered the question. I kept a wary eye out for claws and had completely despaired of receiving a response when one came. *Safve*.

I frowned at him, not sure if he was trying to say "Safe" or "Save". *What are you talking about? What do you know?*

Safve. He began kneading harder, pulling at the tanned skin with abandon.

"Cut that out," I hissed, completely forgetting my desire not to wake Carlos as a possessive streak I didn't even know I had burned through me.

"He's fine," Carlos mumbled.

I dragged my gaze away from my insane familiar to a now very awake Carlos. "I'm sorry. This isn't like him."

"Like I said, está bien, feels good. Besides, he's warm." He closed his eyes and hummed appreciatively in time with Sigurd's incessant purr. I glared at the cat and fought the impulse to knock him off the bed like some caveman.

You're a menace.

In blatant rebellion, he purred louder, and faint tendrils of indigo emanated from his paws as he infused Carlos with his magic. The possessiveness I'd felt before paled compared to what washed through me then.

"That's it." Rather than risk getting swiped at, I used a simple levitation spell to forcibly remove him from his commandeered perch.

He hissed furiously at the rude treatment and glared at me as I moved him to his new position on the floor.

Mine. Not yours.

"Hey, ¿qué pasó? He wasn't hurting anything." Carlos angled up onto his forearms to look over at me.

"I can put him back. Or...." I flicked the sheets down and slid over to sit on his thighs.

He snorted a laugh. "Your familiar may be heavy, but he's not people heavy, pendejo."

"True, but I figured you'd enjoy this massage better." I kneaded Carlos' beautifully tanned back. Not so unlike what Sigurd had been doing moments before. Just like it had the first time I'd touched his bare skin, magic flowed out of me, water flowing from an area of high pressure to low, as if needing to be part of Carlos. I still didn't understand it. My magic had never done that before, at least not without direction. But as a deep moan emanated from where Carlos' face was now pressed into the pillow, I didn't care.

"Mierda, Theo."

"Still prefer the cat?" I dug my fingers in a little harder, pushing the magic deeper, claiming Carlos in exactly the same way Sigurd had been attempting.

"Nunca. Fuck. ¿Por qué se siente tan bien?" He panted and writhed beneath me, his groans bringing a feral grin to my face.

"You okay, baby?"

"Si. Tus manos son increíbles. Mucho mejor que el gato."

I chuckled and leaned down to place a kiss on his neck. "I can't help but feel like if I even knew half of what you were saying…"

"Nunca," he interjected. "Nunca aprendas español. Entonces no podría decir cuán agradable creo que es tu polla y sabrías lo desesperado que me pones."

"That's what I'm talking about." I rubbed my hands hard along his sides, leaving swirls of purple in their wake, miniature galaxies of magic on his dark skin. "Some of that sounded dirty."

"Eso es porque lo es. Mierda. Me estás matando." He lifted his hips as high as my position would allow and pressed back. I dragged a possessive hand down his spine to squeeze the globe taunting me. I didn't need to know Spanish to understand that.

"Still with me, sweetheart?" I asked as I shifted off his thighs to kneel between them instead.

"*Eres* una amenaza," he groaned loudly, face still pressed firmly into the pillow.

"That sounds promising." Cheating, I magicked supplies out of the nightstand and set them within reach. Then I grabbed his hips and pulled until his spectacular ass was at a better height.

I looked down at the incredible sight of the man before me. His back a sinuous arch, his arms stretched out above his head, that dark mop of curls begging for my fingers. A band squeezed around my heart even as it skipped a beat.

"Carlos." He moaned lightly into the pillow, but didn't respond. "Look at me."

It took a second, but he finally shifted to look at me over his shoulder. The sight of his pupils blown so wide the brown was all but gone was exactly the confirmation I needed. Carlos didn't just like my magic touch. He fucking loved it.

"Tell me when you're getting close," I said as I trailed a finger buzzing with magic down his crevice. His eyes rolled back, and the moan that fell out of him instantly had me grabbing my aching erection.

"Ahora. Mierda. Ya estoy cerca."

I took it as a point of pride that Carlos had given up on English. My lips pressed into the hollow at his back, then followed the same path as my finger. A cascade of moans and more colorful Spanish fell around me as I tasted and teased. When the unmistakable sounds of ecstasy dissolved into desperate whimpers and what I hoped were pleas for mercy, I grabbed the supplies. Too far gone myself to go slow, I drove home to a collective groan from both of us. Even thoroughly worked over, Carlos' tight heat strained my control.

"Ay. Sí, sí, sí. No pares. Nunca pares."

I sent a silent prayer to all the Norse gods that he was as close as I hoped he was, because I sure as hell wasn't going to last long. I continued to rove my hands over his smooth skin, the visual contrast driving me every bit as wild as the sounds coming out of his mouth.

Carlos fisted his fingers into the sheets as his orgasm ripped through him. "Theo!" The shout bounced off the walls to land squarely in my chest, where it buried deep and became a part of me. I gasped at the force of it and clung to his hips for dear life as my release slammed through me hard enough to make stars dance at the edges of my vision.

Suddenly, Carlos's entire body flushed in an echo of the magic I'd been layering into him, including the indigo remnants of what Sigurd had laid. He dragged in a shuddering breath, then collapsed onto the mattress. Wisps of magic continued to swirl lazily beneath his skin, fading more and more with each second that passed.

I stared down in shock at the unfinished indigo protection rune dancing between his shoulder blades. With a shaking hand, I trailed a light finger along his back, completing the symbol.

It shimmered briefly, then sank into his body. A muffled groan that sounded suspiciously like defeat emanated from the pillow Carlos was once again buried in.

Feeling more like pudding than a person, I flopped down beside him, Sigurd's words playing through my mind more confusing than ever. Carlos shifted just enough to look at me, exhaustion and the post-orgasmic high shining brightly in his stunning brown eyes.

"Hey," he said, his voice husky.

"Hey," I quipped back, unable to resist the tease. "Better than the cat?" He smiled, and it was like the noonday sun filled the darkening room. I shuffled closer until every part of our bodies was tangled and touching, then stole a sweet, albeit deep, kiss from his tauntingly plush lips. By the time I pulled back, his breathing was shallow, and one of his hands had snaked its way into my hair.

"Definitely better than the cat," he said, then promptly snared my mouth again.

Chapter 10

Theo

The thin plastic of the bag dug into my palm while I waited for Carlos to unlock the door to his dorm.

"You sure you're cool with hanging out earlier? I know you typically meet up with your witch colleagues today," Carlos inquired as he turned the antiquated key in the equally antiquated door.

I shrugged and walked in after him. He led the way to the modest kitchen and placed his own bags on the counter. I followed suit and started unpacking the groceries.

After a minute of the unusual silence, he glanced over at me. "I take it the project isn't going well?"

"You could say that," I grumbled. "Not going well" was the understatement of the century. Our last attempt at a cohesive binding circle had resulted in me nearly losing a hand. If Essen's counterspell hadn't activated in time, I would have. I glanced at Carlos out of the corner of my eye as he took out the requisite pots and pans. Between lying to Carlos, the lack of success, and recurring visions, I was most definitely in a mood.

"Anything I can do to help?"

Could it really be that easy?

I swallowed hard, my anxiety suddenly through the roof. How many times had I gotten close to coming right out and asking for his true name? Now that an opportunity had presented itself, trepidation coiled in my gut. He filled a pot with water and flipped the burner on, then moved on to prep the ingredients. "Still can't believe you cook," I said to stall for more time.

He laughed and pushed his glasses up his nose. My mind flashed to the heartbreaking image of tears sitting heavy on those long, dark lashes from the vision that had been torturing me of late. I couldn't imagine ever doing anything to cause him such pain. I wanted him to always be smiling like he was now.

"What makes it so unbelievable?" he asked, drawing me away from the troubling thoughts.

"First off, I was led to believe Miguel was the chef of your obscenely large family, and second, you're making Greek, not Mexican. Where'd you even learn this?"

"Well, *first off*," he teased, "mi madre made sure all of us could cook. And second, Miguel is actually the one who taught me. He knows how to make many dishes."

"Really? Why doesn't he do fusion food then? That would sell like crazy in a college town like Sieben Hügel."

Carlos threw his hands up in the air. "¡Eso es que lo dije! He won't listen to reason. Cabrón has a gift and refuses to embrace it."

I couldn't help but chuckle at his emphatic indignation. "You're a smart man."

"Charmer," he scoffed with a wry smile. Between one blink and the next, his demeanor shifted. His shoulders sagged and I could practically see him withdrawing into himself as he turned away from me. I didn't know what could have possibly prompted the sudden change and instantly missed the warm vibrancy of the moment before.

Without a second thought, I snagged his arm and spun him around. He let out a small squeak of surprise right before I captured his mouth. I used my other hand to hold his face steady as I explored his mouth and lightly teased his full lips with my teeth.

Much as I would have preferred to keep going and strip him down right here, I didn't really think Carlos would be interested in going at it in his kitchen. An impromptu handjob was one thing. Propping that perky ass on the counter to fuck him senseless was entirely another. Reluctantly, I pulled back.

Carlos's eyes searched mine when I released him, both of us a little hard up for air. "What was that for?"

I smirked back at him. "Because you have a mouth made for kissing."

"Just kissing?" he taunted, a wicked gleam in his eyes. My grin wouldn't be contained. I loved that Carlos was secretly a bit devilish.

"Naughty boy," I played along, stealing another kiss for good measure.

"No tienes idea. Me pregunto cómo sería tu cara si te dijera que estaba pensando en inclinarte y follarte aquí mismo en la cocina." He blinked at me after all of that. The picture of innocence, despite the fact that I was fairly positive that whatever he'd just spouted off was far from it. In fact, I suspected it was positively filthy and would have made me harder than a steel rod. Hell, I was clueless and still halfway there. Suddenly, the urge to blurt out the truth about everything rose up like a force of nature inside of me—who I was, why I'd pursued him, how I was starting to feel about him.

"Carlos—"

"I'm not sleeping with anyone else." His eyes widened, and his cheeks darkened as if he hadn't meant to blurt that out. "I mean seeing. I'm not seeing anyone else. Well, sleeping too, but that's not... Mierda." He pinched the bridge of his nose, forcing his glasses higher up his face. He took a deep breath, then straightened them on the exhale. "What I'm trying to say is that you're the only person I've been seeing, and I'm good with that."

Joy exploded inside me, and I had to fight hard to keep from grinning like a lunatic. I was so fucking relieved to learn he wasn't exploring other options. I wasn't dumb enough to think I was the only guy in school who recognized how attractive Carlos was, but I also hadn't wanted to think about other men lusting after him, either.

He cleared his throat, though it did nothing for his persistent blush, and averted his gaze. "Anyway, yeah... Thought you should know." He turned back to the stove and added, almost too low to hear, "And I'm negative."

Every cell in my body reacted to the information. All the impulses I'd been pushing aside returned with a vengeance. My fingertips buzzed with energy, my breathing all but stopped, and my heart pounded mercilessly in my chest. It wouldn't have surprised me if, on top of everything, my hair and eyes had reverted to their natural lavender shades. For once, I didn't give a shit if the entire world could see I was a Wisteria, I'd explain it away as some kind of magical backlash if I had to, but right now, all I cared about was getting my hands on Carlos Barrera.

No sooner did my fingers brush his hip than the door to the dorm opened. Carlos's roommate spared us a look that could have petrified wood. To my surprise, Carlos completely ignored the openly hostile expression.

"Hey, Nessa. Hungry? I'm making salmon with couscous, olives, and feta. There should be more than enough for all of us."

Nessa made a noncommittal grunt and stalked across the dorm to disappear into his room.

"What a prick." My hand finished its journey to Carlos's side. The contact settled me, though the impulse to take him right now had abated. "I don't understand how you can be so nice to him. Especially since he's so clearly homophobic."

Carlos glanced towards his roommate's closed door. "Actually, I don't think it's us, or not just us anyway."

I pressed into him, enjoying the warmth of his body against mine. "Of course not. We're fabulous." He laughed like I hoped he would.

"What I mean is, I don't think it's that we're two guys."

I stepped back so he could continue moving about, substantially more intrigued by this twist than I would have anticipated. "So, what do you think his deal is?"

"Honestly?"

I snickered. "No, lie to me." He chuckled and shook his head. "Come on," I prompted. "Let's hear this earth-shattering theory."

"I think all sex grosses him out. Like genuinely freaks him out."

Well, that was a theory I certainly hadn't entertained. Maybe lashing out because he was jealous. But against all sex? Who was against *all* sex? "And how did you come to this conclusion?"

"Putting together little things. Realizing what he focused on whenever he'd express having a problem." He cast a coy look at me that had my heart shamelessly doing somersaults. "Also, I may have done some digging into his past roommates."

"Why would you do that?"

"This guy I've been seeing thinks I should stick up for myself. Figured it would be good to get my facts in order first." All my insides turned to goo at the casual statement. Before I got the chance to say something as inane as how proud I was of him, his cheeky grin melted away. "It's okay, you know."

"What is?" I asked, confused by the gearshift.

His gaze fell, and the color rose in his cheeks once more. "If you're seeing other people. You told me upfront that you only did casual. I don't want you to think that I was expecting anything by telling you I wasn't seeing anyone else."

I fought to keep the devastation plaguing my heart from registering on my face. Did he really think that I was screwing around on him? That he was one of many?

Of course he does, dumbass, you practically told him that.

"Are you asking me if I'm exclusive?" I asked in an attempt to lighten the suddenly somber mood.

He blinked and met my gaze without faltering. "Are you?" The way he asked sent an arrow right through my heart. I looked back at him, more shaken than I cared to admit. It was a simple question and should have had a simple answer, but nothing in my life had ever been simple. I didn't expect that to suddenly change because I'd stumbled across a genuinely good guy.

"I could tell you anything. Lie. Why would you believe me?"

He offered a small smile that softened his features. Empathy I didn't deserve shone in his brown eyes as he said, "You could, but I don't think you will."

Years of being jaded, of being used, prevented me from taking the plunge my heart so desperately wanted me to. "Why are you so confident about that?"

He shrugged. "It's a feeling I have. Plus, I trust you. You've been honest about everything else. Why would you lie about this? Besides, like I said, it's okay if you're not. I just wanted you to know where I stand."

Guilt slammed through me and froze my tongue. I'd been anything *but* honest with Carlos. I was a horrible person, and here he was saying he trusted me without any reason to do so.

"Right," he said and spun back to the stove in blatant dismissal of the unfinished conversation. "I never told you why I needed to meet early."

My frozen tongue was still numb as it formed an appropriate response. My heart, on the other hand, was burning to ash. I didn't deserve to have someone like Carlos in my life, and he certainly didn't deserve to have someone like me.

Carlos

I skidded into the small room and immediately braced my hands on my knees as I puffed for breath.

"Damn, primo. Cutting it a bit close, don't you think?" Miguel said.

I made a vague flapping gesture and immediately returned to trying not to pass out. The dead sprint I'd done to get here in time, a not so friendly reminder that while I may have been skinny, I was not what anyone would call "in shape". I glanced up at my cousin's uncharacteristic silence and found him eyeing me rather judgily with his arms crossed over his chest. "What?" I panted.

"Estabas con eso brujo."

"Shut up. Now you have a problem with it? Your idea, remember?" His hand came down with a hard smack on my shoulder that nearly sent me crashing to the ground.

"Me acuerdo. I also remember you were supposed to give me the details."

I rolled my eyes and straightened up. "Not happening." Miguel didn't need to know that I'd given Theo head before bolting out of there like a bat racing the dawn or that I'd come this close to begging him to reconsider his no dating policy. And he *definitely* didn't need to know how freaking pathetic I'd sounded admitting to Theo that I had no intention of seeing anyone else while I was seeing him.

The stricken look on Theo's face when I'd told him that I'd be leaving a week early to prepare for Dia de Muertos had almost made up for the horrified one he'd given me at the desperate confession. Already I missed him, which was stupid, and as if that wasn't embarrassing enough, I'd sworn to myself no less than three times not to text him the whole week como un pegajoso.

I refused to meet Miguel's gaze as I pushed my glasses up my sweaty nose and straightened my rumpled shirt. One small mercy was that I hadn't needed to bother with bags since I still had plenty of clothes in our home outside of Oaxaca. "How long have you been waiting?"

"Not too long. Didn't have anything nearly as entertaining to hold me up." I couldn't help but glance up at the hint of envy in my cousin's voice. Never in a million years would I have ever guessed the self-confident, endlessly suave Miguel Rivera might be jealous of *me*. He offered a crooked grin and wiggled his eyebrows. "So... what *did* you two get up to that made you so late?"

The laughter that burst out of me was a surprise, but I didn't hold it back. "Nice try, cabrón. Ask all you like, you're not getting a play-by-play of our sexual encounters."

"Ha! So you have had sex con el brujo."

"Fine," I said, throwing in the metaphorical towel, "if you must know, I made him that Greek dish you taught me last year."

Miguel's eyes brightened, and he immediately launched into wanting a play-by-play of that instead. It never failed, mention food and Miguel was instantly sidetracked. Why he insisted on being so damn stubborn about not pursuing his true passion, I'd never understand.

An attendant came out to let us know the portal would be opening soon and to stand back. We listened attentively to the directions, though we'd done this enough times to quote them back. When they were finished, they vanished back into the control room, satisfied that we were ready.

Miguel glanced over at me as we stood shoulder to shoulder and waited for the pearly galaxy to come to life before us. "You really like this guy."

"Yeah, I kind of do," I admitted, since it'd be pointless to even try to deny it.

"I'm happy for you, primo. But if you don't want mi hermana to hit you with a million questions, you might want to wipe that stupid grin off your face."

The smile I hadn't even realized I was sporting fell. "What makes you think I haven't told Gabbi?"

Miguel snorted and stepped toward the milky scene swirling to life on the wall. "Porque tu amante es un brujo." Well, that was rude. Theo wasn't my "piece". He spun around to walk backwards through the portal. "Also, I know you, primo." Another step and he was gone. I hastened to join him before the attendant closed the portal and I was left stranded in the wrong hemisphere.

The world was still a blinding array of starry white when an ear-shattering squeal pierced it. I let out an "Oof" as arms wrapped around me in a tight hug that threatened to squeeze out every ounce of air my lungs had ever held. "Hey, Gabbi," I wheezed.

As quickly as it had arrived, the embrace vanished, and a fist slammed into my arm. "Cabrón. You don't call or text. What gives? ¿Ya no me quieres?"

I blinked away the last of the afterimages and smiled at the sight of my cousin and best friend scowling at me with her hands on her hips, the very picture of mi Tía Carmen when we'd gotten in trouble, no less fierce for her short stature. Unlike Tía Carmen, however, Gabbi's dark curls and round face bore a much more striking resemblance to her brother's, which wasn't all that surprising considering they were twins. I smiled as I realized just how much I'd missed her.

"Of course I still love you. And it's good to see you too."

She gave an exaggerated huff, looped her arm through mine, then promptly propelled us away from the isolated grotto towards where she parked her hatchback not far off. "Tell me everything. I feel so left out with you and Miguel away at school. Are classes good? How are your friends?"

"School is school, nothing really to report there. Still hanging with the usual crowd," I replied.

"Ugh, I refuse to believe your life is as boring as you make it sound. There has to be more than that," she needled.

"You should ask him about the guy he's been hooking up with," Miguel hollered back. "Total cutie."

Gabriella's mouth fell open, and she turned a wounded expression on me. "You're dating someone, and *Miguel* knows?" She squealed. "¿Qué carajo, Carlos?"

I shot my cousin a death glare as he sauntered away to a safe distance. "We're not dating, pero es muy guapo."

She squeezed my arm hard enough that I feared for blood flow. "Spill. I want all the dirt. And don't leave out any of the juicy bits. You owe me. Tienes hasta we get to the Rubios' to convince me not to hate you forever for telling my brother first."

I couldn't help but laugh at her insistence. Luckily, the drive from here to the Rubios' was at least twenty minutes. While she and Miguel differed in many things, in this they did not. Miguel had even slowed down, sensing the inevitable collapse of my resolve to withhold details.

"Pagarás por esto," I warned him before succumbing to Gabbi's persistent demand for every detail I could scrounge up, including why I'd almost missed our portal. The only particular I didn't share was the fact that Theo was a witch. Miguel naturally picked up on the omission, but thankfully didn't point it out and land me in even hotter water than I already was. Still, he gave me a knowing look that I caught it in the rearview mirror as we made our way to the outskirts of town and to our first household to see what relatives we'd be retrieving from across the bridge next week.

Chapter 11

Theo

In the twenty-three years I'd been alive, I'd never been quite so put out as when Carlos informed me he'd be gone an entire week for Dia de Muertos... and then some. Of course, it made sense when he explained everything that had to be done in preparation, but that didn't make his absence any easier to bear. Somewhere along the line, I'd gotten used to seeing him practically every day. That I hadn't even noticed how much time we were spending together should have troubled me. It didn't, which troubled me more.

"Hey, sour puss, pull your head out of your ass and get to work."

I showed Warren my teeth in what was meant to be a smile, but likely resembled more of a snarl, judging by the hateful look I got in return. Essen sidled up to me as I resumed mashing the ever-loving shit out of moon rocks coated in fairy moss. She placed a gentle hand on my shoulder and I stiffened at the touch.

"Everything okay?" she whispered.

"I'm fine," I forced out between gritted teeth.

"If that was true, you wouldn't have combined cemetery dust with essence of fright in that last attempt and made a necrotic acid that's probably eating its way to the core of the planet," Warren snapped, pouncing on my latest disastrous attempt. While his assessment of the results was unfairly inflated, I *had* produced an acid, something I knew how to avoid. "I'm telling you, Kavren, we need a different witch. Theo may be a top-potion maker where he came from, but he's not impressing anyone here."

I threw the pestle down to clatter in the marble mortar and rounded on him as Kavren made a calming gesture with his hands. "Go fuck yourself, Warren," I snarled. Rather than wait around for a comeback, I stormed out the back door of this week's meeting spot. The basement of the abandoned house had been useless, and the room we were working in was far too small, but it was far enough from prying neighbors that the inevitable failures wouldn't attract notice.

I walked right up to the low stone wall encircling the small yard and let out a breath that misted before me. The stones were cold beneath my hands. I invited the chill deeper to quench my out-of-control temper. A glance down revealed the lurid glow of electricity dancing between my fingers in the dreary evening light.

I have got to pull it together.

"Theo?" At Essen's soft whisper, I clenched my hand to hide the telltale purple lightning.

"Yeah?"

She stepped up beside me, and I hoped she hadn't seen anything. "You sure you're alright? You've been on edge the last few sessions."

My shoulders slumped. I thought of Carlos's full mouth tilted up in that smile that warmed his eyes, the way he pushed his glasses up whenever he was nervous, which was practically all the time, and how his laugh was always deep and genuine. Longing rose inside of me as well as the unshakable knowledge that I was falling for my mark... hard. I didn't want to hurt Carlos in any way and everything we were doing virtually guaranteed it. But I couldn't exactly tell Essen about my internal conflict and risk getting replaced, as Warren had suggested. Much as I wanted to spare Carlos, I *needed* this. He could survive this. I couldn't.

"Just... frustrated is all," I finally said. "I feel like this should be going so much smoother than it is. None of us are novices. We all know what we're doing, in theory at least, but nothing is coming together right. Even when I develop a stable compound to create the circle, either the design, the invocation, or both trigger a critical failure." I dug my fingers, thankfully absent any condemning sparks, into the numbing rocks.

Essen nodded in understanding. Seeing as how she was virtually the only reason the rest of us hadn't perished in some of those critical failures, I was surprised she wasn't more frustrated herself. She crossed her arms to fend off the autumn chill and shifted her feet. "Don't let Warren get to you so much. He's not doing any better. Like you said, we all know what we're doing to an extent. Kavren wouldn't have brought any of us on if he didn't believe we had the skills to pull this off.

"Try to remember we're making this up as we go, pulling from stories older than dirt and hearsay diluted by generations to cobble something together that *might* work, and that we may only get one shot at. We could come up with the perfect everything and it still won't mean a witch's twitch if we can't crack the true name. Add to that the fact that all of us are desperate for this to succeed. It's no wonder we're fracturing beneath the pressure."

Guilt and curiosity warred inside of me as I cast her a sidelong look. Getting Carlos's true name was supposed to be my job, and I was doing a piss-poor job of it. On the other hand, this was the closest the enigmatic witch had come to admitting she had a stake in this. I resisted the urge to push for more information to understand just how much everyone had to lose, but recognized that such an intrusion would invite questions as to my own motives.

We stood in awkward silence as the sun continued to set and stars emerged to dot a quickly darkening sky. Cygnus winked back at me, and I wondered if Carlos called it the same thing and if he was looking up at it now. Our locations weren't so far apart that the constellation that wouldn't appear in his sky at all, though it likely would be in a different position. I amused myself working out exactly where it would fall upon the midnight canvas where he was.

The heavens, the great unifier.

When Essen spoke again, I nearly jumped out of my skin, having completely forgotten she was there as my mind yet again drifted to thoughts of Carlos and what he was doing hundreds of kilometers away.

"It's my grandmother."

I turned to her, unable to resist encouraging her to continue sharing. "Oh?"

Her head slowly rose from where she'd been intently staring at the ground to look out into the distance over the hilly land-scape blanketed in shadow. "She's sick, real sick."

"Are you trying to prevent her from dying?" I asked carefully, anxious about how close our motives might be.

She shrugged and let out a huff, dropping her arms only to bring them back up again. "I don't know. Maybe? She's in so much pain and I've tried everything else. When Kavren approached me, it seemed like the universe was finally offering me a chance to help ease her suffering. And before you say anything about death being a release, you should know it's more complicated than that."

"We're witches. Isn't it always more complicated than that?"

She gave a dry laugh. "You have a point. Shouldn't come as a surprise, then, that magic is involved. The curse that's killing her will also trap her soul for a tortured eternity."

Fuck, that was some dark magic. I wanted to ask who the hell her grandma had pissed off, but knew better than most that some curses transcended the cursed to affect generations to come. My own family's "gift" had been the result of just such a curse. Moral of that cautionary tale—don't fuck with oracles, even if you *do* have the patronage of Norse gods.

"Anyway, that's why I'm here. And I get that you and Warren butt heads on, well, everything, but go easy on him. His reasons are just as dire. He has until his twenty-fifth birthday to prove himself, or his coven will strip him of his powers and banish him to live among mortals."

I nearly swallowed my tongue. "Warren is a Licentia? That coven is..." Insane was the first word that came to mind. "Intense," I finished instead.

Essen clicked her tongue in agreement. "Now you get it. We all know why Kavren is doing this." I couldn't help but roll my eyes. Leave it to the ringleader to be the stereotypical, power-hungry witch. "Exactly, but the rest of us... we all have something to lose." She gave me a knowing look, though I clearly hadn't shared my motivations. When I didn't fill in the blank for her, she stepped back and turned to fully focus on me.

"I'm only going to ask you this once, Theo. Are you all in, or do we need to find a different potions expert?"

As conflicted as I was, I didn't hesitate. "I'm in."

"Good. Then let's cut the shit. What's your real deal? I've seen the potions you've come up with in class. You're a total whiz and have a propensity for thinking outside of the box, but your work lately has been subpar at best. Is it the Kisin?" I gave an involuntary wince, which undoubtedly prompted her next question. "You know you don't actually have to sleep with him, right? I mean, do whatever you want, but needing to keep a close eye on him doesn't mean sex. I don't care what Kavren is smoking. You're your own person and shouldn't do anything that makes you uncomfortable."

I leaned down on my forearms and chuckled. What was it with everyone thinking the sex was such an ordeal? Sex with Carlos was out of this world. "It's not that," I said at last.

"Okay... Then what is it?"

"He's currently out of the country. Left a week early to do what Kisin's do best. So my current problem has more to do with the fact that I *don't* have eyes on him than whether I should be having sex with him." Essen frowned, and I quickly added, "Don't worry, he's coming back. Few days after All Hallows Eve he'll be back on campus and within reach."

No sooner did she let out a sigh of relief, than Kavren burst out of the house, waving a sheet of paper he'd torn free of a notebook. "I've got a new design." He passed me the page, and I held it up to the faint light.

The room was almost completely devoid of light. The singular source being the lurid glow of orange emanating from swirls painted into an elaborate pattern on the ground. Inside the circle stood a man I'd recognize anywhere. Carlos threw his head back in a silent scream as he transitioned against his will from human to skeletal. Horror wrapped around my heart and squeezed the air from my lungs. In the eerie silence, there was only one thought: What have I done?

I blinked and combed a shaking hand through my hair at the same time I passed the image back to Kavren. As unwanted as the vision was, it provided the first sign of any real guidance. We'd find the spell, Carlos would be held, and this was the circle that would do it. "Looks promising."

Chapter 12

Carlos

I straightened my jacket as I entered the room where Gabriella was essentially holding court. Several members of our family filled the room, mingling and chatting as they awaited their turn to have mi mejor amiga do their makeup. The Rivera twins were both artists, though where Miguel's medium was food, Gabbi's was paint.

While Miguel and I had leapt at the opportunity to attend the prestigious Arminius University halfway across the world, Gabbi had opted to stay in Mexico. Now her artwork graced walls around the state both as elaborate murals and highly sought after pieces hanging in galleries.

I watched as she amicably chatted away with Tío Marco and created her latest masterpiece. Warmth flooded my chest, and a smile tugged at my mouth. Seeing our family always made me happy, but there weren't words to express how proud I was of her for pursuing her passion and refusing to give up on her dream.

Gradually, the crowd thinned out until at last it was my turn. I pocketed my glasses and called up my true face as I took a seat before her. "¿Mis ojos finalmente murieron o was that Tía Olga?"

"Your eyes are fine, cabrón." She switched her brushes for fresh ones and reached for a pot of golden orange.

"Since when does she let anyone but Rosa do her day-of makeup?"

Gabbi snickered. "Since she learned that she didn't have to have spiderwebs and crosses." We both laughed. For as long as either of us could remember, Tía Olga had been la reina araña and terrifying children every Dia de Muertos. Apparently, she was done being the spider queen. "So..." she began when we sobered up. The wet brush flowed smoothly over my cheek. Despite the appearance of nothing but bone, I was physically aware of each delicate brushstroke.

"So," I prompted when she didn't go on.

She paused and looked at me. "Are you gonna do it?"

"Do what?" Knowing Gabbi, it could be anything from grabbing coffee or streaking through town. Thankfully, I'd only ever let her talk me into the latter once, and I'd been drunker than a goat on tequila.

"Ernestito."

Sadness enveloped my heart. Learning of the poor boy's passing as we made our rounds to all the local houses had been heartbreaking. "You know how hard it is to bring children back."

"Lo sé," she sighed and dipped the brush in green paint. "I still can't believe it. I saw him just last month for an art lesson en la escuela. É era un bebe. Sus padres están devastados."

Of course, they were devastated. Their six-year-old son had fallen down a ravine and broken his neck. "It's too soon. El chico necesita tiempo to adjust, to accept." Sudden death was always the worst when trying to bring someone across the bridge, mostly because often they didn't realize they were dead. Add to that the mind of a child...

"Todavía podrías intentarlo. We knew him, he was like familia."

My fingers clenched against my thigh at the persistent plea. "There are risks, Gabbi," I argued, knowing full well that she was trying to appeal to my bleeding heart. "What if he won't return al final del día? He'd be stuck on the wrong side of the veil. La Llorona no necesita otra alma perdida."

"Don't say that punta's name," Gabbi hissed as she drew the cross over herself to protect her own soul from the wretched spirit.

"Gabbi—"

"You'll protect el alma del chico and return him home. You've done it before." I opened my mouth to argue some more, but she cut me off with a gentle hand on my knee. "Te amo, Carlos, and I understand your concerns, pero eres el mejor con los niños. Even abuela says so and you know how she can be." I chuckled, earning myself a light smack for moving before the paint was dry. Our abuela was notoriously particular with her favor. At present, only three people in our entire family were enjoying it—myself, Miguel, and my baby sister Julissa.

"That was a fluke."

"Tienes un regalo. How many other people do you know who've saved a soul from that traidora? Eres un heroe."

"I'm no hero, prima. And I don't have some special gift. I was just in the right place at the right time." She snorted and switched colors yet again. I gently touched her elbow and met her stubborn gaze. "I'll try. Bueno?" I withdrew my hand and shook my head at my inability to say no. "Hopefully, he's not too scared," I said with a defeated sigh. It was always worse when they were scared.

"No way. You're fucking beautiful, primo." Gabriella put down what appeared to be her last brush and clapped her hands gleefully. "This might be my best work yet." She passed me a large handheld mirror.

As I gazed at the elaborate artwork decorating my skeletal face in the reflection, I was inclined to agree. I reached up, stopping just shy of touching the still drying paint. How anyone could accomplish such detailed shading in such a short amount of time with only the supplies I could see boggled my mind. Her creation looked practically three-dimensional. "You outdo yourself every year."

She preened beneath the compliment. "So..."

Laughter burst out of me at the repetition of our earlier start. "So," I echoed, curious what turn this would take.

She made a big show of cleaning her brushes and putting away the paints. At last she cast me a downright malevolent look out of the corner of her eye. "Miguel tells me you're pretty into this chico nuevo."

I stiffened, instantly wary. There wasn't much else Miguel could have added to what I'd already willingly supplied, except for everything I wasn't eager for the entire family to know. "No es un chico. And what else did Miguel tell you?"

She gave me an exaggerated eye roll. "Fine, hombre muy guapo. And he said you spend more time with this guy than him now. Not that that's a bad thing. Mi hermano needs his own life, and it's good to see you getting out there. I just want to know what the deal is."

"Deal? No hay un deal."

She quirked an eyebrow. "¿Verdad? Then why haven't I heard about him before now? ¿Dienes novio nuevo y no me dices? What gives, primo? We used to tell each other everything."

"Theo no es mi novio. It's casual," I mumbled, averting my gaze as I patted my jacket pocket to make sure my glasses were secure for when I changed back to my human visage. She smacked my chest, and I looked up as she settled the elaborate headdress of chrysanthemums and roses on her head.

"We should send him a selfie."

"Absolutely not," I adamantly refused, as I reached back to secure my hat and place it on my head.

She paused in her adjustment of the cut flowers. "Does he not know what you are?"

"Él sabe."

"¿Entonces, cuál es el problema?" She was already reaching for where she knew my phone rested inside my jacket pocket with my glasses. "You look fucking fierce, primo. You need to share that shit."

I barely secured the device before her grabby hands got a hold of it. As if on cue, it beeped. Out of reflex I looked down and opened the message waiting. My stupid face split into a wide grin as the image file popped up with Theo's own mischievous smile and dazzling baby blues.

"Ay, primo, este es el chico? You've been holding out on me." I rolled my eyes at the near perfect echo of what Miguel had said upon seeing Theo for the first time. Gabbi and her brother definitely had the same taste in people. "Looks like he's at some kind of Halloween party. His witch costume is on point."

Rather than correct her that his outfit was not a costume, I let her believe what she will. Plus, she was right. Theo looked amazing. The hint of violet eyeliner made his eyes pop and paired great with the lavender hair spilling out from beneath an archetypal witch's hat, point and all. Damn if my mouth didn't water at the sight of his handsome face smirking at me. Why the hell had I not texted him again?

No sooner did the question surface than Gabbi snatched the phone right out of my hand. "He's hot, Carlos. You have to send a pic now."

"I do not," I argued, making a play for the phone, which she expertly held out of reach. "Give it back."

"Not until you take a selfie with me. Come on, it's like the universe giving you a sign."

"What if he freaks?"

"So what? As far as he could know, you're dressed up for the holiday."

"I already told you he knows what I am, why I'm home too," I grumbled.

"Then take the damn picture with me."

"No."

"Yes!" She looped an arm around my neck and I managed a begrudging smile as she snapped a picture. She didn't even review it before sending it off and tucking the phone back in my jacket pocket. If I didn't love her so much, her self-satisfied smirk would have driven me nuts. As it was, I didn't bother arguing with her further. What was done was done. I held out my arm, and she looped hers through it. Together, we walked out of the house and joined the rest of my family on the lawn.

Bright colorful faces smiled back at us, an air of anticipation electrifying the space. In the distance, a soft yellow glow touched the near-perfect night, the light from hundreds of candles at the nearby cemetery illuminating the darkness with hope.

"Ready?" Gabbi squeezed my arm in eager anticipation.

I smiled back at her and called my Xolo, Azul, to my side. Even he hadn't been spared a few colorful brush strokes. "Always."

As one, my entire family, all the way down to second and third cousins old enough to make the trip, stepped forward. The coolness of the veil rippled over me. I reflexively closed my eyes, even as Theo's question came back to me. *Why make the journey if the price is so steep?*

The peculiar coolness dissipated, and I opened my eyes onto the most incredible vision. Beneath our feet, petals of deep orange marigolds littered the trail to form the bridge leading to the land of the dead. On the other side, a spectacular city sprawled across as far as the eye could see.

Lights in colors of every imaginable shade winked back at us from windows and balconies. At the foot of the bridge, countless souls waited impatiently to be reunited with their loved ones. Azul danced in front of me, his hairless body now glowing with bright blue fur that still held the intricate markings of Gabbi's paintwork. I pulled my attention back to the happy, smiling faces waiting for us.

Because it is so very beautiful.

Theo

I flagged down Jessica Carmen, my usual partner in crime at these events. As distant cousins, she was one of the few family members I could look forward to seeing on witch holidays. Her magical talents lay with plants and her florist shop was dominating the scene in southern France. I knew everything there was to know about Jessica, mostly because she never seemed to stop talking, but she was less knowledgeable about some of my particular gifts. It was just safer that way.

The rare aptitude for lightning she was well aware of, as I'd accidentally shocked her when we were four. The visions, however, I'd managed to keep to myself. As far as anyone was concerned, my mom and grandma were the only witches left with the ability.

"Nice hair, cuz," she said, teasing the long strands.

I swatted her hand away. "Maybe if you'd paid more attention to practical charms than herbology, you could change yours at will too."

"As if I would ever need to," she said, flipping long, straight platinum blonde hair over her shoulder. I smiled, but would never tell her that I used her hair as a basis for whenever I was with Carlos. "How's uni? I heard you switched schools. Why would you ever do that?"

Damn if witches didn't gossip like a bunch of bored old biddies. "Arminius has the curriculum I need."

"Whatever." She eyed her nails, each one artfully done to a point as if they were talons. "We miss you at school, but you do you, boo."

"Hey, you haven't seen any more of the family around, have you?" I asked, changing the topic. The last thing I needed was for any of my family sticking their noses into why I'd transferred. I didn't need another lecture about the futility of avoiding prophecy.

Jessica blew a large bubble of bright neon pink, popped it, and kept chewing. "Pretty sure I saw Auntie Pearl a little while ago."

"Cool. Find you later?" I'd barely finished asking, and she was already off, waving in agreement as she disappeared into the throng of the gathered coven. I shook my head and went in search of my aunt. Thankfully, Auntie Pearl was vain and ostentatious. It took all of five minutes to find her.

I slipped through a line of witches arguing about the semantics involved in preserving a warding charm against malicious insects. A few offered vague gestures of greeting before returning to what was proving to be a rather heated argument. I shook my head and stepped closer to my mother's sister, Pearl. "Hello, Auntie," I said, greeting to the woman with nearly white hair. Only the faintest hints of purple still colored the rebellious locks that were topped with a violet, pointed hat that mirrored mine.

"Well met, Theobald. How does this Hallow's Eve find you?"

"Well enough, Auntie," I replied, gracing both of her cheeks with a kiss. "You haven't seen my mother by any chance, have you?" The possibility of my in-demand mother being present was slim, but I was unrealistically optimistic.

Her wrinkled face drooped into an empathetic expression of sorrow. "Oh Theo, you know the family can't risk too many of us in the same place. The overlapping amplification of magic could jeopardize the cover we have all so meticulously maintained."

Even though I recognized the logic of the situation, my heart still sank. The last time I'd seen my mother was when we'd argued about my switching schools from our alma mater. "Yeah, no, of course."

She reached out to caress my face with a wizened hand. "My dear boy, she'd be here if she could. It's already pushing things to have us in proximity. Fates be praised that your cousin Jessica is too far removed to have the gift."

I nodded in understanding, because I did understand. I didn't like it, but I got it. A sliver of jealousy wormed its way into my heart. Carlos was home with his big, loving family, and I was lucky to see two of mine on a significant witch's holiday. "How is grandmother?"

Auntie Pearl adjusted her velvet cape. "As well as any woman of ninety-three can be expected to be."

I glanced around before asking, "Any significant insights I should be aware of?"

"Unless you follow American sports, no."

My shoulders sagged as I recognized the flimsy hope I'd held that Grandmother Wisteria would miraculously have a vision that clarified the circumstances of my untimely demise. "She'll outlive us all," I said, instead of the thoughts plaguing my mind.

"From your lips to the Crone's ear." Her gaze slid over my shoulder to the crowd behind me. "If you'll excuse me, dear Theobald, I believe I see Elzibeth. That witch owes me a tonic for that spell I provided. Blessed be."

"And merry meet," I replied, though she was already winding her way through a host of witches.

The evening's festivities had started early with the rising of the moon and had reduced to a cacophony of mingling. My gaze wandered over the gathered people, some of which were distantly related, most of which weren't related at all. Not for the first time, I wished my family didn't have to live in such absolute secret. Being a Wisteria was lonely.

Unsurprisingly, my mind wandered to Carlos and how he might be spending his evening. Was he surrounded by his extensive family and all the love he could stand? Was he calling his dog Azul into the realm of the dead to lead souls back to their families? Did he know I was missing him?

I'd already taken out my phone by the time I registered what I was doing. A whole week I'd waited for Carlos to message me. Even something as flippant as Happy Halloween would have been enough, and yet nothing had come.

Fine, if he won't message me, then I'll message him.

I typed and deleted half a dozen messages before giving up and snapping a picture of myself in full witchy getup. My thumb smashed send before I could second guess the wisdom of such an image. Then I stared obsessively at the screen, which remained obstinately blank.

What the fuck was I thinking? He's probably on the other side of the veil. There's no cell service there. He wouldn't have even—

The phone dinged, and I nearly dropped the damn thing trying to open the message. The image took a second to load and then my eyes were greeted by impressive marigolds in various shades of yellow, orange, and gold encircling empty eye sockets and butterflies in a multitude of colors hovering at the fringes of a face made of bone. Each line was exact and stunning, a work of art that I hadn't anticipated when opening the message.

Though I'd never seen this side of him, I didn't need anyone to tell me who I was looking at. I barely even saw the person next to him, though their headdress threatened to dominate the screen. I ran a delicate finger along his pronounced cheek, angled up in a smile, and my breath caught at the sheer beauty that was Carlos Barrera in his true form. Even without the traditional paint for his trip beyond the veil, he was stunning.

Suddenly, I knew exactly what my potion for the circle had been missing. I couldn't create any generic solution. It needed to be specific to Carlos, and this image had all the answers I'd been missing. The phone slammed home into my pocket as I raced out of the room filled with witches chatting away about nothing of consequence. I exited the room and raced down the hall to find a potions lab, eager to test my theory.

The vision of Carlos screaming trapped in the circle Kavren had constructed filled my mind and my frantic run ground to a halt. Yes, I had my answer, but if I did this, Carlos would suffer, possibly die. Sharp pain constricted around my heart. My life might be saved, but the life of the man I'd inexplicably fallen for would be forfeit. For the first time in my life, I questioned if it was actually worth it.

Chapter 13

Carlos

The red paint turned brown at the edges of where it flaked away from the wood. Tiny cracks ran down the surface like miniatures fissures in clay earth left to bake in the merciless heat of the August sun. Except it wasn't summer, and I wasn't looking at the ground outside la casa de mi familia.

My gaze focused so exclusively on every detail of Theo's faded door, it wouldn't surprise me if I dreamed about the damn thing. Considering how long I'd been standing there like an indecisive lump, I could've painted the whole thing twice over.

What am I doing? I should've called.

Despite the logic, I hadn't called. My hand didn't even move towards the phone shoved in my pocket. Instead, my feet remained firmly rooted in place and my hand continued to hover inches away from the door. My heart pounded hard against my ribs as my gaze shifted to another patch of peeling paint that looked like it had been boiled into submission over a decade ago.

I nearly jumped out of my skin at the soft click of a door handle. My head swiveled to the side in time to see someone vacating an adjoining apartment. Their key scraped in the lock and they shot me an anxious glance, no doubt because I was standing around like some tonto.

I offered an awkward smile as my knuckles closed the distance to rap on the distressed door. The hollow thud of the knock sounded unnaturally loud in my ears, and I swallowed past a nauseating wave of trepidation.

Looks like he's not here. Definitely should have called. Dropping by unannounced was dumb. Soy un idiota. I should leave.

I was all set to bolt when the knob turned, and the door finally opened. I raised my head to meet the gaze of a perplexed Theo. His brows pulled together in a frown and his face still had creases from sheets as if he'd been asleep.

"Carlos?"

"Um, hi," I replied pathetically, trying valiantly not to think about reasons why Theo would feel the need to take a catnap in the middle of the afternoon—reasons that involved another body—and failing miserably. I swallowed past a suddenly dry throat and pushed my glasses up before they slid clean off my stupid, sweaty nose.

Theo combed fingers through the same light lavender hair from the photo he'd sent me. As they raked through the fine locks, the color shifted to the platinum I was more familiar with. For some reason, I was sad to see the purple go. "What are you doing here?" he asked as his hand fell free.

My stuttering heart fell with a sickening thud to the bottom of my stomach. "Yeah, of course, right..." I paused to clear my throat before my voice could pitch any higher.

Mierda, I'm such an idiot. He's with someone. ¿Qué estaba pensando?

"Carlos?"

"What? Oh. I... uh, got back early," I lied through my teeth. "Figured I'd pop by, but you're busy. It's cool, I should have called." I added a shrug, as if that would somehow lend credence to the sheer fabricated nonsense spewing out of my mouth. Theo didn't look remotely busy in his relaxed sweats and over-sized shirt barely clinging to one shoulder. An observation further emphasized by the confusion now scrunching his face. I pushed my glasses up again, though if they went any higher the nose pads would literally be in my eyes. "I'll go."

I'd already spun around fast enough to fall over when his hand shot out to grab my arm. "No, wait."

I glanced back at him, uncertainty making my stomach roll. "Yeah?"

"Sorry, you caught me off guard." He released me and stepped back. "Come in."

It didn't seem possible to be more nervous that I already was or than I'd been the first time I'd come here, and yet, I had to wipe sweaty palms on my pants and my heart wouldn't stop racing as I stepped deeper into Theo's gloomy lair. The door slammed shut, and I jumped at the sudden noise.

"Storm's coming in. Pressure change pulled the door shut," he said in explanation as he moved to stand before me. He shoved his hands into his pockets only to immediately take them out and fold his arms, threatening the hold of his already precariously perched shirt. "Thought you weren't due back for a few more days." Of course he would think that. It's exactly what I'd told him.

"Um, yeah..." I stalled, my gaze rebelliously sliding over to stare at his mostly closed bedroom door that I was fairly certain hid another person. If only the door was open a little more, then

I might get a glimpse of its occupant. On cue, Theo's familiar slipped through the crack without so much as nudging the door an inch. I ripped my disappointed gaze away from the narrow opening to zero in on the haughty Skogkatt sauntering towards me. "I, uh, was going to stay the full time, but I... didn't," I finished awkwardly.

As if knowing I was in desperate need of a buffer, Sigurd finished crossing the distance, then promptly launched himself into my arms. Wholly unprepared for the massive cat to do such a thing, I nearly didn't catch him in time. Theo's eyes widened in what might have been anger, while his fingers tightened on his arm until the tips turned white. Rather than address the awkwardness festering in the room, I focused all of my attention on the welcome distraction that was Sigurd, who was now pawing at my arm like he was shaping putty.

"You miss me, buddy?" I asked, scratching the feline behind his tufted ears. His purr could've passed for an earthquake and he immediately shifted from kneading my arm to kneading my chest. Faint tingles reminiscent of what I felt when Theo touched me permeated the cotton. "Well, aren't you affectionate for someone who's supposed to be grumpy?" I chuckled, fully aware that I was hyper-focusing on the familiar to avoid looking at Theo, who'd yet to say anything beyond asking why I was here.

My eyes squeezed shut as the fear I'd been fighting since before I'd left Oaxaca washed over me. I buried my face in Sigurd's extensive coat to hide the expression.

I never should have let Gabbi talk me into taking that picture. Knowing what I am is one thing. Actually seeing me in full Kisin form... And now he wants nothing to do with me.

Theo

Carlos stood in my tiny ass apartment sounding anxious and looking adorable as fuck, like some manifested vision—which he was. The exact same vision, in fact, that had led to me originally inviting him here weeks ago. The foresight had clearly conveyed how surprised I'd be. It had failed, however, to include the fact that I'd also be blindingly jealous—of my familiar.

Even standing there, gripping my arm tight enough to bruise, I couldn't believe my eyes. Carlos was actually here, the very man I'd been dreaming about when a knock had woken me, and he couldn't even be bothered to look at me. Meanwhile, my mangy beast of a familiar pawed at his chest and lapped up all of his lavish attention. When wisps of indigo magic drifted from between his paws, I had to bite my cheek to keep from shouting at the wretched creature. Then Carlos buried his face in Sigurd's coat and I about near lost what was left of my shit.

Carlos cleared his throat as he straightened. "Lo siento. I can see myself out." I barely even heard the odd statement over the roaring in my ears as he gave Sigurd one last thorough pet and lowered him to the ground.

My body practically vibrated with impatience as I waited for the insufferable feline to get the hell out of the way. Then in two giant steps I closed the measly distance separating us. I fisted a hand in Carlos' shirt and yanked him forward to mash my mouth against his. He let out a squeak even as the plush lips that tortured me daily molded against mine. My body arched into his, aching for more, but first...

I pulled away enough to smooth the wrinkles out of his shirt and forcibly replaced Sigurd's magic with my own. As my hands ran over Carlos' chest, the rest of the world slipped away.

I wasn't touching Carlos anymore. He stood with his back to me amidst an intricate circle of orange light and glowed head to toe in luminescent violet. Every inch of Carlos' body emanated the color that I would recognize anywhere—the color of my magic. Hope rose like a tidal wave inside of me. This could actually work...

"Theo?"

I blinked away the last tendrils of the vision and looked into Carlos' warm brown eyes touched with worry. "I'm exclusive." No sooner had the words cleared my lips than I was sampling his again. My fingers slid along the back of his neck to keep him there even as he pulled back.

"What?"

I licked my lips while I stared, entranced by his. Heavens above, I'd missed him more than I'd ever missed someone I was supposedly just hooking up with. Not even celebrating my favorite holiday with some of my family could distract from the depression that had plagued me when he'd left. "You never let me answer before." I stole another kiss, only to have him pull away again. I barely suppressed a growl of frustration.

"What are you talking about?"

I let out an exasperated huff and met his confused gaze. "I haven't seen anyone but you in months, longer even." He stared back at me and for a heartbreaking moment, I didn't think he believed me. My thumb traced his ample bottom lip as I whispered, "It's only you, Carlos." I was too afraid to meet the doubt in his eyes, so I kept my gaze focused on the path my lighter thumb was taking on his darker lips. The panicked beating of my heart emphasized what I already knew—if Carlos walked away right now, it would shatter me. I didn't do relationships—ever—yet here I was solidly three months into one.

At last, I steeled my nerve to raise my gaze. His eyes held all the doubt I feared.

I can't let him go, not when keeping him safe means finding a way to saturate him with my magic.

I wasn't even thinking as I shifted my thumb to brush along his cheek, trailing a glittering streak of violet in its wake. Carlos' breath hitched and his long lashes fluttered. Selfishly, I didn't want to save Carlos just to save him. I wanted to save him for me. I searched his face for any sign of rejection, even as I pulled him close once more to drink from those delectable lips.

Carlos

I stood stiller than a statue as Theo pressed his mouth to mine. His words continued to tumble over and over in my mind until, at last, they came to rest. Theo wasn't seeing anyone else. There wasn't some other guy behind that door passed out naked on Theo's bed. Coming back early hadn't been a mistake. My skeletal visage hadn't scared him off.

My lips tingled with the magic I'd quickly become addicted to, and I sighed as Theo pulled away. I couldn't help but track the path his tongue took along his glistening lips. "Anything else?" I asked, not even recognizing my voice.

Theo's eyes sparkled with the same mischief that worked his mouth up into a half smile. "I'm negative. Like I said, it's just you."

The repeated words grounded me forcibly back into my body. I lurched forward like some depraved lecher to capture his mouth. He groaned into me as I wrapped my arms around his neck, mindless of his own hand still between us. I didn't care that I was probably coming across as desperate. I'd forsaken my family just to return early because of how much I'd hated being away from him.

Just me.

Theo's hands wriggled free and fell to my waist, where they promptly latched on to my hips. He used his hold to grind me against him, and a moan forced its way past my lips. Suddenly, those same hands slipped beneath my shirt and sent waves of ecstasy-inducing electricity across my skin.

"Me encanta eso. Más. Muchisimo más. Fuck, Theo. Yes," I hissed, barely clinging to sanity. My hands scrambled to conquer the shirt, currently losing its fight to stay on Theo's body. The flimsy material puddled on the floor just in time for Theo's own deft fingers to rip mine off.

His gaze fell on my chest, then, like earlier, he ran his hands up my torso. Only this time, the force of magic that danced through my skin threatened to make my knees buckle. I reached down to palm my aching cock, only to have Theo snare the appendage. Shock rippled through me as he intertwined our fingers and dragged me toward the bedroom.

To my shame, I let out a relieved breath when the door opened and revealed absolutely no one on the other side. Theo's eyebrows rose at the traitorous sound. "Didn't believe me?" Before I could respond, Sigurd slipped into the room. To my shock, Theo let out a low growl. He snatched a quick kiss and said, "You get that sexy ass naked and on the bed. Join you in a sec."

I moved to do as he said, my erection grateful to finally be free, and crawled onto the bed. I placed my glasses on the nightstand, then leaned back on my elbows to try to figure out what on earth Theo was doing. When he dove out of sight and reemerged with an angry ball of gray fluff, I had to bite my tongue to prevent laughter from erupting out of me. He walked over to the open door and tossed the poor creature out, then promptly closed the door and locked it.

"Really?" I teased at the excessive measures.

Theo spun around as if suddenly realizing he'd had a witness for that little spectacle. When his gaze landed on me stretched out, naked though, his eyes dilated with hunger. "Fuck, you're beautiful." The flush that spread across my chest at that heated look paired perfectly with the pounding of my heart.

"¿Empiezo sin ti or are you going to finish getting undressed?" To add weight to the threat, I shifted to balance on one elbow and reached down. Theo's gaze riveted on my hand as I wrapped it around myself, then slowly slid it up and back down my shaft. Almost instantly, his own hands became a flurry of movement. I'd never seen anyone get undressed that fast and strongly suspected magic had been used.

Soon enough, a liberated Theo was crawling up my body. I relinquished my hold in order to dig my fingers into his silken hair as he kissed me deep enough to steal my breath. He abandoned my lips to trail kisses along my jaw and onto my neck while sparklers trailed over one of my sides. When he returned to my mouth, I realized he'd fished out supplies from the drawer. I kissed him deeper and arched into him in search of friction. He set the supplies within easy reach and devoted both hands to exploring.

My whole body came alive at his electric touch, and his blond hair fell in his face as he returned to tease my lips with another sparkling kiss. I moaned into him while my hands splayed across his back. "For the record, I'm a fan of the purple," I said when he shifted his focus to my collar.

Theo pulled back a few inches and looked down at me. Even a little blurry, I could tell he was confused.

"Your hair," I elaborated, brushing the straight strands out of his eyes. "The lavender seems to suit you best."

Without warning, he rocked back to rest on his heels and stared at me. The longer the heavy silence stretched, the more I feared I'd crossed some kind of boundary.

Mierda. Why did I have to open my big mouth? ¿Por qué me importa el color de su pelo?

With each passing second, my anxiety grew until it threatened to reach my earlier waiting at the door levels. Finally, he blinked, and my heart dared to beat again. He cocked his head to the side and seemed to consider me another insufferably long minute.

"The purple, huh?"

I nodded, not trusting my voice not to betray my bout of nerves.

"Give me your hands." He held out his and a small part of me worried this was some kind of trap. I shoved la paranoia deep down and let him pull me into a seated position. His fingers were gentle as he rubbed his thumbs across my knuckles before adjusting his hold. My uncertainty tripled when he raised my hands up, then promptly turned to awe as he guided my fingers through his hair.

Magic tingled through my hands as they coasted through the silken strands. Theo's eyes drifted shut, and he gave a soft sigh as he continued to move my fingers along his scalp. Where they passed, the shade of his hair altered from nearly white blond to an almost silvery light purple. Once my hands were through and every strand had changed, he released them. He slowly opened his eyes again, and in their depths shone an insecurity I hadn't seen before. He struggled to meet my gaze, his eyes focusing instead on the space between us.

I reached out and combed my fingers through the remarkable tresses. "Que lindo."

He huffed a dry laugh, and those baby blues finally met mine. "I have no idea what that means."

I smiled and caressed his face. "It means beautiful." I leaned forward to brush his lips with mine. "You're beautiful. Now, how about some more of those magic hands? Sabes lo que me hacen."

The kiss Theo captured me with next was nowhere near the sweet, tame ones we'd been sharing. It was assertive and dominating and paired perfectly with the flood of electricity cascading over my body. I groaned into him, and bright spots of light danced behind my eyes when a charged, slick finger slipped past my rim.

"Theo," I panted, digging my fingers into his shoulders as I opened up more for him.

"That's it, sweetheart. Just relax. The world is going to be upside down by the time I'm done. Nothing but stars, baby." He curled his fingers, and the promised stars danced crystal clear across my blurry vision.

"¿Cuántas estrellas? Y el mundo ya está patas arriba. Eres un…" My words trailed off into a strangled moan with another expert crook. The fact that I couldn't seem to string two English words together anymore only seemed to encourage him. A hand sparked its way up my thigh while Theo's mouth closed on my neck. I couldn't take much more of this. I was going to die if he didn't fuck me soon. "Por favor. Me estás matando. Solo fóllame ya."

Theo pulled back so fast, it was a wonder I didn't have whiplash. I blinked blearily past my lust-fogged gaze to find him securing the rest of the supplies. He hadn't even torn a corner before I plucked the condom from his nimble fingers.

"Eres negativo, ¿sí?"

"Yes."

"Estás seguro?" I asked, quirking an eyebrow.

"Yes, I even got tested again after you left."

"Bueno." Without so much as a second thought, I tossed the foil and brought Theo back down for another toe-curling kiss. We spent another few minutes lost in tangled tongues and touches short-circuiting my system. Finally, he adjusted, but instead of driving straight home, he hesitated. "¿Cuál es el problema?" I asked with maybe a touch of impatience.

"Are you sure?"

The thoughtfulness of the check-in had my heart doing all kinds of ridiculous flips and filled my chest with light. Except this wasn't the time for unfounded feelings and certainly not *those* feelings, so I channeled my inner bitch instead. "Deja de estancarte y mete tu polla dentro de mí," I snapped.

There wasn't a chance in hell Theo had understood my demand for him to stop talking and put his dick in me already, but he sank deep just the same. I hissed past the initial burn and curled my fingers in the sheets. Then his hands caressed my sides, and sparklers were everywhere, inside and out. My grip turned white-knuckle as my back arched off the bed in response to the overwhelming sensation.

"Ay. Mierda. ¿Qué es eso? Madre de Díos."

"Easy, baby. I've got you." The overwhelming current dimmed slightly as Theo traced a hand up my side to my arm, then on to my hand, where he unknotted my fingers from the sheet, only to lace them with his. Then he leaned down to complete the connection with our lips. He rocked into me, and my grip tightened while he swallowed my moan. "Fuck, Carlos, you feel incredible."

My free hand tangled in his hair while my legs locked around his back. I used them to pull him even closer, and for a second, everything was purple. Theo was purple. I was purple. The whole fucking room was purple. Then the sparklers returned. I gasped out in shock, and my entire body seized with the sudden onslaught of sensation. The room was definitely upside down or inside out or not right-ways up. Whatever it was, it was incredible.

"Carlos." Theo's breath came in hot puffs on my fevered skin as his pace picked up. I could scarcely manage a moan. His grip pushed my hand deeper into the mattress, and suddenly I realized where his other hand was going.

"No te atrevas. Lo juro por Dios..." There was no way I'd keep it together if he put a hand sparking with magic on my cock. "No lo hagas," I pleaded, desperate to continue clinging to this impossible precipice. "No estoy listo para caer."

"Let go," he whispered against my lips, not remotely deterred. His hand reached its final destination between us, and I exploded like a rainbow-colored firework. My body bowed off the bed... and didn't come down. Wave after wave of pleasure crashed over me. Lightning ricocheted between every nerve as Theo thrust one last time and cried my name.

Chapter 14

Carlos

My hand flailed blindly, bumping into several things, until at last it settled on my glasses. I slipped them on and opened my eyes. Almost immediately, a smile tugged at my lips. Theo lay curled toward me, his soft hair spilling across his forehead in a lavender curtain. I reached out to brush it out of his eyes, and he made a small sound of contentment. Joy filled my heart near to bursting. Forget the mind-blowing sex. Theo had said he was exclusive—con migo.

I sighed happily and continued to stare at him. My fingers were millimeters away from stroking his soft cheek when something moving on the bed caught my attention. My gaze shifted to find that at some point Sigurd had finagled his way back into the room and now lay curled up between Theo and me.

"Tu bribón," I chuckled quietly. Sigurd lifted his head and flicked a long tufted ear at me. "Tu compañero no va a ser feliz." Unsurprisingly, he didn't respond to the admonition that his companion wouldn't be happy about this, but settled back down. I ran a hand over his silken head and onto his back, impressed with how similar in feel his coat was to Theo's hair.

Perhaps witches and their familiars influence each other more than I thought. Theo did say Sigurd didn't take to most people. Perhaps he was actually talking about himself.

My smile widened as I returned my gaze to Theo's face. To my surprise, his baby blues were waiting for me. They seemed to twinkle in the half light slipping through the partially pulled curtains. I pulled my hand away from Sigurd to caress Theo's adorably sleepy face, miraculously clear of so much as a shadow of growth. Like most things Theo, I suspected magic was at play there. As my hand neared its destination, his eyes flicked to the coyote-sized cat curled between us and narrowed to slits.

"What the—"

"Calmate," I whispered. "He's not doing anything. He's fine." Despite my words, Theo didn't look by any means swayed.

He glared at the harmless cat and hissed, "Get the fuck off." Sigurd merely raised his head and looked back at Theo without indicating that he had any intention of following such an order. To add insult to injury, he settled back down and promptly scooted closer to me. I watched Theo go from irritated to livid in the blink of an eye. Then it finally clicked.

Hijo de puta. He's jealous of the cat.

Before Theo could escalate his fury beyond angry words into violently removing his familiar, which looked closer and closer to murder by the second, I intervened. "Mi amigo, ¿te importaría comerciar con lugares? Your spot is so warm, y tengo frío."

For a minute, I feared Sigurd wouldn't understand my intent enough, that asking for a favor—in Spanish—would be lost on him, but my faith was rewarded. He took his time uncurling and then gracefully leapt over me, all beneath the watchful gaze of his witch. I quickly scooted closer to Theo and tangled my legs with his lest he decide to take issue with the fact that Sigurd was still technically in the room. Also, decided it was best not to mention that now his familiar was curled rather tightly against the small of my back.

"That's better, no?"

Theo dragged his gaze away from where Sigurd had vanished from his sight and looked at me, concern darkening his eyes to ocean blue. "How are you feeling?"

I slipped a hand around his waist and pulled him closer. "How do you think I'm feeling?" His face softened slightly, but the worry was still etched clearly in his furrowed brow. "Besides, I feel like I should be asking you that." He smirked like I hoped he would and leaned forward to brush my mouth with a soft kiss that held trace hints of sparklers. I licked my lips and smiled like an idiot.

"You blacked out," he teased.

"So did you." His gentle laugh warmed my chest, and my stupid grin only got stupider. "Sex that good?" I poked.

"Fuck yes," he groaned. "But it was also likely all the magic. It's a wonder I have any left."

I snuggled closer to him as his fingers threaded through my hair. "How long does it take to come back?"

"Not too long. Takes rest mostly. And food," he replied absently as he twirled a curl around his finger. Abruptly, his gaze snapped back into focus. "You should let me cook for you."

I snorted. "You cook?"

"Don't sound so surprised. I may not have had a million people teaching me ancient family recipes, but I'm pretty decent."

"And humble too."

"Shut up." He gave me a playful push that was matched by Sigurd's own paws pressing into my back. Like earlier, the sensation of mild sparklers emanated from the contact. "Come on, let me cook for you. It's only fair." Sigurd's paws ventured higher up my back, kneading little bits of electricity as they went. Part of me recognized that I should probably be a little wigged out about being sandwiched naked between the guy I was sleeping with and his cat, but I wasn't. Sigurd was an extension of Theo, though I didn't think Theo saw it that way at the moment.

"Okay."

"Perfect, I know just what—"

I tightened my hold on his waist to prevent him from going anywhere. "But only on one condition." Theo cocked his head to the side and looked for all the world like Sigurd had when I'd woken up. "Answer a question for me."

"What?"

"Try not to get mad. I'm just curious." Theo rolled his eyes and made an impatient face. I took a steadying breath, suddenly very concerned for the fluff ball's safety. "Can Sigurd do magic?"

Despite my attempt to head off a negative reaction, anger instantly clouded Theo's eyes. "What makes you ask that?"

"For starters, unless you sleepwalked and opened it, that door was closed and locked."

Theo's anger abated a bit. "Right, of course. Yes, familiars are capable of holding the magic of their witch. That's actually why most witches have one, to help with spells beyond their capacity without having to pull in another witch. There are limits, of course, but..."

Fascinating as this insight into witch culture was, I wasn't done. "But Sigurd is different."

Theo's eyes instantly became wary. "Sigurd is different. Skogkatt can produce their own." Why was I not surprised?

"It's very similar to yours," I stated as evenly as I could. Contrary to what I expected, Theo didn't fly off the handle. He let out a resigned sigh.

"Yeah." He traced patterns on my arm that seemed like smaller versions of what Sigurd was currently doing to my back. The two really were like perfect echoes of each other. "He's used his magic on people before, mostly defensive stuff, but never like what he's done to you. I honestly don't know what he's on about."

"Have you asked him?"

"Yes. Little shit is obstinate and no help," he grumbled. Admittedly, I was impressed that Theo'd asked in the first place. Theo's hand flattened over where he'd been drawing, and the faintest wave of tingles ran down my arm. "*Now* can I cook for you?"

I pressed my lips to his in a chaste kiss. "Yes."

"Thank the stars, because I'm starving," he declared and virtually launched himself out of the bed in a flurry of sheets. "There're lounge pants in the bottom drawer, if you're interested. I'm going to go ahead and get started." He finished pulling on his sweats from earlier and slipped out of the room.

I followed suit and left the cozy warmth of the bed. The more relaxed pants fit well enough, though they seemed to be clinging to my hips through sheer wishful thinking. I rolled them a bit in the hope that the added bulk would help them keep their perch and made my way to the en suite. A glance back at the rumpled bed revealed a rather disgruntled Sigurd.

"Lo siento, mi amigo." His tail flopped with a muted thump on the bed and he gave me an indignant glare, the same one Theo had given him earlier. I laughed to myself as I slipped into the bathroom to clean up as best I could, amazed at how similar the two were.

In short order, I was presentable again and made my way out to a kitchen that already smelled amazing. It would seem that Theo had quite the secret talent. I walked around the peninsula to lean against the counter beside him to watch as he worked. There were waters on the counter, and I gratefully took the fuller of the two. When most of the liquid was gone, Theo gestured to the fridge.

"I refilled the filter, so it might not be very cold."

"No me importa. You gonna tell me what you're making?" I asked once I'd refilled my glass and resumed my previous position. My attempts to guess from what was still out were futile as he'd already put most of it away again.

"It's a surprise." He winked, then opened the oven to slide in a full baking pan.

"Not even a hint?"

He laughed and set a timer. "Let it be a surprise. I promise, it'll be worth it."

"I don't doubt it, but I'm curious."

He snagged his half-full glass and proceeded to empty it. "Not telling."

"Well, it's obviously una cazuela of some sort," I proffered, refusing to give up so easily.

"Stop guessing."

"But I want to know."

Theo moved to stand in front of me and leaned forward so that his hands were resting on the counter on either side of me. "Knowing isn't everything." He shook his hair out of his eyes, and I kind of loved that he hadn't changed it again.

"Says you." I reached up and caressed his face like I'd intended to in bed. His eyes lidded as I pulled him forward to taste his lips.

My heart beat fast and slow all at once, and time itself seemed to stand still as I got lost in the kiss.

Our tongues came together in a dance designed just for the two of us. Steps I'd never known before came naturally when I was with Theo. Our lips moved slowly, but purposefully and perfectly in sync. The warmth that washed over me was like stepping into the sun after swimming for hours in the coldest stream, like returning from the land of the dead to be embraced by mi familia, like coming home.

When I pulled away, it was to hover a breath away while my lips tingled. Theo's eyes stayed shuttered, his soft breaths mingling with mine, and suddenly I couldn't hide from it anymore. I'd been terrified at the prospect that Theo might be seeing other people, because somewhere in the last three months, I'd completely fallen for him.

"Theo, I—"

The scream of a timer tore through the air. Theo's eyes flew open, and his head snapped to the side to look at the stove. And just like that, our fragile bubble shattered. He scrambled to stop the offending noise, but even as it vanished, my heart continued to race.

What was I thinking? I can't tell Theo I'm in love with him. He just told me he's not seeing anyone else, *and we're still avoiding labels. Ay Dios mío, I'm such an idiot. One mention of the "L" word and he'd vanish faster than las tamale de mi abuela on Christmas.*

No sooner had I pulled myself back together and far away from the precipice of stupid I'd nearly toppled over, than Theo was turning back to me. "What were you saying?"

Theo

Carlos' Adam's apple bobbed sharply, and he pushed his glasses up his nose. The intrusion of the timer had effectively obliterated whatever beautiful moment we'd been enjoying. A moment I'd do just about anything to resurrect. I'd never been so tempted to use a rewind spell in my life. It wouldn't take much, a minute at most, but time magic was not something someone used without proper preparation and, given my current drained state, not the wisest course either.

"Guess this means I'll get to find out what's for dinner," he quipped.

I moved back in front of him and slid my hands up his arms. "What were you going to say first?"

His gaze flicked briefly to mine before skittering off somewhere safer. There wasn't a doubt in my mind that he would have pushed his glasses up again if he could have. He swallowed again, and my breathing went shallow, even as my heart hammered against my ribs in anticipation.

Please say it. Please, Carlos. I need to hear you say it.

I didn't give a shit that we weren't sitting or that tears weren't resting on his lashes or that he didn't look sad. The future changed all the time; it wasn't fixed. There could be many paths to the same destination, and right now, all I cared about was hearing Carlos say three words I'd never wanted to hear from anyone.

"I missed you."

My heart sank somewhere down by my knees, and my absent breath came out in a whoosh as if I'd been punched in the gut. At the wayward sound, Carlos finally looked at me. The uncertainty and self-doubt shimmering in his brown eyes made me want to tear my hair out. He'd given me three words all right—the wrong three.

"Is that okay?"

Fuck, I'm such an asshole.

"No. I mean, yes, it's okay." I moved my hands to cradle his head and stole a deep kiss that pulled a surprised squeak from him. "In case it wasn't abundantly obvious, I missed you, too."

He offered a shaky smile, and I debated explaining that I'd never told anyone before that I'd missed them, not even my family, though I did. Wisterias were self-sufficient and independent by necessity. And it was true. I'd missed Carlos more than I had the words to express.

Before I could do anything as absurd as tell him I loved him or, ancestors help me, cry because I couldn't, I asked, "Still hungry?"

His smile gained confidence, and my heart rallied enough to climb up into my stomach. "Claro que sí."

"I'll take that as a yes," I responded, which prompted him to chuckle. I stepped back and pulled down plates. Each of us got a generous helping, with just enough left over for two more modest ones.

Carlos eyed the plate I set before him on the peninsula. "Are you trying to imply that I'm too skinny?"

I quirked an eyebrow and sat my equally heaped plate beside his. "Are you trying to imply I'm fat?"

He glanced up at me. "I would never," he said with as somber an expression as I'd ever seen him have. He blinked, and we both burst out laughing. "Sorry, it's just... come up before."

That it had come up enough times to make him defensive broke my heart. I reached out and trailed light fingers through his thick curls. "You're perfect the way you are." Carlos batted those insanely long lashes at me while his lips parted in shock. I took it as an invitation. His full lips molded against mine and for the second time in less than ten minutes, the rest of the world simply fell away.

My eyes were closed, but I knew I was safe even though I was surrounded by people I barely knew. Joy danced in my chest as a woman's voice scolded me to stop smiling. Almost immediately, Carlos' voice filled the darkness and my rebellious smile broadened.
"Oye, get your grubby hands off of him."
The woman huffed, and I sensed movement. "But I paint everyone."
"Not him, you don't. And not today." A wet brush delicately touched my face and spun out in a confident stroke. "You really do have to stop smiling, though, mi corazón."

I pulled out of the kiss and tried not to think about how happy I'd felt in the vision or that of all the Spanish Carlos had spouted at me over the last few months he'd never said mi corazón. I cleared my throat and focused my attention on the plate. "Aren't you going to guess what it is?"

Carlos shifted his gaze to stare intently at the piled high plate of food. "Ummm... well, there's onions and potatoes, and uh, an egg," he said, essentially listing ingredients as he poked at them. "Yeah, no lo sé."

"It's Tiroler Gröstl."

"And that is..." he trailed off as he tentatively loaded his fork.

"A traditional hodgepodge of things easily thrown together in a microscopic apartment kitchen." His face twisted in confusion, and I laughed. "It's an Austrian dish. My Great Aunt Jolene used to make it all the time when I spent winters with her." Of course, Great Aunt Jolene had also been nuttier than a fruitcake, driven mad by visions of her husband's death for twenty years before she even met the poor sap.

Clarity brightened Carlos' beautiful brown eyes, and he looked down at his plate with a hair less skepticism. "Oh. Why'd you put it in the oven? Most of this looks like it was cooked beforehand."

"Because I like cheese on mine." With that, I helped myself to a generous bite.

Chapter 15

Theo

Carlos plucked at his wrinkled shirt and scrunched his face in disapproval. "Ugh, I need fresh clothes...and a shower."

"There was a shower." I ran an adventurous hand up his sadly now khaki-encased leg.

"*That* was not a shower. Shower implies the use of soap."

"There was soap."

"You know what I mean."

I snickered, because I one hundred percent knew what he meant. Our attempt at bathing the evening before had quickly devolved into hands and mouths pretty much anywhere we could get them. My hand continued to venture and Carlos' chest started to rise and fall faster. He was so focused on the path

I was taking that he didn't even seem to notice his glasses were in danger of sliding right off his face.

I pulled my hand off his leg right as it reached his inner thigh in order to fix them myself. He mumbled disparagingly, but didn't argue when my lips found his. As adorable as his quirks could be, I loved how he forgot to be nervous when we were together.

"Mm, clothes," he hummed against my lips.

I sat back, momentarily thwarted by his insistence on returning to his dorm. What was the big deal? I had clothes, he could use those. Worse came to worse, I should have enough magic restored to summon brand new shit if he really wanted. Except what he *wanted* was apparently his own damn clothes.

"Mírame." He tipped my chin up. "I didn't say I didn't want to spend time with you anymore. I just want to bathe..." I opened my mouth to interject and he cut me off, "*properly* and change. It's not like I wouldn't come back. Or, you know, you could always come with me." He released me and shifted to get up.

I kind of hated how easily he could read me and the fact that I would most definitely be going with him if only to ensure he did, indeed come back. He fit in my apartment. My space felt more like a home than a box with furniture when he was there.

That the distinction was so notable made my skin itch, but not enough to prevent me from doing whatever it took to bring him back and sequester him in the modest apartment for as long as I could. I now had a much better appreciation for all of the ridiculous stories about witches locking away their heart's desires far out of reach of mortal grasps. Perhaps there was a bit more truth to the impulse than I'd been led to believe.

"You coming?" Carlos asked from the open doorway. I rolled my eyes and immediately walked toward him. He ducked his head as he turned to leave as if that could in any way hide the brilliant grin threatening to dominate his face. I glanced back into the apartment before shutting the door just in time to catch Sigurd's own mocking sending of my expression. By his account, I appeared the dopey goof with my own grin splitting my face in two.

Shut up and go chase your lady friend.

He twitched his tail once then leapt onto the windowsill. Summarily dismissed, I finished closing and locking the door. Carlos led the way to the dorm, and I followed after like some smitten fool, anything to stay near him for a little longer, a sentiment that would have alarmed me to no end three months ago. But now? Now I didn't give a witch's twitch as long as I could be close to him.

Sadly, he drew the line at my hopping in the shower with him when we arrived at the dorm. Something about no actual showering happening the last time. In support of his ridiculous request to get clean by himself, I remained in the living room.

I let out a huff and crossed my arms over my chest as I leaned against the wall and fantasized about my hands spreading slippery soap all over his deliciously dark skin. The fantasy was all of thirty seconds away from being a reality when the door opposite Carlos' opened.

I did my best to smile at Nessa as he emerged into the communal space, though I strongly suspected it came out more of a sneer, one which he returned. His withering gaze slid past me to Carlos' door. It wasn't until his eyes returned to me, wide and mildly alarmed, that I realized small sparks of lightning were playing across my forearms. He seemed to debate whether to say something, his jaw working as if trying out words. Then he wisely escorted his scaly ass out of the dorm without uttering so much as a peep.

I rolled my eyes and shoved my hands in my pockets. Cool metal welcomed the tips of my fingers. I removed my right hand

and the prize that had been hiding there. The nondescript coin could have belonged to any currency, yet it belonged to none. I closed my fingers around the trinket and quickly peeked into Carlos' room to see if he'd emerged yet. Reassured that he was still in the shower, I returned my attention to the coin and the spell I'd been crafting.

Carlos

Theo's laughter wrapped around me, much like his arm draped over my shoulders. I struggled to think of a way this moment could get any more perfect. A shower and fresh clothes had me completely rejuvenated and ready to spend another full day with the man by my side.

"Juan Carlos Barrera."

I lurched forward and out of Theo's welcome embrace. Just like that, my perfect moment blew up. It took two tries to swallow past my suddenly Shara-dry throat. "Mamá." I pushed my glasses up with a hand that I hoped no one could tell was shaking.

Ay Dios mío. What kind of grown man is afraid of his mother?

Fácil, easy. The kind sneaking around with a witch behind her back.

My mother placed her hands on her ample hips and quirked an eyebrow. Her reddish-brown hair lay in a braid pulled over her shoulder, and her brown eyes bored into me like they knew I'd been stealing galletas from the pantry. With her fierce demeanor and imposing presence, Catalina Barrera was every inch a modern Mayan warrior, albeit uncharacteristically tall and about five hundred years too late. She even had an elaborate jaguar pendant hanging from her neck. A pendant whose emerald eyes were currently flashing as fiercely as my mother's brown ones.

"¿Vas a presentarme a tu amigo, mijo?"

Introduce him, of course. I summoned moisture from somewhere and wet my mouth enough to speak. "Mamá, this is Theo Kendal." I angled to include him and gestured back at my mother. "Theo, this is mi madre, Catalina Barrera." My mother's eyes crinkled in a good-natured smile, and I dared to breathe.

"Mucho gusto, Theo." She stepped past me and extended a hand in greeting. I turned to see what Theo was making of this detour of today's plans. To my horror, as he reached out to accept her hand, his other rose to his hair. I shook my head vehemently, but either he didn't see me or had no idea what I was referencing. My mother's fingers closed around Theo's at the same time his passed through his hair—changing the lavender to platinum.

My mother went stiller than a statue, and all the blood drained from my face. She looked over at me and fire might as well have been flying from her eyes as she said in scathing Spanish, "A *witch*, Carlos? Have I taught you nothing?"

"Mamá, it's not … bueno, it is, pero puedo explicarlo," I said, tripping over my tongue and fluctuating between English and Spanish. There had to be a way to make her understand without getting completely disowned, but for the life of me I was drawing a blank.

Theo glanced between the two of us, his now freed hand hanging awkwardly in the air. "Um...should I go?"

"Sí." "No," my mother and I said at the same time. Her eyes narrowed, and I have no idea where the steel in my spine came from, but I glared right back.

"What is the meaning of this? You know what people like him do to us. Untrustworthy pigs, all of them," she hissed angrily in Spanish.

I winced at the swine comment, and I was more than aware of witches' reputations as I'd been raised on countless stories of the atrocities they'd committed against demonkind, but she didn't stop there.

"And here I find you in intimate company with one of them. Have you lost your mind?"

"Don't talk about my boyfriend like that," I snapped. Shock splashed across my mother's features, then dissolved into an expression of surprised disbelief.

"Your boyfriend?" It wasn't until she repeated my words back at me I realized what I'd called him. I blanched and thanked all of my lucky stars that Theo didn't speak Spanish. He'd admitted to being exclusive less than twenty-four hours and I was already tossing around labels.

I opened my mouth to say something, anything, to mitigate the inevitable explosion. Mi madre held up a hand.

"Is that why you're abandoning your family, your sacred duty? To go back to this user? Does he know what you are?"

My hand tightened into a fist at my side, and I stood a little straighter. "Stop it," I said firmly in English. She had no right to judge me. I would never give up my sacred duty. And Theo wouldn't use me. He wasn't like that.

"So this gringo is your boyfriend. Truly?" The condescending look and tone, on top of the insulting question, pushed me past the last edge of reason.

"English, Mamá. It's rude to speak about someone in front of them in a language they don't understand."

Against all laws of physics, my mother's eyes widened even more. "You have a boyfriend I've never heard of—a witch—and he doesn't even speak Spanish? Is he even your boyfriend?"

"Of course I am." My mother and my head snapped around at Theo's cavalier response to her cruel question. He raised his eyebrows at our open shock. "You didn't really think your son would date someone and not at least attempt to teach them Spanish, did you? I may not be able to speak it, but I'm not entirely hopeless. After all, Spanish is a Latin-based language, and in *that* I am proficient." He shifted his focus to me, and a light breeze could have knocked me over. All the things I'd said to him over the last few months—last night—came rushing back to me.

Estoy tan jodido. I'm so fucked.

While I silently freaked out at this horrible revelation, my mother eyed Theo with a new level of speculation. "My son has a boyfriend?"

"He does," Theo answered without blinking.

My mother's sudden smile frightened me more than her earlier rage. "Maravilloso. I actually came to retrieve my stray hijo for dinner. You must join us." Her smile broadened, revealing perfectly aligned teeth. "The family would love to meet you." Her words sank like a stone in my stomach. She turned that sinister grin on me and added, "I can't wait to hear what tu abuela has to say."

For a second, I worried I'd shifted to my skeletal form, because there couldn't possibly be any blood left in my face. I surged forward and inserted myself between the two of them. "I don't think that's a good idea."

"¿Por qué no? You can't keep este secreto para siempre, Carlito."

I shook my head while I floundered to find the words that could get us out of this mess without making a bigger one. Getting busted with a witch was bad enough. Coming out to my entire family that I was dating said witch was tantamount to turning my back on all of our traditions and becoming the next La Llorona. A warm hand closed around my arm. My mother's gaze sharpened as she took in the familiar touch.

"I'd love to meet your family."

Victory blossomed across her face. I chanced a look over my shoulder at Theo. "You don't know what you're agreeing to."

Theo's unshakable blue eyes softened, and his thumb brushed lightly on my arm, sending out the smallest of sparks to caress the exposed skin. "Sure I do, baby. Your family wants to meet your boyfriend."

"Theo, I—"

My mother's clap cut me short, and I flinched at the abrasive sound. "Then it's settled. We'll do dinner." She grabbed the two of us right as a portal ripped open mid-sidewalk. I knew I'd be in trouble for bailing on the festivities early, but it was much worse than I'd anticipated if she'd come by private portal. And now a witch was involved. "Estoy muy contento de que tus hermanos decided to stay another day."

"What!" I yanked back on my arm. "No. No, we can reschedule. Mamá, por favor no. No me hagas esto. Not abuela and mis hermanos."

"And tus tías y tíos también."

I shot Theo an apologetic look as the portal swallowed us whole. It had been nice while it lasted.

Chapter 16

Theo

Shock hit me like a bolt of lightning when the word boyfriend came out of Carlos' mouth. A shock that was quickly replaced by another as he stood up to his mother and defended me. My amazement took a back seat, though, as I defended him in turn. Never mind that I didn't date, that relationships could be dangerous for me, and that one with a Kisin might literally be the dumbest thing I'd ever live to do, if Carlos had the gall to set his mother down, then I had his back. Then I agreed to dinner.

"You don't know what you're agreeing to." The concern in Carlos' eyes as he argued against the impromptu invitation could only be matched by the hope I saw shining there as well. That tiny glimmer decided me, if his family liking me was important to him, then it was important to me. I'd move the heavens if I had to.

"Sure I do, baby. Your family wants to meet your boyfriend." Touching Carlos even as mildly as placing a hand on his arm felt odd beneath the critical gaze of his mother, but it was nowhere near as disconcerting as hearing the actual word boyfriend coming out of my mouth.

Uncertainty and fear warred right alongside that ember of hope in Carlos' dark brown eyes. "Theo, I—" His mother's timely clap cut him off, and I took the opportunity to lace our fingers together as a show of silent support. Mama Barrera proceeded to lead the way through what smelled an awful lot like a pop-up portal. Carlos shot me an apologetic look as we stepped through. Before he could follow it up with a verbal one and betray that until five minutes ago we hadn't actually been in a relationship, I spoke up.

"How much family are we talking, Mrs. Barrera?" Deep down I recognized the question for what it was—a stalling tactic.

She gave a dismissive wave of her hand as she marched across grass tormented by a blistering summer and an impending winter. "Only una pequeña gathering de la familia."

Carlos groaned as if that were the worst news possible. "¿Todos mis hermanos?"

"Claro que sí."

I shoved my free hand into my pocket and established a link so magic would pour directly into the coin without my having to recharge it. The cost of keeping the interpretation spell fueled would be large, but I had a feeling I was going to need every second of it. The link took its sweet time siphoning off the energy it required, and I missed the first part of Carlos' persistent argument.

"Lo crucificarán. You can't do this to him." I did my best to quell my alarm since he basically just said that they were going to crucify me.

His mother glanced over her shoulder to spare me a troubling grin. "He agreed."

"He doesn't *know* what he agreed to. The whole family, Mom? That's a bit much for a first introduction. Are you *trying* to scare him off?" I bit my tongue to prevent myself from answering his obvious concern with a reassurance that I wasn't going anywhere. I didn't care how terrifying his family was. Only the emphasis of his native accent gave away that all of that had originally been in Spanish... which I shouldn't know, or at least not that well.

Mama Barrera narrowed to slits. "Trial by fire. His kind is used to that."

Carlos scowled at his mother's receding form while I struggled to manage my reaction to such a scathing comment. Suddenly, I had a much better understanding of Carlos' initial reluctance to give me the time of day. His family clearly distrusted witches on a fundamental level, and here their son was bringing one of the terrible things home like a stray cat. What was worse was that I couldn't even dispute my kind's deplorable reputation. It had absolutely been earned through hundreds of years of abuse and manipulation. After all, wasn't that why I was here? To keep tabs on him so I could ultimately use him for my own gain?

I pushed the wretched truth away.

This is more than that.

I tightened my fingers around his, and he looked at me askance. Before I could say anything, a loud screech filled the air. I tore my gaze and troubled thoughts away from Carlos in time to see a door rebound off a stucco wall. A girl who couldn't be more than twelve launched herself out of the sprawling home and straight at Carlos' mom, a medium-sized hairless dog hot on her heels.

"Mom!" she shouted in translated Spanish. "Jorge is picking on me again! He said my braids are stupid and only little girls wear those. I told him he was wrong and that *he* was stupid, but he just laughed and pulled my braid." The dog pulled to a stop beside her, then caught sight of the two of us and bounded over.

Mama Barrera paused in her march to address who I now assumed was Carlos' younger sister. "Your braids are lovely, my beautiful girl. Your brother is simply jealous that his hair is not so pretty."

"But Mom!"

"Julissa, stop yelling. We have a guest." She gestured to me, and I offered a small wave. The little girl's eyes widened to the size of saucers, and her mouth fell open as her gaze slid over to me and her brother standing hand in hand. We finished walking up to where she'd remained frozen while her mother ventured into the house.

"Hey, Juli." Carlos' greeting seemed to snap her out of whatever fog she'd gotten lost. She blinked and whipped her attention to Carlos.

"Who's this? And why is he so white?"

"Oh my God, Julissa, you can't go around asking people why they're white. And what does his skin color have anything to do with it, anyway? Rude little girl." He shook his head and reached out to stroke a hand along the dog's wrinkled back.

She crossed her arms and huffed indignantly. "Well, who is he? And he's not just white, he's like white-white. A ghost."

Damn kid, not all of us can tan.

Carlos winced at her persistence. "This is Theo. He's my..." He cast me an anxious glance as he floundered for what title to give me.

"I'm his boyfriend," I filled in, dropping to her level in order to pet the peculiar animal that was undoubtedly Carlos' dog, Azul. Her brown eyes went wide, then she drew in a deep breath and spun around to race back into the house, the contested twin braids flying behind her.

"Javier, Jesús, Jorge, José—Juan has a boyfriend!" She screamed as loud as her tiny lungs would permit as she careened into the house. Carlos grimaced with each listed name, and the apologetic look returned.

I gave the remarkably friendly Azul one last pat and straightened up. "She's a bit of a tattletale."

"You have no idea."

No longer hand in hand, we followed after the remarkably dramatic preteen into the house where literally nothing could have prepared me for the sheer volume of people that awaited us. My hand shot out to encircle Carlos' arm like a vice and hold him back even as he let out a relieved breath.

"What's the matter?"

"Your mom said a small gathering," I hissed.

Carlos looked around the room at all the curious eyes turning on us. "This *is* small. The good news is, despite what my mom said, it looks like my aunts and uncles left, which means fewer cousins."

"Carlos, there have to be twenty people in here."

His face scrunched up with confusion. "I'm assuming by your tone that you find that unusual, but it's perfectly normal here. Truthfully, this is very small." My mouth threatened to gape. Meanwhile, four guys that all bore a striking resemblance to Carlos, if Carlos had a goatee, or no hair, or was three inches shorter, or was built more like a soccer player, descended upon us like a pack of vultures.

"Juanito, you came back!" Goatee exclaimed in Spanish as he slapped Carlos on the back.

"What's Julissa saying about you having a boyfriend?"

"You're dating? Like a real person?" Baldy snickered.

"Why didn't you tell us?" Shorty rounded out the interrogation.

"Probably because he's a witch," Mama Barrera said as she passed behind the group like some kind of sinister wraith. All questions died, and an oppressive silence enveloped the room. The curiosity in their eyes turned to distrust as each of the people Carlos called family stared at me. I swallowed and licked my lips, desperate to find the words to persuade them I was anything but a manipulative witch out for themselves—but they would have been a lie.

"What's this about the savior of lost children seeing a witch? Surely not *my* Juanito." The thin voice of an old woman shot through the silence with the precision of an arrow, splitting it apart with abandon.

"It's true, Mother. Carlito has brought home a witch to meet the family." Mama Barrera's statement missed the truth by a mile. Carlos had been coerced into coming home, and I'd stupidly agreed with the blind assumption that I could handle it. Wrong didn't come close to describing how out of my depth I found myself. A handful of people I could charm, maybe a dozen. But a room full of Carlos' closest relatives all looking at me like I was planning on sacrificing their beloved brother, son, cousin? Add to that the fact that it's exactly what I planned on doing to save my worthless hide.

"Move aside. Move aside. I want to see this witch." The sharp, aged voice snapping out startled me enough that I jumped. Meanwhile, the people between me and who I suspected might be the scariest member of the family separated like the Sea of Barreras to reveal a tiny, wrinkled woman sitting at a small table. "Come closer. Let me get a good look at you."

I did as bidden and approached the wizened crone with her bright eyes and iron-gray hair pulled into a long braid. She stared at me unblinkingly, and the whole room seemed to hold a collective breath.

"Grandmother Margarita, this Theo," Carlos offered from where he hovered like a ghost at my side.

"You're a witch," she declared.

"Yes."

Her eyes narrowed, emphasizing lines earned from years of laughing and smiling. "Are you really?"

I couldn't fathom why anyone in their right mind would think it would be funny to pretend to be a witch in this house. "Last time I checked."

She threw up a wrinkled hand in frustration. "But can you do real magic? Because the last witch I met could barely do more than parlor tricks at a circus. Fraud couldn't even tell the future."

I glanced over at Carlos, who looked every bit as confused as I felt. "Um...the ability to see the future—foresight—is an incredibly rare ability. They likely couldn't."

She huffed and smacked the table. "Well, what *can* you do? Tarot? Palm reading?"

A smile twitched at the corner of my mouth. "Both, actually, but I don't have any cards."

"Julissa! Get my playing cards." The young girl that I hadn't even noticed standing on the periphery of the blast zone scrambled to retrieve the requested items. A scant five minutes later, I found myself sitting across from the intimidating woman, a deck of cards in hand and the rest of the house, once again going about their business.

"You don't have to do this," Carlos leaned down to whisper in my ear.

"I got this, babe. Tarot is first-year stuff. Though admittedly I'm a bit rusty and this isn't my usual deck," I added louder. His grandmother grunted and waved for me to get on with it.

"Come on, let's see what you've got."

I raised my eyebrows and shook my head as I shuffled the cards, pulling a little magic into them with each bridge. Finally, I doled out three cards in a traditional past, present, future spread, then without batting an eye, I flipped the first card. "The Tower."

Her eyes opened wide, and I couldn't help but smirk as she stared down at the transformed card. "Your past was turbulent and filled with trials that threatened to break you," I spoke as I flipped the next card, the seven of wands. "But you persevered, built a family and a life when the world told you it was impossible. You have many healthy children who have brought much joy to your life." I turned over the final card—ten of cups—and smiled. "And your future will bring you a joy you never expected."

Carlos squeezed my shoulder, and my grin grew. His grandmother's gaze darted up to him, then settled back on me. "It would seem yours does as well." My smile slipped, and she smacked the table again. "You've proved your mettle, witch. Now my grandson."

"Grandmother—"

"I really shouldn't..." I argued in time with Carlos.

"Don't be silly, of course you can."

Out of curiosity, I peeked at the top card. The Hanged Man. Cold flooded through me and I quickly shuffled the cards back together, restoring them to their natural state, and shoved them back in their box. "No." They both gave me peculiar looks at the abrupt action and decisive answer. Without really meeting his eye, I asked Carlos, "Didn't your mom mention something about dinner?"

His worried frown relaxed into a smile. "Yes. If we're lucky, there will still be some of my grandmother's tamales left."

The woman in question pushed up from her seat and reached up to pinch Carlos' face. "My precious boy, you know I always save you some. I suppose you could share some with your boyfriend." The look Carlos gave me over his five-foot grandma made all the awkward stares worth it. I'd find a way to rewrite the stars if he'd look at me like that forever.

Carlos

I finished rinsing off our dishes, then slipped back out into the large family room, where I continued to be surprised by Theo's presence in my home. The fact that mi abuela had barely batted an eye at his presence continued to astound me, and with her passive acceptance of his presence, everyone else had fallen in stride. Already, he'd met and charmed my brothers as well as their wives and girlfriends. He didn't seem the least bit intimidated by all the prying questions or side eyes, and he was still *here*.

"What are you smiling about?" He asked as I passed him a can of fresca. My cheeks burned at getting caught thinking of him, and I pushed my glasses up.

"Just impressed with how well you're handling all of this."

"All of what?"

"All of the people."

He shrugged and took a drink. "They're just people. And I think your grandma is nicer than she lets on." I barely registered his conspiratorial wink as I was too wrapped up with trying to figure out if I'd ever heard a witch refer to a demon as a person before.

I cleared my throat and pushed the observation away. "Still, doing the whole meet-the-family thing is a bit much, especially considering we're not really…" I trailed off, more than a little embarrassed about this whole thing. Theo hooked a finger in my belt loop and tugged me closer to whisper in my ear.

"We're dating Carlos Barrera. Get used to it." He brushed his lips along the shell of my ear, and I shivered. "Besides, I like your family." I swiveled to stare at him in surprise.

"Really?"

His blue eyes sparkled with merriment. "Yes, though I do have two questions."

"What might those be?" I asked, enjoying how natural this felt.

"First, where's your dad? I'm surprised he's not here."

"What, twenty Barreras not enough for you?" I teased. He nudged me with his elbow before taking another sip of his drink. "He's at the shop. Mamá says a special order came in and he had to be there to receive it."

"Special order? What sort of shop is he running?" The light laughter at the edge of his words brought a smile to my lips, and it suddenly occurred to me that Theo would probably love to see our family shop.

I'll have to take him sometime.

"Years ago, mis bisabuelos opened a books and antiquities in downtown Oaxaca." Theo's eyes lit up as if he'd discovered an unexpected treasure.

"Would this store be where you developed your love of all things mythos?"

I stared at Theo for a solid minute and fought the urge to ask him to be my boyfriend for real. "Yes," I finally managed once I had the impulse back under control. "You had another question?"

Theo set his drink aside so he could talk with his hands. "Yes. I would really like to know why everyone keeps calling you Juan."

"Because it's my name."

He plastered a hand to his chest and assumed a look of affronted shock. "You told me your name was Carlos. You *lied* to me?"

I couldn't help but laugh at the theatrics. "My name is Juan Carlos, after mi abuelo."

"I take it he's no longer with us?" I shook my head and glanced down at my forgotten drink. Theo's voice softened. "Do you get to see him on the other side?" My heart swelled like it did every time Theo put together the small pieces that made me who I was.

"I do, but visits tend to be short and far between. He's quite busy." Questions about his own family were on the tip of my tongue when someone turned the music up and a familiar tune played through the speakers. My head snapped around to find the culprit was none other than my brother, Jorge. He grinned like an idiot as he did a quick salsa move and beckoned toward the open floor. I put down my drink and slashed a hand through the air. "No. Absolutely not. You turn that off right now."

"Oh, come on, Juanito, don't you wanna dance with us? I'm sure tu novio would like to dance," Jesús shouted as he joined my obnoxious brother.

"Yeah, show him your moves," Jorge added as he swung his hips low in a suggestive arc, then he and Jesus proceeded to laugh their asses off

"Leave him out of this."

"Hermanito, you used to *love* Elvis Crespo," Javier insisted as he and Jose appeared beside us.

"Don't you dare." I glared at my oldest brother.

"What are they talking about?" Theo asked as Jorge turned the music up even louder.

José threw an arm around Theo's shoulders and leaned in close to be heard over the blare of trumpets. "You see, when mi hermano era joven, he became obsessed with the artist after hearing nuestra madre playing it one day. Mamá has always had a soft spot for salsa."

"Made sense," Javier cut in. "The music is good, and the songs are fun." My brothers shared a conspiratorial look, and I wanted to crawl under a rock.

"But that's not why Juanito liked el cantante so much." José leaned forward to leer at me while keeping his hold on Theo. "Something about his hair, right, hermanito?" He glanced over at Theo. "Al menos eres consistente." For the love of God, I did *not* need my brother pointing out I had a thing for pretty hair.

"Juanito's obsession with Crespo is how we all figured out he was gay," Javier said, with an evil smirk.

"Where did he even find all of those posters? They covered his entire room. Literally, floor to ceiling, Crespo everywhere." José's laughter made me want to transition and cross the veil right there to escape.

"Ustedes son los peores," I groaned, simultaneously covering my face with my hands and knocking my glasses askew. They really were the worst.

One of my idiot brothers grabbed hold of my wrist and pulled me forward, tossing me into Jorge and Jesús. I tried in vain to escape them, to no avail. Jesus spun me around, and I caught sight of an equally captive Theo with José. He shrugged at me and fell into the rhythm like he'd been born to dance. I stood staring in amazement at how easily he flowed with the music when Jesús jerked on my hips, reminding me to move. If anyone had told me as early as yesterday that a witch would be laughing and dancing con mis hermanos in my family home, I would have laughed in their face. Yet here we were.

The song changed, and dance partners rotated. Jesús snagged his wife, Jorge stole Theo, Javier grabbed me, and José shimmied next to his pregnant girlfriend. Halfway through the second chorus, everyone shuffled again. Inches away from Theo, Jorge traded places with Javier and danced me away from my desired dance partner. I let out a frustrated huff, but went with it. It wasn't until the fourth such change that the irritation reached a boiling point.

I extricated myself from Jesús and made my way through the impromptu dance party that now included my mom and several of my nieces and nephews in order to get to Theo. When I finally spotted him amid the throng of people crowding the floor, he was dancing sandwiched between Jorge and José and looked like he was having the time of his life. His hands sat easily on José's hips while his hips moved in time with Jorge's behind him. Cold washed over me as if someone had dropped me in the creek in the dead of winter.

This is my ex all over again.

Unable to stomach coming in second to my brothers yet again, I turned and bolted.

Chapter 17

Theo

I'd never given much thought to the fantasy of being passed around by a bunch of attractive men, but I was definitely starting to see the appeal. Carlos' brothers were easily as handsome as he was and clearly had no qualms dancing with another man, spoken for or not. The only shame was that I hadn't actually gotten to dance with Carlos yet.

Jorge grabbed my hips and set a fast enough pace that I had to hang onto Jose or fall over. I threw my head back and laughed at the improbability of it all. One minute I'm positive the family is planning an old-fashioned witch burning in their backyard. Next, everyone's dancing and having a good time. Even grandma was getting her groove on.

I leaned forward to ask José where Carlos had gone when I spied him approaching out of the corner of my eye. My smile widened in anticipation as I turned in time to see the look of sheer horror stamped across his face. Without so much as a word, he spun and ran. All the happiness that had been filling me evaporated in the blink of an eye.

Guilt slammed through me as I pushed both Jorge and José away, ignoring their shouts as I tore after Carlos. I made it all the way to the opposite side of the house and what was clearly the domicile wing, where I finally lost my heading. I ground to a halt and swiveled around in search of any indication as to where Carlos had gone.

"Carlos? Carlos, I'm sorry. I fucked up. I'm not here for them. I'm here for you." I hazarded a few steps deeper into the warren of doors. "Carlos, please. I'll leave if you want, but at least talk to me. I'm sorry. I—"

A tanned arm reached out and yanked me through one of the open doors. I caught a brief glimpse of a bedroom, then everything went dark as another door slid shut. The hand that had snared me relinquished its hold in favor of my face and guided me through the inky black to a pair of familiar, full lips. Carlos captured my muffled groan as he dominated my mouth with a persistence that set me on fire.

"Carlos," I moaned and wrapped my arms around his waist.

"Hands," he demanded breathlessly, nipping at my lips.

I snaked my fingers beneath the hem of his shirt. He let out a groan the moment the electric touch hit bare skin. The sound instantly had me scrambling for his belt. Within seconds, I had my hand wrapped around his length while he conquered my mouth with a determination that blasted away all other awareness. I continued to stroke him even as I got lost in this perfect bubble of sensation Carlos had created. With my free hand, I trailed sparks of lightning along his arm.

Hues of purple lit the dark space as Carlos' teeth sank into my lip. His fingers curled in my hair and held me close, his tongue diving deep to steal whatever was left of my reason as he fucked into my hand. I moaned and squeezed a little tighter on my next stroke, nearly losing my rhythm in the frenzy.

Adrenaline and joy wove together in a tangled knot while Carlos kissed the hell out of me. Despite avoiding serious relationships like the plague for the better part of my life, I'd give anything for this feeling to last forever. To be his rock and safe harbor. To be the reason he was brave. To be the one to make him feel good. To be his everything.

Suddenly, white light illuminated the closet, and a shrill voice shattered our shadowed oasis. "Oh. My. God. Mom!"

"Shit," Carlos hissed as he struggled to put himself away and do up his pants at the same time.

We stumbled out of the closet too late to catch Julissa before she vaulted into the hallway. I looked at Carlos to gauge the severity of our situation. "What do you think she saw?"

"Enough. We have to catch her before she finds my mom. Little brat lives to get me in trouble." His zipper slid home, and we raced after his sister. The maze of rooms didn't appear half as daunting with Carlos by my side, and after only two turns, we spied Julissa sprinting down the last stretch of hallway. We picked up speed, but weren't fast enough to stop her from skidding to a halt among a circle of people curious as to the ruckus.

"Mom, I found Carlos in the closet!" The little tattletale shouted.

Javier laughed and elbowed Jorge. "Cute Juli, but Carlos has been out of the closet for years."

Carlos rolled his eyes at the terrible joke and stepped forward to restrain his sister and prevent her from saying anything else. "Let it be, Julissa."

She tore free of his grasp. "Oh yeah? Well, Theo was—"

"Julissa!" Carlos shouted over her. His brothers snickered, no doubt guessing where this snitch-fest was headed. Meanwhile, Mama Barrera entered the ring and stared down her youngest son with her arms crossed over her chest.

"What were they doing?" she asked in Spanish. Her tone had both myself and Carlos swallowing down a sudden wave of anxiety.

Julissa threw a self-satisfied smirk over her shoulder at her brother. Carlos squeezed his eyes shut and seemed to brace himself for the worst, but not even I could have anticipated what would come out of her mouth next.

"Theo made Carlos sparkle," Julissa replied in English. Carlos straightened up and looked over at me with the same confused expression that now dominated everyone's faces.

Carlos

Theo stepped closer to me. "Carlos—"

"What is she talking about?" I asked just as quietly.

"No soy mentiroso," Julissa argued with Jose, stamping her foot. "He did sparkle, I swear."

"Hermano, what is she talking about?" Javier asked, stepping forward. I searched Theo's face a moment longer, then turned to address my brother.

"I—"

"It's magic," Theo interrupted before I could admit that I didn't have a clue.

"See? Te lo dije. Do it again," Julissa demanded. I glanced back at Theo even as Jesus spoke up to echo my little sister's demand.

"Let's see this magic." His voice was joined by several others, including mi abuela's.

"Theo?" I asked.

He let out a sigh and ran his fingers through his hair, though the shade remained miraculously platinum. "O-okay."

"What are they talking about?" I whispered. "What did she see?" Theo met my questioning gaze, and for the first time since I'd met him, he actually looked embarrassed. He averted his gaze and swallowed.

"I probably should have told you about this sooner." He placed a hand on my arm just below my sleeve and added even quieter, "I promise to make the voltage really low." I was all set to ask him what the hell he was talking about when it finally clicked. My eyes widened in horrified realization a microsecond before the familiar tingles trailed down my arm.

I nearly swallowed my tongue in an effort to keep my mortified whimper to myself. A blotchy red suffused Theo's cheeks as his fingers finished their trail at my wrist. Up close, it looked as though tiny bolts of electricity leapt from his fingers to my arm. In their immediate wake, violet sparkles danced along my skin, lingering like glitter before fading away.

Theo snatched his hand away and stuffed it in his pocket, but refused to meet my gaze again. "I'm sorry," he mumbled. My mouth opened and closed uselessly as words evaded me. How had I never noticed before? Had I really been that out of it? And was that fucking *lightning*?

"Mierda, hermano. What kind of kinky shit are you into?" Jose asked into the dead silence of the room.

Mi madre smacked him in the arm. "Cuida tu lengua." Heh, like he'd ever watch his tongue.

"Lo siento, Mama. No quise decir nada con eso," he apologized, rubbing the injured appendage, as though he really hadn't meant anything by it.

Suddenly, Javier barked out a laugh. "Always knew you had a sparkling personalidad. Now the rest of you sparkles too." The rest of mis hermanos laughed as well, while Julissa scowled in disappointment. Javier spared me a wink, then announced loudly that he was going to eat the last of the tres leches. His brood of children squealed in protest along with Jose and Jorge, and the lot of them raced to the kitchen and the cake in question.

I continued to stand there at a complete loss amid the chaos of voices and stared down at where a miniature galaxy of purple stars had sprung to life on my arm. Gentle fingers combed through my hair. I looked up from the now perfectly normal flesh and straightened my glasses before looking into my mother's concerned eyes.

"¿Te está lastimando?" she asked softly.

I glanced around, mildly amazed she'd ask me bold as brass in front of Theo if he was hurting me, and realized that at some point he'd vanished. "¿A dónde fue—"

"He slipped away to the bathroom. Por favor, responde la pregunta, mijo." I stopped searching for Theo as the worry in my mother's voice registered.

"No. He's not hurting me, Mama. He's been nothing but respectful and honest with me. Yo confío en el." I didn't realize how much I trusted him until I said the words out loud. "Me gusta mucho, mamá." I more than liked him if I was honest with myself.

She smiled and ran her fingers through my hair again, like she'd done when I was little. "Puedo ver eso. I think he likes you, too. You should have seen how fast he ran after you."

My mouth fell open before I regained my senses. "Why would you tell mis hermanos to do that?"

She shrugged and stepped back. "We had to be sure. Y fue idea de tu hermano Javier. Now go find that boyfriend of yours before el muere de vergüenza." She gave me a light shove in the general direction Theo must have disappeared, and my smile broadened to mirror hers.

Theo

I splashed cold water on my face to cool the burn in my cheeks and stared at my reflection. The awful redness may have gone down, but guilt still shone in my eyes.

What am I doing? I need to talk to Carlos.

With a sigh of resignation, I wiped my face dry and hung the hand towel back up.

All I can hope is that he doesn't hate me.

I didn't think I could stand it if Carlos didn't actually want to be my boyfriend after all of this mess, because I sure as fuck wanted to be his. Anytime I was with Carlos, I forgot to worry about the future or that I might not have one, it was enough to be with him. The idea that I might have screwed all of that up by not being upfront about my magic or briefly entertaining that ludicrous fantasy left a sour taste in my mouth.

No sense in stalling.

I opened the bathroom door and came face to face with Julissa. "Um...hey," I said lamely. A quick glance down the hall showed she was alone. Her mouth turned down in a scowl that darkened her face. She tightened her skinny arms across her chest and continued to glare at me. "Can I help you?"

"You bet your white ass you can help me."

I recoiled at the verbal abuse and looked back at her, substantially more concerned about her presence. "Should you be here by yourself?"

She sucked her teeth and rolled her eyes. "It's my house, dumbass."

"Right..." I tried to skirt past her toward the relative safety of the main living space where I'd left Carlos, but she maneuvered to block the way. "What do you want, you little sprite?"

"You're gonna make me sparkle like Carlos."

I snorted. "No, I'm not."

"Yes. You. Are." Her glower returned with a vengeance.

I crossed my arms and met her petulant stare with a stubborn one of my own. "No. I'm. Not."

Her mouth twisted up in an evil, crooked smile. "Oh, yes, you are or I'm gonna tell mom that you and Carlos were fooling around in the closet."

"You're bluffing. You didn't see anything," I countered, not sounding nearly as certain as I wanted to. If I knew how much trouble we were risking, maybe I could've been a little more assertive.

"Oh yeah?" She drew in a deep breath, much like she had when I'd first arrived, and I quickly slapped a hand over her mouth.

"Cool it." I kept her mouth covered for a minute, then slowly removed my hand.

"Make me sparkle."

"I don't think that's a good idea," I sidestepped. While this would be the perfect opportunity to test my theory about how my magic reacted with Kisin demons, I'd much rather not risk my hypothesis blowing up in my face. Not to mention the side effects...

"Sparkle. Now." She narrowed her eyes at me. "Or else." I squeezed my eyes shut and grimaced at her insistence.

Carlos is going to kill me. But do I really want to chance getting him in trouble over something so simple as a magic trick?

Against my better judgment, I caved. "Alright, you menacing munchkin." She immediately dropped the glower and jumped up and down, clapping her hands excitedly. My gaze swept the corridor for witnesses, and I held up a finger to stall her enthusiasm. "One arm. That's it."

"Two."

"One. Final offer."

She huffed, but held out her arm without further argument. *Please don't let me regret this.*

Like I'd done earlier with Carlos, I reduced the voltage as much as possible before trailing a single finger along her outstretched arm. The moment her eyes widened, I knew I'd made a terrible mistake. "Julissa..."

"Oh. My. God."

Oh no.

"Magic is... Amazing!"

"Would you shut up? What happened to not getting me in trouble?" My words went unheard as she traced the same path my finger had taken and stared at her arm in wonder.

Her gaze snapped up, and all the trouble I'd been hoping to evade came tumbling out of her mouth. "I can't wait to tell grandma!" She promptly spun on her heel and ran toward the main room. My fingers stirred the vacant air a millisecond too late to catch her.

"Fuck." Rather than chase after the malicious devil child, I went in search of Carlos. Thankfully, I found him quickly as he was currently walking down the hall toward me. For a brief second, I forgot why I'd been looking for him so earnestly when I saw the relief in his eyes.

"There you are. Can we talk?"

"Sure thing, but first we gotta go. Like now." I grabbed his arm without slowing down and propelled us back the way he'd come.

"What are you talking about? It's still early."

"You're menacing, little sister cornered me."

"What did she do?"

I winced. "It's more what I did."

Carlos ground to a halt. "Theo, what did you do?"

I gave him an apologetic look. "She threatened to tell your mom what we'd been doing."

"What did you do?" he repeated.

"She wanted to sparkle."

"Theo!" he hissed.

"I know, okay? I tried to get out of it, but she wouldn't let it go."

"That's no excuse. You're an adult. She's a kid."

"She's bossy, and she blackmailed me. But seriously, can we argue about this somewhere else?"

Carlos opened his mouth, undoubtedly to insist on having this argument right here, when Julissa's voice rang loud and clear through the house. "When I grow up, I'm gonna marry a witch so I can sparkle all the time!"

Carlos turned a face plastered with horror to me. "We gotta go. Now." He grabbed my hand and resumed our quick pace. We burst into the living room, and several heads swiveled around. Carlos offered a half-hearted wave of farewell. "Totally forgot we have an exam, gotta go."

"Juan Carlos Barrera..." Mama Barrera's threatening tone chased after us as we beat a hasty retreat.

"Bye, Mom, talk to you later." The same door we'd entered through hours ago smacked shut behind us. Twenty paces from the house, Carlos pulled up and glanced around. "Shit, how are we going to get back?"

"Stand back, babe. I got this." I rubbed my hands together and added what I was about to attempt to the long list of poor choices I'd made today.

Chapter 18

Theo

We fell through the portal and into my front door, the burnt smell of ozone all around us. I leaned on the door a moment for support as the last of my magic reserves vanished and my connection to the coin in my pocket snapped.

"Holy shit, I had no idea you could make a portal. Can all witches do that?" Carlos asked in amazement.

"Not really." I unlocked the door and stepped into the gloomy room, simultaneously hoping he wouldn't probe too much into the other things I could do.

"So, you're just really impressive then."

"You could say that," I responded with a half-hearted shrug.

The room took on an oppressive air as we stood beside the peninsula in awkward silence. I cast a glance around the apartment and was relieved not to see Sigurd. The last thing I needed was a lecture from my familiar about depleting my magic so completely. Carlos cleared his throat, and I glanced over at him as he pushed his glasses up his nose while staring resolutely at the ground.

"Guess I'll be going."

"What?"

He shrugged much like I had and mumbled, "You're probably sick of me by now." My heart sank to rest uncomfortably in my stomach, and I took an absent step toward him.

"Why would you say that?"

"Seriously, Theo? Like getting abducted to spend the afternoon with the clan of Barreras isn't bad enough? I'm aware of how intense my family can be. Not that I don't appreciate you keeping up appearances, but it's not like you actually signed up to be my boyfriend. So I'll go now, and I completely understand if you don't want to see me again."

My heart finished falling to the floor. I didn't think I could bear it if he walked away. "What if I am signing up?" I blurted a little too quickly. Carlos raised his gaze to mine. Misery battled with confusion in his dark brown eyes.

"What?"

"I know I had a lot of missteps today, but…" I trailed off, not sure if I was ready for what I was about to commit to, then I thought of how he'd smiled at me when his grandma had essentially given her blessing. "But I'd really like to be your boyfriend… if you'll have me." My heart thundered nauseatingly while I waited for an answer.

Carlos' eyes darted across my face as if weighing my sincerity. "¿De veras?"

"Yes," I sighed. "Also, my interpretation spell expired when I made that portal. I'm back to not knowing Spanish." His lips twitched with the makings of a smile.

"That's how you did it."

"Were you really that worried?" I chuckled.

"No tienes ni idea." He gave an exaggerated roll of his eyes and held out a hand in invitation. "Mi novio. Me gusta cómo suena eso."

"Yeah, see, no clue what you just said." I stepped closer to him. "You know, you could always actually teach me Spanish if I *am* going to be your boyfriend."

"Nunca," he teased and stole a soft kiss that banished the last of my tension.

"You sure? Because I wasn't kidding about being fluent in Latin, I will eventually figure it out. And of course, there's always this." I removed the spent coin from my pocket and held it up. Carlos plucked the trinket from my fingers and tossed it over his shoulder to clatter on the floor in the kitchen.

"You won't be needing that."

I leaned in to taste his lips. "Fine, keep your dirty secrets."

He threaded long fingers through my hair and held me close. "Gracias, lo haré." The following kiss reestablished my heart in its proper place, hammering wildly in my chest.

"Mm..." I hummed. "That reminds me. We were in the middle of something..." I teased his lips with the tip of my tongue as I worked his belt loose once again. He moaned into my mouth when my fingers wrapped around him. I gave a decisive squeeze as I stroked up, loving the feel of his steel beneath my fingers.

"Si bien to mano asombra, to boca es la que nombra," he said in a husky voice that instantly had my erection straining painfully against my fly.

"I may not be able to understand what you're saying anymore, but I think I have a good guess." He smiled against my mouth as I abandoned my hold to lift his polo over his head.

He recaptured my mouth and kept it occupied with sultry kisses while I ran my hands over his warm, smooth skin. I ground into him, eliciting a moan from deep in his throat, which I promptly swallowed. Then, I gently pushed him back into the peninsula so my mouth could follow the same path as my hands.

Carlos' head tilted back and set free another encouraging moan. Despite the fact that I didn't have an ounce of magic left in me, it didn't stop me from trying to produce the very touch he craved. At best, my caress managed to create a muted buzz, as I ran my hands over every inch of exposed skin I could reach.

His breath hitched when I sucked him into the deep wet of my mouth while his hand reached out to once again thread delicately in my hair. The sheer tenderness of the touch made my heart skip. I glanced up at him through my lashes, and the rest of the world fell away at seeing the relaxed ecstasy on his face. Today had been insanely dangerous on so many levels, agreeing to be his boyfriend even more so, but it was all worth it if only to make him happy.

His fingers tightened in my hair, letting me know how close he was. I gripped his pronounced hips and took him deep as he gasped out his release. When his breathing leveled out, he relaxed his hold and softly brushed my hair back. I placed a soft kiss on his hip and worked my way back up again to brush my lips on his.

"Carlos..." I had no idea what I intended to say. Whether it was to apologize for the lack of magic and all my mistakes today or tell him the truth about how we'd come to this moment.

He curled his fingers around the back of my head and brought me back in for a slow kiss that melted me from the inside out, then took the decision completely from my hands. "Take me to bed, Theo," he whispered.

"I meant what I said. I'm completely out of magic." I let out a defeated sigh and rubbed my hands along his smooth sides as if to emphasize my point.

He stole another sweet kiss, then took my hand. "I'm not with you for your magic."

The words slipped right to the center of my heart and took the whole organ over. I practically floated behind him to the bedroom and continued to stand at the foot of the bed in a daze as he divested himself of the last of his clothing and laid out on the bed. My gaze wandered reverently over every centimeter of gorgeously dark skin, that somehow seemed even duskier in the half-light seeping through the drawn curtains. "You're beautiful."

Carlos shifted to kneel on the bed before me, his hands beyond gentle as they cupped my face and brought our lips together once more. "Come to bed, Theo."

I reached back and pulled my shirt over my head. My hands continued to move by rote, efficiently removing every article they encountered, though I couldn't have told a soul what happened to my clothes once they left my body. All of my attention remained focused solely on Carlos watching me with a tenderness I'd never encountered in a partner before.

Finally, I was free of the last barrier standing between us. I reached out and held his face, eager to reunite our lips and the connection forged whenever we came together. Every move I made found our lips pressed together. Hands drifted up his legs, with their fine hair, to the soft skin at his waist. My entire body hummed like a tuning fork when he moaned into me as my slick fingers teased his entrance. Even without magic enhancing the touch, Carlos bowed off the bed and clung to me when I quested for that ultimate bundle of nerves.

His name became a soft chant falling from my lips to echo around the room. I pulled him close as I sank deep into his inviting warmth and the promise of more, the promise of everything. He wrapped his legs around me, encouraging me deeper even as he claimed my mouth, his arms draped around me in a hold I never wanted to leave.

We rode the swell of sensation together. No gasped words of passion passed between us, only an intensity that rivaled anything I'd ever known. When the wave finally crested, I was already drowning in the endless depths of his brown eyes. Much like a wave crashing on the shore, our mouths crashed together to create a perfect circuit of rapture. Words I'd never said to any man tingled on my tongue and burned in my eyes. Too afraid to say them aloud, I whispered them again and again in the secret confines of my heart.

I'm in love with you, Carlos Barrera.

Carlos

Theo's chest rose and fell in the steady breathing of deep slumber. I reached out to brush back the lavender hair falling across his face. It had changed back almost the second we'd cleared the portal, a skill I hadn't even known he possessed. I'd feigned ignorance, but that was definitely next-level stuff. It would seem Theo Kendal was full of many surprises, higher magical abilities being the least of them. Never in my wildest dreams would I have ever imagined a witch capable of winning my family over.

He'd survived the twisted tests of my brothers, the machinations of my younger sister, garnered the approval of mi abuela, and even charmed my mother. Not to mention how he'd already stolen my heart. And something had definitely shifted between us in the last forty-eight hours.

While I may not have much experience, even I could tell that there had been a different kind of magic tonight. I couldn't even bring myself to be upset that he'd passed out the second he'd hit the pillow. He'd quite literally given me everything he had and then some. My heart felt full near to bursting as I ran my fingers through his silken hair and contemplated lavishing his face with featherlight kisses.

At last, I gave up my staring to slip free of the sheets and ventured to the en suite to clean up, then returned with a warm cloth to give him the same care. He didn't so much as twitch. I couldn't help but smile and stroke his cheek. Miraculously, he leaned into the caress, and my smile grew.

"What am I going to do with you?" I whispered to myself before withdrawing to the living room to search for the only thing I knew could help him.

The lamp emitted a soft yellow glow, lending the room the same kind of effervescence that seemed to permeate the bedroom. I glanced around until I found the object of my quest. The enormous feline nearly obscured the entire back of the chair he was draped over. His long gray hair turned silver in the moonlight from an open window.

I shivered as the chill air wrapped around me and leeched away my meager body heat. Sigurd looked up at my approach, and the faint roll of a purr reached my ears. "Hola mi amigo," I said as I ran a hand along his soft fur. He pressed his head into my palm and purred harder when I made a second pass. "Think I could trouble you for some help?"

He blinked eyes that were eerily luminescent in the near darkness.

"Your companion needs you," I added. Without further explanation, the gray Skogkatt extricated himself from his perch and landed with a soft thump on the floor. He then padded over to the open door of the bedroom.

By the time I caught up with him, he was already atop the bed. He glanced back at me, then carefully picked his way over Theo's sleeping form. Curious, I drifted around the edge of the bed and found Sigurd making himself comfortable, stretched out along Theo's back. I let out a relieved breath when the faint glow of indigo emanated from where the two touched.

"Thank you," I whispered softly. Sigurd's light purr remained gentle enough not to disturb his exhausted companion. After a few more minutes, I slipped back into bed.

I'd scarcely settled when Theo's hand drifted out. When he met resistance, he coasted the same hand over my waist and tugged me close. I curled into him, and he buried his face in my neck, letting out a nearly silent sigh as he resettled. My heart soared past the moon to land among the stars Theo held in such reverence, and I prayed this enchantment would survive the light of morning.

Theo

Wakefulness brought with it a horrible feeling of being scraped bare, coupled with the contradictory sensation of being heavy and filled to the brim. A groan rose out of my bone-weary body as I rolled from my side onto my back. I hit resistance and started the rest of the way awake.

"What the hell?" I twisted around to find the source of the obstacle.

"Don't be mad."

I ceased my mindless search at the sound of Carlos' voice. "What?"

"I invited Sigurd into the bed," he elaborated as he finished making his way into the room. He bore a tray laden with every breakfast item I had in the kitchen and wore a pair of my sweats that clung to his hips with a wish and a string. I dragged my gaze up his body to his face as his words finally registered.

"Why would you do that?"

He set the tray aside and sank onto the bed. When he leaned forward for a soft press of lips, I gladly met him halfway. "Familiars hold their witch's magic. I asked him to help you." I twisted around again in order to see my drained familiar laid out beside me. Come to think of it, I'd never asked such a boon of him.

"And he listened?"

Carlos' warm chuckle spread through my chest and recaptured my attention. "Don't sound so surprised. You and Sigurd are like dos caras de la misma moneda. You're as much a part of him as he is of you." I blinked in astonishment at the astute deduction, then glanced between the copious amount of food and my boyfriend's warm smile.

Boyfriend. I agreed to be Carlos' boyfriend.

No, not agreed. Asked.

"It takes food and rest to replenish. ¿Verdad?"

For a solid second, I forgot to breathe. I continued to sit there half-propped on the pillows and blankly stared at Carlos. The last time I'd used all of my magic, I'd been left to my fate. No one had cared for me, no one had brought me food or sought out my familiar, and definitely no one had stuck around.

"You okay?" The hint of insecurity in his tone threatened to overtake his previously happy demeanor.

"Is this what relationships are like?"

Confusion clouded his features. "What do you mean?" I couldn't help but glance around the room, taking in all the evidence of Carlos' kind heart and thoughtfulness. I doubted I'd ever met anyone as remarkably selfless.

"Everything. The... kindness," I finished, for lack of a better word.

A smile twitched on his lips. "I'm not sure exactly what you mean, but let's go with yes."

"But, I didn't—don't—have any magic," I corrected myself. "I couldn't give you what you want. Why...why would you stay?"

"I already told you, Theo, I'm not with you for your magic." As if to lend credence to his words, Carlos leaned forward and pressed our lips together once again.

We stayed frozen like that, while I fought the urge to argue, to find some logic to explain why anyone would want anything to do with me if I didn't serve some higher purpose. Our breath mingled between slightly parted lips and brought into question everything I'd thought I'd known about myself, about the world. I was in love with a demon, not for what he could do for me or what I could use him for, but because of who he was, his beautiful smile and his even more beautiful heart.

He shifted to pull back, and panic drowned all the doubt. My hand shot out to wrap around the back of his head and keep him in place while I lost myself in a kiss I felt all the way to my core. His fingers brushed featherlight along my exposed shoulder, and I shuddered at the gentleness of it. I forced myself to relent on the needy kiss and let it dwindle to soft tastes. Didn't hurt that I was also now substantially light-headed.

"Sorry," I croaked as my hand slid from his head to drift down his neck and shoulder to his chest. The stubborn thing stopped right over his heart, that I likely imagined fluttering beneath my palm. Ancestors knew mine was doing all sorts of ridiculous things at the moment.

"Don't be." He sat back and gave me a self-satisfied smirk. "Any other preguntas tontas?"

"No Spanish, remember?" His smile widened, letting me know he very much remembered. I rolled my eyes and took a stab that he was referring to any other dumb questions. "Don't suppose you have any other names I should know about?" The moment the probing question was out of my mouth, I wanted it back. How could I go from being amazed that he didn't want to use me for my magic to returning to try to use him in a matter of minutes? What was wrong with me?

"Just Juan. Though I suppose if we're getting technical, I also bear my mother's maiden name as well. Which would make my full name Juan Carlos Barrera Velazquez."

"Because that's not a mouthful." I winked at him, and he threw his head back in a loud laugh that I had no idea how much I needed to hear.

"You must be feeling better. You've got jokes."

"What are you talking about? I always have jokes. But seriously, no other names I should know? I'd rather not get blindsided again if it's avoidable," I said as I crawled away from Sigurd's warmth in pursuit of Carlos. His eyes danced with amusement as I kept talking. "No secret pet names, weird, ancient ritual titles, or true names?"

"If I have any other names, I don't know them. Besides, the whole true name thing is a myth."

"Thought myths were your specialty," I purred. Carlos' eyes lidded as I stole another taste of those plush lips. I took advantage of his distraction to yank him down and straddled his hips. "All myths are rooted in reality. ¿Verdad?" I added, echoing him from earlier. His laughter bubbled up, and I drank up each delectable sound.

"Verdad. But no more Spanish for you. Hearing it out of your mouth is weird."

I gave him a crooked grin and raised my eyebrows, but didn't vacate my perch. "Semper potui loqui Latine. But then there's the risk of accidentally doing a spell. Unforeseen consequences and all that." His brown eyes widened at the same time a deep rose stained his cheeks.

"I refuse to admit how hot that was."

I leaned down, my lips brushing against his ear as I whispered, "I think you meant to say that in Spanish."

"Mierda," he hissed, then threw me to the side so he could pounce on me. I laughed even as I hungrily devoured his mouth.

A low growl emanated from my right. Carlos and I pulled away to stare at each other, somewhat abashed at having completely forgotten Sigurd was there.

The image of two mangy mutts in heat going at each other projected directly into my mind. I let out my own strangled yowl at the insulting image and was met with the Sigurd equivalent of a snicker.

"What did he say?"

My head snapped back to Carlos leaning over me, his glasses askew, and his lips wonderfully dark from kissing. "Nothing."

He laughed and sat back. "Whatever he said, enough of that. You need to eat."

I'd rather eat you.

Carlos gave me a knowing smile before plopping the tray on my lap. "Eat up, Destellos."

"What does that mean?" I asked as I attempted to reposition myself without knocking anything over.

"Nothing." Ooh, I really did love playful Carlos.

That same love helped me clear the outrageous amount of food with next to no help from Carlos, got me into what mostly constituted a real shower, and even got me dressed. It also was the reason I turned into a mopey disaster the second Carlos said he needed to go.

"You sure you can't stay a little longer?" I prodded, not even caring how pathetic I sounded. To my amazement, Carlos seemed to find my inexplicable neediness endearing. I didn't care what he found it as long as he stayed.

He shook his head and released my hand to flop dejectedly at my side. "No es posible. My lit paper should have been finished days ago. As it is, it'll take the rest of the weekend to cobble together something remotely passable."

"Oops," I responded unapologetically.

His smile sparkled in his eyes as he trailed fingers through my wet hair, then rubbed a thumb beneath my bottom lip. "Totally worth it." I stepped into the touch and claimed his mouth one last time. My arms wrapped around his narrow waist and pressed him as tightly as I could against me.

Yeah, totally worth it.

His hand flattened on the back of my head and urged the kiss deeper. I moaned into him, and a tiny spark of hope that he'd changed his mind burst into life.

"Theo..." His body molded perfectly to mine, and the ember grew, only to be extinguished the moment it tasted life. "I have to go, Gordito."

I pushed him away, a smile still playing on my face. "Why does that sound mean?"

"Guess you'll never know," he fired back and stepped farther away. At the door though, he turned back, his eyes soft like dark caramel. "I'll talk to you later, Cariño." While I had no idea what that endearment meant anymore than the last, it made my heart flutter something fierce. Maybe it was the way he said it, like it was something precious, treasured.

I continued to stand in the middle of the apartment long after he'd left. The emptiness of the space only rivaled by the light overflowing inside of me. Of course, Carlos was right, we had other responsibilities demanding our time: school, family, subverting a prophecy. Sigurd's tail swished on the floor, and I twisted to look down at him.

"I'm gonna do it. I'm going to tell Carlos the truth—about everything."

I didn't even register the pain as my knees crashed into the floor or Sigurd's loud howl of distress. The apartment flipped upside down, and I fell straight into a waking nightmare.

"Let him go!" I yelled. Kavren snickered and pushed me back. I stumbled, barely catching myself. "Please, I'm begging you, don't do this. You'll kill him!"
"So what? He's a demon, nothing more. You knew what you signed up for."
That was the worst part, wasn't it? I'd known exactly what I was signing up for—anything to save my own life.
"Please," I sobbed.
Kavren stepped away and into a room where I wasn't. The circle glowed a lurid orange, and the creature inside gave a scream that scraped along bone. "You're mine now." The menace in Kavren's victorious words sent chills down to my very soul. The captive creature spun around at the voice, but there was no life in the skeleton's eyes, only death...

Sigurd's paws pressed relentlessly into my chest. I blinked around bleary-eyed at a world out of focus. Slowly the leg of a chair solidified, then the base of the side table and the shattered remains of a lamp.

How'd I get on the floor?

I slowly turned my head to look up at an incredibly distraught Sigurd. "Wh-what happened?" I angled to sit up, and the weight of the vision I shouldn't have been able to have stripped as I was of magic crushed down on me. Sigurd barely got out of the way in time before I lost every scrap of the meal Carlos had so thoughtfully fed me.

Gradually, my heaves dissolved into gut-wrenching sobs. My worried familiar rubbed along my side, offering what little comfort he could while repeating over and over, *Safve Safve Safve.*

I shook my head as snot stretched from me to the floor. "I can't. I can't tell him." My chest spasmed, and I squeezed my eyes shut. "What have I done?"

Chapter 19

Theo

Considering that I continued to have crippling visions the second there was even an iota of magic in me, it was probably best that I didn't see Carlos for the next few days. I ran out of tears as vision after vision assaulted my mind, each worse than the last, until finally I concluded that there was no safe way to warn Carlos, not so much as a hint. Then the visions stopped.

With a crushed spirit and more exhaustion than any magical being should ever be forced to bear, I pushed open the door to our latest meeting space. Essen took one look at me and instantly morphed into a mothering hen, clucking and tutting about with worry.

"Sweet nimbus, you look terrible."

"Thanks," I responded without much bite as I slumped into an available chair. Dust puffed up around me from the relic, but not even that could get a reaction from my swollen sinuses.

"You're late." Warren glowered at me from his own perch on an equally dilapidated chair.

"I'm aware."

"Well, you're here now, so we can get started. Where are your supplies?" Kavren looked around like the bag I usually carried would magically manifest out of thin air. The sound of his voice alone was enough to make my heart race unpleasantly.

I shook my head and forced memories of his demented pleasure and insane laugh from my thoughts. That was one future among many, not remotely definitive. Besides, in some of them he'd died too. "No magic."

Essen's face paled, and she looked from me to the others. "When you say no magic..."

"Plum out. Not a drop to be had." It was mostly true. I'd scrounged up enough to make a healthy supply of potions to hide my eyes and thankfully the charm for my hair required next to none, but past that, I couldn't so much as light a candle, let alone imbue a circle.

"What kind of idiot uses all of their magic?" I couldn't even muster the energy to snap back at Warren's scathing rebuke.

"The kind that followed their mark all the way to Oaxaca and then had to bring them back without help," I responded flatly. While I didn't want to overplay my hand and give them any sort of insight into how much magic I truly possessed, it couldn't be helped. Perhaps the fact that I remained drained so many days after the event would distract from any unfortunate assumptions.

"You made a portal? On your own?" Much as I liked Essen, I kind of hated her right then.

"Took everything I had." I failed to mention that I'd technically been nearly drained the day before or that I'd been fueling a potent spell for the better part of an afternoon.

"You followed the Kisin to Mexico?" The begrudging respect in Warren's voice almost made me smile.

I straightened up a little and glanced at each of them. "Yeah. Probably not the brightest thing I've ever done. I know I won't be of much use as far as creating the circle goes, but I hoped the reconnaissance could help make up for it." I put as much as I dared into the feeble plea. More than anything, I needed time to figure out how to fix this whole mess.

Kavren perked up, holding his chin as he considered me. "Reconnaissance, you say? What kind of intel are we talking?"

"Considering I was there with his whole family? A lot."

Warren leaned forward and placed a hand on my knee. He mumbled something in what sounded a lot like Arabic, and some of the exhaustion plaguing me lifted. I gave him a grateful look, and he offered a small nod in return. "I'm sorry, Theo. I was wrong about you. A whole nest? That took guts. What if something had gone wrong?"

"Several somethings did go wrong, and for a bit I was sure I'd be on a spit in the back, but we made it through." I thought about the spark in Carlos' grandma's eyes as I passed her weird test and the way his brothers had welcomed me with open arms. His whole family had set aside their very founded prejudices, all because Carlos vouched for me. They trusted him, and he trusted me. Somehow, that was enough.

Suddenly, a warm glass was being pushed into my hand. I looked over at Essen, who offered an encouraging smile, then down at the mug of tea she'd magicked for me. I wanted to thank her, but my throat was too tight to push out words. "Drink up. There's an enchantment in the brew that should help. It may not bring your magic back any faster, but it can ease the ache of its absence."

I nodded and took a sip, then made my big play. "I asked his name." Their concern at the danger I'd willingly put myself in order to obtain such information vanished as all three leaned forward, an eager hunger in their eyes.

"Well?" Essen prompted me when I didn't keep speaking.

"He said they don't have true names. It's a myth."

"Of course he would lie," Warren scoffed, his begrudging respect now a thing of the past. I shook my head and let out a strained breath.

"He wasn't lying."

"How do you know?" Essen asked softly. I looked at her and hoped how deeply I'd fallen for Carlos wasn't written clear as tea leaves across my face.

"I just do. As far as he knows, they don't exist, and he's never heard of another demon having one. Face it guys, we're trying to accomplish the impossible. Without a true name, everything else falls through."

Essen turned away to stare listlessly at the floor. Warren looked as though he was trying to keep himself from falling apart. Kavren, however, rested his forearms on his knees and eyed me speculatively. The longer he sat unblinking, the more my skin crawled. Finally, I couldn't stand it anymore.

"What? I know it's not what any of us wants to hear, but I can't change the facts." I could barely change the future.

Kavren narrowed his hazel eyes, the dark auburn hair hanging over his forehead casting an ominous shadow on his grim features. "I'm not ready to give up. Just because he doesn't believe it, doesn't mean it's non-existent. Now, tell me everything, everything you saw, everything you heard."

My heart crumbled in my chest, and I fought to keep the pain from my face. While I hadn't been optimistic that they'd decide to drop the endeavor on their own, a tiny part of me had dared to hope. I shoved my heartache as deep as it would go and opened my mouth.

"His full name is Juan Carlos Barrera Velazquez..." My insides twisted as I proceeded to tell them almost everything I'd seen and heard while at Carlos' home in Oaxaca.

They learned his full name, the peculiar title his grandma had given him, even the silly nicknames his brothers had used. And with each word, I hated myself more, but no visions came rushing out of the ether to curtail my actions. This was the course—one of many—I just had to find the one that didn't result in Carlos being hurt anymore than avoidably possible. According to my now shredded calendar, that fine line of fate wasn't going to be easy to distinguish.

Carlos

Grisham's laugh rumbled low, shaking the table and his neatly trimmed beard. He glanced up from the phone he'd been obsessively typing away on for the last ten minutes at the three faces surrounding him. "What?" He asked softly enough to respect the fact that we were in the library.

Patty and I smirked at each other in agreement on how goofy a smitten Grisham was. For a big bad dwarf who could probably crush solid rock with his bare hands, he was an absolute mush when it came to his harpy girlfriend. Lena frowned and spared us each a look colored with reproach.

"Hush, you two. I think it's marvelous Grishy got his girl back," Lena cooed, patting a rather puffed up Grisham on the arm. "Maybe now we can go on that double date."

Patty threw her hands up and flopped back in her seat. "Are we going to study or is this going to become a relationship circle?"

"Ignore her. I'm really happy for you. Felicidades." I smiled at my friend who, despite all his hard edges, was a bigger softy than Lena.

"Thanks man." His broad grin crinkled his eyes and threatened to split his face in two. "I know you all think I'm a hopeless romantic, but I feel like Cara and I are meant to be. Fate. You know?"

Patty opened her mouth, no doubt to argue as she put it the improbability of something as fickle as fate, only to have Lena clap a hand over it. I ducked my head to hide my laugh while Patty glared daggers at Lena. Unperturbed, Lena shot her a look right back before softening her gaze and turning back to Grisham.

"All that matters is that the two of you are happy. Don't let Miss Bitter Britches get you down simply because she can't hold down a partner for more than a month." Patty ripped Lena's hand off her mouth.

"I broke up with him! Son of a sand flea cheated at riddles. Who does that?" While perhaps a grievous affront to her sphinx capabilities, I saw her last boyfriend's efforts to keep up endearing. She clearly disagreed.

Lena rolled her eyes, but didn't bother containing the resident sour puss further. "Maybe it is fate."

Patty snorted. "How is that fate? Might as well have fallen for one of the merfolk."

"Are you trying to drown me? You know dwarves don't swim. Sink, but never swim."

"But flying you can manage?" she fired back, relentless. Grisham's face crumbled into dark thunderclouds and I quickly intervened before we could find out who would get us kicked out first.

"Hey, Lena is right. You believe whatever you like. I don't know if I believe in destino, but I do know that the world can surprise you."

A wicked smile flashed across Patty's face, highlighting the golden undertones of her sepia features. "Don't you mean people, Carlos?"

"I don't know what you're talking about," I sidestepped. My textbook fell open to a random page that in no way coincided with the day's notes that I was now fastidiously studying.

Lena let out a happy little squeal and clapped her hands. "Oh, come on, chipmunk. Tell us about your beau. It's not like he's here yet." Heat burned its way down my collar. While I hadn't technically told any of them Theo and I were official, they apparently had come to their own conclusions weeks ago. "You going to do holidays together?" she teased lightheartedly as she poked my arm with a pencil. "Maybe matching shirts?"

Grisham yanked his gaze away from where it had once again become riveted on his phone to stare at me in open wonder. "So it's official? You actually caught the wind?"

"You make him sound flighty." I scowled at my friend.

Patty shrugged her sweater-encased shoulders. "If the broom fits. I'm not saying that he gets around... just, well, yeah, that's exactly what I'm saying." While I may have been too far to retaliate, Lena was not. She smacked Patty sharply on the arm. "Ow. What was that for? Don't pretend like you haven't heard the same things I have."

Lena narrowed her eyes at Patty and darted them at me. A less than subtle way to get Patty to stop talking. I sighed inwardly, hating everything about this unfortunate turn of attention. Even if I hadn't heard the rumors about Theo being a bit of a charmer, I could have guessed. I spun my pen on the table and took solace in the fact that while Theo may be an incurable flirt, I believed him when he said he hadn't been with anyone in months.

"Chipmunk…"

"His specialty isn't even flight magic," I finally said. Grisham choked on a laugh while Patty looked like she'd swallowed an egg whole.

"Oh?" Lena piped up, leaning eagerly across the table. "What is it?"

Lightning. Real, actual, electrifying lightning. And it feels fucking incredible.

"He's a winter witch," I echoed the lie he'd asked me to go with, because apparently people knowing you could generate lightning like a Tesla coil was a bad thing. I glanced up and was surprised to note the concern on Patty's face. "¿Qué?"

"I know you probably don't want to hear this, but I did some digging." She immediately held up a hand to forestall an indignant Lena. "More than the rumor mill and student center gossip. Did you know he transferred from Dreifacher Mond?" Grisham and my head snapped around, but it was Grisham who found his voice first.

"*The* Dreifacher Mond?" Disbelief dripped from his question and mirrored my own. Patty nodded sagely and Grisham sat back, stupefaction making his face slack. "What witch willingly transfers from there? I've heard of witches selling their souls to get in that place."

"That's clearly an exaggeration. Who would collect the tuition?" Lena countered.

"Maybe, maybe not. Still, makes you wonder." Grisham's gaze slid over to me, where I was as equally flabbergasted as the rest of them. Finally, I pulled myself together.

"Why ever he transferred, I'm sure he had a good reason." One which I planned to ask him about at the first opportunity. I buried myself in finding the section of the text in the hope it would distract from how uncomfortable I now was while they continued to come up with endless arguments why no witch in the history of ever would walk away from a school like that. "Besides," I added, "it's enough that my family likes him." The muted bickering came to an abrupt halt. I glanced up at three pairs of shocked eyes.

"He's met your family?" Patty asked at last.

"Sí. Last Saturday."

"And you're just now telling us?" Lena's squeal of disapproval garnered several scathing looks from nearby patrons. I shrugged. It couldn't possibly have anything to do with the fact that I still wasn't certain where Theo and I stood, even after our incredible few days together. There was something a bit jarring about being borderline ghosted after putting a label on things. I understood Theo was frustrated that his magic was taking longer than he wanted to replenish, but I couldn't help but feel a little left out in the cold.

As if the sphinx could now miraculously read minds, Patty crossed her arms and leaned back in her chair, a dark eyebrow arched high. "So, where's the sprite now?"

On cue, Theo rushed up to the table. "Sorry, I'm late." He leaned down, snared me with a kiss, then slid his pack to the ground and began taking out books and paper. I sat there staring at him until he turned back to me. With a gentle finger, he pushed my glasses up my nose and stole a softer kiss. "I'm sorry about this morning. I overslept. What did I miss?"

Patty cleared her throat, and I finally blinked. Without missing a beat, Theo offered a wave to the table.

"Hey guys. Don't worry about catching me up. I'll figure it out." Beneath the table, his hand slid warmly over my thigh and gave a light squeeze. Just like that, all of my previous anxiety poofed out of existence. If Theo hadn't told me about the transfer, it was because he didn't think it was relevant. I placed my hand over his and laced our fingers. Out of the corner of my eye, I caught the barest hint of a smile tugging at his lips.

"*Now,* can we study?" Patty asked, beyond exasperated.

Grisham threw a balled-up piece of paper at her. "I thought Cara was supposed to be the harpy." We all snickered at that, even Patty, and at last turned to our notes.

For the next hour, we did get some studying done. Grisham untangled timelines, Lena earmarked the footnotes Professor Roman loved to sneak into exams, and Theo got all caught up on the lesson he'd missed that morning. It wasn't until we started packing up to go our separate ways that I realized our fingers had stayed linked almost the entire time. I bit the inside of my cheek to keep from smiling like un cabrón.

"Oh hey, before I forget. Derrick and I were going to hit up the cafe on Main Friday night to see a local band. I hear they're pretty awesome. Any of you interested in joining?"

I hadn't seen live music in ages. "That sounds–"

"We have plans," Theo said over me. I turned to look at him, and he winced.

"We do?"

"I mean, I hope we do. Probably should have asked if you wanted to go out before assuming you'd say yes."

"Like...on a date? A real one?" I felt a bit like a broken record. All that was missing was the scratch. Theo's face softened into the sweetest expression.

"Yeah, like a real one." My heart pounded and skipped and did all sorts of impossible things in my chest. It took every ounce of restraint I had not to throw myself across the small distance separating us and kiss my boyfriend silly.

"For the love of the pharaoh, get a room," Patty bemoaned. "If you two get any sweeter, I'm going to have to see the Tooth Fairy."

Lena smacked her for the second time. "That's speciesist."

"What? She's a literal fairy who decided to become a dentist. She knew what she was getting herself into."

"What do you say?" Theo asked just loud enough for me to hear. "Go out with me this Friday?"

I spun back to Lena, who was mid-lecture on the harmfulness of feeding into stereotypes. "Maybe next time. I've got plans with my boyfriend."

Grisham gave me a rather obvious thumbs up, Lena tittered happily, and Patty gave an exaggerated roll of her eyes that coupled nicely with her small grin. Meanwhile, Theo's pleased smile seemed to mirror my own. The only way things could have gotten any better was if I had any clue what these supposed plans were.

Chapter 20

Theo

So far, the only difference between Friday evening and any other time Carlos and I hung out was the fact that we were calling it a date. Of course, we also hadn't gotten to the best part. I led him around the small fence that discouraged absolutely nothing, least of all trespassers, and angled us toward one of the famous seven hills that gave Sieben Hügel its name.

"Should I be worried that you're leading me to some sort of ritual sacrifice?"

I missed a step and tripped up the hill. Despite his playful tone, panic zipped down my spine with the force of a lightning strike. Was it possible he'd found out? Discovered some clue at my apartment? Heard something he shouldn't? I glanced over at him and hoped like hell my sudden alarm wasn't written all over my face. Whatever Carlos saw, he barked out a laugh.

"Dios, no soy serio. I'm kidding. Made the same joke about me sacrificing you months ago. Remember?"

I did remember, but it did nothing to ease the guilt souring my stomach. Air filled my lungs and exited in a conscious breath as I forced myself to take another step. "Right, yeah, of course."

"You're awfully keyed up considering we're doing the same things we always do." I couldn't help but smirk at the near perfect echo of my own thoughts.

"It's not entirely the same. This is different," I countered, and hell if that wasn't the understatement of the decade. I laced our fingers together and basked in his soft smile a moment before resuming our trek with renewed purpose. "It's...been awhile since I've done this with anyone."

"Walk up a hill?" he teased.

"Ha-ha. It's what's at the top."

"You mean the ritual sacrifice."

This time I was more prepared for the nihilistic humor and barked out a laugh. "I have no intention of sacrificing you, Carlos Barrera." And I really didn't. I just had to figure out how to make sure no one else would either. My gaze darted over to him when he didn't immediately offer a comeback. He bit his bottom lip and glanced away, pushing his glasses up.

"You're really not going to tell me?"

"What's with you and surprises?" He'd never mentioned anything in his past that might have led to such an aversion, but his obvious trepidation made me anxious and instilled in me a strong desire to explain. "I don't really do this with anyone, and I'd like to do this with you. That okay?"

"But you're not even going to give me a hint?" He turned what could only be described as puppy-dog eyes on me, and I realized I'd been played. Not a difficult feat considering how wrapped up I was in the man beside me. Two could play that game.

"Nope." I used our joined hands to drag him the rest of the way up the isolated hilltop. Trees fell away to reveal an unobstructed view of the surrounding landscape as well as the quickly darkening sky. Already hues of magenta gave way to deeper notes of indigo and the inky darkness of a cloudless night. I released Carlos so he could take the last few steps to the pinnacle on his own.

"Wow. Theo... Talk about a view." The awe in his voice as he spun in a circle taking it all in warmed me in a way totally untouchable by the chill bite of air. "How did you find this place?"

"I looked."

"Sabelotodo," he fired back.

I shoved my hands in my pockets and stared up at the sky, my breath misting before me as Carlos continued to take in the stunning scenery. High overhead, in the sea of deepening night, a single star winked back at me. The old nursery rhyme my grandmother used to tell me rose from my memories.

Star light, star bright,
First star I see tonight,
I wish I may, I wish I might,
Have this wish I wish tonight.

My breath misted again, and I willed the rhyme to hold magic and the power to grant my greatest wish.

Please let me find a way to save Carlos.

No sooner did the wish form in my mind than the landscape vanished.

"How could you do this to me? You said you loved me!" Carlos screamed inches from my face as Kavren and Warren fought to keep him under control. In the background, the circle lay waiting, pulsing a muted orange in anticipation of its prisoner.

He yanked an arm free and grabbed my shirt in a tight fist, yanking me to my toes. "Tell me why, Theo. Tell me!"
Warren's hand shot out to free me from Carlos' clutches while I stood powerless to stop any of this from happening. "I'm sorry. I'm so so sorry," I sobbed.
"All of you witches are the same! I never should have trusted you."
Warren finally managed to liberate my shirt, and they dragged a kicking and screaming Carlos back. Off to the side, Essen waved a charged wand of hazel wood and suddenly Carlos hung suspended in the air, his furious gaze boring into me.

The vision launched me back into my body without a shred of mercy. I slipped on the slick hillside and barely caught myself from crashing into the earth. My fingers dug into my chest as if they could keep my breaking heart in one piece. I hunched over and fought the urge to lose dinner.

"Theo? Are you okay?" Carlos' worried voice snapped me into action.

"I...I'm fine." I stumbled to my feet and lurched off to the side, where I knew a small public restroom existed for hikers.

"You don't look fine." He took a step toward me, and I quickened my pace.

"Just give me a few minutes." My hand flailed behind me in an absent wave as I all but ran to the shack-like facilities. I slammed the door behind me and locked it for good measure.

The light flickered overhead, dimly illuminating the stall with a sickly yellow glow. Cobwebs glinted in the corners while various nocturnal entities scurried away from the intrusion. I paid none of them any heed as I walked straight for the wash station, where I hung my head and braced myself on the sink.

"Get a grip. It's not true."

Not yet.

My hands tightened on the porcelain as the image of Carlos' hate-filled gaze stripped me bare. I let out a gasp that sounded eerily like my sob from the vision as it ricocheted around the room.

"I won't let it happen. I won't. I'll die first." Violet eyes, the trademark of the Wisteria line, stared back at me from the age-spotted mirror while my lavender hair stuck to my forehead in sweaty strands.

I took an uneven breath and fished out a tiny vial from inside my coat with shaking hands. In one gulp, I downed the shimmering liquid and returned my attention to the mirror. I watched as the violet slowly faded to cornflower, then periwinkle, and finally settled on the baby blue that the world associated with Theo Kendal.

A light knock on the door caused me to drop the container. It bounced to the ground with a tinkle of glass, but didn't shatter. I quickly swept it up and pocketed it right as a concerned voice breached the feeble barrier separating me from its owner.

"Theo? What's wrong?" Carlos's evident worry stabbed at my heart, and I bit back a fresh sob. I didn't deserve someone as pure and good as him, and nothing I did would ever change that. But selfishly, I couldn't bring myself to walk away, either.

"Dinner didn't agree with me, that's all. I'll be out in just a second." I turned on the water and rinsed my mouth out to lend credence to the lie, then ran still-shaking fingers through my already damp hair.

"Maybe we should go. If you're not feeling well..."

I flung the door open before he could finish. "And miss why we came out here in the first place? Not a chance." I'd hoped the hint that we'd come here for a specific reason would pique his interest. No such luck. "Come on." I tried to push past him, but he was having none of it.

"Wait. Let me look at you." He held my face delicately with both hands as he looked at me with worry, creating a line between his dark brows. My heart stuttered and ached beneath that caring gaze.

I love you so much. I don't want to hurt you, but I'm afraid I won't be able not to.

He stroked a thumb across my cheek and brushed my lips with a light kiss. "You sure you're okay? We don't have to stay." I removed one of his hands from my face and pressed a kiss into his palm.

"I want you to see this." He gave a small nod and let me lace our fingers once more as I brought him back to the top of the hill.

Carlos

Theo magicked a blanket seemingly out of nowhere for us to sit on and another that he wrapped around us to fend off the early winter chill. We settled on the ground, and I leaned against him. But even encircled in his arms, I wasn't convinced he was miraculously better. Whatever it was that had sent him scurrying off had shaken him far more than a few stomach cramps.

"Comfortable?" The whispered question puffed warmly against my neck, and I shivered. He tightened his hold around me. "Warm enough?" Almost immediately, an unnatural heat suffused the blanket.

"Si, cariño. Plenty warm." To emphasize my words, I snuggled back into him. In return, he nuzzled my neck and nipped playfully at the thin stretch of exposed skin. I laughed and squirmed away, but captive in his embrace, there was nowhere for me to go. He continued to nibble, and my laughter turned to muted squeals. "Stop it. Ya basta. You win."

"And what do I win?"

My heart.

Dios, did Theo ever have my heart. My breath caught as the sudden urge to tell him I was in love with him overwhelmed everything. The words filled my mouth and demanded to be set free. While I was terrified those three little words would send him racing off the hill faster than he had earlier, I also wasn't sure how much longer I could keep them to myself. I turned to face him, but before I could set them free, he caught me in a kiss that sparked on my lips and sent tingles all the way down to my toes.

"You're supposed to be looking at the stars." He stroked a thumb laced with the tiniest amount of electricity over my cheek.

The stars. Of course, Theo had taken me stargazing. He loved the stars. My heart struggled to contain the surge of love threatening to burst it. "Theo, I–"

"You're going to miss it."

Momentarily derailed, I glanced up at the sky. "Miss what?" He chuckled and leaned further back, taking me with him until we both lay on our backs staring up at a crystal clear, star-studded sky. I searched the heavens for some clue as to why else we could be out here besides making out under the stars. "What am I supposed to be looking at?"

The arm still around me squeezed, bringing me close enough for him to whisper in my ear while the other stretched out toward the sky. "There."

I followed the path his finger created, but no amount of squinting brought any clarity. Then I saw it. A tiny ball of light burst into life, streaked across the expanse, and vanished.

Santa Madre de Dios, he brought me to see a shooting star.

Not even the beating of my heart disturbed the silence left in its wake. I made to turn to him once more only to have him nuzzle into the side of my neck. "Keep watching."

I did as he asked and turned fully forward again, sinking into his warm embrace. Seconds ticked by with nothing more eventful than an owl hooting in the distance. Then another star raced across the sky, followed by another and another. I gasped at the sheer wonder of it, my hand involuntarily going to my mouth, while I tried to remember how to breathe. "It's...it's..."

"A meteor shower. Leonids, to be exact."

"Why is it called that?" I whispered, as if my voice might scare away the incredible sight.

He reached toward the sky again. "You see that cluster of stars? That's the constellation Leo. And that one just below it is Hydra and the ones over there, Cancer and Gemini."

I listened in a daze as Theo pointed out constellations and major stars all to a backdrop of meteors zipping across the sky. After a while, he stopped talking, and we simply lay together with the soft hush of the hilltop wrapped around us.

"It's nice to share this with someone." He said it so softly, I almost didn't hear him.

I twisted around, forsaking our cocoon of warmth to prop on my elbow and look down at him. His face was almost completely obscured by the night, but I didn't care. "Theo, when you said it had been a while since you'd done this with anyone...did you mean ever?" The heavy silence confirmed my suspicion that this was a part of Theo he didn't share with anyone. "What about your family?"

He reached up and tentatively ran his fingers through my hair. "I don't get to see my family very often, and I haven't done something like this with one of them in a very long time." My heart broke for the sadness that laced his words.

"Why did you transfer from Dreifacher Mond?"

"Found out about that, did you? I won't even ask how." He let out a sigh and dropped his hand to my shoulder. "Some things are more important than school. I needed to be here, so

I was. I'm a legacy though, so when—if—I decide to go back, there will be a place for me."

I didn't understand at all, but it was substantially more of an answer than I'd expected. He seemed to be waiting for me to dig deeper, an air of resignation settling over him like a physical thing. Rather than give into the temptation to pry for more information, I opted to share my own truth. "I'm glad you're here."

He let out a relieved sigh that misted in the air between us. "Me too." His thumb traced small circles on the back of my neck, leaving a delicious trail of sparklers.

"You don't have to do that. I already told you, I'm not with you for your magic, and I know how frustrated you are that it's taking so long to replenish." His thumb stopped circling so his fingers could comb up through my hair and spread the tingling sensation.

"Guess I should come clean about that."

I forced myself to ignore the incredible feel of tiny lightnings dancing along my scalp and focused on him. "What do you mean?"

"It's not on purpose. Well, most of the time." I heard more than saw his cheeky grin. "I've actually spent most of my life learning how to control my magic so I don't inadvertently hurt someone. But with you... it's completely involuntary. Has been from the start."

"Why me?"

"I don't know. Might have something to do with what kind of magic you have or your true nature. Whatever the reason, it's like my magic wants to be part of you."

"That's, um..." I trailed off, not sure what to say.

"Creepy. It's okay, you can say it," he said with a laugh.

"I don't think it's creepy. It's..." I floundered for the word. "Special."

Theo shifted to be slightly more propped up, which brought our mouths wonderfully closer together. "You have no idea, Carlos Barrera. Lightning magic is incredibly rare and incredibly dangerous, and yet, it doesn't hurt you. Even more than that, as much as you like my magic, you like me without it. No one's ever wanted me for more than my magic."

That sounded awful. What kind of a people only valued what you could give? The obvious answer, of course, was witches. But as I looked back at Theo in the darkness surrounded by stars, I knew even beyond his magic, Theo wasn't like other witches.

I closed the distance, fully intent on kissing him absolutely stupid... and missed. "Hijo de puta," I cursed under my breath, though not quietly enough to avoid Theo hearing. He laughed softly and shifted beneath me.

"I've got you, baby." A small orb of light appeared beside us, washing out his features in its pearly blue light. He wrapped an arm around my waist and tugged me closer even as his hand on the back of my neck guided me forward. "Come here."

Different stars danced across my eyes as our lips came together. He started slowly, teasing me with small tastes and lingering presses. I let out a gasp when his tongue trailed along my lip and he stole a deeper kiss, just as he'd stolen my heart.

<h1 style="text-align:center">Chapter 21</h1>

Theo

The music pulsed around us, the beat radiating out to fill every nook and cranny of the dark room spotted with multicolored strobe lights. That, combined with our drinks and Carlos grinding against me, made for a heady mix. And *fuck* could Carlos dance. Not that I was surprised after getting roped into the impromptu dance party at his house. But dancing with his brothers didn't come close to the thrill currently thrumming through me at Carlos' hands guiding our hips in perfect sync.

The confidence he exuded on the dance floor was intoxicating, and I definitely wasn't the only one drunk off of it. I'd lost count of the people who had tried to work their way into our sphere of syncopation. He'd ignored every last one, keeping all of his focus on us—on me.

He leaned closer, his plush lips brushing my ear while his long fingers tightened on my hip where they'd slipped beneath my shirt. "Having fun?" The heat of his breath made me shudder and ache in the best way. A laugh bubbled out of me, carefree and so freaking happy. I loved how being with Carlos made me forget everything else and live in the moment.

"So much."

"Too much to leave?" His husky voice came out like crushed velvet, caressing every nerve and sparking it to life. I angled to look back at him over my shoulder and found dark brown eyes clouded with lust, waiting for me.

Oh, hell yes.

I flashed him a Cheshire grin and grabbed the hand torturing my fevered flesh. His own smile threatened to split his face as I dragged us to the nearest exit. Bodies parted before us as we wove our way to the far wall, past high tops surrounded by smiling people, around the bar clustered with eager patrons, and right by several couples engaged in their own teasing dances. Only the bright red exit sign kept us heading to the metal door that all but disappeared into the wall. I pushed it open and the cacophony inside drowned out the squeal of rusty hinges.

We spilled out the side door of the crowded club directly into an alley. Bitterly cold air instantly cooled the sweat on my skin and dampened my shirt, but couldn't touch the heat burning with abandon inside of me. I yanked Carlos close, mashing my mouth against his before the echo of the door slamming shut had even dissipated.

His groan poured into me, and I tangled my fingers in his sweat-damp curls, the feel and smell of him driving me wild. I sucked his tongue deeper in my mouth, desperation for the man in my arms scrambling my brain. His hands slipped beneath my shirt once more, their warmth a sharp contrast to the cool night. He crushed me against him and swallowed my resulting groan.

"Apartment," I gasped.

"Apartment," he echoed, equally breathless.

Hand in hand, we stumbled out of the alley onto a side street, giggling like a bunch of overeager teenagers. And I gave zero fucks. Everything about Carlos made me feel light and free. I didn't even know it was possible to be this happy, like I'd swallowed a star and the light was bursting out of me. I loved Carlos with everything I had, and I had every intention of worshiping him body and soul the second we stepped foot in the apartment.

He glanced over at me, the crooked grin teasing his lips, hinting at his own lust-filled thoughts. With one look, he made the fire burning inside of me go from barely contained inferno to full-blown supernova. My heart sprouted wings and soared while my body seemed on the verge of combusting. And fuck, we weren't going to make it to the apartment.

I veered into the nearest cross-alley, pulling an illusion spell across the entrance. The magic hooked, effectively hiding us in plain sight, and I sought Carlos' mouth once more. His lush lips molded to mine just as they had the first time I'd ever kissed him. Fuck, I loved his mouth, so plush, so pliable... so mine.

He pressed forward, and I tripped over my feet as he pushed me into the wall and took control. My brain short-circuited. I tightened my fingers in his hair as he tangled our tongues. I moaned into him, bowing off the bricks to get closer. His fingers dug into my sides in a punishing grip that sent me spiraling even higher. He abandoned my mouth to conquer my neck with wet kisses that drove me wild.

"Theo," he groaned against my throat. The vibrations of his deep voice rocked me to my core. Need burned up my spine, stealing my breath and threatening to make my knees buckle. He angled his thigh between my legs, and I shamelessly rubbed against the firm muscle. My entire body ached for more. Each moan thrummed through me, and reality slipped farther away.

I practically crawled up his body, hungry for more of him, all of him. It wasn't even a want anymore. I *needed* Carlos to take me, to make me his. It had been years since I'd trusted anyone enough to let them top me, but I trusted him. I trusted him with everything.

"Carlos." His name came out more of a strangled moan as he sucked my tongue back into his mouth. I clung onto him for dear life as he simultaneously conquered my heart and my body. He pressed me harder against the wall and rolled his hips. My eyes rolled back, and I nearly blew my load right there.

Abruptly, he ripped his mouth away and turned to stare back down the alley. A quick glance reassured me the illusion spell was holding—wouldn't do a thing about all the noise we were making, but I was way past caring. Carlos slowly turned back to me, his curls in wild disarray from my greedy fingers and his glasses tilted precariously on his nose. My heart raced with anticipation as the distance between our lips reduced to centimeters. I leaned forward to close the meager gap, hungry for more, only to be denied yet again as he glanced back once more.

"What?" I asked with the little breath in my lungs and a touch of irritation.

"Do you hear that?" He turned to me, concern pulling at his brow. I struggled to hear anything over my own labored breathing and the blood rushing in my ears.

"Hear what? There's nothing there. Now bring those luscious lips back over here."

The desired lips quirked up in a smirk. He didn't even make it to centimeters this time, however, as whatever it was snagged his attention for the third time. "*That*. You can't hear that?"

"Again, no idea what you're talking about," I grumbled as irritation and frustration worked to kill my erection.

"It sounds like a kid crying for help."

Aaaand boner gone.

I let out a huff, which he ignored. "Seriously, Carlos? Let their parents deal with it."

Without warning, he pulled the rest of the way away, his attention still off in the distance, focused on the phantom sound. I yelped as I slid down the wall, now that his leg was no longer holding me up.

"What the hell?" I brushed my quickly freezing hands on my pants and straightened my rumpled shirt, anger now dominating my irritation.

I looked up when he didn't deign to respond just in time to see him step through the illusion, his eyes searching the night. More than a little put out, I moved to follow him and drag his distracted ass back where he could finish what he'd started.

Suddenly, he stiffened, and he swiveled his head to focus intently to the east. A solid beat passed, then he sprinted down the road, heading straight for the hills and out of town.

Carlos

The hollow echo of my feet hitting the pavement chased me out of Sieben Hügel. I skidded to a stop at the edge of town, my gaze wandering over the countryside. Not a soul could be seen amidst the fog-shrouded hills, not even rogue car lights traveling the narrow, winding road. I searched the vacant landscape for the source of the cry that had dragged me away from my very hot and undoubtedly now very pissed boyfriend.

Cold mist wrapped around my rapidly cooling body, reminding me we'd forsaken coats when I'd suggested going to the club tonight. Strain as I might to hear, perfect silence ruled the night. Even my own sharp breathing seemed to be muffled by the expanse of nothing. Goosebumps erupted along my arms half a second before a small sound, almost like the pitiful cry of a wounded dove, lilted through the night.

My head snapped around to face north, where the road twisted into the trees a ways down and vanished. I stared intently into the unforgiving dark, haunted with clouds of vapor trapped on the ground. Then the cry came again...far away from the road. The cold caressing my skin was downright warm as a summer breeze compared to the cold dread that settled in my stomach.

I know that sound.

Without another thought, I resumed my run, only slowing down enough not to slip on icy patches. My fingers went numb and my breath misted in labored puffs, leeching the last of my body heat. Heavy fog obscured the ground, and I barely stopped in time to prevent myself from tumbling over the steep slope of the hill I'd apparently been running up.

I braced my hands on my knees and gasped for breath even as I searched the ground below. Swirls of white eddied and pooled like a phantom river beneath the fat moon overhead. Search as I might, though, nothing stood out.

Mierda. I know it was coming from here.

Where are you?

I pushed my glasses up my nose with shaking fingers and looked harder. One of the swirls coalesced and a small child stumbled out of the eerie mist, their waif-like cry stabbing at my heart.

"Found you." I glanced around for a safe way down that didn't risk me slipping and breaking my neck. Funny thing about being a Kisin Demon - while we could cross the veil at will while we were alive, once we died, we stayed on the other side, just like everyone else...except for one. Unfortunately, no matter how I searched the hillside, no path emerged to get me down the treacherous hillside.

"There has to be something," I muttered in frustration.

I glanced back to make sure the child hadn't vanished into the fog that had spawned it. My heart squeezed as their own frantic gaze searched the area, but for what I knew not. From this distance, I couldn't even tell if it was a boy or a girl, but their mournful cry ringing out once more was enough to get me to searching again.

My gaze roved over the hillside until it caught on movement down below, at the edge of the tree line and several meters from the fearful child. I stared into the ephemeral river and willed it to be still. Another form solidified in the creeping mist. My heart froze and sank like a stone as a woman with long, dark hair that seemed to float around her stepped free of the white. Even from here, I could see the otherworldly hunger burning in her eyes.

It's another La Llorona.

I shook my head as if it could alter the figure ghosting down below.

That's not possible.

I squinted through my glass and really looked at the apparition approaching the lost child. The mist clung to her faded red dress, which seemed to belong to another century, and trailed behind her in an ephemeral train. The more I looked, the more certain I was that she wasn't one of my kind, nor had she ever been. My gaze bounced between her and the child still keening their distress. Kisin or not, she clearly had every intention of devouring the defenseless child. My hand tightened into a fist at my side and I took a small step forward.

Sobre mi cadaver.

"Carlos."

I pulled up short and turned to look at Theo, loathe to lose sight of the two below.

"What the hell?" He panted, his breath coming out in thick white puffs.

"I don't have time to explain. That kid needs help." I glanced back down. Fortunately, the malevolent apparition hadn't gained much ground. Unfortunately, the child seemed to have spotted her and was now warily drawing closer.

Mierda.

"I don't see anything. Only mist," Theo said beside me. "No one is down there."

I frowned and looked at him.

"What?"

"The people down there aren't alive. They're ghosts. You can't see them?"

Theo stepped back from the edge with a huff of misted air. "First off, not all witches can see ghosts. That's not my curse. Second—people? You said child."

I chanced another look down and, much as I feared, the two were closer. "There's a woman too. I'm guessing she's a trapped spirit. Pretty sure she's going to eat them."

"What? How do you—"

"You're just going to have to trust me." Theo shook his head, confusion still plastered on his face as I tucked my glasses into my shirt. Down below, a soft lullaby drifted out of the fog, haunting in its sweetness. My chest constricted, and I swiveled back to Theo. "I'm going down there."

"W-what?"

"Stay here. And whatever you do, don't interfere." I patted my glasses to make sure they were secure and inched closer to the edge, where I gazed down at the incline with trepidation.

His face paled, a notable distinction given how washed out the moon already made him. "What are you going to do?"

"Stop her." Theo's hand stirred the air at my back as I stepped forward and started to slide down the hill, transitioning into my Kisin form as I went.

"Carlos!"

I ignored his shout and focused on keeping my footing. Miraculously, I didn't fall on my ass when I reached the foot of the hill. I spared the intimidating incline a victorious look and nearly swallowed my tongue at the sight of the near vertical slope. It hadn't looked quite that steep from up above. I shook off the sudden rush of nerves and turned back to the task at hand.

The thick, billowing fog seemed even more like a river now that I was in it. Unpleasant thoughts about the River Styx and the myths surrounding it threatened to steal my focus. Whether it was some manifestation of the river or not, it wasn't my soul I feared for. I took a hesitant step, carefully testing the unseen ground.

I have to be out of my mind. How am I supposed to find anything in this? And without a speck of paint on me, the kid is likely to run screaming in terror from the skeleton man.

Suddenly, the fog opened up and my gaze fell on the bedraggled child—a small boy clutching a worn teddy bear with tear tracks etched on his dirty cheeks. He reached out with the hand not clutching the stuffed animal toward something I couldn't see, his bottom lip quivering. That's when I registered the lullaby. My gaze followed his hand and found the source of the unnerving sound. Her eyes were set deep in a gaunt face and glowed a disturbing red that matched the pendant hanging around her neck. She reached out a clawed hand of her own as if to minimize the distance between them.

The lullaby grew louder, though I couldn't make out any of the words, and the boy took another step. I lurched forward into his line of sight, and he stumbled backward in fright.

"Estás bien. No voy a hacerte daño," I said as I held out my hands in a placating gesture.

His eyes widened in obvious terror, and his gaze swiveled between me and the horrifying woman.

"Mierda. No Spanish. Right. It's okay, little boy," I tried again, taking slow steps towards him, arms low and non-threatening. "I'm not here to hurt you. I want to help."

The boy sniffled and blinked wet eyes at me. "Mama." The small, desperate sound nearly broke my heart.

I shook my head and pointed at the gruesome figure getting closer with each step. "That's not your mother. She doesn't want to take you home." The child didn't look convinced, and the singing took on a more plaintive tone. I stepped back into the kid's immediate view to draw his attention. "Hey, what's your name? Can you tell me your name? What about your friend?" Unease crawled along my skin as I sensed the woman approaching behind me. I swallowed down my fear and waited for the child to answer.

"Dis is Oscar." He squeezed the bear tighter to his chest.

"And you are?" I prompted softly, inching closer.

"I'm Emil."

"That's a rather nice name, Emil. Are you lost?" My heart hammered in my chest as the prickling along my spine grew worse.

His eyes welled, and he nodded.

"Sh, sh, that's okay. I'm going to get you home. Would you like that?" Another nod. "Good. First, I need you to take my hand." Emil stared uncertainly at my skeletal fingers. Precious seconds slipped by, each one intensifying the malevolence wrapping around us. "It's okay. I won't hurt you. I just want to take you home, where you'll be safe."

With a shaking hand, the boy reached out. The moment he touched my fingers, I tightened my hand around his tiny, pearlescent one and swung him around my back as I stood to confront the creature bearing down on us. An unearthly cry of outrage rang through the chilly air. Birds nested for the night erupted out of the trees, and the boy cowering at my back burst into tears.

"Give him to me," the woman hissed, her voice like water hitting hot coals.

I pushed the kid farther behind me, shielding him with my meager skeletal frame. "No."

She snarled at being denied her prize. "Your kind have no place here, demon." I swelled up and refused to be cowed by her overbearing menace.

"Go back to the hell that spit you out."

"Never. Give me the boy."

"Not a chance." I took a step back, but she mirrored it and took a larger one forward, cutting the meter between us in half. The stench of her rotting soul hurt the marrow of my bones and stung my hollow eyes. "Leave."

"Give him to me!" She launched forward, claws extended, to take the boy by force. I raised my hand, and it landed squarely on her chest, right over the pendant. It burned to the touch, but I stayed firm.

"No." The one word echoed through the fog thick as the River Styx with finality. Then I did what Kisin do best. I tightened my hold on the amulet, ignoring the pain, digging deep into the magic that lay within, and ripped the wretch's soul from the stone.

The apparition let out an ear-splitting shriek. Her image lingered for a moment and vanished. The empty amulet bounced to the ground with a muted thud, its red glow equally gone. I quickly pocketed it and turned back to the distraught child.

"Ready to go home?" He nodded, his voice gone once more, and reached out for me to pick him up. I did so without hesitation. His tiny arms wrapped around my neck, and he buried his face in my chest despite the fact that there was only a thin layer of cotton between him and the bones beneath. I glanced up the impossible hill as I rubbed his back. "Don't suppose you know how to get up this thing?"

He wriggled free an arm and gestured off to the side where there was the tiniest of trails that switchbacked up the hill. I straightened my spine with resolve and began the climb. When we eventually reached the top, I was beyond exhausted and still didn't know what I was going to do with the poor soul. We were far from Oaxaca and the lands I traveled. I didn't even know what was on the other side of the veil here.

A wave of relief washed over me when I found Theo still there, his gaze searching the ground far below. "Theo," I called softly.

He swiveled around, his eyes wide, then rushed up to me as I made my way over. "What happened? I lost sight of you." He glanced at the kid on my hip. "Who's this?"

"You can see him?"

"I did a spell. It's temporary though, and I don't know how much longer it will last."

"Spell, of course. That reminds me." I pulled the ruby amulet from my pocket and held it by its antique chain. "I believe this is more your department."

His face clouded with confusion as he carefully took the cursed jewelry. "Okay... But, Carlos, what did you *do*?"

"I separated her soul from the pendant. And this is Emil. Sorry, I didn't catch a last name."

Theo's gaze flicked to the child as he tightened his hold on me and back to my face. Suddenly, it occurred to me that he was seeing me in my true form—no paint, no costume, just me—and he wasn't running. "You...separated her soul...from the amulet..." He repeated as he stared down at the empty ruby.

"Yeah..." A new sense of unease grew in my chest.

"So..."

"Look, I know it's a little freaky, and it's kind of how Kisin got their bad rap, but it had to be done. She was going to *eat* him," I said in a rush.

A small smile curled at the edge of his mouth as he slowly brought his gaze back to my skeletal face. "So... my boyfriend is kind of a badass."

If I'd had eyelids, I would have blinked. Instead, I just stood there stupidly, staring at him. Emil stirred in my arms, reminding me that my work was as yet unfinished. "I'm really sorry, Theo, but I'm going to have to cut our evening short. I need to get this little guy home."

To my amazement, Theo nodded. "Of course. Mind if I walk with you?"

I wasn't sure how well my smile translated through bone with no paint, but I did it anyway. "That'd be nice, but only as far as town. The rest I need to do on my own."

Chapter 22

Carlos

I paused at the edge of town, just outside the glow of inviting light. Emil tucked his head into my shoulder as the faint sounds of town drifted through the night to us. The move reaffirmed my decision to stay in Kisin form. Without it, I'd only be able to see Emil, not hold and comfort him. I shifted the small boy to sit more solidly on my hip.

"Guess this is where we part ways."

Theo stopped where he stood bathed in the light of street lamps and turned to look back at me. He glanced into town then down at the cobbled road. "Right. Of course."

I shuffled my feet where I clung to the shadows. My free hand rose halfway to my face to push my glasses up before I remembered they were tucked in my shirt. I adjusted course and patted them, somewhat amazed that they'd survived the interaction.

"Suppose I'll take care of...uh...this." He tightened a fist around the amulet, its weathered chain hanging from his fingers.

"See you later?" I ventured, more unsure with each awkward second that passed. In lieu of being able to chew on my lip or swallow my increasing anxiety, I held Emil closer.

The distant pensiveness that had taken hold of Theo's face as he stared down at the captive pendant dissolved into a soft smile. He walked toward me, abandoning the circle of light and I fought the reflex to keep distance between us, to stay hidden. Once he was squarely in front of me, he reached up to touch my face.

"Of course." He brushed a thumb tingling with magic across my exposed cheekbone. Shock rippled through me at the unexpected contact and I was suddenly immensely grateful it couldn't show on my face. "Can you feel that?" He whispered.

I nodded, not trusting my voice.

Theo is looking at me—touching me—in my purest form... and he's not freaking out.

I reached out tentatively with my free hand and hesitated shy of touching him. In a stroke of bravery, I closed the distance and slid long fingers of bone through his soft, lavender hair. He didn't pull away or so much as flinch. The small smile that touched his eyes as I continued to comb through his hair suffused every bone in my body with warmth. If I'd had a heart, it probably would have stopped beating.

"You're not afraid?" I asked, my voice cracking with wonder. His smile grew, and he still didn't move.

"I've seen a lot of terrifying things in this world, Carlos. You're not one of them."

Dios mío, how is it possible to love him more?

Emil shifted in my hold, shattering the moment and drawing attention to the fact that we were standing there in the half-light staring at each other. I quickly snatched my hand back, suddenly self conscious.

"Kid getting restless?" He must have sensed my confusion, because he added, "Spell wore off. You're basically standing there holding an invisible sack now."

I gave a self depreciating chuckle. "Suppose it would look odd to anyone who can't see ghosts. I really should be taking him across."

Theo shook his head as he laughed quietly. "Because a walking skeleton in the middle of a mortal town wouldn't attract attention at all."

"Fair point," I responded and wished Theo could tell I was smiling. His gaze softened once more as the merriment dissipated. He rubbed my cheek again, then leaned forward to place a gentle kiss on the smooth bone.

"Be careful. Okay?"

A light breeze could have knocked me over, but somehow I scrounged up the wherewithal to nod again. He offered a mischievous wink, as if he was fully aware of how much he'd just rocked my world, and walked into town. I lingered a few minutes, watching him go, then turned to my charge.

"Ready to go home?"

Emil nodded enthusiastically against my bony chest. With a renewed sense of purpose, I stepped through the veil... and promptly stepped right back out. "¿Qué carajo?" I whipped out my phone so fast I nearly dropped the damn thing and hit speed dial. "Come on, pick up, pick up. You hijo de cabra..."

"¡Primo! ¿Qué tal?" Miguel's voice poured through the line and relief rushed through me.

Good, he's not too inebriated to answer.

"I need your help."

"Shh, sh," he laughed as he addressed the indistinct voices in the background. "What was that?"

"Miguel, I need your help."

"Little busy at the moment." Decidedly masculine and feminine giggles rippled down the line. I suppressed a groan as I realized exactly what I was interrupting. There was a squeal of delight followed by Miguel's own rich chuckle. "Yeah, I gotta go. I'll catch you later."

"No!" I shouted before he could end the call and startling poor Emil. "Look, I'm sorry, but this can't wait. I need you *now*. I'm at the west edge of town."

"But—"

"Your evening isn't the only one that got derailed. I'm sorry, I really am. Just get here." I glanced down at Emil's phantom head. "And, Miguel? Hurry."

He grumbled something that might have been acquiescence. The happy noises in the background turned to sighs of disappointment and pleas for him to remain. I hung up before I could hear more than I wanted and to give him some privacy to excuse himself, then waited.

The longer it took for him to arrive, the more certain I was that he wasn't coming at all. I paced in place, my anxiety getting the better of me. "Come on, Miguel. I swear, I'll owe you thirty Saturdays at that damn taco truck, just please..."

"This better be worth it." Miguel's irritated voice immediately snagged my attention.

"Thank God."

"You owe me big, primo. Do you have any idea how long it took to get Jeremy *and* Savannah on board? I have two very attractive, very *naked* bodies that are now having a lot of fun without me."

"Would you quit your griping? Yeah, I'll owe you, but this is kind of a big deal." I stepped far enough into the light so he could see Emil. "Miguel, this is Emil and Oscar. Emil, this is my cousin, Miguel. He's like me."

Miguel stood there a moment completely at a loss for words. "Do you think you could..."

He looked back at me, no doubt taking in that I was still wearing my true Kisin form. "Really? Here? Don't get me wrong, primo, I think you're brave as fuck for walking around like that, but some of us still want to get laid."

I glowered at him, one of the few expressions that translated just fine in skeletal form. "You're making him nervous."

"El salvador de los niños perdidos." He shook his head. By the time it came to a stop, all that was there was a white skull with hollow eyes. "Why didn't you take him across yourself? Why call me?"

"¿No crees que pensé en eso? Of course I tried that."

"What do you mean 'tried'?" The wariness in his tone brought back all the anxiety that had led me to calling him in the first place.

"Step through."

"¿Aquí?"

"Yes, here," I snapped, my nerves more than a little frayed after wracking my brain for so long. He held up his hands defensively, but stepped forward. A thin shimmer rippled in the air as he walked through the veil. He couldn't have been gone more than a second or two when he reemerged.

"Holy shit. There's nothing there."

"Now ¿lo entiendes?"

He grabbed my shoulder, the hollows of his eyes wide. "No, primo, there's nothing. Where are the souls? ¿El puente? The welcomers to ferry newcomers? Where is everyone?"

I shook my head as he said aloud the very same thoughts that had gone through my head the first time I'd crossed the veil into that desolate gray. I'd never seen a place so empty, so devoid of everything. "There are no Kisin here. This is not a culture that celebrates the dead or remembers them like we do. The myths are different here."

Miguel glanced at the child still clutching me like I was a life raft. "What do we do with him? Where do they even go?" He whispered.

"I have an idea about that, but…"

"But." He brought his gaze back to me. Even without facial features, I could tell he was dubious about where this was going.

"But, it's deeply rooted in myth and I don't know if it will work, and…I'm kind of afraid to go by myself." Miguel cocked his head to the side, and I braced myself for the inevitable dig about my obsession with myths. To my surprise, it never came.

"What do you need me to do?"

"First, we have to go back to where I found him."

My relief that Miguel was willing to help was only matched by my relief at seeing the river of fog exactly as I'd left it. Much like before, it swirled around as if hitting invisible obstacles, then shifted to keep flowing. Emil burrowed deeper into me, less than enthusiastic to be returning to this place.

"It's okay, little one. She can't hurt you anymore," I said softly. A dark part of me wondered how long the spirit had been feeding off his soul or if she'd happened upon him like I had, having heard his lost cry.

"Carlos, what she?"

"I'll explain later after we find what we came here for."

"Which would be?"

I looked over at him and stepped through the veil. The coolness that touched my skin as Emil and I passed through was barely distinguishable from the chill on either side, only now, instead of fog, we stood on the shallow bank of a wide river that curved its way through a shadowed forest. Miguel emerged a second behind us and whistled lightly through his teeth at the peculiar sight.

"Where are we?"

I tightened my hold on the small. "If I'm right, we're on the River Styx. Now all we need to do is find the Ferry Man."

"The who?"

"Charon." Before Miguel could repeat his question, a shadow appeared on the water. As it drew closer, I could make out the shape of a small boat and a long oar. There was a soft scrape of wood against rock as the vessel beached itself before us.

"Bienvenidos primos." The raspy voice was both strong and frail, an echo of something long forgotten like wind through a hollowed out ravine. With its utterance, the form of the ferryman took shape. A ragged coat that had seen better days draped down to the bottom of the boat, likely hiding knobby knees to match the sinewy figure of skin and bone before us. While his form was ghoulish in appearance and his face gaunt, it seemed to be his natural visage much like the skeletal was ours.

Miguel and I shared a look. ¿Usted habla español?" I asked.

"Claro que sí. I speak all languages. But I confess, it has been many years since I have seen one of your kind at my shores."

"You've had dealings with Kisin before?" Charon turned to face my cousin.

"The dead know the dead, do they not?" He chuckled, a dry laugh that emphasized his hollow form. "What have you brought me, cousins from across the sea?"

Emil chanced a peek at the voice addressing him. My fear that the child would try to bolt upon seeing the gaunt man proved unfounded as Charon's harsh features seemed to melt and soften before our very eyes. Miguel and I shared another look as Emil scrambled to be set down, then stepped out to meet the man.

Charon held out his hand, which held substantially more flesh than it had a moment ago. "Emil Hoeg, es ist Zeit nach Hause zu gehen?"

Miguel leaned closer to me and whispered, "What did he say?"

"No sé." To my amazement, Emil took the ferryman's hand. He then let Charon help him into the boat as it remained perfectly still beneath them, as if anchored in stone. Emil cast the first smile I'd seen from him at me over his shoulder and took a seat. The tension in my chest eased.

"I'll see him where he needs to go." Charon dipped his staff into the water and pushed. As the boat slipped back into the main flow of the river, he turned back to us. "Juan Carlos, should you find any more lost souls in need of a way home..." A hollow ping rang out over the water and a tiny point of light spun in the air. It arced towards us with preternatural precision, and I held out my hand just in time to catch it. When I looked back up, the boat was gone.

"What is it?" Miguel craned his neck to get a look at the item I now held in my hands.

"It looks like a coin." I flipped it over in my hand, the unusual weight both right and unnerving. "There's a skull on one side and a boat on the other."

"How come you get one?"

I frowned, for all the good it did me in this form, and looked over at him. "¿En serio?"

Theo

The amulet weighed down my pocket, but at least the heat charm I drew on my shirt kept me from shivering. When I'd gotten dressed for a sexy night out with my boyfriend, I hadn't anticipated running around town freezing my ass off. I sighed inwardly and hoped Carlos was alright. The spell I'd used to see his rather epic showdown with the cursed spirit may have been rushed, but it had been more than enough to realize that while Carlos was possibly the sweetest man I'd ever met, death was literally his trade.

I can't believe I touched him...kissed him.

The air of shock that rolled off of him, though, had made the bold move more than worth it. I smiled to myself and pushed open the secret door set in a nondescript alley of no importance to reveal a low-key lounge. At first glance, the place was nothing more than a callback to new-age jazz cafes with its scattered tables and oversized velvet couches. An impression further solidified by the indie jazz floating through the air, the lights turned down low, befitting the environment and the hour.

No, nothing stood out as particularly out of the ordinary, not the chill atmosphere nor the fully stocked bar and assortment of hookah pipes available. But for the patrons who knew how to find this place, it was a refuge from the mundane. A trained eye could recognize the tipped ears of the bartender, the orbs floating and glowing without the assistance of electricity, and, of course, the persistent and comforting hum of magic thrumming through the joint.

Thankfully, *Le Breuvage Sorcière* didn't hold its usual number of regulars. After a few moments of searching shadowed corners, I found the person I'd come to see. I snaked my way through the meager crowd, offering enough nods of greeting not to draw undue attention. The last thing I needed was someone thinking I was there for entertainment or worse, an actual purpose.

At last I stood beside a deep green couch currently occupied by two canoodling witches. One had shoulder-length hair shaved on one side in a shade of magenta that I made a mental note to test out later. The color played surprisingly well with the blue undertones of their cool beige skin. Their facial piercings glinted in the low light and gave off a subtle aura, hinting at the magic within. They glanced up at me as I approached, and I offered a small wave. Then, the other witch turned around. Her face immediately brightened with a smile that matched the yellow sweater dress hugging her full figure.

"Theo!"

"Hey, Essen. Hope I'm not interrupting too much. I was hoping to talk to you about something?" I angled my head toward the suite of private rooms at the back.

Her eyebrows rose in surprise, but instead of pressing me for answers, she extricated herself from the couch and her date. "What's this about?" she asked quietly as she stepped close.

"Oh, a couple of things." I flashed the pocketed amulet at her. "Your companion won't mind too much, will they?"

She glanced back at her date with a friendly smile. They offered a finger wave with one hand while they took a sip of their glowing cocktail. "Mischa isn't the jealous type. They know I wouldn't step away if there weren't a good reason. Which there better be," she added quietly as she led the way to the nearest private room.

I let her enter first, then used the cover of activating the silence wards to layer my own spell to ensure nosy practition-ers couldn't overhear us. "Hopefully, this won't take too long. Here." I tossed her the amulet, and she snatched it out of the air with a magicked bit of wind. She let it hover for a minute as she studied its cracked and vacant depths before finally taking hold of it.

"Where did you get this? I haven't seen magic this old since... well, come to think of it, I don't know if I've ever seen anything this old." She glanced up, her brows angled down in a sharp V.

"It's not just old. There was powerful magic in that... soul-binding magic."

Essen let out a yelp and dropped the cursed jewelry like it was a burning ember. "What the hell, Theo?"

I scooped the dead trinket off the floor. "It's harmless now. The magic dissipated when the soul was exorcised."

"How did you manage that? There are whole covens that can't break curses that strong."

"*I* didn't."

"Then who?"

I met her confused gaze without blinking. "Carlos." Her confusion tripled, and she snatched the pendant from me to study it closer, no longer afraid of her own soul becoming ensnared.

"The Kisin? I find that hard to believe." She continued to inspect the trinket with the trained eye of a witch who's no stranger to cursed objects.

"Believe it. I watched him." I stepped closer to her, my excitement at the implications of what I'd seen overriding the terror I'd felt when Carlos had come toe to toe with the tortured soul of the captive witch. "He separated her from the amulet. Literally reached in and ripped her soul clean out. Didn't even break a sweat. Not that skeletons can sweat, but that's beside the point. He pierced layers of ancient magic as if they were nothing. Essen, do you hear me? Do you know what this means?"

Essen stared at me, her green eyes wide with wonder. "It's going to work. A Kisin truly has dominion over death."

"What? No. Well, yes, but that's not what I meant. He can help. Hell, he's nice enough, he'd probably do it if you just asked."

"I'm not following."

"Your grandmother. She's attached to a cursed object, right?" Essen nodded, her face still stubbornly clouded with confusion. I could have pulled my hair with frustration. "He has the power all on his own to break her curse. He doesn't need a witch's guidance or a binding circle or compulsion. I doubt he'd even take payment. Your grandmother is suffering at the edge of life, fighting a fate worse than death. Carlos can break that connection, ensure her soul finds peace and isn't trapped on this mortal plane. He can prevent her from becoming what I saw earlier this night." I stopped talking solely by virtue of having run completely out of air.

"You... saw this happen? And you're sure?" she asked tentatively as she turned the dim ruby over in her hands.

"Yes."

"And you think it—he will help?" The mix of hope and fear in her voice was like music to my ears. I gently took the amulet from her and enclosed it between my palms. I brought it to my lips where I muttered a spell of light, then blew it and a touch of lightning to act as a power source into the ruby. She let out a soft "Oh" as I revealed the lit gem and placed the chain over head.

"I do." The subtle glow of red against the yellow filled my heart with hope. "I do."

Chapter 23

Theo

I scooted infinitesimally closer to Carlos on the couch, mindful of his judgy roommate who'd yet to leave. Carlos glanced at me out of the corner of his eye, the smile teasing his mouth clearly written in his eyes. I smirked and returned my attention to the movie that we were failing miserably at watching.

Most I could deduce was that it was something about a coalition of individuals trying to save the world using their respective supernatural skill sets. Humans had such funny notions of what constituted magic. Had a real witch been involved, a simple spell at the outset would have negated the necessity for such an unusual band of heroes.

Carlos' fingers brushed discreetly along my arm, and a jolt of desire shot down my spine. Why he bothered to entertain modesty for the sake of his awful roommate was beyond me, but it also spoke to how genuinely kind Carlos was, and I loved that about him. I loved quite a lot about Carlos Barrera—his humor, his nervous habits, his intelligence, his thoughtfulness, his mouth, his ass, his eyes, the list could go on forever—but more than anything right now, I loved that I hadn't had a single dire vision about him in nearly two weeks.

I laced our fingers together and held his hand in my lap, heedless of what the judgmental Nessa would have to say about the intimacy. Bastard should count his lucky stars I hadn't tackled Carlos and ripped all his clothes off yet. The happiness radiating off Carlos mingled with mine and might have been making me a tad high. I didn't care. I had Carlos...and I had hope.

Essen now had a viable solution that didn't involve torturing my boyfriend, Warren seemed to be investigating alternative ways to keep his place among the Licentia in case everything fell through, and Kavren had called a hiatus to the meetings in deference to the pending Winter Solstice. Everything was good and right in the world.

Now if only fucking Nessa would leave already.

On cue, a grunt of disapproval emanated from the kitchen. I bit my cheek to keep from giving him a piece of my mind as Carlos gave me a gentle nudge with his shoulder. "What?" I hissed under my breath.

He shook his head, making his thick curls sway. "Be nice. Not much longer."

I grumbled and sank deeper into the couch, taking him with me. His suppressed laughter filled me with light and tripled my desire to tangle my fingers in his hair. Before I could completely give up all pretense of watching the movie and start making out with my insanely adorable boyfriend, Nessa appeared beside us. His glower would have done a Gorgon proud. I ducked my head to keep from bursting into laughter and stayed that way until the door finally clicked shut.

"Thank fuck." I released Carlos' hand in order to dig both of mine into his thick hair and bring his mouth to mine. Mercifully, he was right there with me. His lips parted, inviting me deeper, while he pushed us back into the cushions. "I thought... he'd... never leave," I managed between kisses.

"Your patience will be rewarded. Promise." He rolled his hips, rubbing our straining erections against each other, and I came alive like a live wire.

"Fuuuck yes," I groaned, simultaneously grabbing for his shirt.

A noise like jingling keys came from right outside the door, and we both froze. Carlos and I stared at each other wide-eyed while tense seconds ticked by. Finally, heavy footsteps ventured away from the door. We let out a collective breath—not that I was personally afraid of Nessa, but I figured Carlos would have a problem with me barbecuing his roommate, and I certainly didn't need that sort of attention.

"Bedroom?" I asked, raising my eyebrows.

"Bedroom." He scrambled off of me and we raced into the relative privacy of his room.

The door had scarcely closed when his mouth closed back on mine. I moaned into him and wrapped my arms around his neck. Confident Carlos was hella fun and hot, like really, really hot. Clothes disappeared in a mad show of grabby hands and greedy mouths. The same burning sense of need from the alley came back with an undeniable vengeance as we hit the bed in a tangle of limbs.

"Theo, I—"

"I want you to take me," I blurted before we could get sidetracked.

Carlos pulled back to look at me, confusion and surprise shining in his eyes. "What?"

I struggled to get my labored breathing under control. "I want you to top me." He fell back on his heels, and fear spiked through my system. "Unless you're not into that, in which case forget I said anything. I didn't mean... I just... maybe... and... Fuck, I should have asked. You're so not into—"

He clapped a hand over my mouth, effectively turning my incessant blathering into muted muffles. "I'm definitely into it. But you said that you were always a top." I reached out and gently removed his hand.

"Actually, I said I was *generally* a top, but I... I want this... with you." He searched my face for a long time before finally leaning forward to brush my lips with his.

"Are you sure?" I loved how thoughtful he was. I smiled against his mouth.

"Very sure. Just go slow, okay? It's... uh... been a while." To my chagrin, he pulled away once more, taking that delicious mouth with him, and speared me with an intense look.

"Define 'a while'."

I swallowed, anxious all over again. "Eight years?"

"Dios, Theo. Yeah, I'm totally up for it, but mierda, we don't have to do this today, or at all."

"No! Please, Carlos, I'm serious when I say I want this. I need to feel you inside me."

He squinted at me, skepticism written plain as day on his face. "You promise to say something if you change your mind?"

I drew a cross over my heart. "Promise."

To my surprise, he gently pushed me back, then immediately lay across me, letting our bodies touch from crown to heel, kissing me, slow and deep, like he was learning the shape of my mouth, the hitch of my breath. When he was satisfied, he left my mouth to quest more exploratory kisses along my jaw and down my neck. I moaned and arched off the mattress into him, my hands caressing his back and already buzzing with magic.

"Back or hands and knees?" The husky question vibrated through my core and made me cross-eyed.

"B-back," I panted. "I want to be able to see you." He groaned, his fingers tightening on my hips, and a whimper of want slipped out of me. He stole another quick kiss, then resumed his torturous adventure down my body. His fingers teased and played everywhere they roamed, and I couldn't help but wonder if this was what my magic felt like to him.

By the time his mouth wrapped around my cock, I was positive I was done. He gave me a minute to get back under control, then resumed his focused attention. A surprisingly slick finger tapped at my entrance, and I bucked into his mouth. I glanced down at him, but where I expected to see doubt or concern, I found only challenge. I flung my head back and dug my fingers into the pillow, groaning as his long, slender finger pushed deeper. My gasp as he added another filled the room, only to be replaced by a moan deep enough to raise the dead when he stroked my prostate.

I lost count of how many times he brought me to the edge, only to back off and do it again. My body became heavy with the need for release as he continued to work me. "Carlos, please," I begged, my fingers dragging a higher voltage across his shoulder, anything to hurry him up. I was beginning to think he'd become immune to my touch when the hand caressing my side jerked. Suddenly his fingers, his mouth, everything was gone, and I'd have literally sold my soul if it would bring them back.

I propped up as much as my putty-body would allow and attempted to glare at him. "For the love of all things sacred, fill me before I die."

A self-satisfied smirk tipped his lips as he leaned forward to tease me with a languid pull of my lips. "You're not going to die, mi amado."

The need to correct him rose—everyone died, and I would die sooner than most—but looking into his dark brown eyes, I wanted to tell him something else. That I was okay with dying, that knowing him even for such a small amount of time made it all worth it, that he was worth it. I didn't get a chance to say any of it. He caught me in a mind-numbing kiss as he slowly claimed my body.

"How are you doing, cariño?"

I love you. I love you so much. Please don't ever leave. Stay with me 'til the end.

As air rushed into my lungs, though, none of that came out. I managed a weak, "Great," fisted my hand in his hair and brought his mouth to mine, where I swallowed his groan with a savage kiss. His thrusts found a steady rhythm that once again brought me to the brink and kept me there.

Finally, I couldn't take it anymore and used magic to flip us. I had just enough time to register Carlos' surprise before I was driving onto him with reckless abandon. His fingers dug into my sides as he met my wild ride with sharp thrusts of his own. I wrapped a hand around my pulsing cock and matched the frenzied rhythm.

He gave another deep thrust that hit just right. Everything crystallized, then shattered. My entire body clenched, and I spilled hot streams on his chest at the same time he released deep inside. I wanted to bask in this unbelievably perfect moment, relive it a thousand times, tell him how insanely happy he made me, and that I hadn't trusted anyone this much in years. I didn't do any of that. What I did was collapse into the sticky mess of my cum.

I panted for breath into the side of his neck while his fingers stroked over my bowed spine. Eventually, we managed enough shaky energy between us to get cleaned up. By the time we crawled exhausted back into bed, I could have slept for a week.

I didn't. Instead, I stared up at the ceiling, so filled with love for the incredible man sleeping beside me I couldn't stand it.

I have to tell him. Who cares if he hasn't said it first? To hell with the consequences.

I opened my mouth to finally tell him the truth burning in my heart and choked on a torrential flood of visions. My eyes widened painfully, and tears leaked out the sides as the sheer force of them stole my breath and forced me into the mattress. One after another, they kept coming. Some I'd seen before, like the vision at the library and Carlos yelling that he hated me, but most were new and much, much worse. Gone was the beige ceiling. In its place was a waking parade of nightmares.

Carlos' fingers wrapped around my neck, crushing my windpipe as he stared at me with hollow eyes in a white skull. I scrabbled at his bony hand, sobbing as I begged. "Carlos, please don't do this. This isn't you. Please. I love you." The fingers tightened...

Carlos fell to the ground, screaming his agony in a sea of orange. "Let me go!"
The hands holding me pulled me farther away.
"No!" I screamed. No one listened.

I stood, hand outstretched toward a skeletal Carlos, my other arm hanging limp from my shoulder. "You don't have to do this," I pleaded with him.

He stepped across the disintegrating circle intent on his target—a cowering Kavren.

"I don't understand. I did everything right," the man blubbered as he tried to put more distance between him and Carlos.

Carlos reached out a skeletal hand and seized Kavren. The man let out an unearthly shriek as his soul was ripped forcibly from his body, then crumpled lifelessly to the ground.

Carlos

I woke to find Theo thrashing beside me. All dregs of slumber vanished in the blink of an eye as I moved to hold him down. He bucked beneath my hands, his lids fluttered enough to reveal the whites of his eyes, spittle frothed at his mouth, and his head swung wildly from side to side.

"Theo! Theo!" I shouted in panic. "What's wrong? Please, mi corazón, mi amor, mi vida, háblame." Tears streamed in hot rivulets down my face as the man I loved continued to seize beside me. I didn't know what to do. Did I hold him down? Turn him on his side? Call for help?

Suddenly he dragged in a huge lungful of air and bowed off the bed like something straight out of a possession movie, then collapsed back down. His head lolled listlessly to the side, and he didn't move.

"Theo?" When he didn't respond, I loosened my death grip on his arms in order to gently shake him. "Theo? Please, cariño, wake up," I sobbed. Still nothing, not even his chest moved. In a fresh rush of panic, I leaned in close to hear his breathing. I cupped the side of his face and fought the instinct to see if his soul was still tethered to his body. "Please wake up."

His chest rose with a giant, ragged breath of air, and his eyelids fluttered.

"Theo. Are you okay? What happened?" Abruptly, I realized that my crowding him probably wasn't helping. "I'm going to get you some water and a damp cloth. I'll be right back." I practically flew out of the room, heedless of the fact that I was stark naked, to retrieve a glass of cold water and a dishtowel. By the time I returned, Theo was sitting up and holding his head in his hands, damp, lavender strands spilling over his fingers. "Here," I said, offering him the water as I sat beside him.

He accepted it without looking up and used the cool towel to wipe his forehead, then placed it on the back of his neck. "Thank you," he said, his voice rough and quiet.

"Theo, what happened?"

He set the water on the nightstand, took a deep breath, and looked at me. His face was tight and pale. He looked more like death than a corpse at a wake, but most surprising were his eyes.

"Your eyes... they're purple."

He blinked slowly and looked away. "For the record, this is why I don't date."

"Because you have random fucking seizures?" I snapped suddenly angry. "And why aren't your eyes blue?"

"I... need to tell you something, but... it won't be easy."

I bit my tongue to prevent myself from snapping at him more. Logically, I recognized I was upset, because I'd been so scared—still was—and was lashing out. He glanced up, his shocking amethyst eyes filled with trepidation.

"I don't know what will happen once I start talking. If I start seizing again, it's... it's alright. I'm alright. Just don't let me swallow my tongue, okay?"

"Eso no es divertido. Me asustaste casi hasta la muerte. Now start talking." I didn't give a shit if he didn't understand Spanish. There was no mistaking that I didn't find his flippancy remotely funny or that I'd believed he was dying. He clasped his hands in his lap, the sheet covering him still damp from his fit. I refused to fill the silence as I waited for him to speak.

"My name is Theobald Tibalt Marcel Wisteria."

"But—" He looked over at me, and I snapped my mouth shut.

"I come from a long, ancient line of witches that has made it their business to stay hidden, not just from the mortal world, but from everyone. I have purple hair and purple eyes... and I have been lying to you." He braced himself as if waiting for something to happen. After a second, he relaxed. "Lightning is not the only unusual magic I have. You know how I said that gifts like seeing ghosts and the future are really rare?" I vaguely recalled him saying something similar to mi abuela.

"Are you telling me you really can see ghosts?" I asked, mildly affronted.

"Not ghosts." He let that hang, and I slowly filled in the blank.

"The future?"

"It's called foresight, and it's not a gift—it's a curse." He seemed to brace himself again, then let out a shaky breath. "The Wisterias were cursed to relive the deaths of their lo—the people they cared about centuries ago. Since then, the ability has evolved to cover more, but that is what it is at its core. We've been in hiding for generations. Our name and trademark eyes tell of our true abilities." Sadness filled those amethyst depths as he looked at me. "I haven't seen my mother in over a decade and my grandmother since I was ten. I don't have any siblings, and the only family that's safe to be around for extended periods of time barely has enough foresight to count."

"Why keep it secret?"

He let out a soft sigh and offered a wan smile. "Because, Carlos, witches covet. If there is a power out there greater than ourselves, we want it, will search it out, and we *will* abuse it.

That's not speculation. It's a fact. Right now, my mother and grandmother are the only two witches in the world that have made their abilities known. Like me, they hide their true appearance, and no one has any idea that they're related. Some very powerful people currently employ my mother, and everyone believes my grandmother is senile, driven mad by her *gift*."

He twisted the last word with such bitterness, I couldn't help but reach out. A rogue tear streaked its way down his cheek as he fisted his hand in the sheet and seemed to shake with the effort of keeping himself together. Seeing him in so much pain broke my heart. I scooted closer and gently wiped the tear away.

"You could have told me, Theo. I wouldn't have..." Wouldn't have what? Told anyone? Thought less of him? Tried to use him? "I'm here for you. Why didn't you mention anything before?"

He looked at me with watery eyes, and I could see how the amethyst shade suited him so much better than the baby blue he'd adopted. I brushed back the hair sticking to his forehead. He simply blinked, and the most obvious piece finally fell into place.

"Have you had visions about *me*?"

He slowly closed his eyes and turned away. The lack of answer testament to the truth.

"Your seizure tonight—was that a vision?"

"Yes. Several."

"Were they about me?"

He flinched. "I can't tell you that."

I let out a huff of frustration. "Have you had seizures like that before?"

"No. Maybe? Once."

"Were those about me?"

"I can't tell you that."

"Why did you transfer schools?"

He drew in on himself. "I can't tell you that."

"What *can* you tell me?" I asked finally losing my patience.

"I can tell you about the ones that have already come true." Shock exploded inside of me. Assuming he'd had visions about me and actually hearing him confirm it knocked me for a loop. "You have to understand, the future isn't set in stone. It changes... and anything I do..." He stopped and swallowed hard before going on, "...or say, can affect it."

"O-Okay."

He looked back at me with enough sadness to swallow the world. "It's okay if you're super freaked out. I understand if you want me to go."

"No, I want you to stay and... and I'd like to hear what you can share."

He nodded and did just that, all the while staring down at his clasped hands. He didn't move more than to draw breath to speak, and when he did, it was in a perfect monotone. By the time he stopped, he'd shared no fewer than eight visions and looked like he'd been scraped hollow with a spoon. I, on the other hand, was dizzy with questions and more confused than ever.

He let out a heavy, defeated sigh and sagged beside me. "Can we be done with questions?"

I swallowed my burning curiosity. "Yeah."

"Still want me to stay?"

I finished shifting back beneath the covers and frowned at him. "Esa es una pregunta estúpida. Now, come here." The relief that washed across his face as I held open my arms for him helped to quiet the tumult inside of me. I'd never thought of Theo as fragile before, but he felt like glass snuggled against me. I pushed all the doubt away for later and waited for him to settle, then said, "One more question and I'm done for the night, promise."

He stiffened, and I swear I could feel his heart hammering against my chest. "Okay." When I didn't immediately ask, he glanced up, his purple eyes deep with resignation. I couldn't help but smile as I stroked his smooth cheek.

"Was the sex really that good?"

He barked out a laugh, and his tension evaporated. He stole a sweet kiss that completely melted my heart. "Absolutely."

Chapter 24

Carlos

I set my pen down in order to rub the bridge of my nose. The nose pads of my glasses scratched at my forehead as I pushed them even higher to work out the pressure behind my eyes. Theo could see the future, the *actual* future, and he'd seen mine... several times.

I couldn't help but wonder how much of our relationship was constructed and how much was natural. Did it matter? What if the only reason we were together at all was because he'd seen some future that told him so? He'd certainly shared enough visions of us interacting to support the speculation. Did Theo even *want* to be with me? Did I want to be with him? Did we control our fate, or was it a foregone conclusion?

A small groan escaped me as my thoughts whirled into a new level of chaos and the pounding behind my eyes intensified.

Thankfully, there were minimal witnesses to my silent descent into madness as I continued to obsess over what I'd learned about Theo. If he could lie about his name and who he was to me, what else could he be hiding?

No. I couldn't think like that. Pero... It'd be nice to get another perspective. I glanced at his last text.

Theo

Missing group. Urgent project to finish.

What project could he possibly have? Why haven't I heard about it before now? Does it have something to do with what he told me? Maybe he thinks it was a mistake...

I gave up trying to banish the headache and straightened my glasses. My thumb hovered over the phone's keyboard while I debated how to respond. Unfortunately, I had no more ideas now than I'd had when he'd originally sent it two days ago.

"You okay?" The note of concern in Patty's voice instantly caught my attention. I quickly turned off my screen and pocketed the phone without sending so much as a single character.

"Huh? Yeah, I'm fine," I said, meeting her hazel eyes. Her mouth turned down in an unconvinced scowl. I debated confiding in her, but dismissed the idea. Not that I didn't love and adore Patty, but in her current anti-romantic mood, she wasn't exactly the pinnacle of good advice where relationships were concerned and there wasn't anyone else more sympathetic around. It was just the two of us today.

She finished putting away her notes and spared me a considering look before leaning across the table. She wrapped her around mine, preventing me from clearing my own notes. I glanced at her, noting the warmth and concern on her sepia face. "This isn't about what I said before, is it? I hope you know I didn't mean anything. I was just trying to look out for you."

"I know," I said, softening. Perhaps it was unfair to assume she couldn't be supportive of someone else's relationship drama, because she couldn't handle her own.

"Is it... something else?" she fished, doing a poor job of looking or sounding disinterested.

I sighed and settled back in my chair. What did I have to lose?

"Well, tell me," she demanded, giving up all pretense of polite questioning.

"I... uh... recently learned some things about Theo," I said, choosing my words carefully and doing my damnedest not to meet her prying gaze.

"Aaand..."

"And I can't really go too much into it beyond saying that it's kind of thrown me. Now I'm... questioning things." I quickly held up a hand at seeing the clouds converge on her face. "Before you decide to get all affronted on my behalf, know that it's not cheating or even flirting. I just wasn't expecting... this."

"What, did he kill someone?" she scoffed.

I paled and thanked God she was too busy putting away the last of her books to notice my reaction. Truth was, I didn't have a clue. Maybe? Yes, but not yet? Never in a million years? I hated I didn't know and hated even more that she'd made me think of it. I didn't want to think those things about Theo. He may be a witch, but that didn't automatically make him a killer. Right?

I cleared my throat and sat straighter, pushing my glasses up my nose before folding my hands around the pen once more. "It's not anything like that." *I hope.*

She turned back to me, eyebrows raised. "But you won't tell me what it *is* like."

"Yeah..."

"What can you tell me?" Her question was so like my own from the other night that I squeezed my eyes shut.

He didn't have to share the truth with me. He could've lied, and I'd never have known. That had to count for something. I loved Theo, trusted him. Or at least, I thought I did. Did learning he belonged to some ancient, all-powerful witch family that could see the future really change anything?

Yes. Because he's not telling me something important.

Disturbing as it was to hear him recount all the visions we'd lived through, I was more disturbed by the ones he'd refused to share. Doubt rose dark and menacing, like a storm sent to swallow me whole. I couldn't do this. No amount of wanting to trust Theo could undo the fact that he'd lied to me, that I was sure he was still lying to me.

"He..." I began, ready to spill the truth about everything. "It's complicated," I finished instead. I wouldn't betray Theo's trust that way. No matter how I didn't understand it, I could recognize the sacrifice it had taken to expose that part of himself to me. "We talked about some pretty heavy stuff, but I'm worried he's holding something back." I expected Patty to have a decided opinion about that, like she had an opinion about everything. What I did not expect were gentle words of compassion.

"You sweet thing, you're completely smitten with him, aren't you?"

"What?" My head shot up from where I'd been memorizing the divots in my pen cap.

She rolled her eyes and gave my arm a gentle squeeze. "It's plain as day for anyone near the two of you. You're just as crazy about Theo as Theo is about you."

"You really think so?" I swallowed thickly. If Theo really felt the same about me as I did about him, the truth of who he was would be a lot easier to swallow, though it didn't change that he hadn't trusted me in the first place. It wasn't like *I* was a witch. How could I possibly use him?

"Sphinxes don't think. We know." She offered me a wink and released me. "So he's holding something back, so what? Give it time, he'll open up eventually, or he won't, and you'll have your answer."

"That was about as clear as a river during the rainy season. Tu y tus acertijos."

"All I'm saying is if you care about him as much as you obviously do, then give him a chance to explain whatever you think he's holding back. Did he have to share what he did?"

"No." I shifted in my chair, recalling how his eyes had rolled back and the fear that had gripped my heart. He could have said anything to explain the seizure. There were countless believable fabrications he could have fed me. Instead, he'd given me a dangerous truth. I wanted to believe that was enough, that what we had was real.

She smacked me as she stood up. "There you have it then." I smiled back at her, my spirits lifted by the unusual pep talk. "Alright, alright, don't get too sappy on me. See you next semester?"

"Claro que sí. Professor Roman?"

"Like that's even a question. Sands, he's hot."

"And married," I added with a laugh.

"Pft, doesn't change how hot he is. If anything, it makes him more so."

"You're terrible."

"You still love me." She placed a kiss on my cheek and ruffled my hair much as I imagined an older sister might. I shook my head, because she was right, and I appreciated her insight into my situation even if I hadn't been able to tell her much.

We parted ways, bidding each other pleasant winter holidays, and I made my way back to my dorm. I shot off a quick text to Theo, wishing him luck on his project, determined not to overthink this anymore than I already had, and stepped into my dorm. To my surprise, Nessa was there. I hadn't actually seen him since his gruff departure the night Theo had confided in me, but had seen the evidence of his passing.

"Hey." I raised my hand in a gesture of greeting and let the door lock shut behind me. "Thought you'd be out celebrating or something."

He pushed off the peninsula, scaled, red arms crossed imposingly over his chest. "Club's canceled for holidays." He said the statement with such finality that I almost recoiled.

Why do I try? Like seriously?

I stepped towards my room, looking forward to a hot shower and hopefully some dirty texts with my boyfriend. If I was lucky, maybe I could entice him out of his cave and finally put to rest all of my doubts and insecurities.

"Where's your... the witch?" Nessa asked, pulling me up short and clearly struggling with giving Theo any sort of relevant, intimate title.

I shifted my backpack on my shoulder, simultaneously curious about this sudden interest in my personal life and pleased to see that we were finally making progress. Maybe all my efforts not to shove Theo and my relationship in his face had paid off. Respecting boundaries was important, even if they weren't necessarily for my benefit.

"He's busy tonight with an assignment. Sounds like he'll be tied up with it for a while," I admitted, though I still hoped to spend some actual time with him.

"Oh? He going to be coming by later tonight?"

"Not likely. Will probably be a couple of days before he can come by. Would *you* be interested in hanging out?" I added cautiously, not entirely sure if I wanted him to agree or not.

His eyes lit with a fire both alarming and promising. "Yeah. Let's go." He marched across the room and took hold of my arm with terrifying intensity.

"Whoa, I didn't mean right now. More like mañana o como nunca," I countered with as much conviction as I could muster.

"I think now sounds great." His grip tightened painfully, and my horror tripled.

Alarm sent a wave of cold adrenaline down my spine. I pulled in vain against the iron hold. "Nessa, what are you doing? You're hurting me."

"We're leaving. Now." He yanked my bag free to land with a solid thud on the ground and dragged me towards the door. I fought the momentum with everything I had. My feet dragged in the lush carpet, my fingers dug insubstantial marks on his hardened scales, and my heart threatened to beat right out of my chest.

"Please, Nessa. Whatever it is, I'm sorry. You don't have to do... whatever it is you're doing."

Suddenly, he yanked me close, and pure terror at what he planned to do to me froze the air in my lungs. Without warning, he dug a hand in my pocket. I tried to angle my hips away from the invasion, but Nessa was twice my size, and there was nowhere to go. At last, he liberated my phone. My eyes widened as he crushed it in one hand right beside my face.

"Nessa, please..." I squirmed to get free with every ounce of strength I possessed.

"Time to go."

I opened my mouth, and something solid slammed into my head. I had just enough sense to wonder when Nessa had picked up the book before the darkness took hold.

Theo

I curled my fingers around my chin as I considered the wall of my apartment, which now resembled a murder board. Colorful strings stretched across the plaster expanse, connecting equally colorful push pins and corresponding sticky notes. Each one marked a trigger and a subsequent possible future. Unfortunately, seeing it all spread out wasn't providing any more enlightenment than keeping it all in my head. Even with color-coded lines, the multitude of outcomes looked more like a spaghetti bowl than the revelation of clarity I desperately needed.

My gaze slid to the cluster of black pins, each one representing a death. Warren's, Kavren's, Carlos's... mine. I shuddered at the visceral memory of having my soul separated from my body. The hollow ache, the pain, the desperate pleas for him to stop... I squeezed my eyes shut and ran a hand over my face, but it did little to erase the vision or the array of black pins when I reopened them.

So many... Too many to avoid.

No one had been spared, and multiple futures ended with everyone dying. But somewhere among the chaos, there had to be a line of events that wouldn't end up with Carlos or me dead. I shook my head and dropped my hand, the exhaustion of sleepless nights weighing on me.

"There has to be a way. I won't let him die, and I won't let him become a killer." I twisted to look back at Sigurd, where he lay on the loveseat. He'd taken up the position when I'd begun decorating the wall and hadn't moved since. "Don't suppose you have any ideas?"

His tail thumped heavily on the cushion as he perused the abused wall. After a moment, an image of Carlos glowing purple projected in my mind.

I turned my attention to the wall and one of the few futures that didn't seem connected to the others. Amid a sea of death, it was a sole beacon of hope, and I had no idea where it belonged in the grand scheme of things. At this point, Carlos was so full of my magic it was a wonder it didn't seep out of his pores when he sweat. But it was a stopgap, a precautionary measure, for I didn't know what. I didn't know how or why it was relevant. Not a clue when or *if* it would happen. And didn't even know if when it came to it, if it would work. The chance of an alternate future I hadn't seen yet where it didn't was just as likely.

I ran both hands through my hair, only to tangle my fingers in the messy strands. "I don't know what to do," I agonized. "What does any of this mean?"

I considered the two white pins positioned far outside the realm of uncertainty. They represented the only visions I'd had that felt like they existed beyond all the death, somewhere in a more distant future. The happiness in them provided my only hope that any of this could be survived. I didn't even know if they belonged to the same realm of possible futures, but I wanted them. That joy was worth fighting for. Carlos was worth fighting for. Hell, he now knew my most dangerous secrets, and he hadn't rejected me. He'd... *held* me.

No one had held me like that since I'd had my very first vision about a snake getting into our dove coop. My mother had found me distraught in a violence of feathers, screaming about how I hadn't made it in time. That had been my first lesson about the future being unavoidable. A year later, my grandmother had given me the prophecy of my death. Seventeen years later, I was still fighting it, and that lesson felt more poignant than ever as I stared in defeat at the wall that all but guaranteed the end of everything I held dear.

I'm not ready to lose him.

I swiped away a sudden rush of tears and gave myself a good shake.

"Okay. Okay. I can do this. We're just missing something." I walked up to the rogue dots and brushed a finger over the one with the sticky note beneath it that read "mi corazon". My heart tightened with longing at reading the words. When I'd started this quest to subvert the prophecy of my death, I'd never expected to find love or want it as much as I did. I recognized now the folly of putting off happiness into an uncertain future. Life was too short not to live every second.

I shifted my attention to the plethora of strings and willed the solution to reveal itself. "Tell me what I'm missing," I pleaded with the wall. Despite how fervently I wished, no answer revealed itself. I let out an aggravated cry and spun on Sigurd.

"Come on, you mangy beast. You're supposed to be helping."

His eyes narrowed to slits, and a low growl accompanied his now-twitching tail. He re-sent the image of a glowing Carlos.

"I already—"

Before I could finish, he altered the image to reflect the wall. Upon it, he blazed a mental trail through various visions. It seemed to bounce and double back through things that had already transpired until it snaked its way past gruesome ends and shot through the two white dots.

With a gasp, I swiveled around and immediately started rearranging the board. I'd been so focused on the outcome of triggers, it'd never occurred to me that the timing was also relevant. "My gods, they're out of order. This is it. What I've been missing. They aren't separate. They're related. Why didn't I see it before?" I rambled aloud as I ripped out pins in my madness. Sticky notes drifted abandoned to the floor, and strings hung unconnected. "Almost there. If I can just..."

Sigurd let out a yowl so loud I feared my eardrums would rupture. My latest pushpin missed the wall and stabbed straight into my hand.

"Motherfucker!" I shouted as I pulled it free. Blood welled, bright and red. I shoved the injured appendage in my mouth and sucked on it to stop the bleeding as I turned to confront my familiar. "What the fuck?" My vitriol evaporated as I took in the sight of Sigurd, equally losing his shit.

His yowls of distress bounced off the walls as he darted about the room like he was possessed.

"Sigurd…"

His mad dash circled the room again, and he careened off the couch as if he had wings.

"Sigurd, what's wrong?" I took a wary step closer, anxiety about his unusual behavior making me nauseous.

He let out another grating caterwaul.

I clamped hands over my ears to protect them from the offensive sound. "Sigurd, stop. Talk to me."

His claws scrabbled on the ground as he abruptly shifted direction and came barreling toward me. Fifteen kilograms of fur slammed into my chest, forcing me backward.

My back pricked with pain as protruding pinheads dug into it and all the air rushed out of my lungs. At the same time, a flood of magic, equal parts mine and Sigurd's natural magic, poured into me. I arched off the wall and rose to my tiptoes as my body struggled to contain the inrush. The force of it threatened to pop my eyes out and send lightning lancing up the walls. I fought to control the sudden surge of power and breathe. The tide finally subsided, and air rushed painfully into my lungs. I gasped as I fell to my knees beside where my familiar lay slumped on the floor.

"Sigurd. Sigurd!" I tried again, terrified to touch him with so much power coursing through my veins. Carlos may be immune to my touch, but Sigurd definitely was not. Considering how much power I was currently holding, I'd be just as likely to shock him as burn him to a crisp.

To my infinite relief, he rolled one emerald eye at me. *Save.*

Cold doused me from head to toe. "W-what?"

A shaky image of a glowing Carlos found its way into my mind. Pieces of it fractured off into colorful motes that turned gray and disappeared. *Save.* He closed his eye, the effort of the sending having sapped the last of his strength.

"Carlos." I quickly checked to make sure my familiar was still breathing, then surged to my feet. My gaze roved over the half-organized wall. "I'm out of time."

Chapter 25

Carlos

I opened my eyes, only to immediately shut them against the piercing light. The headache I'd been fighting at the library paled compared to the agony currently ripping through my skull. I let out a groan that echoed painfully between my ears and absently reached up to straighten my glasses. Reassured that they were still on my face, I fumbled around blindly for some clue where the hell I was. My fingers skirted over gritty concrete that was otherwise smooth until my questing hand hit an unseen obstacle and pain lanced up my arm.

"¡Hijo de puta!" I hissed and snatched my burned hand back.

"It works. Those fuckers actually did it."

Icy fear slithered down my spine at the unfamiliar voice. I squinted against the harsh light to get a look at its source. Nothing about the man with auburn hair and a malicious smile sparked any sort of recognition. He stood several meters away, his pale skin a disturbing yellow in the lurid light that encompassed me. While he seemed to be about my age and a little taller, I couldn't have picked him out of any crowd or class. The longer I looked, the more positive I was that I'd never seen him before in my life.

"Who are you?" I asked.

"That's not relevant." He waved a dismissive hand, and the surrounding light flared. I winced at the change in brightness and tried to focus on the room at large to find any sort of hint of where I was.

I don't understand. The last thing I remember is Nessa... Nessa!

My gaze fell on a figure crumpled against the far wall. The hard red scales and overall size betrayed the owner's identity. "¡Dios mío! What did you do to him? Where am I? Who *are* you? ¿Por qué estoy aquí?"

The man snickered and turned to look back at my unmoving roommate. "It served its purpose. And you're where I want you."

"Is... is he alive?" Nessa and I may not be mejor amigos, but I didn't want him *dead*.

"Does it matter?"

"¡Por supuesto que importa!" What the hell kind of question was that? *Of course,* it mattered. Anger burned in my belly. Nessa was hurt, quite possibly dead, and it was obvious this pendejo was responsible.

I forced myself to my feet beneath his creepy, dark gaze. His eyes glinted with malevolence as I took a determined step toward my roommate. Orange light flared around me, and I flew back as if thrown. I hit the unforgiving ground hard and blinked away bright spots of light, then promptly recoiled at the sight of blood on the ground. Mercifully, it didn't seem to belong to me, but the realization offered no comfort. His gleeful cackle surrounded me and made my stomach churn.

"You pitiful creature, you're not going anywhere." His words brought with them the sickening realization of where I was and why the light seemed to bother me so much. I lay at the heart of a witch's summoning circle. Fear strangled my heart as every horror story I'd ever heard about witches flashed through my mind. The ground swam before my eyes, and the world around me seemed to teeter.

I fought back the urge to faint and pushed myself onto my hands and knees. "What do you want?"

His eyes glinted in the peculiar light, and a smile that looked like death spread across his face. "Everything."

Theo

I didn't bother with a spell to unlock Carlos's dorm, just blasted it open with a miniature bolt of lightning. The door rebounded off the wall, narrowly missing me as I surged into the room.

"Carlos!" I spun around in the living area. Nothing seemed out of place. No sign of a struggle. "Carlos!" My gaze fell on his backpack lying on the floor, its contents spilling out. "I'm too late." Despite the knowledge in my heart, I searched the entire space and couldn't find a trace of where he might have gone.

"No, no, no." I pulled at my hair while my heart beat erratically in my chest. "There has to be something. Some clue, some way to find him. I was so close..." The image of my murder wall and Carlos glowing purple leapt to the forefront of my mind. "Magic! Of course."

I dropped my hands and focused on calming down. My riotous heart continued to pound away, but eventually I got my breathing under control and turned my attention inward. Since Sigurd had given me every drop of magic he possessed, there was only one other source that held my magic's unique signature—Carlos.

Precious seconds slipped by as I called to my magic. At last, the responding echo hit my awareness. My eyes flew open, and I raced out the door. I wove through campus past curious bystanders as fast as my feet could carry me, a sense of urgency dogging my steps. When I hit the edge of the university grounds, I didn't hesitate to veer into town.

Streets and alleys became a blur of sun-bleached stone as I careened around corners. Each turn simultaneously slowed me down and brought me that much closer to my destination until I ultimately stood in front of a large metal door. The resonance of my magic pulsed strongly on the other side.

Unlike at the dorm, where I'd simply blasted the door open, here, logic and caution won out. I approached the barrier slowly, sending feelers out to detect any alarm wards or traps. Almost immediately, I met resistance. The door glowed a subtle green and exuded a sense of menace. I drew a steadying breath and took the time I didn't have to spare to dismantle the security. The spell came apart seamlessly without raising alarm, and I let out a sigh of relief. With painstaking slowness, I cracked open the door, leery of what might await me on the other side, and slipped inside.

I blinked a few times to adjust to the dim lighting. A cursory look found what appeared to be a makeshift boxing ring and a few chairs scattered about. However, the overall feel of the place was decidedly of an abandoned warehouse. I shook off a sudden sense of unease and stepped deeper into the room. Try as I might to find some indication of why I'd been drawn to this empty place, I found nothing. It took calling to my magic again to find the small hallway at the back.

I ventured down the tight corridor and came to a quick halt when it abruptly opened up into a smaller version of the previous space. At the far end stood another door, this one with a soft orange glow spilling beneath it.

Found you.

I muttered a quick spell to silence my footfalls and approached the last obstacle separating me from the rest of my magic. The door swung open on silent hinges, and my heart stopped dead in my chest. There in the center of the room, Carlos stood encircled in orange light dictated by intricate swirls set into the ground. It didn't matter how many times I'd seen it in my visions, bile still crawled up my throat at the sight of the man I loved held captive in a glowing cage. A cage I'd help make.

A shadowy figure I hadn't noticed at first beyond the circle made a gesture, and Carlos fell to his knees with a scream of pain that scored into my bones. Without thinking, I stepped deeper into the room. The door slammed shut behind me, and a dark-shrouded Kavren looked up at me. For a moment, all the horrible versions of confronting this heinous person threatened to drown me. I couldn't do it. I'd never succeed. This had been doomed to fail from the start. The small sound of breaking glass snapped me out of the downward spiral.

"Let him go," I demanded, finding my voice at last and taking another step forward. Kavren cocked his head to the side and considered me for a moment as Carlos shakily turned to face me.

"Theo? Theo! He's done something to Nessa!" Carlos shouted.

I frowned and looked in the direction he was pointing. Sure enough, Carlos's roommate lay slumped against one wall, not so much as a breath stirring his form. I didn't need to check for a pulse to know there wouldn't be one and that his body would be cold to the touch.

Nessa? I've never seen him in a vision.

"Theo Kendal." Kavren's ominous tone instantly recaptured my attention. "I should have known you couldn't be trusted when you volunteered to lie with such a creature."

My hands fisted at my side while my lip curled in a silent snarl. "You want to talk about trust? Where are the others, Kavren? Are Essen and Warren hiding somewhere I can't see, or did you stab them in the back like the treacherous snake you are?"

Confused horror splashed across Carlos' face, and too late, I realized the error of my questions. "Y-you know him?" Guilt stabbed at my heart, but I didn't have the luxury of begging for his forgiveness right now. I had to get him out of here before he ended up like Nessa.

I ignored Carlos's stricken face and focused my attention on the present threat. "Let him go. He can't give you what you want. The circle may hold him, but that's not enough."

The sinister smile that curled Kavren's thin lips sent icy tendrils of fear down my back. "I beg to differ." He held out a hand, and the circle that held Carlos burned to life, searing its afterimage into the backs of my eyes. Then he spoke.

The power of his words filled the air, and their meaning settled into my bones. Carlos screamed an unearthly cry that I'd hoped never to hear in real life. Then it cut off abruptly, and he went unnaturally still. Between one blink and the next, Carlos turned from flesh and blood to his pure Kisin form, the white of his bones reflecting the orange light surrounding him.

"No!" I shouted.

"You're too late," Kavren fired back without mercy, his face alight with menacing glee.

"But, but how?" I scrambled to make sense of the knowledge now embedded in my soul. "How did you learn his true name? Where are the others? Why are you doing this?"

"Why? Because I can. Because it's my *right*. As for the others..." He considered me a long second, then turned his attention to Carlos, a horrible sneer twisting his features. "They'll be a great way to test out this new power." His gaze snapped back to me. "But I think I'll start with you."

At the speed of light, lightning shot across the room. Kavren waved his hand, and Carlos lurched to his feet and into the electricity's destructive path. The orange circle still holding him captive glowed angrily in response to the invasive magic while his skeletal body absorbed a blow that would have incinerated the average human with scarcely more than a twitch.

"Oh, ho ho. Lightning, my dear Theo? You've been holding out on me." His mirth dissolved into a scowl. "It's no matter now. You'll die just like the rest of them. I alone control death, and it is impervious to any magic you could possibly use."

I couldn't believe it. I'd played my biggest hand and lost. "Please let him go," I pleaded again to buy time. I could throw bolts until I ran out of magic, but it wouldn't do any good if he kept using Carlos as a shield. What else did I have besides lightning? Then it hit me.

I have the future.

"Never. I hold all the power now." His mocking laughter grated on my raw nerves and threatened to turn me into a gibbering puddle as visions of him ordering Carlos to kill me accosted my mind.

I pushed through the onslaught and held up my hand as he had earlier. "You shouldn't have let me hear his true name."

"What are you going to do?" he scoffed. "I already have dominion over the demon. Saying it again will change nothing. It is under my control."

"That's what you think."

The power of Carlos's true name filled my being and shattered the magic hiding my appearance. I knew without looking that my hair had reverted to its natural lavender and my eyes glowed the trademark Wisteria purple, while tiny arcs of lightning danced along my skin. As I willed the name into being, I called to the magic that resided in the man I loved, magic I'd devoted hours upon hours layering into him, a stopgap I now finally understood.

The final syllable of his true name passed my lips and resonated in the room. Kavren snickered, no doubt feeling his victory imminent. His mirth died as the skeleton, previously awash in orange light, suddenly glowed head to toe in luminescent violet. Every inch of his body emanated a color that I would recognize anywhere—the color of my magic. Hope rose like a tidal wave inside me, joined by a crippling undercurrent of guilt.

Forgive me, Carlos.

Chapter 26

Theo

My lips buzzed with energy. The surrounding air hissed and popped as the lightning dancing on my skin fired off in random directions. I understood now why Kavren seemed half mad. I had a rare natural ability, but was well on my way to being drunk with the foreign power now coursing through my veins. Nothing could stop me. Not the future. Not some prophecy. And certainly not Kavren.

I can do it. I can save us.

At the thought of *us*, the fog clouding my vision cleared, and I crashed back to reality. The skeletal figure remained frozen within the circle, flushed with purple, as if awaiting orders. I swallowed past a painful lump in my throat. "Carlos? Can you hear me, baby?"

He turned slowly to face me, his eyes vacant and lifeless as he considered his new master. While not surprised at his lack of response or even recognition, self-loathing still boiled rancid inside of me.

"It's me, baby," I tried again, though it came out more of a choked sob. Not so much as a twitch came from Carlos. "Please, you know me." Nothing. The man I loved had been pushed aside to become a soulless vessel of power. And it was my fault. I'd done this to him. I held his true name and the ability to make him bow to my command. Bile rose in my throat, and my legs threatened to buckle as the weight of the power I held threatened to bring me to my knees.

"I can't believe it. You really have feelings for this... this *thing*," Kavren sneered.

"Shut your face before I shut it for you!" I shouted at him. "Carlos is a person! He has the kindest, most selfless soul I've ever seen, and he does *not* deserve this!" I didn't want this power. I didn't want to hurt Carlos, to use him for my own end.

"What sort of witch are you?" Kavren scoffed. "Demons are *tools*. Power sources to accomplish a goal. We have it at our mercy. The circle holds. We can still both get what we want..."

I blocked out his entreaties to join forces and focused on the swirls of orange burning on the ground. *The circle.* As long as Carlos was within it, Kavren could re-seize control the moment I released my hold upon him. From my hand in constructing the damn thing, I recognized the defensive runes that prevented anyone outside of the maker from dismantling it, but they didn't account for what could be done from the *inside*.

I lifted a surprisingly steady arm toward Carlos, and he mirrored the move. We stood several meters away, arms stretched toward each other in a sickening display of symmetry. Lightning shot across the space between us, launching from my fingers and vanishing into his.

Kavren's cackle echoed through the room and abraded my ears. "You don't even know what to do with all that power. Best give it back before you hurt yourself. I'd be happy to show you what a *real* witch can do with it."

I ignored the taunt and continued to pour unfettered electricity into Carlos like he was my own personal lightning rod. Then I directed his other hand to point two fingers toward the circle. Enthralled as he was, Carlos didn't even twitch as he rerouted the raw destructive force through his body to burst into the glowing circle holding him captive. Stillness captured the area as the electricity vanished into the floor, then the ground exploded in a shower of concrete and dirt. Embers of orange winked out of existence. Debris rained down and dust filled the space while the bang resonated with near-deafening force.

I held onto Carlos's true name long enough to yank him clear of the blowout like a doll on a string. The moment I relinquished it, he slumped to the ground beside me, once more in his human form. Fear clawed at my spine as I fell beside him and tilted his head up to see his face. Thin lines of red streaked his face where he'd been caught in the violence of the explosion, but overall he was unharmed.

"Thank Freyja!" I exclaimed. He blinked at me, his warm brown eyes somewhat glassy. Worry tightened around my chest as I carefully brushed loose bits of gravel from his face and away from his eyes. At some point, he'd lost his glasses and squinted as if trying to bring me into focus.

"Theo?" He groaned and coughed.

I rubbed his back. "Yeah, it's me. Are you okay?" No sooner did I ask than all the dust clouding the room fell to the ground in an unnatural rush.

"No!" Kavren screamed.

Carlos and I swiveled around at the exclamation of rage. Kavren stood once more, staring down at the destroyed circle, his features twisted with fury and blood dripping down his face from a sizable cut on his forehead. He staggered forward and had to reach out to brace himself on a large boulder of ruined concrete.

"What. Have. You. Done!" He glared at me, his face mottled purple, his teeth bared.

Carlos shrank back and looked up at me, fear and doubt clearly shining in his eyes. Guilt slammed through me at realizing Carlos didn't know whether he was safe with me.

I gave him a gentle squeeze, followed by a nudge. "Get behind me. I won't let him hurt you." Carlos's gaze darted over to the furious Kavren, but he didn't immediately move. I was about to encourage him more forcefully when Kavren spoke again.

"You will suffer for this, Theo Kendal. If it takes the rest of my life, I will destroy everything you hold dear. Starting with your pet." He clapped his hands together and spewed out a discordant rush of Latin.

Without enough time for a counterspell, I threw out another bolt of lightning to intercept the makeshift incendiary spell. The two met meters away from where I still squatted by Carlos with enough concussive force to knock us both back. I threw up an arm to ward off the flare of light and pushed to my feet.

Out of the corner of my eye, I saw Carlos shimmy out of the direct line of fire, though to my dismay, he didn't take shelter behind me where he would be easier to protect. I shook my head as I dusted off. It would have to suffice for now. I could plead and beg for forgiveness once we were out of here, but right now Kavren deserved my full attention.

"Looks like I'm not the only one who has tricks up their sleeves," I said as I stepped forward and more dirt clattered to the ground at my feet.

"That's not all I've got." With practiced ease, a thin rod of polished wood the length of his forearm slipped from his cuff. My eyes widened with horror as his fingers tightened around the wand. "Don't look so surprised. I had Essen make one just in case. Of course, she doesn't know that I stole it or that I replaced all of that ridiculous flight magic with something—how should I say?—a little more potent." The smile that twisted his face also twisted my gut.

Foresight really was fucking useless. At no point ever had he had the wand, and it didn't take a genius to guess that the prepped spells the magical device now held could destroy a city block with minimal effort and leave Kavren's personal well untouched. Even with all the power rioting inside me, he'd bleed me dry long before he had to tap his own reserves. Fucked was a mild way to put our current predicament.

Gravel skidded beneath my shoes as I took a wary step back and held up my hands in a placating gesture. "There's no reason to be rash about this." All hope of reasoning with him went right out the window as his eyes lit with inhuman rage.

"Rash? Rash! You obliterated years of effort! And for what? A demon that would sooner see you dead than share its powers? I'll show you rash." He angled the wand at us. The tip glowed blue, and an icy burst shot forth.

I rattled off a quick blocking spell and threw up both hands to push the magic out as far as I could to protect us. The spear of frost cracked hard enough into the projected barrier to make me stagger. Shards of wicked-sharp ice rebounded to embed themselves in the wall. I didn't dare look over to see if Carlos had escaped unscathed, as I released the hasty spell before it could drain too much of my magic.

There was a reason wand duels were outlawed, and the knowledge of how to make them all but banned—the spells held at the ready could be far stronger than the witch that generated them and there was no telling what was stored until it ripped you apart.

"Just let us go. No one ever has to find out about this." I gestured at the general chaos surrounding us.

Kavren snarled and made several cutting motions with the wand. Instead of using up my entire power supply trying to stop all of them, I redirected them instead and tossed in a few bolts of lightning for good measure. Kavren dismissed and sidestepped the arcs of destructive force as if they were nothing. Chunks of wall exploded into rubble as the various magical bursts slammed into them. I let out a growl and muttered an incantation to detonate a fresh pile of debris next to him. He leaped away, but not before getting caught in the side by the improvised shrapnel.

"You'll pay for that!" he snarled. A green burst of light shot out of the wand, but unlike all the missiles before, this one streaked toward an unsuspecting Carlos.

Carlos yelped and scrambled to evacuate the blast radius as I levitated a volley of debris to intercept and disperse the attack. Acid ate at the rocks as fast as I could put them in its path until the last of the green light vanished, and I sagged from the effort.

"Quick thinking, but neither of you is getting out of here alive. I'll tear down the whole building to bury your body. If you're willing to forsake your own kind to be with a demon, then you can die like one, too."

Against my better judgment, I stole a glance at Carlos. His eyes met mine, wide with terror in a face set with uncertainty. My hand tightened into a fist at my side as I returned my attention to the asshole, willing to get all of us killed for his vendetta.

That's it, no more kid gloves.

"You want to see what kind of witch I am? You got it."

The pressure in the room dropped, and alarm splashed across Kavren's face as I summoned up the extra power Sigurd had given me. Heat lightning mixed with a winter storm capable of tearing down whole castles. I pulled more magic, drawing on the thin hold that still connected me to Carlos through the knowledge of his true name. That would always connect me to him. I didn't call on his magic, though. I called on mine, draining out of him every ounce he still retained. The hair on my arms raised, crackling with electricity as I poured all of it into a sphere. Arcs of lightning leapt off the barely controlled ball of energy hovering between my fingers, building and growing until it threatened to break free.

"Theo." My head snapped down to see Carlos looking up at me. His beautiful curls lie matted to his head with dust and sweat streaked lines in the dirt covering his face to mix with blood. Even a disheveled mess, he was beautiful, still held my heart in his hands. Those soulful brown eyes that had captured me months ago once again held me in their sway. He placed a hand lightly on my arm, and the lightning skittering along my flesh seeped into him as if drawn. "You don't have to do this."

"But... He'll never stop. Never." I shook with the force of restraining the certain death between my hands.

"Please, Theo. This isn't you," he entreated, his fingers digging into my arm. "Don't let him make you a killer."

"But it is. I'm a monster." I stole a glance at Kavren, desperately trying to mount a defense with the remaining spell components from creating the circle. My window of opportunity was shrinking at an alarming rate.

"No, you're not. There has to be another way."

I blinked down at him, as all the possible futures I'd endured over the last five months raced through my mind.

Another way. A way I haven't seen. A way I don't know...

Then it hit me. The future I needed, the one I'd never been able to see, was because I couldn't. Only two types of magic had the power to affect foresight that way—time manipulation and something infinitely more unpredictable.

I gritted my teeth against the pain of absorbing the energy from the lightning sphere. If the insane scheme I had in mind was going to work, then I couldn't afford to be wasteful. I briefly considered invoking Carlos's true name again for an added boost and dismissed it just as quickly.

I will never use him like that.

I gathered the loose lightning that had resisted being reabsorbed and created a missile. Thankfully, this sort of magic came as naturally as breathing to me and required about as much energy. I could spare it so long as it bought me the time I desperately needed.

This better work.

I threw the spear of power at Kavren. It streaked in a jagged line across the room, no less lethal for its lack of accuracy. His head popped up, and he abandoned his efforts in order to throw up a dissipating spell. It was no match for the condensed lightning set to strike in front of him. Much like his attack earlier, the energy hit the counterspell and exploded with enough force to send all three of us flying.

I squinted through the cloud of dust, my ears ringing as I struggled to regain my bearings. "Carlos."

"Here." A shadowy line appeared in the haze, followed by a groan. I rushed over, my gaze roving over Carlos's form once more, searching for more blatant injuries. He coughed and reached out to grab my arms. "You didn't..."

I shook my head, noting his relief. "He's alive. I just hope I've bought us enough time."

"Bueno. Let's get the fuck out of here." He pulled on my arms and turned back to look at me when I didn't budge.

"I can't leave, not yet."

"What are you talking about? Tenemos que irnos. Now," he reiterated, pulling on me again.

"I have to finish this." I took a deep breath and let it out slowly. We didn't have time for this, but Carlos needed to know what was at stake. "He knows your name. Your *true* name."

His face blanched beneath the layer of grime. "What are you planning to do?"

A tear streaked down my face. Of all the ways I'd thought we'd end, this hadn't been one. I cupped the side of his face and almost dissolved into a sobbing mess when he didn't pull away. "I'm going to make him forget. I need you to know..."

It was all worth it. I'm not afraid to die. I love you.

I squeezed my eyes shut against the familiar flood of visions that always accompanied thoughts of telling Carlos how I felt. As expected, when I abandoned the desire, the visions relented. When I finally reopened my eyes, worry and fear dominated Carlos's face. I brushed a thumb across his cheek, leaving a small swirl of purple magic glittering against his darker skin.

"I need you to know that memory spells are dangerous. I don't have the ingredients or preparation required to execute one with precision. They are unpredictable in the best of circumstances..." It went without saying that we were far from an ideal situation for casting such a volatile spell. I swallowed the well of emotion threatening to drown me, so I could explain the most crucial aspect of the endeavor. "I'm going to attempt to target it, but there's a chance other things will get swallowed by the raw casting."

"Theo." His fingers dug into my forearms.

I took a shaky breath and gently removed his hands. "I have to do this to keep you safe. You can't afford for *anyone* to know your true name."

His eyes widened with horrified understanding. "You know my name."

I nodded.

"Don't do this. It's not worth the risk. We can figure something else out," he argued. "I don't care if you know my name!"

"You should care. Even if I never wanted to use it again, I would. It's in my bones and it's in my nature." I sighed softly. He needed to understand. "Witches covet, remember? It could be a day, a year, or ten years from now, but I will eventually invoke it. I won't do that to you."

"Please, no. There has to be another way."

I looked at him sadly. "This *is* the other way. If this works the way I'm hoping, your name will be erased from both of our memories. If... if it doesn't, if it takes more, you can't tell me anything." I took a step back and began gathering every speck of energy I still had, focusing it at my core.

Carlos moved to come after me. "But—"

I held up a hand and shook my head. "Even a hint would risk undoing everything, not just for me, but for him. Please... trust me. There's a chance some memories will come back on their own, but they *have* to come back on their own." I didn't tell him that was all but impossible, that memory spells had a nasty way of claiming everything without distinction. It was entirely likely that I wouldn't just forget his name. I'd forget everything.

I may not have said any of it, but I saw the pain of understanding in his eyes. All magic has a price. His face twisted with agony. Much as I wanted to kiss him one last time, hold him for just a moment, reassure him that everything would be alright, time was running out. Any second now, Kavren would regain his senses and start firing spells again.

"Theo, please." The raw desperation in his voice ripped at my heart.

I offered a wan smile. In lieu of telling him I loved him, I said the only thing I could trust not to trigger a flood of visions. "Tu solus stellam in caelo. Verus Aquilo meus." *You are the only star in the sky. My true North.* I stood looking at him another moment, then turned to face Kavren for what I hoped would be the last time.

"Theo! I don't know what that means. ¡No hagas esto! ¡Te lo ruego! Theo!"

Each shout stabbed at my heart as I knelt to the ground and used focused lightning to carve out a circle. Bluish-white light filled the crevices etched in the ground. Magic poured through me as I manifested Carlos's true name. The circle flared brilliantly at the rush of power that came from such a potent source. I blinked away colored spots of light and let out a sob as my gaze landed on how the information had chosen to corporealize.

Carlos' cries faded into the background as I stared down at the Monarch butterfly perched in the center of the circle, its wings slowly opening and closing. It was so pure, so innocent... so Carlos. The sound of a shoe scuffing dirt and a heavy groan dragged my attention to where Kavren stood braced against a heap of rubble to support himself. The wand in his hand shook, though whether from anger or failing strength, I wasn't sure. Either way, it was perfectly intact.

His arm may have been unsteady as he raised it once more, but the wand remained miraculously steady. "You will regret this."

"Probably." I placed both hands on the electric circle and forced all the magic I had remaining into the spell. Blinding white light and screams filled the room.

Carlos

Light filled every crevice of the room, blinding me and swallowing my last vision of Theo.

"NO!" My shout echoed through the destroyed space. Time seemed to suspend, frozen in one awful moment. Then the light shrank back, and air rushed in to fill the void. It sucked the breath from my lungs, and I collapsed forward, my knees cracking painfully on the devastated earth. I struggled to get back up and squinted through the pain at the blurry haze of the world.

Not far away, a kneeling form swayed, then crumpled to the side.

"Theo!" I forgot all the aches and pains as I scrambled to his side. His blurry outline gained some substance, but details eluded me as the tears welling in my eyes made it even harder to see. I pulled him into my lap and didn't think twice about checking to see if his soul was tethered to his body. I let out a relieved sigh at finding it solidly within.

"Mi amor, por favor, despiertate." I gave him a gentle shake. "Please wake up. Theo." I sniffled and gave him another shake.

His head rolled to the side, and he let out a soft groan.

"That's it," I gasped. Another groan across the room captured my attention. The same guy I'd woken to standing over me pushed to his feet, holding a hand to his head, his auburn hair matted with blood from the wound.

"What... what happened?" he asked, looking around. His gaze wandered around the room, skittering over the lifeless form of my roommate and the destruction until it landed on me. "Who are you?" His focus slid to Theo, lying in my lap, unconscious.

I tightened my hold on him while the other guy frowned like he was trying to remember something. Even without my glasses, I could make out his obvious confusion.

At last, he gave it up and shook his head. "Whatever the fuck happened here, I want no part of it." With a grunt, he pushed off a nearby blur and made his way toward the door.

I recoiled as he came close enough to touch.

He spared me a dismissive glance, his gaze lingering on the burned-out butterfly beside us, its shadow emblazoned permanently on the ground. He offered a noncommittal grunt and continued to shuffle past.

I continued to hold my breath until all awareness of him vanished, then returned my attention to Theo. I brushed lavender hair from his forehead, and his eyes finally fluttered open.

"Did it work?" he asked, his voice rough and his violet gaze intense.

I gasped out a sob. "Yeah, sí, it worked." My heart soared with relief. He was okay. I hadn't lost him.

"Awesome." He glanced around as he pushed himself up. His fingers reached out to touch the butterfly, and it crumbled to ash. "What did I do?"

Just like that, my heart plummeted into the depths of the earth. "W-what? You saved us."

"I did?"

"Why would you ask if it worked if you don't know what you did?" I asked, panic making my voice pitch high.

He shrugged and continued to survey the destruction. "I'm out of magic. Only way that would happen would be if I used it up on a powerful spell." His gaze snapped to me. "I don't know why I told you that. I don't tell anyone about my magic." His eyes narrowed with suspicion. "What did you see? Who are you? Do I... do I know you?"

"Theo, it's me. I'm—" I began, then promptly snapped my mouth shut. Theo had warned me not to tell him anything, not even the smallest hint. Much as it pained me, I let it go, because regardless of what had transpired today, I trusted Theo. If he said the memories could come back on their own, then I would do everything in my power to help them along. "We should probably get you back to Sigurd."

His eyes widened with shock. "How do you know my familiar?"

Mierda. How am I going to do this? This is impossible.

"You... uh... have talked about him before."

Theo cocked his head to the side, his face a jumble of confused skepticism. "Why would I do that?" Had he always been this distrustful, and I'd missed it?

"Because of... my studies," I floundered as I pushed away and went in search of my glasses, anything to escape his curious gaze, absent of any recognition. "You learned I studied mythos in literature, and you mentioned you had a Skogkatt," I added as I tentatively approached the devastated remains of the circle that had held me.

Whole chunks of the ground lie several meters away from their origin. A surge of relief went through me as I spied the glint of wire frames. A relief that shriveled up at seeing the cracked state of the lenses. I reached down to snare them and gently blew the layer of dust off, leery of popping the broken glass out of its tentative hold on the frames.

"Well, fuck."

"What is it?" Theo asked beside me.

I jumped and placed a hand over my struggling heart. "My uh... glasses are broken." I slid on the warped frames and peered through the filthy lenses.

"Ouch, that is bad. Bummer. I'd offer to repair them, but you know." He shrugged as if being completely stripped of magic was commonplace, which I knew it wasn't. The affected nonchalance only elevated my concern. "Anyway, we should probably get out of here before someone finds this mess and tries to pin it on us."

I cast a wary glance back at Nessa, whom Theo had not remarked upon at all. "Yeah, I guess." It wasn't like I could carry him out of here. I'd have to come back or call the authorities. At that thought, my stomach twisted. What would I even tell them? I was the only one left standing who had any memory of what had transpired. And telling anyone risked undoing the spell Theo had sacrificed everything for.

What am I supposed to do?

"You coming?" The question tore me out of the troubling thoughts, and I scurried to catch up with Theo. He gave me another considering look. "Who are you again?"

"Carlos Barrera," I said evenly while sending up a silent prayer that hearing my name would trigger something.

He looked me over from head to toe. "Have we..." He trailed off, the implied question of whether we'd been intimate clear and obviously troubling him.

"We're classmates."

"Oh, cool. Which class?" he asked as he led the way through the door. I swallowed my heartbreak and followed him.

Chapter 27

Theo

I pinned up the calendar and once again wondered where the other one had gotten to. It wasn't like me not to keep a record of my visions. Of course, neither was transferring schools. Not even speaking with my Aunt Pearl and Cousin Jessica at the yuletide festivities had offered enlightenment.

"I don't get it, Sigurd. I only had a year left. Why would I leave?" I glanced over at the massive feline, who remained stoically silent. He'd been even more of his characteristically taciturn self since I'd returned to my apartment weeks ago, covered in dust from a witch battle I had no recollection of fighting. He merely flicked his tail at me. I rolled my eyes and returned my attention to the blank calendar. It was unusual for me to go so long without a vision.

"Why did I leave?" I repeated. Knowing me, it likely had something to do with the prophecy about my death. I'd only been obsessed with subverting it since I'd first heard it. Odd thing was, now when I thought of my inevitable demise, the usual accompanying despair wasn't there. I felt... resigned, at peace. I shook my head of the troubling observation and scooped up my backpack.

"Guess I'll see you later. Try not to destroy the place with any wild parties." The humor fell flat as he met it with a low growl. "Fine, suit yourself, you cantankerous fluff. I'll take my jokes where they're more appreciated."

I shut the apartment door and activated all the wards as I locked up. While I had little memory of why I would have set such powerful aversion charms, I trusted I had my reasons. I hiked my bag higher on my shoulder and set out for Advanced Demon History II, though I hadn't the faintest idea of what I needed with such an obscure class.

It's not like they teach you to summon demons.

I snickered to myself as I found a vacant seat in the auditorium-style classroom. Slowly, the room filled with other students. I let my gaze wander in the hope that I'd find something or someone that would clue me in as to why I'd signed up for the damn class. A fellow student pulled up a seat next to me, and I did a double take.

Well, well, well. What do we have here?

I took in the guy who was undoubtedly a demon, judging by his aura. His light eyes and freckles reminded me of a trip I'd taken to southern France with my grandmother years ago. We'd spent a day collecting wildflowers with a local family of witches for love charms. I offered him my most charming smile and wondered what he thought of the impressive shade of magenta that graced my hair today.

"Hey, name's Theo."

He offered a light chuckle that was a hair higher than I would have expected. "Wren, but before you get your bristles in a bunch, I'm here for her." He gestured with his pencil toward the front of the room. The woman in question had vibrant aqua hair that cascaded down her back like a waterfall and light brown skin that reminded me of sand. If I had to guess, she was either a water nymph or an actual mermaid. The aquatic beauty also happened to be standing behind a delicious specimen of a man that barely looked older than me.

"Nice. You can have her. I'll take Mr. Tall-dark-and-dreamy."

My companion laughed quietly again. "You and half the class, buddy. Some days, I wonder if anyone is here to actually learn or just to ogle Professor Roman."

I arched an eyebrow at him and took in the plethora of dreamy expressions currently being directed at the man in question. "I see your point."

The professor started scratching on the board, and I turned my focus to the day's lesson. By the end of the class, I was no more enlightened than at the start about why I would have enrolled and inching closer to transferring back to Dreifacher Mond, though I was loath to do so mid-school year.

Maybe they'll take me back. I was already ahead in my studies. I could...

I lost my train of thought as I ran into someone. They turned around, and it took me a moment to recognize them without all the dirt. "It's you."

The guy's smile shone in his brown eyes behind repaired glass. "Hey, Theo." The way he said my name stirred something, but when nothing solidified, I ignored it.

"You're the guy from... that day," I finished, dropping my voice low so as not to be overheard. I'd listened to the news for days to see if any clues would surface to explain why either of us had been there, least of all with a dead wyvern. I was fairly confident I hadn't killed the dude and was equally confident the guy in front of me couldn't hurt a flea, let alone murder someone. "Sorry, I don't remember your name."

His smile slipped, though he did a good job of catching it. "Carlos."

"Right. Barrera?" I hazarded. He nodded, and his shoulders sagged, though his plastered smile remained firmly in place. "How have you been? You in Professor Roman's class too?" I asked conversationally.

"Sí. I... I've been okay." He glanced over his shoulder at a woman with warm brown skin and golden undertones.

"Oh, I'm keeping you from your girl. I'll let you go."

His head snapped around so fast it made his dark curls bounce. "What? No. Patty and I aren't... We... We're just friends. Actually, we have a... uh... study group, if you'd like to join," he stammered out. He pushed his glasses up his nose, though they weren't sliding, and kept his skittering gaze focused on the ground.

Poor guy was awkward as fuck, and while not normally the kind of person that made up my crowd, he was one of the few people I seemed to know, or used to, at least.

Maybe he can fill in some of the missing pieces.

"When and where?"

His gaze darted back to my face, and I wasn't sure if it was genuine or a trick of the light, but they seemed to be filled, oddly enough, with hope. "The library. Six o'clock every Tuesday and Thursday. Our table is over by the astronomy stacks."

I perked up. "I love astronomy."

"I know." He winced and pushed his glasses up again. I was getting the impression the move was a nervous tick. "Qué tonto soy. Él no sabe que tú lo sabes," he grumbled to himself.

I couldn't help but chuckle. "You'll have to forgive me. Spanish is not my forte. Latin I can handle. Spanish, not so much."

"Right, lo siento." He groaned. "I mean, sorry. We start meeting tonight. See you there?"

"Six o'clock." I winked, and a deep rose infused his tan cheeks. Before I could get myself into too much trouble, I turned and made my way out of the building for my next class.

Carlos

I sank deeper into my chair beneath the watchful gaze of my friends, possibly more miserable than I'd ever been in my life. There was no suppressing my wince as Theo laughed at whatever not-funny thing the student librarian said. I knocked my glasses askew as I covered my face, as if it could somehow block out the sound. My fingers cracked apart in the hope that this was all some horrible dream, but nope, the cute guy was still there... aaand giving Theo his number.

This isn't happening. Alguien me mate. Seriously, someone kill me.

A warm hand covered mine. My gaze flicked from Theo to Patty's concerned face. The look was one shared by most of the table, though Griffith also looked about ready to throttle Theo. The only mercy was that I was sure he'd restrain himself—pretty sure. I'd told them as much as I dared and stressed the importance that Theo's memory having to come back on its own. Given how little I'd been able to explain, they had still agreed to go with it, because I had asked, though now they seemed to be second-guessing that decision.

"This isn't right," Leah whispered.

No. No, it wasn't. Not by any stretch of the imagination. When I'd accepted that I'd have to wait for an extended time for Theo's memories to return or possibly win Theo all over again, I'd never imagined that I'd have to endure... *this*. Weeks of watching him flirt with practically any male with a pulse was beyond demoralizing—he'd even made a half-hearted pass at Griffith. What he had not done, though, was spare me so much as a second glance.

Another laugh.

The sound pierced through my heart so sharply it was a wonder I didn't grunt at the pain. Without a second thought, I scooped all of my notes into my bag, heedless of crumpling them beyond recognition. My chair caught on the carpet and nearly fell over as I launched out of it. "I gotta go."

Theo turned away from his latest conquest at the commotion, his face clouded with confusion. "You're leaving?"

I refused to meet his searching gaze and directed my response to the others. "I'll see you guys later."

"Chipmunk." The sympathy in Leah's voice only made my eyes sting more. I feigned straightening my glasses to wipe away a heavy drop before it could spill and destroy the little composure I still had.

"Estoy bien. I'll get caught up another time."

Theo stepped away from the guy as if to stop me, but not before promising to call him later. Pain constricted my chest and threatened to bring me to my knees. I quickly brushed past, keeping my head down lest I completely lose it.

"What was that about?" Theo's question chased me out of the library until I burst through the main doors onto a warm spring day. Except the sun couldn't touch the cold of despair spreading through my chest. I'd tried practically everything short of outright telling him we were in a relationship. In hindsight, maybe I should have been honest about that from the start when he first asked me who I was. But I'd been so stricken that he didn't remember me at all that I'd panicked.

I leaned against the stones of the massive ancient library and gulped for air. My breaking heart, however, seemed to have no intention of slowing its rapid pace. "I don't understand," I said aloud. "I've recreated how we met almost perfectly. Why... why..." A rogue sob cut me off. I squeezed my eyes shut, and the tears I'd been holding back slipped free.

Why won't he look at me?

The truth I'd been avoiding danced at the edge of my grief. I pushed it violently away, back to the wretched depths that had spawned it, but this time it wouldn't be denied. Cold, the likes of which I'd only felt at the shores of the River Styx, seeped into my bones.

What if the only reason he saw you the first time was so he could get your name? Use you? That's all you've ever been to him—a means to an end. Nothing less. Nothing more.

I took off my glasses and scrubbed my face. It couldn't be true. It just... couldn't. I'd watched Theo these past weeks. He was... different, not the Theo I knew.

Did you ever know the real Theo?

I lashed out at the contrary voice in my head. I *did* know Theo. I knew he was careful about touching people because he was afraid of shocking them. I knew he was using magic to hide his natural eye color and hair, because being a Wisteria made him a target. And I knew that no matter how many guys he slept with, he wouldn't stay the night and he wouldn't take any of them back to his place, because he was afraid a vision would blow his cover.

My fingers dug into the fabric of my khakis as I braced myself on my knees. With a shaky hand, I replaced my glasses and forced myself to straighten. I'd always been timid when it came to going after what I wanted. Maybe I needed to be bolder about wanting to be with Theo. Even as I thought it, my heart sank. Bold wasn't really in my wheelhouse.

"What am I going to do?" I asked myself.

"Excuse me, you're Carlos Barrera, right?"

I averted my gaze from my study of the overcast sky. The woman before me stood several inches shorter than me, her light brown hair curling around a round face. She wore a green sundress that seemed to invoke the spirit of spring as it flowed around her full figure. I'd never seen her before in my life.

"How do you know me?" I asked bluntly.

Her hazel eyes dropped to the ground, and she toed a pebble with a sandaled foot. "Theo." She briefly flicked her nervous gaze up. "From before he... I know he doesn't remember."

I pushed off the wall, and she squared her shoulders. "You're one of the witches he was working with."

Her face paled, but she held her ground. "My name is Essen. And... yes. Kavren doesn't remember anything either. If you're worried about that." Truth be told, I hadn't spared the hijo de puta a second thought since he'd walked out of the rubble-filled room. Maybe a small part of me had hoped he'd walked outside and gotten swallowed by a sinkhole, but nothing past that. Theo had consumed all of my thoughts.

"What do you want?" I asked, a little sharper than I might have given different circumstances.

She flinched, but still didn't leave. Instead, she took a deep breath and steadily met my accusatory glare. "I'm sorry. About everything. He... he hid it well, but Theo clearly cared about you." My heart really couldn't take this kind of abuse after spending the last few weeks doing everything short of begging Theo to come back to me.

"You still haven't answered my question. Dime la verdad. I can't handle anymore lies. Why are you here?"

Her gaze finally fell to skitter about the gravel-strewn path. "Theo... Theo said you could help me. Said you'd probably help if I just... asked. That you would likely do it without payment, because that's who you are."

My eyebrows rose in curiosity despite myself. "I don't understand. What are you talking about?"

Her hand went to a shiny silver chain hanging around her neck. She dug out a pendant that glowed red despite no source of light to make it shine. "It's my grandmother."

I swallowed hard and took a nervous step back, but the wall behind me prevented me from going any farther. "Where did you get that?"

She glanced at the ruby and back at me. "It's not possessed anymore. Theo made it glow when he gave it to me. That's also when he told me about what you did. You see, my grandmother's cursed and will end up just like the witch you exorcised if I can't prevent it." She paused only long enough to refill her lungs. "That's why I was working with Kavren. To save her. I was desperate, but... Theo helped me see you aren't a tool.

"You deserve the same happiness the rest of us are chasing. Please, Carlos, help me save my grandmother. It never occurred to any of us that we could just ask *or* that you might say yes. I'm so sorry. We've made so many mistakes, but we need to be better. *I* want to be better." Her hand tightened around the amulet until her knuckles turned white. "I'm begging you, don't let my grandmother suffer like this witch did."

My eyes grew wider with each word that rushed out of her mouth as if she was afraid that if she didn't get them all out at once, she'd never get them out at all. I blinked a few times as I tried to absorb everything she'd said. Theo had talked to her about me? I stared at the pendant glowing between her fingers. She'd been part of the witches that had wanted to hold me captive, use my real name to conquer death, then toss me aside like I was nothing.

But... she worked with Theo.

"Why was he doing it?"

Her face went ghost white. "I... I don't know. He kept his reasons to himself."

"They must have been damn good," I mumbled to myself, falling into the familiar trap of wondering what could have driven Theo. "He transferred from Dreifacher Mond during his final year, after all."

"Did you say Dreifacher Mond? I knew he transferred to Arminius, but I had no idea from where. I can't believe it. We had a bona fide Princeps Sacerdotum, in our midst... Warren is going to blow a gasket when he finds out."

"You didn't know?"

She shook her head. "No, and I'm sorry I can't answer your question about his motivations. Seems Theo shared even less than I thought. I understand if you don't want to help me." Her evident despair plucked at my bleeding heart. While it would be easy to assume she believed I wouldn't help her because of her role in trying to use me, I knew from my conversations with Theo and hearing his own perspective that wasn't all of it. She believed I wouldn't help her because she had nothing to offer in return.

I licked my lips and pushed my glasses up. Theo had believed in me, had told her I could—that I *would* help—because helping people is what I did. Maybe... maybe not all hope was lost. He knew me once. He could know me again. "Tell me about your grandmother."

Her head shot up, eyes brimming with tears, and she gasped out a sob. "Thank you. Thank you so much."

Chapter 28

Carlos

I stuffed my hands into my pockets while the smell of braised pork filled the air. I rolled my head to the side to follow the last patrons of the day leave the small square housing the taco stand. Miguel stuck his head out of the pickup window as if to make sure I was still there. I raised my hand and offered him a sardonic wave. He scowled, then ducked back inside to finish cleaning up for the day. I let out a defeated sigh and pushed my glasses up before once again shoving the appendage in my pocket.

I don't know why I agreed to this.

That was a lie. I missed my cousin. That's why I was here. But I wasn't eager for the lecture that seeing him was likely to bring. Judging by his sour expression, it promised to be a hell of an aturdido. Miguel stepped out and pointed aggressively at one of the ironwork tables. He continued to scowl at me until I shifted off the wall I'd been leaning against for the last half hour. I rolled my eyes and shuffled my feet over the dusty cobblestones as I complied with his silent demands.

The metal was warm from baking in the sun, but shy of burning. Even in late spring, Austria had pleasant weather. I had even needed a light jacket earlier in the morning. Despite the cheery sun overheard, my thoughts turned dark.

Spring with summer right around the corner.

It certainly didn't feel like almost three months since Theo had spelled his memory away. At the same time, it felt like an eternity, an eternity slowly chipping away at my soul and at my resolution.

"That. That shit right there. Eso tiene que parar. This has to stop," Miguel repeated as he stalked up to the table, wagging a finger at me.

I sighed and pushed up my glasses. "What are you talking about?"

His hand smacked onto the table so hard I jumped. "Sabes muy bien de lo que estoy hablando. Don't you dare sit there and pretend you don't know what I'm talking about. Look at you." He waved his hand to take in my overall state. "You're a wreck."

"I'm fine."

Miguel let out a loud, exasperated sigh and dragged both hands through his curly hair. My heart tightened at the gesture, remembering how Theo did the same whenever he was anxious. "No, primo, you're not." He took a seat across from me and rested his forearms on the intricate swirls of iron. "Please, nosotros estamos preocupados por ti."

I scoffed and crossed my arms as I leaned back to put what little distance between us my seat would allow. "What's this 'we' bullshit?"

"Don't pretend you haven't been avoiding me *and* Gabbi. She says you haven't so much as texted in weeks."

I shifted in my seat, no longer appreciating the warmth beneath me. "There hasn't been anything to report."

"Report? Primo, pull your head out of tu trasero."

"Excuse you?"

"You heard me. You've been moping around como un espectro for months."

I narrowed my eyes at my cousin, suddenly rethinking the wisdom of coming here. "Watch yourself, Miguel. That sounds dangerously close to suggesting I'm becoming a spirit like La Llorona."

"Are you?" Miguel asked without missing a beat.

"No," I snapped. "And I didn't come here for a... un... ¿Cómo se dice?" I surged up from my chair as I struggled to find the right word. "Una intervención," I managed at last. "You and Gabbi can take your concerns and accusations and mételos en el culo."

"Primo. Carlos!"

"No," I repeated with all the force I could muster as I attempted to free myself from the heavy seat my shirt was now caught on. "I'm done with this conversation. No debería haber venido aquí." I pushed my glasses up with a hand that shook so badly it might have been safer to take them off altogether.

"You need to let him go. I don't understand how you can still want to be with someone who tried to use you like that."

I rounded on Miguel, my shaking anger loud in my response. "He saved my life!"

"He's the reason your life was in danger in the first place!" It had been a horrible mistake telling Miguel the truth, one I could never take back.

"I don't care."

"You *should* care. I get it. He had everyone fooled. We all believed he was genuine. But face it, primo, he's a witch just like the rest of them," Miguel argued, rising to pursue me in my retreat.

"You're wrong. He had it. He had all the power he needed, and he gave it up."

"It doesn't change the fact that he took advantage of you. Please, primo, te lo ruego, let him go before you find yourself on a path you can't come back from." The danger in his words, the concern, plagued my heart.

I fisted my hands at my sides and squeezed my eyes shut, willing it not to be true. "I love him."

"I understand, but—" His mouth snapped shut as my eyes flew open and I speared him with a ferocious glare.

"I love him, and I'm not giving up." I turned on my heel without sparing a backward glance and marched out of the intimate square I'd come to with the misguided hope of receiving compassion and support.

Theo

My fingers slipped through thick locks, tangling and tightening as pleasure wrapped around my spine. I groaned into the darkness, my fingers once again convulsing in the soft hair. Man had one hell of a talented tongue that seemed determined to keep me at the edge, aching with need. He pulled off, then ventured up my torso, his full lips planting hot kisses along my abdomen and chest until at last they reached my mouth.

I curled a hand around his shoulder, urging the kiss deeper even as I ground up into him. His moan vibrated through me, and suddenly I couldn't wait any longer. I desperately needed to be inside of him. We rolled, and his hands found my ass. He gripped tightly, pushing me forward to rub our erections together, the glide gloriously smooth. Our dual moans echoed in the room consumed by night and hiding him from my sight.

What's his name?

I dismissed the thought as fast as it came. My sex-addled brain couldn't be expected to provide such details confronted with sensations like this. I knew his name, of course I knew his name. If only I could see him, it would certainly come back to me. Except, the only light in the room was coming from the faint glow of purple where my hands coasted possessively over his sides. My entire body jerked as I registered my magic being used. I'd never—*would* never—risk a partner's life like that, or exposure.

This is a dream.

I refused to let reality spoil the moment. Not to mention, as far as fantasies went, it felt real enough. I slid into the delusion that I could ever have something like this without fear and deep into him. His gasp resonated in my core, and I found his mouth once more. He tangled his gifted tongue with mine while his fingers carded through my hair.

"Theo." The husky whisper set every nerve aflame, and my heart stuttered in my chest. Not even the heat wrapped around me could rival the burn in my chest, a burn of want and longing... and love.

Need to know.

If the glow of my hands was all I had to see by, then I'd be damned if I wouldn't manipulate this dream to figure out why it felt so real.

Who are you?

My hands slid along his torso, past dark nipples and a smattering of darker hair, as they inched slowly toward their destination, dragging purple galaxies in their wake.

Is this a vision?

It didn't feel like one, and I hadn't had a real vision in months. I'd be worried if I wasn't also relieved. I rolled my hips, and he arched off the bed, baring his throat. My thumb brushed lightly over his Adam's apple while my heart hammered a crazy rhythm, equal parts anticipation and hovering at the edge of the precipice.

Almost.

His head started to lower, and my hand ventured to his cheek. Meanwhile, my other hand wrapped around his pulsing cock between us. His entire body seized, and the wave I'd been staving off crashed me into oblivion as he tightened around me.

I lurched up, breathing hard and drenched in sweat, my shirt twisted around me. "Son of a fucking bitch," I hissed and ripped off the sheets. While the creeping stain of cum on my sweats wasn't a surprise, it only further enraged me. "That's it, no more. I'm done with this shit." I scrabbled out of the rumpled bed and made short work of the soiled clothes, yanking on fresh pants with a tad more force than necessary and straightening my shirt nearly hard enough to tear it.

The door to the bedroom hit the wall with a loud smack as I made my way into the living space. "I need to get laid for real. No more of this deluded fantasy bullshit."

Sigurd's head popped up at my angry diatribe. I glared at him. Because apparently my vivid, repeating sex dreams were his fault as well as my months-long dry spell. He twitched his tail at me unhelpfully. Not that I'd expected any input. He'd been exceptionally tight-lipped since I'd returned to find him nearly devoid of all magic, including the magic that extended his life and kept him tethered to me. Restoring him while also being magically bankrupt had been a tricky endeavor and not a process I was eager to repeat.

I stalked across the room to the narrow desk. Of the three drawers, I reached for the one on the right, which was where

I'd squirreled away all the numbers I'd acquired over the last fourteen weeks. Hell, if I knew what compulsion had led me to discard all of them without so much as a single call, but suddenly I was grateful that the same compulsion had made me keep them.

My fingers hovered centimeters away from the handle when a massive gray paw slashed out.

I snatched my arm back as three sizable welts started bleeding red. "What the fuck!" I held the injured arm against my chest and made to reach out with the other.

Sigurd let out a low, menacing growl that instantly made all the hair on the back of my neck stand up.

I bared my teeth at him in a snarl while he squatted on the desk, his bushy tail thrashing high above him. "What is your problem?" No response. "I can call whomever I want. It's *my* life."

His growl lowered an octave, and his nails slipped free to scrape threateningly on the worn wood.

"Fine! Fine. Keep the damn numbers or whatever it is you've hidden in there. I'll get new ones."

The nails disappeared, and the growl eased up, but he didn't move. Finally, with a huff, I rerouted to the kitchen to clean up the stinging disaster on my arm. I hissed at the pain as I pressed a wet towel into the freely bleeding wounds and started searching for the first-aid kit.

"You better not give me bubonic plague or something, you mangy beast. I oughta punt your fluffy ass outside for that shit!" I hollered back at my familiar, who unsurprisingly had not vacated the aged teal desk.

My fingers found the small box containing the meager medical supplies. I pulled it down and set it on the counter next to a letter that hadn't been there a second ago. "What do we have here?" I mused as I broke the nearly black, red seal. An

elegant script flowed across the thick vellum page, highlighted with gold. I read it all the way through, then read it again.

A snicker slipped free as I let the elaborate, personalized letter
fall back to the counter. They may not know my true identity,
but they knew I was gifted, important, and unquestionably
connected. I couldn't even imagine how much they'd trip over
themselves if they knew I was a Wisteria and could see the
future. My mouth turned down into a frown. Considering all
the applicants had signed in blood, it was quite possible they *did*

know and were merely saving the information to use at some advantageous time.

I shook myself to loose the sudden funk. This was good news. Whatever their agenda, they were still the premiere academy for witches, and they were willing to take me back mid-semester, no questions asked. Where I expected relief, tightness filled my chest. Why wasn't I excited to go back to the school that had been all I'd ever dreamed about? A way to get out, to be free? Yet, here I was at some lackluster university open to all, and I... didn't want to leave.

What's wrong with me? I should be leaping at this chance.

I balled my hand into a fist, and fresh streaks of red made their way down my arm. "Damn it." I debated going to the infirmary as I pressed a cotton swab saturated with disinfectant on the last scratch. Then my gaze caught on the time. "Fuck." I dropped the swab into the waste bin, snagged a small foil filled with antibiotic, and scooped up my backpack. "Look what you've done," I continued to berate the cat. "Now I'm going to be late for my study group. I don't even know why I joined the stupid thing in the first place. It has nothing to do with my major, and half the time it's awkward as fuck."

An image of Carlos Barrera with dirt all over his face and his round glasses cracked beyond all repair came to mind. Of course, he was why I'd agreed. He seemed to be the only person willing to talk to me, almost like we'd been close before I'd lost my memory. Like friends.

I snorted to myself as I toed on my shoes. "As much time as I spend with the guy, you'd think I'd have gotten his number by now."

I paused and considered that for a moment. Why *hadn't* I tried to pick up Carlos? He was definitely cute in that I've-been-a-nerd-my-whole-life sort of way, if a tad skinny. And his blushes were a special kind of adorable. As it was, I was practically orbiting him. So... why not?

I shouldered my bag and spared one last hateful look at my familiar. "Probably has something to do with the fact that he barely looks at me and walks around on eggshells like I'm going to smite him. It's ridiculous." I grumbled to myself—more put out than I cared to admit—that the reason I hadn't hit on Carlos was because he seemed to have zero interest in me. "Not all witches are bad," I added glumly. "So what if he's a demon? What do I care?"

Sigurd's tail flopped heavily from side to side, his eyes shining emerald in the afternoon light as he stared at me.

"Don't look at me like that. I don't. Even if he is a demon of death, nothing he does will change my future. I'm already slated to die. Might as well make the most of whatever time I have left." With that, I pulled the door shut and raced over to the library on campus to meet with a guy that I probably still wouldn't hit on, even after that little speech.

Chapter 29

Carlos

I straightened my notebook for what had to be the millionth time and looked toward the stacks anyone approaching this table would have to venture through. Theo was late. He was never late.

Does this mean he's not coming?

Did I miss my chance?

A familiar ache spreads through my chest, winding its way through my body to reach all the way to my fingertips and the soles of my feet. Miguel's argument rang loud in my mind. I stood by what I'd said, though. Theo wasn't the villain Miguel needed him to be, the villain *I* needed him to be. He was a witch of a different caliber and had sacrificed everything to keep me safe—even from himself. Perhaps it was time I returned the favor.

The table bounced and tilted as I pushed my glasses up. I tucked my hand beneath my leg to hide how badly it was shaking and took a steadying breath that only made me feel fainter. If I truly loved Theo, I'd let him go. My heart thumped painfully in my chest, and I squeezed my eyes shut as I forced myself to think about what I'd been avoiding for weeks.

Theo's memory wasn't coming back, probably never would. My breath came in short gasps. He'd likely lied when he said it was possible they might return to prevent me from stopping him from doing the spell. Which I would have in a heartbeat. I didn't care if Theo knew my true name. I trusted him, even if he didn't trust himself. Hell, I'd tell him it myself if I thought it would change anything. But it wouldn't. I knew that now. The Theo I'd fallen in love with was gone. In his place was some earlier version that didn't trust anyone and wouldn't look at me twice.

"Hey," Theo said. I slowly raised my head as he dropped his bag to the floor and took the seat beside me, where he promptly started removing his books and notes.

"What happened to your arm?" I asked, catching sight of the greasy red marks streaked in glaring contrast to his pale arm.

He glanced down at the injured appendage briefly before resuming settling in. "My stupid familiar."

"Sigurd attacked you?" Worry spiked through me, momentarily eclipsing my grief.

Theo's head whipped around. "It's nothing." He seemed to debate saying more, but asked, "Where is everyone?"

"Not here," I responded, my voice coming out more of a croak as my grief returned twofold.

"Oh? Why not?"

I wanted to do this in private.

My heart broke all over again as he immediately turned away and focused all of his attention on the morning's lesson.

I can't do this. I'm not strong enough.

"So... where are they?" he asked again, still not looking at me. If the last of my hope died any louder, it would start attracting attention. Theo remained oblivious, his yellow highlighter squeaking across the page. "Is the group disbanding or something?" The note of disappointment was likely a figment of my imagination, a final ember of desperate hope flaring one last time.

I swallowed hard and extricated my hand from beneath me in order to straighten my glasses. "Theo."

"Yeah?" He reached across the table to flip to a new page in the text.

"Theo," I said more forcefully.

He started and leaned back in his chair slowly, but refused to look at me. Suddenly, he leaned forward again and snapped his book shut, then promptly jerked it off the table and stuffed it in his bag. "Look, if the group is dissolving, you could've just told me. There was no need for this... this... *production.*" Each angry word hit me like a physical blow until I couldn't stand it anymore.

I hooked a finger under his chin and turned him gently to face me. He blinked those baby blues at me, questions and a touch of hurt apparent in their depths. Against my better judgment, I shifted to cup the side of his face, soaking up the warmth of his cheek one last time. Sorrow swelled in my chest as I stared at the man who had stolen my heart.

"Carlos?"

Tears sprang to my eyes unbidden at hearing my first name on his lips for the first time since he'd lost his memory. "Sh," I whispered as I brushed a thumb lightly over his cheek and willed the tears not to fall.

Before I could second-guess myself, I leaned forward and pressed our lips together. A tiny spark of lightning arced between us. He let out a small gasp, and our breaths mingled for a bittersweet second until I pulled away. He didn't pursue me, and what was left of my breaking heart finished shattering. I swallowed past the emotions clogging my throat and said the three words I'd sworn to myself I wouldn't.

"I love you." *Goodbye.*

Theo

Time hung suspended around me as I stared at Carlos and fought the simultaneous urge to yank him back for another kiss and the need to hold him close. The unshed tears hanging heavy on his lashes made my chest hurt, while the tingling in my lips had me ready to burst with light. I licked my lips, tasting the bittersweetness of his kiss. Slowly, as if stepping free of a fog, dozens of kisses flooded my memory—passionate, sweet, desperate, loving.

Carlos.

My heart threatened to soar right out of my chest, while a sense of inevitability settled over me. Finally, *finally*, I'd found my way to the one vision that mattered. The smile that spread across my face wouldn't be contained as I said the words that would bring everything full circle.

"I knew I could get you to say I love you first."

Carlos drew in a sharp breath, and his gaze flicked to mine. My smile broadened at the hope I saw shimmering in his warm brown eyes. "Theo?"

"Hey, baby."

His hand flew to his mouth to stifle a sob. The move caused the pooled tears to streak unhindered down his face. "Is... is it really you?"

In lieu of answering, I reached up and dragged my fingers through my hair, turning the platinum to lavender. Another sob tore free of him, then he was leaning forward again and snaring me with a salty kiss. I tangled my fingers in his thick curls and returned the fierce kiss as if it could ease the ache of need in my chest and his.

Abruptly, he pressed a hand into my chest and pushed me away. I watched as his tongue glided over swollen lips and he struggled to process what was happening. "It really is you."

"Who else would it be?" I teased, so fucking happy I thought I might explode.

Just like that, his tentative hope flashed to anger. "Lo juro por Dios, if this has all been some elaborate scheme to get me to say it first, I will *personally* rip your soul from your body and escort it across the veil." I was viscerally aware of the blood draining from my face. This wasn't at all like this was supposed to go. I was back. We were together. That's all I'd ever wanted. We'd fought for this.

"Carlos—" I reached out, desperate to reassure him, only to have my hand slapped away. I swallowed past a surge of unease. "You did it, baby. You found me. I knew you would."

"No."

I recoiled at the vehemence of the declaration. "What?"

"Do you have any idea of the hell I've been through these last four months? I want an explanation, and I want it now." Where he'd been shaking with nerves when I'd arrived, he was undoubtedly shaking with anger now.

"Carlos," I tried again.

"*Now.*"

I glanced around at all the eyes our conversation was attracting. "Maybe this would be a chat better held elsewhere? I'll answer any question you have, baby, I promise. But not here. Okay?" I worried my bottom lip while I waited for him to respond.

His eyes narrowed to angry slits, not unlike the death glare Sigurd had given me earlier. "Answer one thing for me first."

"Anything," I said, a hair too quickly, and prayed he wouldn't ask anything too dangerous where so many prying ears could overhear.

"Your memory loss. Was it all a ruse to get me to say I love you first?" The danger glittering in his eyes made it clear there was most definitely a right answer.

"No." I let out a defeated sigh and wished more than anything that there was some other answer I could give beyond the muddled truth. "And yes."

He relaxed only to immediately puff up again, then scooped all of his untouched books back in his bag. "¿Qué clase de respuesta es esa?" he snapped, fury evident in every line of his body. "Me voy. I should have left a long time ago instead of torturing myself." He stood, zipping his bag so violently I feared for its contents.

I shot out of my chair and grabbed his arm before he could storm off. "Please, Carlos. I can explain. I can. Come back to my apartment. I'll show you everything you want to know. Please, please don't leave." He eyed me warily, and I dimly became aware of the magic leeching out of me to suffuse his warm, tan skin. I tightened my hold and swallowed. "Please."

He nodded stiffly, and I magicked the rest of my books into my backpack in order to keep up with him as he stalked out of the library. We walked in silence back to my apartment, my trepidation growing with each step. What if he didn't understand? What if he couldn't forgive me? I couldn't even feign ignorance of my actions over the last four months. I remembered everything now. Every face, every flirtation, the judging looks from the rest of the study group... and Carlos' stoic silence through it all.

My steps stalled meters from my chipped red door. Carlos had most definitely been through a living hell. I certainly wouldn't forgive me. Why did I expect he would? I dragged my gaze away from the cracked walkway to meet his stern one.

Because he didn't give up.

Because he's here.

"Change your mind already?" The challenge in his question spoke volumes about his level of hurt. My chest spasmed in response. I'd give anything, *anything* to take that away, but more than that, I wanted to prove to him we had a future together, even if it was a short one.

I cleared my throat and stepped up beside him onto the crowded landing. The key clicked in the lock, and I pushed open the door. "Never."

Carlos

Anxiety ran rampant through me as Theo led the way into the apartment. After all the days, all the sleepless nights, I'd given up hope that this moment would ever come. Yet here we were. Theo glanced over his shoulder as he walked deeper into the space, like he wasn't sure I'd follow. The door clicked shut behind me, and for a tiny second, every instinct screamed this was a trap. I took a deep breath and let it out slowly. As much as my head didn't believe this was real, my heart needed to know.

"We're here. Explícate."

"Right. I..." He twisted his hands together and looked over at the far wall. Before he could venture any closer to it, a head popped up from the couch.

I had just enough time to register tufted ears when a streak of gray zipped across the room. The massive feline didn't hesitate to catapult himself into my arms. I let out an "Oof" at the sudden weight, and a rebellious smile slipped free as I threaded my fingers through his long, soft fur. Sigurd pressed his head under my chin and purred hard enough to rattle my bones.

"He missed you." Theo's soft voice was barely audible over the thunderous noise vibrating through my chest.

My gaze flicked up from the happy cat to an obviously sad Theo, and my smile slipped. "¿Y tu?"

Pain flashed across his face. He turned and finished walking toward the far wall, then paused. "You once asked if I'd had any visions about you."

I set Sigurd down and stepped closer, his tone making me anxious. "Sí."

"I told you I could only share the ones that had already come to pass."

"The future is uncertain," I echoed from what felt like eons ago.

He nodded. "These are the ones I didn't share." He waved his hand, and a ripple passed over the wall. In a matter of seconds, it went from bland, painted plaster to a chaos of strings and pinned notes.

My eyes widened as I took in the multitude of colors stretching from pin to pin and clusters of paper. "Theo, what is all of this?"

"When I was six years old, my grandmother gave me a prophecy... about my death."

I ripped my attention away from the wall that looked more and more like a murder board the longer I stared at it. "That's—"

He held up a hand, sadness clear in his eyes. "Please let me finish."

I closed my mouth and offered a small nod.

He let out a shaky breath. "I have spent my entire life since trying to subvert that prophecy. Everything I've done has been in pursuit of that. It's why I transferred schools, why I found you, and why... why I planned to use your true name."

My heart sank with each word. Miguel had been right. What a fool I'd been to think someone like Theo could ever really love me. I quickly wiped away a sudden tear. Just when I thought my heart couldn't break anymore than it already had, here it was cracking loud enough to raise the dead.

"I shouldn't have made you bring me here. I'll go." I turned to beat as hasty a retreat as I could and still maintain some modicum of dignity, but a hand wrapped lightly around my arm pulled me up short. Tingles radiated from the contact, small sparklers dancing along my skin that I'd never thought I'd feel again. I squeezed my eyes shut against a fresh wave of heartache. "Please, Theo." My voice cracked on his name, and it took every ounce of self-preservation I had left to finish. "Let me go."

"Wait. Please, you can still go if you want, but please let me finish. I owe you this much, at the very least." He glanced down at where his hand rested on my arm, then slowly released me.

I tried to ignore the pain of its absence and turned back to face him. "Okay."

He gave me a curt nod and stepped up to one array of sticky notes. "You'll recognize most of these. The study group in the library. Racing back to your dorm. Seeing you with Sigurd." He pointed at the corresponding notes as he spoke, building a timeline of our time together. His finger came to rest on a note, and a smile ghosted across his lips. "In the closet at your house."

I ignored the pain that spiked through my heart at the beautiful memory and gestured to an alarming cluster of black strings. "And those? What does the black mean?"

His face lost all expression. "Black means death."

I took an involuntary step forward. Abbreviated notes jumped out at me in lurid detail. Everywhere my gaze fell, it found a different death, each more horrific than the last, and names, many of which were repeated. "Essen, Warren, Kavren..." Only two of those I had a face for, but it was how they died that made my stomach churn. All the blood drained from my face as the final name leapt out amid a myriad of notes pinned haphazardly one on top of another.

My hand shook as I fingered the note on top. *Severed soul.* I ripped it off. *Strangling.* Another. *Knife through the heart.* My stomach heaved, and the acrid smell of bile burned my nose.

"No. It's not possible." In a frenzy, I tore another and another, but no matter how many I removed, they all were the same.

"Carlos..." Theo's placating tone snatched my attention away from the horror before me.

I whirled to face him, crumpling the torn notes in a white-knuckled grip and shaking my head. "These say you die." Bile threatened to crawl up my throat and right out of my mouth. I swallowed it down. "They say *I* kill you." I turned my panicked gaze back to the other names and looked closer. Several of their deaths were also at my hands. "No. I... I'm not..." I stammered, unable to wrap my head around what I was seeing. "I'm not a killer."

"Sh, it's okay, baby. I was never going to let that happen. Never. You understand me? Whatever the cost, I would have paid it."

My throat constricted at the obvious emotion in his voice, and what I hoped was sincerity. "When—" My voice cracked. I cleared my throat and tried again. "When did you have these?"

"I had the first one the morning after we returned from Oaxaca."

The room pitched in time with my stomach's violent heave. I stumbled backward, my hand flying to suppress a gasp. If my head shook any harder, I'd lose my glasses. "But... that was five months ago. You've been living with this the whole time? How could you keep seeing me? How could you keep..." I let it hang, because I couldn't bring myself to ask him how he'd stomached having sex with someone that he'd seen kill him... numerous times. I searched his face, terrified that the real reason was because he was that desperate to save his own life... at the expense of mine. "How?" I repeated.

"Because I love you." I blinked back at him even as a laugh burst out of him. He clutched his hand to his chest and looked at me. "You have no idea how good that feels to finally say out loud."

I frowned. "I'm not following."

"I love you. I've been in love with you for months." His smile radiated from his face as he stepped toward me.

"Why didn't you say anything before?" I asked, my confusion finding new levels.

"I wanted to—so many times—but..." He glanced back at the wall of horrors, then dropped his gaze to the floor. "Every time I thought about telling you the truth, how I felt, why I was here, everything..." He gestured to the black lines.

"No creo eso. I *can't* believe that. You're telling me that admitting how you felt resulted in people dying, in my becoming un asesino?"

He winced at the force of my words. "You have to understand. I tried every angle I could think of, wracked my brain to come up with a different path." He pointed to a pinned note. "Even running away together. Despite leveraging every spell I could think of, Kavren still found us. He was so furious that he tortured us, then buried us alive with a curse."

"Mierda."

"Yeah," he sighed and ran a hand through his hair, his gaze distant, as if reliving the atrocity. "There was only one vision I had that gave me any sort of hope." His fingers brushed a sticky note far removed from the others, with a white pin and no strings connecting it to anything else, like an island of light in a sea of darkness. Understanding finally sank in.

"You needed me to say it first."

"I'm so sorry, Carlos. I wanted to tell you. I almost did once. It didn't go well." His forlorn gaze fell once more to the floor.

I stared at him in silence while Sigurd weaved through my legs and I absorbed everything he'd said. Then it clicked. My heart instantly ached for him. "That night. When you had the seizure."

He nodded and looked back at me, sadness filling his eyes. "I don't expect you to forgive me."

I turned to face the wall again and the staggering array of visions Theo had endured in the brief time we'd known each other. Notes connected by dizzying colors clustered together in sections denoting good, bad, and worse. My gaze traveled over each group, tracing the lines to each consequence. From this angle, the grouped notes kind of resembled the constellations Theo had pointed out when he'd taken me stargazing. I couldn't help but wonder if he'd had an ulterior motive or if it had been a vision that had sent him racing off.

How much of our relationship was real?

I reached out to touch a lone white post-it note, no strings, no extra notes, just two words—mi corazón. *My heart.* I flashed back to the first and last time I'd said those words to Theo. I'd never been more scared in my life than when Theo had been in the throes of that seizure—not when Nessa had kidnapped me, not when I'd woken up in an orange circle I couldn't escape, and not when Kavren had taken complete control of me using a name I didn't even know I had. I'd been afraid because I loved Theo.

I scratched my nail over the scribbled Spanish. I meant to ask about the note, since technically this had already happened, but that was not what came out of my mouth. "How many did you sleep with?"

Chapter 30

Theo

It took me a second to process what Carlos was asking. He wanted to know how many guys I'd had sex with since we'd been apart. It was a fair question, to be sure, though not the one I'd been expecting. I looked deep into his brown eyes at the fear and doubt flickering there and suddenly knew the real reason I'd kept all the numbers.

"None."

He gave a derisive snort. "I find that hard to believe." Of course he would. I'd been a shameless flirt before I'd met him, and worse when I'd forgotten him, desperate to fill a void I couldn't name.

"I'm serious, not a one. Never even called them." I walked past him to get to the teal desk that Sigurd had kept me away from before. This time, he didn't stop me as I pulled open the drawer. My stomach swooped uncomfortably at the sight of all the scraps of paper with their scribbled numbers nestled inside.

"I fail to see how that is supposed to convince me." He crossed his arms across his chest while he fought to keep the hurt from his face. I yanked out my phone, unlocked it, and slammed it on the desk. His arms loosened slightly, and he jumped at the abrupt noise.

"Check my call history. You'll see, none of these numbers has ever been dialed." Disbelief clouded his face, and panic gripped me. He had to believe me. "If you're convinced I've deleted the history, I know a witch who's great with tech spells. She also kind of hates me, so she'll be more than willing to scrounge up any dirt she can get her pointed nails on." I moved to stand in front of him and stopped shy of reaching for his hand. "I promise, not a single call, not a single touch."

Please believe me. I can't lose you again.

As I stood waiting for an answer that might never come, the magic hiding my eyes wore off. I'd never been so physically aware of how exposed and naked that made me feel as I stared fearfully back at the only man I'd ever trusted with the truth. I had no right to ask for his forgiveness, but that didn't change how much I wanted it. My life had been empty and meaningless before Carlos, an endless quest to stop the inevitable. Meeting him had reminded me how beautiful life could be, that it was worth living now, not eventually.

"It's only you," I added as the silence stretched my nerves tighter. My heart hammered against my ribs, torn between beating out of my chest and stopping altogether.

Carlos chewed on his bottom lip, his eyes searching my face from behind his glasses. Then, his full mouth tilted up in a tentative smile. "Deja de hablar y bésame ya." Hope burst like a damn inside of me.

"Still don't speak Spanish," I responded with a half-smile.

"We'll have to fix that." Before I could process the promise of his words, Carlos reached for my face and mashed our mouths together.

For a split second, I froze, not sure if I'd finally gone mad or not. Then, the heat of him registered, the subtle hint of spices from his cologne, the taste of his lips. I kissed him back every bit as fiercely. His fingers tangled in my hair, and he pulled me closer, deepening the kiss and stealing my senses.

"I love you, Theobald Wisteria."

A groan that bordered on a growl rose out of me. I nipped at his bottom lip before sucking his tongue back into my mouth. He moaned into me and tried to pull me closer. I slipped my hands beneath his shirt to caress his sides. He whimpered, and I was glad I'd kept the voltage low. I teased his lips while he adjusted to the sensation he hadn't felt for months. Only when he let out a stuttering breath did I venture more, the intensity of the lightning dancing along his skin slowly increasing. He rubbed against me every bit as hard as I was and moaned again.

"Tell me how you like it, baby," I whispered, my voice husky and ragged. My fingers scraped along his back, spreading arcs of electricity everywhere they roved.

He gasped, breaking the kiss. His head fell back, and his breath came in uneven spurts while I continued to up the voltage. He let out a groan that sounded like it'd been scooped from his core. "There, there," he panted, and I almost came on the spot, completely untouched. "Eso es perfecto. Dios, Theo. Necesito más. Por favor más."

I groaned against his throat while my hands continued their exploration of whatever they could reach of him. "I love you." I pressed a hot kiss on his neck. "I love you." My fingers dug into his hips, crushing him against me and pushing my magic deeper. "I love you."

He whimpered again and clung to me through it all. His reactions told me everything he hadn't said. The hurt I'd caused wouldn't go away overnight, but he was still here, still mine. I abandoned my hold on him in order to drag his face back to mine, capturing him in a kiss that conquered him as much as it conquered me. Whatever it took to regain his trust, I'd do it.

Carlos

My brain forgot how to function as Theo claimed me in all the ways I'd needed him to these last four months. Electricity twisted with desire and brought me to the edge of melting into a boneless jellyfish right there in the middle of his apartment. I scraped together what was left of my senses and finally squeaked out, "Bedroom."

Theo snatched at my lips one last time, then with a wordless growl dragged me into the bedroom like un cavernícola. And mierda, if I didn't love it. We tore at each other's clothes in a flurry of hands, but always coming fiercely back together and always that electric touch. Theo only paused when he reached for my glasses. He arched a questioning brow and waited for me to nod before removing them and magicking the frames to the nightstand.

I tangled my fingers in his lavender hair and yanked his mouth back to mine, because, fuck if that didn't make me love him more. It didn't matter how many times we'd been intimate; he always checked in, had from the start. My heart rioted with feeling as we stumbled back toward the bed. How could I ever doubt this man? Even when he'd been supposedly using me, he'd still put my thoughts and feelings before his own.

The mattress sank beneath our combined weight, the cool kiss of sheets at my back in contrast to the heat of Theo on top of me. I moaned at the ecstasy of sensation, a thousand tiny sparklers dancing up my torso, and the man who had stolen my heart touching me like I was the most treasured thing in the world. A tide of emotion welled up inside me, an infinite sadness tinged with sharp pangs of joy. I bit my cheek and looked back at the headboard as I willed the stinging in my eyes to go away.

"What's wrong?" Theo's concern stabbed at my heart.

All the feelings I'd held at bay since he'd asked me who I was came rushing in. I took a shuddering breath, and the traitorous tears escaped.

Theo caressed my cheek and gently wiped the salty streams away. "Hey, don't cry, baby. I'm right here. Sh, sh, I'm right here and I'm not going anywhere."

My chest spasmed, and a sob broke free. "I missed you so much."

His gaze softened, and he stroked my cheeks with his thumbs, trailing subtle sparklers. "I missed you too."

I barked out what was meant to be an ironic laugh, but it came out more of a disbelieving sob. "How can you miss someone you don't remember?" My lip quivered, and I sank my teeth into it before I could completely fall apart.

He leaned down and gently tugged it free, then brushed his lips against my now very salty mouth. "I dreamed about you, about our time together. Before you ask, no, I didn't know it was you I was fantasizing about, but this," he took my hand and placed it over his heart, "wasn't willing to let you go."

A sob wracked my body as the dam officially broke. He shimmied back enough to scoop me in his arms and held me close. I clung to him as if he were a life raft as I cried into his shoulder. My arms wrapped tightly around him like they could prevent him from ever leaving again. I'd thought these last few months had wrung out every tear I had. I was wrong.

The room grew dark while my heart simultaneously broke and tried to mend itself. Never once did Theo shift or try to pull away. If anything, he held me tighter.

Finally, when there was nothing left to purge of my heartache, I pulled back. To my surprise, the amethyst eyes looking back at me were rimmed with red and framed with damp, lavender lashes.

"Sorry," I said, my voice hoarse and my head pounding. He ran his thumbs under my puffy eyes, and some of the pressure eased.

"Don't apologize, my love." Despite how many times he'd said it now, my heart still skipped to hear it.

I offered a watery smile. "This isn't exactly el reconexíon apasionada I envisioned."

"If you need space and want to go, I understand." There he was, checking in again, willing to give me all the time I needed, even though his eyes looked like that was the last thing in the world he wanted.

"I'd... I'd actually like to stay. If that's okay?"

He surged forward and snared me with a kiss that made my heart flutter.

"Ew, I'm gross," I argued, half-heartedly pushing him away.

"You're perfect."

"Mentiroso."

"Still don't speak Spanish."

"And we have all the time in the world to fix that." I cupped his face, fully prepared to kiss him again, despite that I was a snotty mess.

"About that." He gently took my hands and held them in his. "*Theo.*"

He took a deep breath and let it out slowly, then finally raised his gaze from our joined hands. "The prophecy could still be in play."

"But…" I looked past him in the direction of the wall covered in possible futures.

He squeezed my hands and brought my attention back to him. "I know what we've been through, and it's entirely possible that I have subverted the prophecy, but prophecies are a tricky business. They rarely mean what you think they do, and by the time you realize that, it's too late."

My poor, abused heart sank. "What are you saying?"

"I could still die. It could be tomorrow, next month, maybe a year from now."

"Is there any way to be certain? You have foresight, there has to be something you can—" I cut myself off mid sentence. Wasn't that exactly what Theo had done? Used his visions to navigate an uncertain future? And what had that gotten us? Nearly killed, heartache, and more uncertainty.

"Speaking to my grandmother would help, but I haven't seen or heard from her in years. I'm not even sure I could find her. She's always been a wily old bat and more astute than most at hiding in plain sight. But…" He paused and licked his lips. "But if it's okay with you, I'd like to spend whatever time I have left with you."

"Cuidado, that sounds awful close to vows," I teased, desperate to find some light in all of this darkness.

"Do you want them to be?"

His sincerity struck a chord in me I didn't even know I had. "What if I do?"

A soft smile lit his face and shone in his eyes. "Then they are."

I coughed out a laugh and rubbed my face. "Are we really doing this right now?"

"Why not?" He shrugged, and I laughed again, more light-hearted than I'd ever been in my life.

"Because I'm a lío cubierto de mocos."

He trailed a buzzing finger from my crown to my chin. The tears dried, the puffiness went down, and the snot vanished.

"There's magic for that?" He gave me a cheeky grin, and I rolled my eyes. "Of course there is." I reached for my glasses, but he was already holding them for me. I bit my lip to stop from smiling like un cabrón as I took them and slid them onto my face.

"Full disclosure. You'll pay for that later. All magic—"

"Has a price," I finished for him. "I believe you were asking me something?" My stupid smile slipped free, mirroring the one gracing his own lips.

"Is it weird that I'm proposing while we're naked?"

A laugh bubbled out of me, genuine and freeing. "This is us. It might be weirder if we weren't."

"Fair point." He chuckled, then he took a deep breath, and his playfulness took on a more serious note. "Carlos, nothing would make me happier than to spend the rest of my life with you. Be it a day, a decade, or a century, I want every minute to be with you. My life was so empty before you came into it." He cupped the side of my face, and I leaned into the caress. "I know we didn't come together under the most honest circumstances, and I never expected to fall in love with such an amazing person."

My cheeks burned, and I tried to duck away. "I'm not *that* great." I pushed my glasses up to cover my embarrassment.

"But you are." His mouth twitched with a smile. "I love the way you mess with your glasses whenever you're anxious. I love how adorable you are when you blush. I love how you can be shy, but you're also incredibly confident, especially in the bedroom," he added with a wink.

"Are you calling me a bossy bottom?" I scoffed.

"You are absolutely a bossy bottom and a wonderfully tender lover. I love how your compassion knows no bounds. I love how you didn't run away when you learned about my powers. I love how you stood up to your mom for me. And I love how you accept everything I am."

My heart thudded hard, and my eyes misted. "Ay Dios mío, Theo, please tell me we're nearing the end before I start crying again."

He stroked the side of my face, and his amethyst eyes held all the love I'd ever wanted. "Juan Carlos Barrera Velazquez, will you marry me?"

I nearly burst into tears anyway. "Sí, yes. Oh my God, yes. Theobald Tibalt Marcel Wisteria, I will absolutely spend the rest of my life with you." I threw my arms around his neck and pulled him close for a kiss, mercifully free of salt or snot. When he pulled away and looked back at me, though, there was still a nugget of doubt in his eyes.

"I can't promise you decades of growing old together. I meant what I said. I could die tomorrow."

"That goes for everyone, Theo. And you forget, death is no barrier to me." I flashed to my Kisin form and barely switched back in time to prevent Theo from cracking his face on pure bone as he pushed me back into the pillow. The kiss started with all the fire and passion our relationship had begun with, then evolved into deep pulls that set my soul alight the same way Theo's magical touch did to my body. "I love you," I gasped out when I had breath to spare.

"I love you too." Sparklers trailed down my side, and I arched into him.

"Theo," I groaned, suddenly back where we'd started and desperate for him.

"Hands and knees, handsome," he hummed against my throat.

Chapter 31

Carlos

Theo phased through my bedroom wall with a cheeky grin and a dark promise in his eyes. My first instinct was to admonish him for being here in the first place, my second, to call for reinforcements. The house was filled to the brim with family and anyone of them could be here in a matter of moments with a single shout.

I did neither. Instead, I put my glasses back on the nightstand and pulled the covers back in invitation and blatant disregard for the very real danger of getting caught together today of all days. Ten minutes later found me on my hands and knees, my sleep pants tossed who-knew-where, and at his complete mercy. The last of my doubts vanished as his tongue plunged deep in my ass followed by a finger sparkling with electricity.

"¡Coño! Dios mío. Hagas lo que hagas, no te pares." I writhed beneath him, already seeing double. "Are you sure the silencing spell worked?"

He nipped lightly at my sensitive rim, and I nearly swallowed my tongue. "It works." My arms gave out and my chest sank into the bed at the same time as a groan rolled through me.

"Mierda. Te quiero. Te quiero mucho," I moaned, my words all but lost in the multitude of blankets. "Pero si no me mete la polla en el culo pronto, voy a morir." Okay, I probably wouldn't *die* if he didn't get his dick in me right this second, but it sure felt like it.

He slid his fingers slowly in and out one last time, taking care to brush my prostate. I whimpered, and my hold on the base of my cock tightened. Theo may have been a good witch, but there was something unholy in how fast he could get me to the edge and keep me there. He placed a tender kiss at the base of my spine as his fingers shifted to kneading the globes of my ass. I sighed heavily into the mattress at the momentary reprieve.

"You still with me, baby?" The gentleness of the question, the affection, the love, filled me with thousands of dancing lights.

"Siempre."

His hands coasted delicate waves of sparkling energy along my back and sides as he repositioned. He stole a precious few more minutes of torture as he added lube to the equation. Finally, he pressed slowly inside. Our moans filled the hopefully sound-proofed room, and my body turned to pudding as he bottomed out. He brushed a spark of electricity where we connected, and I yelped at the intense sensation, reflexively tightening around him.

"Fuck, baby, you feel so good. Et non interius amore tibi. Sic et stricta calidum."

I groaned and pressed back, dangerously close to coming despite my hold on myself. "No... no Latin."

He pulled almost all the way out and slid back in, somehow deeper than before. "Videris tantopere similis."

"Theo," I squeaked out, unable to keep the pleading from my voice. Another slow roll of his hips.

"Don't worry, baby, I've got you. I'll always have you." My sharp retort to stop toying with me evaporated as he laid across my back, his entire length filling me perfectly, in order to place a kiss on my neck. "Everyday like it's our last, right?" he whispered in my ear. It wasn't the first time he'd said it, and while we'd lived the last seven months exactly like that, the words never failed to fill me with joy.

I nodded. "Sí. Todos los días como si fuera el último. Te amo con todo mi corazón." I shifted my hand, and he laced his fingers with mine. He gave a light squeeze and started to move in earnest.

The world fell away, replaced with a kaleidoscope of sensation. Theo released my hand to caress my sides with mind-numbing waves of his magic, pushing it deep as he drove in and out at just the right angle. I curled my fingers into the sheet with one hand while I reached back with the other to grip his side, needing to touch him. He brushed another small jolt of electricity along my rim. My back bowed, and I cried his name as fireworks exploded in a chaos of color. Per usual, I was the firework.

He grunted as he thrust twice more and came deep. His sweat-coated forehead pressed into my equally damp back along with a kiss. The heat of his breath tickled my shoulder as he whispered over and over, "I love you." He gently tugged us to our sides when my legs started to shake.

I reached for him again, my heart fluttering like a million butterflies in my chest. When my hand found his once more, I pulled it around to hold it against my chest. He took the cue and curled around me. I placed a kiss on his palm as he nuzzled into the back of my neck.

We stayed like that for a while as we caught our breath, the world slowly waking up around us. Eventually, he pulled away and retrieved a rogue towel from a corner of the room. I propped myself against the headboard so I could watch him as he padded around the small room that had been mine for the last ten years of my life. He glanced around in search of something and eventually grabbed my leftover water from the night before.

He used the damp cloth to clean up, then crawled back onto the bed. He stole a kiss before giving me the same treatment. I moaned lightly into him when his delicate touch found my sensitive hole. "How are you doing? You going to be okay to walk?" he teased.

I snorted and kissed him again. "¿Cómo crees que lo estoy haciendo?"

Instead of responding, he kissed me deeper.

I wrapped my arms around him and pulled him close. "You better get going before someone catches you here," I said when he pulled away from yet another deep, sensuous kiss.

His eyes twinkled, their amethyst depths catching the morning light. "You haven't changed your mind?"

I fought hard to keep my ridiculous grin under control. He'd asked me the same thing practically every day since I'd agreed to marry him. My answer was always the same. "No. ¿Y tu?" My eyebrows rose in mock sincerity.

He leaned forward and snared me with another toe-curling, albeit quick, kiss. "Never."

I set my smile free and tangled my fingers in his silken hair as I dragged his mouth back for another taste. "I love you." The declaration was a tad huskier than I intended, fueled by renewed desire, but that didn't stop Theo from melting into me.

"I love you too," he sighed, his lips ghosting over mine. Much as I didn't want to let him go, I pulled away so we could start this momentous day.

"En serio, vete antes de que mi prima te encuentre aquí y nos mate a los dos." Gabriella would totally murder us both if she found him here.

His happy chuckle filled me with light while his hand trailed sparklers down my leg as he got up, wreaking havoc on my senses. "You know, for die-hard pacifists, your family sure does threaten to kill each other a lot."

"Eh, it's a Mexican thing." I shrugged. "It's said con amor."

"Amor duele."

I chuckled at his mock-serious response that love hurts. "No siempre," I responded, vacating the rumpled bed in order to cage him half-dressed against the wall. His breath hitched, and I teased his bottom lip before sliding my tongue into his mouth to play.

The moan that vibrated through my chest only encouraged me to dive deeper. His hips curved off the wall and rubbed against me. It took an active force of will not to spin him around and take him right there, schedules be damned. I leaned back and gave myself a mental high-five at the glassy look in his eyes.

"So... see you later?" he asked, as if there was any doubt.

"Sí. And you better be there or you'll get to find out whether those death threats are serious." He smirked, and I snaked my hands down his backside to squeeze his ass. "Also, si no fuera obvio, *this* is mine tonight." I had the immense satisfaction of watching his eyes dilate.

"Yeah?" The raw question seriously tested my resolve.

"Me reservo el derecho a follarme con mi esposo cuando me apetezca." God, I couldn't wait to fuck my husband whenever I felt like it.

A wicked smile spread across his face. "Esposo, huh?"

"You got a problem with that?"

"Nope." His smile grew into a devilish grin.

"¿Qué?" I asked suddenly concerned.

"You said it first."

My jaw dropped. "No es lo mismo," I argued.

"Oh yes, it *is* the same. Still counts in Spanish. You said husband first, which means..."

"I know what it means," I grumbled.

"Love you." He placed a peck on my cheek, and I offered a wry smile and rolled my eyes. I was still debating arguing whether it mattered if it would technically be true by the end of the day, when Gabbi's voice drifted down the hall.

"Despierta, lazybones! Ready or not, here I come!"

"¡Espere! I'm not decent," I shouted as I reached for the sweats hanging precariously off the dresser.

The door rattled in blatant contradiction of my cry. "Oye, ¿qué pasa? Open up." The doorknob shook again.

"Damn it, Gabbi, give me a minute!" I nearly fell over as my foot caught in the pant leg.

"She can't hear you," Theo chuckled. "Told you the silence spell worked." He waved a hand and stepped closer to the already shimmering wall.

"Wait," I hissed, now painfully aware that my cousin could hear me. "What about..." I waved dramatically at the very obviously sex-tossed room.

He snickered and conjured a bag of potpourri, which he tossed at me before stepping through the wall. He was still passing through when the door flung open and my overeager cousin exploded into the room.

I quickly spun around and prayed she hadn't seen him. "Gabbi."

"Levántate y brilla, primo. You're getting married today!" Theo's quiet laughter reached my ears right as Gabbi's nose wrinkled. "¿Por qué huele a sexo aquí?" Her gaze fell on the clutched bag in my hands, and she narrowed her eyes. "Carlos! How could you? Ahora, todo el día está arruinado. You know it's bad luck to see the groom before the wedding!"

Chapter 32

Theo

The sound of Carlos's cousin yelling at him followed me through the wall into the room on the other side. I laughed and shook my head. Perhaps it had been a touch cruel to abandon him in a room that smelled strongly of sexual satisfaction, armed with nothing more than a meager bag of dried petals. I chuckled again, remembering the look on his face, and quickened my step.

The hallways were mostly empty as I made my way through the family wing. However, the closer I got to the main part of the house, the more people I saw. One thing was for certain: Carlos's family was *not* small, and they all loved him dearly, their Savior of Lost Children. Not that I could blame them. Carlos Barrera was an incredible man, and I couldn't wait to spend the rest of my life with him, however long or short that might be.

"Buenos días. ¿Estás listo para el gran día?" Javier, Carlos' oldest brother, asked as he passed me in the hall.

I slipped a hand into my pocket and rubbed a bit of magic into the coin there. Carlos may have been teaching me Spanish, and while I could guess a good portion using my knowledge of Latin, today was not the day for guessing.

"More than ready," I responded with a giant Cheshire grin, turning to keep him in my sights. My first mistake was turning my back. My second was assuming Javier was traversing the halls alone. Air rushed out of my lungs as someone crashed into me from behind and wrapped me in a bear hug that lifted me off the ground.

"You better be, brujito. Trust me when I say no one will find the body," Jorge growled in my ear.

I laughed and tapped out. He released me far more gently than he'd scooped me up. I wasn't surprised to find that he was joined by José. Those two were thick as thieves, though hadn't taken kindly to me pointing out they were Irish twins. "Where's Jesús?"

The man in question sauntered up behind the other two. "Thinking of switching brothers already?"

"Not on your life," I responded to the very straight, very married man. It had taken a bit to get used to the good-natured ribbing all the time, but now I recognized it for what it was—affection and acceptance. Being embraced by Carlos' family meant more to me than words could ever describe. I blinked back the sudden sting of tears.

"Hey, wait, he's not serious." Javier reached across me to smack his brother. "Stop upsetting the groom."

I waved a hand to dismiss all of it. "It's not that. Just... a really big day. One I never thought I'd get." As one, the four brothers tackled me in a group hug. They may have looked intimidating from the outside, but the lot of them were just a bunch of big softies. "You assholes keep that up and you're gonna find out why Carlos is so keen to marry me." More laughter as they released me, then promptly began dragging me through the house to where I was supposed to be getting ready.

I nodded to Carlos' dad, who eerily looked like all five of his sons despite all of their differences. He offered a small wave and returned to speaking with two of his own siblings. The brothers deposited me in a room crowded with formal suits, chairs, and, of course, stiffer drinks than any sane person would consume before noon. I downed two before Miguel showed up.

He glowered at me in that brooding way he and his sister shared before finally breaking into a grin. Out of everyone, he had been the hardest to win over. I suspected it had a lot to do with the fact that he knew more than anyone else about what had actually happened. While I was grateful he hadn't shared some of the uglier particulars with Carlos' entire family, I was more grateful for our hard-won friendship.

"Come here, you weird purple witch," he demanded, opening his arms wide.

I laughed and willingly stepped into the hug.

"How are you doing?"

"Mostly trying not to throw up."

He pushed me to arm's length and scowled.

"Those are helping, though." I gestured at the magically refilling cocktails.

He laughed with me and guided us over to the festive clothes.

I was halfway through the buttons on my light purple button-down when a sudden bout of nerves hit. I worried my bottom lip, and glanced over at Miguel, who unsurprisingly had caught onto the mood shift. "He'll show right?"

Miguel gave me a sympathetic smile and finished doing up the last of my buttons. "You really worried?" He grabbed my jacket and held it out for me.

I turned and dipped my arms into the sleeves, then spun back to face him. "No. Yes. Maybe?" I hated how freaked I sounded. "I haven't seen this." Truth be told, I hadn't seen much of anything. I did my best to keep my growing concern to myself, but Carlos had noticed anyway and clearly shared his worries with his cousins.

Miguel tugged on my lapels to straighten them, then flattened the fabric down with firm hands. "He loves you, Theo. So much so that I fear for him if you do leave this world early." Guilt stabbed through my chest.

"Maybe I shouldn't have asked. I should have let him go. I have enough magic saved up. I could create a portal, be gone before—"

Miguel's hold on my jacket tightened and stopped my rambling. "You stand him up at the altar and I'll be the reason you leave this world early."

I swallowed thickly and nodded.

He let out a heavy sigh and smoothed the fabric he'd bunched. "He'll be there."

"I don't deserve him." I expected another threat on my life, or possibly a good dose of teasing, not the soft smile curving Miguel's lips.

"Yes, you do. Now stop working yourself up. It's time to get painted." He slapped me on the back and led me out of the dressing room to a pavilion where he sat me down and ordered me to close my eyes and keep still on yet another pain of death. I chuckled once again at ease and did as I was told.

Minutes passed by with the early afternoon sun warming the chill autumn air. Voices rolled in a steady hum around me. I answered the odd greeting, but dutifully kept my eyes closed. At last, the lilt of Gabriella Rivera's voice rose above the others.

"There's my canvas."

"Good morning to you too," I quipped as the sound of her paint kit clicking open filled the air. "Do you have it?"

"Don't get smart with me. I know what you did this morning." Of course, she did. Carlos couldn't keep a secret from his best friend to save his life. "And of course I have the weird paint you insisted I use. What is this stuff anyway?"

I cracked an eye enough to see her holding up a jar half full of subtly glowing purple paint. "Magic."

"Smart ass."

"Well, it is. Think of it as a bit of my culture too. Especially since..." I trailed off and swallowed the sudden lump in my throat. Especially since my family couldn't be here. I knew the dangers of that much potent magic in one place. We'd be like a beacon to any and everyone who wanted a piece of us.

She placed a gentle hand on my knee and gave me a reassuring squeeze. "In spirit, right? They'd be here if they could."

"Yeah." Of course, Gabbi didn't know that I hadn't actually told any of my family I was getting married in the first place, lest I put any of them at risk. Not to mention, I had no idea how to find most of them.

She smacked my chest. "Quit being so dire, cabrón. It's el día de tu boda for fuck's sake."

I couldn't help but smile as her words slipped into a mix of English and Spanish. Clearly, the little magic I'd infused the coin with had run out. I'd have to recharge it for the ceremony, but that could wait.

"Stop smiling," she scolded. "You'll ruin all of my hard work."

"Oye, get your grubby hands off of him." At the sound of Carlos' voice, my rebellious smile broadened.

Gabbi huffed, and the paintbrush rattled against a container as it was discarded. "But I paint everyone."

"Not him, you don't. And not today."

Her skirts brushed against my legs as she vacated her seat of prominence in favor of my husband-to-be. I blindly reached out until my fingers found the fine woven fabric of his pants. He ran a thumb over my knuckles, then turned his full attention to the task at hand.

The metal ferrule tapped on glass, then a wet brush delicately touched my face and spun out in a confident stroke. It warmed my heart that Carlos wanted to do this himself. I knew what that meant and that he undoubtedly put in hours of practice. The brush vanished only to return a moment later, and I couldn't fight the happiness pooling in my chest.

"You really do have to stop smiling, though, mi corazón."

I could have died a happy man right then. Instead, I schooled the joy from my face and sat stiller than a stone until he gave me leave to open my eyes.

"Do you want to see?" Carlos asked, holding a large mirror at his side.

"Not yet." I stared at the absolute masterpiece Gabbi had created on the love of my life's face. Swirls of glittering purple wove perfectly with rainbow-colored butterflies and flowers encircling his eyes. To my surprise, he wasn't in his Kisin form, but his human, with his round spectacles perched on his nose and his dark, curly hair styled into submission. "How long does this take to dry?"

"Why?"

"Because I really want to kiss you right now. And judging by the menacing looks your cousin is shooting us, she'll kill me if I ruin her handiwork."

"In that, you would be correct. And the kissing, I fear, will have to wait until the end of the ceremony." I frowned as he replaced the lid on the paint jar. "Don't look so put out. That's basically right now." I made to surge up from my chair, but his hand stopped me. "Wait. Please look." He shifted the mirror, and I caught a glimpse of doubt in his beautiful eyes before they were eclipsed by my reflection.

I sucked in a breath and tentatively reached for my face, stopping just shy of actually touching my cheek. "Carlos. This is... You came up with this design?"

"You like it?" Even hidden, I could make out the undercurrent of anxiety.

"I love it. What does it all mean?"

"The purple flowers around your eyes are for life and longevity. The stars are all you." Much like his own butterflies, they were in an array of colors, though where his were vibrant and rich, mine trended toward the paler side of the spectrum. "I know you're not big on astrology, but the grouping on the right cheek is the constellation Leo. It's for your sign and the meteor shower you shared with me. All the symbols are there to represent who you are as a person. Except for the little yellow butterfly above your left eyebrow. That's me."

I swallowed down a flood of emotion and gently pushed the mirror away. "It's absolutely beautiful. Are you sure I can't kiss you?"

He simply laughed and helped me to my feet. "Tan pronto como se dicen los votos."

"Then let's get on with it." My eager declaration was met with a chorus of laughter from nearby relatives making their way to the ceremony site. Before I could forget, I infused more magic into the translation coin and stepped away from the painting station.

My gaze caught on Sigurd sitting in the shade, looking rather dapper with the bowtie someone had procured for him. Beside him was the ever energetic Azul, his tail wagging up a dust storm as he stared at my familiar as if awaiting instructions.

"You coming?" I asked and gestured for him to lead the way.

With all the pomp and circumstance only Sigurd could manage, he extricated himself from the shadows and made his way toward the latticed gazebo where the ceremony would officially be held. He spared me a glance, and I winked in return as Carlos laughed quietly beside me.

"Those two are a mess," Carlos said.

"At least Sigurd didn't turn him into a mouse and eat him," I responded as I made my way with him toward a cluster of his family that was still standing.

"Oh good, it wasn't just me who was worried about that."

My laughter caught at the sudden expression of worry that shone in his eyes. "What's the matter?"

"Who are they?"

I turned to search for who he was referring to, and my heart nearly stopped in my chest. Beside Carlos' immediate family, including his grandmother, were a dozen people that hadn't been there before.

Mama Barrera twisted to face us, a smile on her lips and in her eyes. "I believe these people are here for you, Theo."

My lungs may have forgotten how to pull oxygen from the air, but my feet had a life of their own as they closed the distance. I stared in wonder at the host of people before me, unable to believe my eyes. My cousin Jessica winked at me, her platinum hair cascading in waves over her shoulder onto a deep plum colored dress. Auntie Pearl offered a shy smile, while several other distant cousins offered their own greetings, dressed equally in hues of purple.

A woman separated from the group of witches that I doubted had ever all occupied the same space outside of technology and all the remaining moisture in my mouth dried. Even in her fifties, with white streaking through her silvery purple hair, she was beautiful. Her amethyst gown flowed and rippled in the light breeze, perfectly matching her eyes. *My eyes.*

"Mom," I croaked. Those same eyes crinkled with a soft smile.

"Hello, Theo."

"But... but..." My gaze swiveled around to take in all the people—all the family—I had in this world, all in one place. "But what are you all doing here? What about the risks? I didn't send any invitations," I added belatedly.

She clucked her tongue and waved a dismissive hand wrapped in delicate lavender lace. "One doesn't really need an invitation when they can see the future. And I imagine a veritable army of Kisin should suffice in warding off any enterprising souls." She arched an eyebrow. "Besides, I couldn't very well miss the wedding of my only son. Now could I?"

A sob tore free of my throat, and I launched myself at the woman I hadn't seen in over a decade, heedless of what it might do to the paint on my face. "I can't believe you're here."

"There, there, my sweet boy." She wrapped me in a firm hug and rubbed my back. "I've missed you too."

"I don't understand. I haven't seen anything for months. How could you—"

"There she goes again, taking all the credit," a familiar old voice huffed.

I pulled away from my clinging embrace and stared in amazement at the wrinkled woman with more white than lavender in her hair. "Grandmother?"

"Atta boy, Theobald."

"You saw this?"

She stepped forward and took both of my hands in hers. "Many, many years ago." She glanced over my shoulder to where I could feel Carlos' presence. "Is this your betrothed?"

I nodded and glanced back at Carlos long enough to see the happiness misting his eyes. "Carlos, this is my grandmother, Winifred Wisteria. And this is my—" My voice broke, and I had to try again. "This is my mother, Katherine Wisteria. And... and the rest of my family."

Everyone waved, and Carlos placed a reassuring hand on my shoulder.

I returned my gaze to my grandmother, who looked pleased as punch with herself. "I still don't understand. You saw this? But the last foretelling you told me... You said I was going to die."

"Did I? I may be getting a tad senile in my old age, but I'm pretty sure I said that you would be courted by death and life as you knew it would be over." She glanced once more at Carlos, then back at me. "I would say being courted by a Kisin certainly qualifies, given their unique relationship with the afterlife. And I'm sure everyone here would agree that marriage is the end of one life and the start of another."

There was no telling what sort of mess I'd made of Carlos's paintwork as I stood there and reevaluated every assumption I'd ever made about the dire prophecy bequeathed to me at the tender age of six. "You... you let me believe I would die. Was that ever a possibility?" All the horrible decisions I'd made, the danger I'd put Carlos and myself in, the visions *I* had seen...

A darkness passed over my grandmother's face, and she shared a look with my mother.

"I warned you," Katherine Wisteria said rather ominously.

"What is she talking about?" I asked.

Sadness filled my grandmother's eyes as she cupped my face. A tingle of magic emanated from the touch, and I realized she was spinning back time to restore the artwork. "Some prophecies must be self-fulfilled. I am sorry for the heartache it brought you, but I trust you agree that it was worth it."

Anger bubbled inside me. "That's no excuse. My actions put both of our lives in jeopardy! I've lived a half-life consumed with preventing that stupid foretelling. Who lets a child believe they're going to die and doesn't offer any help?" Carlos' hand tightened on my shoulder, drawing attention to my rapid breathing and the lightning sparking between my fingers. I curled them into a fist, but the lightning continued to dance around my hand until Carlos laced our fingers and absorbed the rampant magic.

Winifred Wisteria may have been older than time, but her eyes were still sharp. She zeroed in on the interaction... and the result, then raised her penetrating gaze back to mine. "If I had given you any sort of guidance, you would have graduated from Dreifacher Mond, top of your class, and gone on to lead a miserable existence. A year after accepting the position of High Priest of Hecate, you would have been assassinated in your sleep. And for what?

"The man you love would be dead now, exploited by the very coven you joined, and your family would still live in the shadows." Her eyes narrowed to frightening glints of amethyst. "If you hadn't believed you were dying, you wouldn't have transferred out of that cesspool of a school. You wouldn't have taken any risks, and you would never have met the man whose hand you're clinging to for dear life. When you've had enough visions to know that sometimes the only right path is the one that seems to cause the most pain, then you can berate me."

I wanted to keep being angry, to throw her out of the wedding and never speak to her again... except I'd had visions like that, knew the difficulty of traversing an unknown future in pursuit of a singular goal. I released Carlos's hand and stepped forward to wrap her in a hug. "I do know, Grandmother," I whispered in her ear.

"You poor boy," she said as she patted my back with frail hands. "I wish I could have done more." She shifted, and I let her step back and wipe her eyes with a kerchief from her sleeve. We stayed like that, a moment frozen in time, then she scoffed and flapped the napkin. "Enough of all this mush. I was told there would be a wedding and a party to die for."

My newly refreshed face scrunched in confusion even as my mother rolled her eyes. "Wait. Told? You said you had a vision."

My grandmother merely shrugged. "Foresight is a tricky thing and absolutely useless, as you well know. I may have had a little help." She gestured, and Carlos's grandmother stepped up.

"Abuela?" Carlos's confusion mirrored mine.

My grandmother held out her arms and embraced the other woman as if she'd known her for years and not seconds. "Margarita and I go way back. We were bosom buddies nearly a century ago. It's been too long, my friend."

"I met Winnie at a fair long before I met my Juan Carlos. She read my fortune, then told me the future." She smiled warmly at my grandmother. "I always assumed it would be Julissa who tried to bring a witch home. Never imagined it would be my Carlito. She warned me and even gave me signs of what to look for. When Theo refused to read Carlos' future, I knew I'd finally found the boy who would tie our families together." Abuela Margarita released her old friend and pointed at rows of seats filled with curious faces. "I don't know about you, but my old bones could use a rest. What do you say we get this show started?"

That was all it took for everyone to break apart and secure their seats. All of my family made sure to send a smile and an invocation of luck and a happy future toward me and Carlos as they mixed with Carlos' family. A mere fifteen minutes later, I stood before Carlos in front of everyone and made my promise of forever.

"Carlos Barrera, to you I give my everything. All my knowledge, all my power, all my memories, and all my love. Tu solus stellam in caelo. Verus Aquilo meus."

The magic paint tingled on my face as I called it to life. Carlos' rich, brown eyes widened as his paint did the same. I'd warned him that the ancestral magic that would bind our spirits together would feel weird and given him several opportunities to opt out of the long-forgotten tradition. He'd insisted on going forward with it. I smiled at his expression of wonder and sealed the spell with a kiss.

"You are the only star in my sky. My true North," I whispered amid a cacophony of cheers. "I love you."

What's Next?

Haven't had enough of our Kisin Demons? Keep an eye out for Miguel's book:

In the meantime, be sure to check out the Playlist for Courting Death!

Acknowledgements

Writing Theo and Carlo's story has been one heck of a roller-coaster, and I couldn't have done it without the most amazing support group. To my alpha readers, Goose and M. L. Eaden, thank you for all your encouragement and help with world-building.

And an extra thank you to my critique group. Sam Drake, Evie McGlynn, Court Stephens, TA Nieman, and Cyd Sidney. All of you are incredibly talented authors, and I am forever grateful for your support. You helped make Courting Death truly sparkle!

Lastly, I want to give a special shout-out to Icelica De La Torre for helping me make the Spanish in Courting Death accurate and more representative of the culture.

About the Author

S am Bolanos (she/they) is a genderqueer author and founder of Chaotic Neutral Press LLC. They believe in love, equality, and the Oxford comma. When not playing with her three dogs or spending time with her incredible husband, she's probably agonizing over edits or escaping into her latest fantasy.

NEWSLETTER: SUBSCRIBE

WEBSITE: SBOLANOS.COM

FACEBOOK: @SBOLANOS

READER GROUP: SAM'S SUNBEAMS

INSTAGRAM: @SBOLANOSBOOKS